KT-364-177

# THE SANDMAN

## LARS KEPLER

Translated from the Swedish by Neil Smith

HARPER

This novel is entirely a work of fiction.
The names, characters and incidents portrayed in it are
the work of the author's imagination. Any resemblance to
actual persons, living or dead, events or localities is
entirely coincidental.

*Harper*
An imprint of HarperCollins*Publishers*
1 London Bridge Street
London SE1 9GF

www.harpercollins.co.uk

This paperback edition 2015
1

First published in Great Britain by HarperCollins Publishers 2014

Copyright © Lars Kepler 2012
Translation copyright © Neil Smith 2014
All rights reserved

Originally published in 2012 by Albert Bonniers Förlag, Sweden, as *Sandmannen*

Lars Kepler asserts the moral right to
be identified as the author of this work

A catalogue record for this book
is available from the British Library

ISBN: 978-0-00-746781-5

Printed and bound in Great Britain by
Clays Ltd, St Ives plc

All rights reserved. No part of this publication may be
reproduced, stored in a retrieval system, or transmitted,
in any form or by any means, electronic, mechanical,
photocopying, recording or otherwise, without the prior
permission of the publishers.

# THE SANDMAN

| DUDLEY LIBRARIES | |
|---|---|
| 000000750561 | |
| **Askews & Holts** | 02-Mar-2015 |
| | £7.99 |
| LYE | |

It's the middle of the night, and snow is blowing in from the sea. A young man is walking across a high railway bridge, towards Stockholm. His face is as pale as misted glass. His jeans are stiff with frozen blood. He is walking between the rails, stepping over the sleepers. Fifty metres below him the ice on the water is just visible, like a strip of cloth. A blanket of snow covers the trees and oil tanks in the harbour are barely visible; the snow is swirling in the glow from the container crane far below.

Warm blood is trickling down the man's lower left arm, into his hand and dripping from his fingertips.

The rails start to sing and whistle as a night-train approaches the two-kilometre-long bridge.

The young man sways and sits down on the rail, then gets to his feet again and carries on walking.

The air is buffeted in front of the train, and the view is obscured by the billowing snow. The Traxx train has already reached the middle of the bridge when the driver catches sight of the man on the track. He blows his horn, and sees the figure almost fall, then it takes a long step to the left, onto the oncoming track, and grabs hold of the flimsy railing.

The man's clothes are flapping around his body. The bridge is shaking heavily under his feet. He is standing still with his eyes wide open, his hands on the railing.

Everything is swirling snow and tumbling darkness.

His bloody hand has started to freeze as he carries on walking.

His name is Mikael Kohler-Frost. He has been missing for thirteen years, and was declared dead seven years ago.

# 1

The steel gate closes behind the new doctor with a heavy clang. The metallic echo pushes past him and continues down the spiral staircase.

Anders Rönn feels a shiver run down his spine when everything suddenly goes quiet.

As of today, he is going to be working in the secure criminal psychology unit.

For the past thirteen years, the strictly isolated bunker has been home to the ageing Jurek Walter. He was sentenced to psychiatric care with specific probation requirements.

The young doctor doesn't know much about his patient, except that he has been diagnosed with: 'Schizophrenia, non-specific. Chaotic thinking. Recurrent acute psychosis, with erratic and extremely violent episodes'.

Anders Rönn shows his ID at level zero, removes his mobile and hangs the key to the gate in his locker before the guard opens the first door of the airlock. He goes in and waits for the door to close before walking over to the next door. When

3

a signal sounds, the guard opens that one too. Anders turns round and waves before carrying on along the corridor towards the isolation ward's staffroom.

Senior Consultant Roland Brolin is a thickset man in his fifties, with sloping shoulders and cropped hair. He is standing smoking under the extractor fan in the kitchen, leafing through an article on the pay gap between men and women in the health-workers' magazine.

'Jurek Walter must never be alone with any member of staff,' the consultant says. 'He must never meet other patients, he never has any visitors, and he's never allowed out into the exercise yard. Nor is he . . .'

'Never?' Anders asks. 'Surely it isn't permitted to keep someone . . .'

'No, it isn't,' Roland Brolin says sharply.

'So what's he actually done?'

'Nothing but nice things,' Roland says, heading towards the corridor.

Even though Jurek Walter is Sweden's worst-ever serial killer, he is completely unknown to the public. The proceedings against him in the Central Courthouse and at the Court of Appeal in the Wrangelska Palace were held behind closed doors, and all the files are still strictly confidential.

Anders Rönn and Senior Consultant Roland Brolin pass through another security door and a young woman with tattooed arms and pierced cheeks winks at them.

'Come back in one piece,' she says breezily.

'There's no need to worry,' Roland says to Anders in a low voice. 'Jurek Walter is a quiet, elderly man. He doesn't fight and he doesn't raise his voice. Our cardinal rule is that we never go into his cell. But Leffe, who was on the night-shift last night, noticed that he had made some sort of knife that he's got hidden under his mattress, so obviously we have to confiscate it.'

4

'How do we do that?' Anders asks.

'We break the rules.'

'We're going into Jurek's cell?'

'You're going in . . . to ask nicely for the knife.'

'I'm going in . . .?'

Roland Brolin laughs loudly and explains that they're going to pretend to give the patient his normal injection of Risperidone, but will actually be giving him an overdose of Zypadhera.

The Senior Consultant runs his card through yet another reader and taps in a code. There's a bleep, and the lock of the security door whirrs.

'Hang on,' Roland says, holding out a little box of yellow earplugs.

'You said he doesn't shout.'

Roland smiles weakly, looks at his new colleague with weary eyes, and sighs heavily before he starts to explain.

'Jurek Walter will talk to you, quite calmly, probably perfectly reasonably,' he says in a grave voice. 'But later this evening, when you're driving home, you'll swerve into oncoming traffic and smash into an articulated lorry . . . or you'll stop off at the DIY store to buy an axe before you pick the kids up from preschool.'

'Should I be scared now?' Anders smiles.

'No, but hopefully careful,' Roland says.

Anders doesn't usually have much luck, but when he read the advert in the *Doctors' Journal* for a full-time, temporary but long-term position in the secure unit of the Löwenströmska Hospital, his heart had started to beat faster.

It's only a twenty-minute drive from home, and it could well lead to a permanent appointment.

Since working as an intern at Skaraborg Hospital and in a health centre in Huddinge, he has had to get by on temporary contracts at the regional clinic of Sankt Sigfrid's Hospital.

The long drives to Växjö and the irregular hours proved impossible to combine with Petra's job in the council's recreational administration and Agnes's autism.

Only two weeks ago Anders and Petra had been sitting at the kitchen table trying to work out what on earth they were going to do.

'We can't go on like this,' he had said, perfectly calmly.

'But what alternative do we have?' she had whispered.

'I don't know,' Anders had replied, wiping the tears from her cheeks.

Agnes's teaching assistant at her preschool had told them that Agnes had had a difficult day. She had refused to let go of her milk-glass, and the other children had laughed. She hadn't been able to accept that break-time was over, because Anders hadn't come to pick her up like he usually did. He had driven straight back from Växjö, but hadn't reached the preschool until six o'clock. Agnes was still sitting in the dining room with her hands round the glass.

When they got home, Agnes had stood in her room, staring at the wall beside the doll's house, clapping her hands in that introverted way she had. They don't know what she can see there, but she says that grey sticks keep appearing, and she has to count them, and stop them. She does that when she's feeling particularly anxious. Sometimes ten minutes is enough, but that evening she had to stand there for more than four hours before they could get her into bed.

# 2

The last security door closes and they head down the corridor to the only one of the isolation cells that is being used. The fluorescent light in the ceiling reflects off the vinyl floor. The textured wallpaper has a groove worn into it from the food trolley, one metre up from the floor.

The Senior Consultant puts his pass card away and lets Anders walk ahead of him towards the heavy metal door.

Through the reinforced glass Anders can see a thin man sitting on a plastic chair. He is dressed in blue jeans and a denim shirt. The man is clean-shaven and his eyes seem remarkably calm. The many wrinkles covering his pale face look like the cracked clay at the bottom of a dried-up riverbed.

Jurek Walter was only found guilty of two murders and one attempted murder, but there's compelling evidence linking him to a further nineteen murders.

Thirteen years ago he was caught red-handed in Lill-Jan's Forest on Djurgården in Stockholm, forcing a fifty-year-old woman back into a coffin in the ground. She had been kept in the coffin for almost two years, but was still alive. The woman had sustained terrible injuries, she was malnourished, her muscles had withered away, she had appalling pressure sores and frostbite, and had suffered severe brain damage. If the police hadn't followed and arrested Jurek Walter beside the coffin, he would probably never have been stopped.

Now the consultant takes out three small glass bottles containing yellow powder, puts some water into each of the bottles, shakes them carefully, then draws the contents into a syringe.

He puts his earplugs in, then opens the small hatch in the door. There's a clatter of metal and a heavy smell of concrete and dust hits them.

In a dispassionate voice the Senior Consultant tells Jurek Walter that it's time for his injection.

The man lifts his chin and gets up softly from the chair, turns to looks at the hatch in the door and unbuttons his shirt as he approaches.

'Stop and take your shirt off,' Roland Brolin says.

Jurek Walter carries on walking slowly forward and Roland quickly closes and bolts the hatch. Jurek stops, undoes the last buttons and lets his shirt fall to the floor.

His body looks as if it was once in good shape, but now his muscles are loose and his wrinkled skin is sagging.

Roland opens the hatch again. Jurek Walter walks the last little bit and holds out his sinewy arm, mottled with hundreds of different pigments.

Anders washes his upper arm with surgical spirit. Roland pushes the syringe into the soft muscle and injects the liquid far too quickly. Jurek's hand jerks in surprise, but he doesn't pull his arm back until he's given permission. The Senior Consultant closes and hurriedly bolts the hatch, removes his earplugs, smiles nervously to himself and then looks inside.

Jurek Walter is stumbling towards the bed, where he stops and sits down.

Suddenly he turns to look at the door and Roland drops the syringe.

He tries to catch it but it rolls away across the floor.

Anders steps forward and picks up the syringe, and when they both stand and turn back towards the hatch they see that the inside of the reinforced glass is misted. Jurek has breathed on the glass and written 'JOONA' with his finger.

'What does it say?' Anders asks weakly.

'He's written Joona.'

'Joona?'

'What the hell does that mean?'

The condensation clears and they see that Jurek Walter is sitting as if he hadn't moved. He looks at the arm where he got the injection, massages the muscle, then looks at them through the glass.

'It didn't say anything else?' Anders asks.

'I only saw . . .'

There's a bestial roar from the other side of the heavy door. Jurek Walter has slid off the bed and is on his knees, screaming as hard as he can. The sinews in his neck are taut, his veins swollen.

'How much did you actually give him?' Anders asks.

Jurek Walter's eyes roll back and turn white, he reaches out a hand to support himself, stretches one leg but topples over backwards, hitting his head on the bedside table, then he screams and his body starts to jerk spasmodically.

'Bloody hell,' Anders whispers.

Jurek slips onto the floor, his legs kicking uncontrollably. He bites his tongue and blood sprays out over his chest, then he lies there on his back, gasping.

'What do we do if he dies?'

'Cremate him,' Brolin says.

Jurek is cramping again, his whole body shaking, and his hands flail in every direction until they suddenly stop.

Brolin looks at his watch. Sweat is running down his cheeks.

Jurek Walter whimpers, rolls onto his side and tries to get up, but fails.

'You can go inside in two minutes,' the Senior Consultant says.

'Am I really going in there?'

'He'll soon be completely harmless.'

Jurek is crawling on all fours, bloody slime drooling from his mouth. He sways and slows down until he finally slumps to the floor and lies still.

Anders looks through the thick reinforced glass window in the door. Jurek Walter has been lying motionless on the floor for the last ten minutes. His body is limp in the wake of his cramps.

The Senior Consultant pulls out a key and puts it in the lock, then pauses and peers in through the window before unlocking the door.

'Have fun,' he says.

'What do we do if he wakes up?' Anders asks.

'He mustn't wake up.'

Brolin opens the door and Anders goes inside. The door closes behind him and the lock rattles. The isolation room smells of sweat, but of something else as well. A sharp smell of acetic acid. Jurek Walter is lying completely still, with just the slow pattern of his breathing visible across his back.

Anders keeps his distance from him even though he knows he's fast asleep.

The acoustics in there are odd, intrusive, as if sounds follow movements too quickly.

His doctor's coat rustles softly with each step.

Jurek is breathing faster.

The tap is dripping in the basin.

Anders reaches the bed, then turns towards Jurek and kneels down.

He catches a glimpse of the Senior Consultant watching him anxiously through the reinforced glass as he leans over and tries to look under the fixed bed.

Nothing on the floor.

He moves closer, looking carefully at Jurek before lying flat on the floor.

He can't watch Jurek any longer. He has to turn his back on him to look for the knife.

Not much light reaches under the bed. There are dustballs nestled against the wall.

He can't help imagining that Jurek Walter has opened his eyes.

There's something tucked between the wooden slats and the mattress. It's hard to see what it is.

Anders stretches out his hand, but can't reach it. He'll have to slide beneath the bed on his back. The space is so tight he can't turn his head. He slips further in. Feels the unyielding bulk of the bed-frame against his ribcage with each breath. His fingers fumble. He needs to get a bit closer. His knee hits one of the wooden slats. He blows a dustball away from his face and carries on.

Suddenly he hears a dull thud behind him in the isolation cell. He can't turn round and look. He just lies there still, listening. His own breathing is so rapid he has trouble discerning any other sound.

Cautiously he reaches out his hand and touches the object with his fingertips, squeezing in a bit further in order to pull it free.

Jurek has made a short knife with a very sharp blade fashioned from a piece of steel skirting.

'Hurry up,' the Senior Consultant calls through the hatch.

Anders tries to get out, pushing hard, and scratches his cheek.

Suddenly he can't move, he's stuck, his coat is caught and there's no way he can wriggle out of it.

He imagines he can hear the sound of shuffling from Jurek.

Perhaps it was nothing.

Anders pulls as hard as he can. The seams strain but don't tear. He realises that he's going to have to slide back under the bed to free his coat.

'What are you doing?' Roland Brolin calls in a brittle voice.

The little hatch in the door clatters as it is bolted shut again.

Anders sees that one pocket of his coat has caught on a loose strut. He quickly pulls it free, holds his breath and pushes himself out again. He is filled with a rising sense of panic. He scrapes his stomach and knee, but grabs the edge of the bed with one hand and pulls himself out.

Panting, he turns round and gets unsteadily to his feet with the knife in his hand.

Jurek is lying on his side, one eye half-open in sleep, staring blindly.

Anders hurries over to the door and meets the Senior Consultant's anxious gaze through the reinforced glass and tries to smile, but stress cuts through his voice as he says:

'Open the door.'

Roland Brolin opens the hatch instead.

'Pass the knife out first.'

Anders gives him a quizzical look, then hands the knife over.

'You found something else as well,' Roland Brolin says.

'No,' Anders replies, glancing at Jurek.

'A letter.'

'There wasn't anything else.'

Jurek is starting to writhe on the floor, and is gasping weakly.

'Check his pockets,' the Senior Consultant says with a stressed smile.

'What for?'

'Because this is a search.'

Anders turns and walks cautiously to Jurek Walter. His eyes are completely shut again, but beads of sweat are starting to appear on his furrowed face.

Reluctantly Anders leans over and feels inside one of his pockets. The denim shirt pulls tighter across Jurek's shoulders and he lets out a low groan.

There's a plastic comb in the back pocket of his jeans. With trembling hands Anders checks the rest of his tight pockets.

Sweat is dripping from the tip of his nose. He has to keep blinking hard.

One of Jurek's big hands opens and closes several times.

There's nothing else in his pockets.

Anders turns back towards the reinforced glass and shakes his head. It's impossible to see if Brolin is standing outside the door. The reflection of the lamp in the ceiling is shining like a grey sun in the glass.

He has to get out now.

It's taken too long.

Anders gets to his feet and hurries over to the door. The Senior Consultant isn't there. Anders peers closer to the glass, but can't see anything.

Jurek Walter is breathing fast, like a child having a nightmare.

Anders bangs on the door. His hands thud almost soundlessly against the thick metal. He bangs again. There's no sound, nothing is happening. He taps on the glass with his wedding ring, then sees a shadow growing across the wall.

His shiver runs up his back and down his arms. With

his heart pounding and adrenalin rising through his body, he turns round. He sees Jurek Walter slowly sitting up. His face is slack and his pale eyes are staring straight ahead. His mouth is still bleeding and his lips look weirdly red.

4

Anders is shouting and pounding at the heavy steel door, but the Senior Consultant still isn't opening it. His pulse is thudding in his head as he turns to face their patient. Jurek Walter is still sitting on the floor, and blinks at him a few times before he starts to get up.

'It's a lie,' Jurek says, dribbling blood down his chin. 'They say I'm a monster, but I'm just a human being . . .'

He doesn't have the energy to stand up and slumps back, panting, onto the floor.

'A human being,' he repeats.

With a weary gesture he puts one hand inside his shirt, pulls out a folded piece of paper and tosses it over towards Anders.

'The letter he was asking for,' he says. 'For the past seven years I've been asking to see a lawyer . . . Not because I've got any hope of getting out . . . I am who I am, but I'm still a human being . . .'

Anders crouches down and reaches for the piece of paper without taking his eyes off Jurek. The crumpled man tries to get up again, leaning on his hands, and although he sways slightly he manages to put one foot down on the floor.

16

Anders picks up the paper from the floor, and finally hears a rattling sound as the key is inserted into the lock of the door. He turns and stares out through the reinforced glass, feeling his legs tremble beneath him.

'You shouldn't have given me an overdose,' Jurek mutters.

Anders doesn't turn round, but he knows that Jurek Walter is standing up, staring at him.

The reinforced glass in the door is like a screen of grainy ice. He can't see who's standing on the other side turning the key in the lock.

'Open, open,' he whispers as he hears breathing behind his back.

The door slides open and Anders stumbles out of the isolation cell. He stumbles straight into the concrete wall of the corridor and hears the heavy clang as the door shuts, then the rattles as the powerful lock responds to the turn of the key.

Panting, he leans back against the cool wall. Only then does he see that it wasn't the Senior Consultant who rescued him but the young woman with the pierced cheeks.

'I don't know what happened,' she says. 'Roland must have lost it completely, he's always incredibly careful about security.'

'I'll talk to him . . .'

'Maybe he got ill . . . I think he's diabetic.'

Anders wipes his clammy hands on his doctor's coat and looks up at her again.

'Thank you for letting me out,' he says.

'I'd do anything for you,' she jokes.

He tries to give her his carefree, boyish smile, but his legs are shaking as he follows her out through the security door. She stops in the control room, then turns back towards him.

'There's only one problem with working down here,' she

says. 'It's so damn quiet that you have to eat loads of sweets just to stay awake.'

'That sounds OK.'

On a monitor he can see Jurek sitting on his bed with his head in his hands. The dayroom with its television and running machine is empty.

## 5

Anders Rönn spends the rest of the day concentrating on familiarising himself with the new routines, with a doctor's round up on Ward 30, individual treatment plans and discharge tests, but his mind keeps going back to the letter in his pocket and what Jurek had said.

At ten past five Anders leaves the criminal psychology ward and emerges into the cool air. Beyond the illuminated hospital precinct the winter darkness has settled.

Anders warms his hands in his jacket pockets, and hurries across the pavement towards the large car park in front of the main entrance to the hospital.

It was full of cars when he arrived, but now it's almost empty.

He screws up his eyes and realises that there's someone standing behind his car.

'Hello!' Anders calls, walking faster.

The man turns round, rubs his hand over his mouth and moves away from the car. Senior Consultant Roland Brolin.

Anders slows down as he approaches the car and pulls his key from his pocket.

'You're expecting an apology,' Brolin says with a forced smile.

'I'd prefer not to have to speak to hospital management about what happened,' Anders says.

Brolin looks him in the eye, then holds out his left hand, palm up.

'Give me the letter,' he says calmly.

'What letter?'

'The letter Jurek wanted you to find,' he replies. 'A note, a sheet of newspaper, a piece of cardboard.'

'I found the knife that was supposed to be there.'

'That was the bait,' Brolin says. 'You don't think he'd put himself through all that pain for nothing?'

Anders looks at the Senior Consultant as he wipes sweat from his upper lip with one hand.

'What do we do if the patient wants to see a lawyer?' he asks.

'Nothing,' Brolin whispers.

'Has he ever asked you that?'

'I don't know, I wouldn't have heard, I always wear earplugs.' Brolin smiles.

'But I don't understand why . . .'

'You need this job,' the Senior Consultant interrupts. 'I've heard that you were bottom of your class, you're in debt, you've got no experience and no references.'

'Are you finished?'

'You should give me the letter,' Brolin replies, clenching his jaw.

'I didn't find a letter.'

Brolin looks him in the eye for a moment.

'If you ever find a letter,' he says, 'you're to give it to me without reading it.'

'I understand,' Anders says, unlocking the car door.

It seems to Anders as if the Senior Consultant looks slightly more relaxed as he gets in the car, shuts the door and starts the engine. When Brolin taps on the window he ignores him, puts the car in gear and pulls away. In the rear-view mirror Brolin stands and watches the car without smiling.

## 6

When Anders gets home he quickly shuts the front door behind him, locks it and puts the safety chain on.

His heart is beating hard in his chest – for some reason he ran from the car to the house.

From Agnes's room he can hear Petra's soothing voice. Anders smiles to himself. She's already reading *Seacrow Island* to their daughter. It's usually much later before the bedtime rituals have reached the story. It must have been a good day again today. Anders's new job has meant that Petra has risked cutting her own hours.

There's a damp patch on the hall rug around Agnes's muddy winter boots. Her woolly hat and snood are on the floor in front of the bureau. Anders goes in and puts the bottle of champagne on the kitchen table, then stands and stares out at the garden.

He's thinking about Jurek Walter's letter, and no longer knows what to do.

The branches of the big lilac are scratching at the window. He looks at the dark glass and sees his own kitchen reflected back at him. As he listens to the squeaking branches, it occurs to him that he ought to go and get the shears from the store-room.

'Just wait a minute,' he hears Petra say. 'I'll read to the end first . . .'

Anders creeps into Agnes's room. The princess-lamp in the ceiling is on. Petra looks up from the book and meets his gaze. She's got her light brown hair pulled up into a ponytail and is wearing her usual heart-shaped earrings. Agnes is sitting in her lap and saying repeatedly that it's gone wrong and they have to start the bit about the dog again.

Anders goes in and crouches down in front of them.

'Hello, darling,' he says.

Agnes glances at him quickly, then looks away. He pats her on the head, tucks a lock of hair behind her ear, then gets up.

'There's food left if you want to heat it up,' Petra says. 'I just have to reread this chapter before I can come and see you.'

'It all went wrong with the dog,' Agnes repeats, staring at the floor.

Anders goes into the kitchen, gets the plate of food from the fridge and puts it down on the worktop next to the microwave.

Slowly he pulls the letter out of the back pocket of his jeans and thinks of how Jurek repeated that he was a human being.

In tiny, cursive handwriting, Jurek had written a few faint sentences on the thin paper. In the top right corner the letter is addressed to a legal firm in Tensta, and simply constitutes a formal request. Jurek Walter asks for legal assistance to understand the meaning of his being sentenced to secure psychiatric care. He needs to have his rights clarified, and would like to know what possibility there is of getting the verdict reconsidered in the future.

Anders can't put a finger on why he suddenly feels unsettled, but there's something strange about the tone of the letter and the precise choice of wording, combined with the almost dyslexic spelling mistakes.

Thoughts about Jurek's words are chasing round his head as he walks into his study and takes out an envelope. He copies the address, puts the letter in the envelope, and sticks a stamp on it.

He leaves the house and heads off into the chill darkness, across the grass towards the letter-box up by the roundabout. Once he's posted the letter he stands and just watches the cars passing on Sandavägen for a while before walking back home.

The wind is making the frosted grass ripple like water. A hare races off towards the old gardens.

He opens the gate and looks up into the kitchen window. The whole house resembles a doll's house. Everything is lit up and open to view. He can see straight into the corridor, to the blue painting that has always hung there.

The door to their bedroom is open. The vacuum cleaner is in the middle of the floor. The cable is still plugged into the socket in the wall.

Suddenly Anders sees a movement. He gasps with surprise. There's someone in the bedroom. Standing next to their bed.

Anders is about to rush inside when he realises that the person is actually standing in the garden at the back of the house.

He's simply visible through the bedroom window.

Anders runs down the paved path, past the sundial and round the corner.

The man must have heard him coming, because he's already running away. Anders can hear him forcing his way through the lilac hedge. He runs after him, holding the branches back, trying to see anything, but it's far too dark.

# 7

Mikael stands up in the darkness when the Sandman blows his terrible dust into the room. He's learned that there's no point holding your breath. Because when the Sandman wants the children to sleep, they fall asleep.

He knows full well that his eyes will soon feel tired, so tired that he can't keep them open. He knows he'll have to lie down on the mattress and become part of the darkness.

Mum used to talk about the Sandman's daughter, the mechanical girl, Olympia. She creeps in to the children once they're asleep and pulls the covers up over their shoulders so they don't freeze.

Mikael leans against the wall, feels the furrows in the concrete.

The thin sand floats like fog. It's hard to breathe. His lungs struggle to keep his blood oxygenated.

He coughs and licks his lips. They're dry and already feel numb.

His eyelids are getting heavier and heavier.

Now the whole family is swinging in the hammock. The summer light shines through the leaves of the lilac bower. The rusty screws creak.

Mikael is smiling broadly.

We're swinging high and Mum's trying to slow us down, but Dad keeps us going. A jolt to the table in front of us makes the glasses of strawberry juice tremble.

The hammock swings backwards and Dad laughs and holds up his hands like he was on a rollercoaster.

Mikael's head nods and he opens his eyes in the darkness, stumbles to the side and leans his hand against the cool wall. He turns towards the mattress, thinking that he should lie down before he passes out, when his knees suddenly give way.

He falls and hits the floor, trapping his arm beneath him, feeling the pain from his wrist and shoulder in the sleep to which he has already succumbed.

He rolls heavily onto his stomach and tries to crawl, but doesn't have the energy. He lies there panting with his cheek against the concrete floor. He tries to say something, but has no voice left.

His eyes close even though he's trying to resist.

Just as he is slipping into oblivion he hears the Sandman pad into the room, creeping on his dusty feet straight up the walls to the ceiling. He stops and reaches down with his arms, trying to catch Mikael with his porcelain fingertips.

Everything is black.


When Mikael wakes up his mouth is dry and his head aches. His eyes are grimy with old sand. He's so tired that his brain tries to go back to sleep, but a little sliver of his consciousness registers that something is very different.

Adrenalin hits him like a gust of hot air.

He sits up in the darkness and can hear from the acoustics that he's in a different room, a larger room.

He's no longer in the capsule.

Loneliness makes him ice-cold.

He creeps cautiously across the floor and reaches a wall.

His mind is racing. He can't remember how long it's been since he gave up any thought of escape.

His body is still heavy from its long sleep. He gets up on shaky legs and follows the wall to a corner, then carries on and reaches a sheet of metal. He quickly feels along its edges and realises that it's a door, then runs his hands over its surface and finds a handle.

His hands are shaking.

The room is completely silent.

Carefully he pushes the handle down, and is so prepared to meet resistance that he almost falls over when the door simply opens.

He takes a long stride into the brighter room and has to shut his eyes for a while.

It feels like a dream.

Just let me get out, he thinks.

His head is throbbing.

He squints and sees that he is in a corridor, and moves forward on weak legs. His heart is beating so fast he can hardly breathe.

He's trying to be quiet, but is still whimpering to himself with fear.

The Sandman will soon be back – he never forgets any children.

Mikael can't open his eyes properly, but nonetheless heads towards the fuzzy glow ahead of him.

Maybe it's a trap, he thinks. Maybe he's being lured like an insect towards a burning light.

But he keeps on walking, running his hand along the wall for support.

He knocks into some big rolls of insulation and gasps with fear, lurches to the side and hits the other wall with his shoulder, but manages to keep his balance.

He stops and coughs as quietly as he can.

The glow in front of him is coming from a pane of glass in a door.

He stumbles towards it and pushes the handle down, but the door is locked.

No, no, no . . .

He tugs at the handle, shoves the door, tries again. The door is definitely locked. He feels like slumping to the floor in despair. Suddenly he hears soft footsteps behind him, but daren't turn round.

## 8

Reidar Frost drains his wine glass, puts it down on the dining table and closes his eyes for a while to calm himself. One of the guests is clapping. Veronica is standing in her blue dress, facing the corner with her hands over her face, and she starts to count.

The guests vanish in different directions, and footsteps and laughter spread through the many rooms of the manor house.

The rule is that they have to stick to the ground floor, but Reidar gets slowly to his feet, goes over to the hidden door and creeps into the service passageway. Carefully he climbs the narrow backstairs, opens the secret door in the wall and emerges into the private part of the house.

He knows he shouldn't be alone there, but carries on through the sequence of rooms.

At every stage he closes the doors behind him, until he reaches the gallery at the far end.

Along one wall stand the boxes containing the children's clothes and toys. One box is open, revealing a pale-green space gun.

He hears Veronica call out, muffled by the floor and walls: 'One hundred! Coming, ready or not!'

Through the windows he looks out over the fields and paddocks. In the distance he can see the birch avenue that leads to Råcksta Manor.

Reidar pulls an armchair across the floor and hangs his jacket on it. He can feel how drunk he is as he climbs up onto the seat. The back of his white shirt is wet with sweat. With a forceful gesture he tosses the rope over the beam in the roof. The chair beneath him creaks from the movement. The heavy rope falls across the beam and the end is left swinging.

Dust drifts through the air.

The padded seat feels oddly soft beneath the thin soles of his shoes.

Muted laughter and cries can be heard from the party below and for a few moments Reidar closes his eyes and thinks of the children, their little faces, wonderful faces, their shoulders and thin arms.

He can hear their high-pitched voices and quick feet running across the floor whenever he listens – the memory is like a summer breeze in his soul, leaving him cold and desolate again.

Happy birthday, Mikael, he thinks.

His hands are shaking so much that he can't tie a noose. He stands still, tries to breathe more calmly, then starts again, just as he hears a knock on one of the doors.

He waits a few seconds, then lets go of the rope, climbs down onto the floor and picks up his jacket.

'Reidar?' a woman's voice calls softly.

It's Veronica, she must have been peeking while she was counting and saw him disappear into the passageway. She's opening the doors to the various rooms and her voice gets clearer the closer she comes.

Reidar turns the lights off and leaves the nursery, opening the door to the next room and stopping there.

Veronica comes towards him with a glass of champagne in her hand. There is a warm glow in her dark, intoxicated eyes.

She's tall and thin, and has had her black hair cut in a boyish style that suits her.

'Did I say I wanted to sleep with you?' he asks.

She spins round slightly unsteadily.

'Funny,' she says with a sad look in her eyes.

Veronica Klimt is Reidar's literary agent. He may not have written a word in the past thirteen years, but the three books he wrote before that are still generating an income.

Now they can hear music from the dining room below, the rapid bass-line transmitting itself through the fabric of the building. Reidar stops at the sofa and runs his hand through his silvery hair.

'You're saving some champagne for me, I hope?' he asks, sitting down on the sofa.

'No,' Veronica says, passing him her half-full glass.

'Your husband called me,' Reidar says. 'He thinks it's time for you to go home.'

'I don't want to, I want to get divorced and—'

'You mustn't,' he interrupts.

'Why do you say things like that?'

'Because I don't want you to think I care about you,' he replies.

'I don't.'

He empties the glass, then puts it down on the sofa, closes his eyes and feels the giddiness of being drunk.

'You looked sad, and I got a bit worried.'

'I've never felt better.'

There's laughter now, and the club music is turned up until the vibrations can be felt through the floor.

'Your guests are probably starting to wonder where you are.'

'Then let's go and turn the place upside down,' he says with a smile.

For the past seven years Reidar has made sure he has people around him almost twenty-four hours a day. He has a vast circle of acquaintances. Sometimes he holds big parties out at the house, sometimes more intimate dinners. On certain days, like the children's birthdays, it's very hard indeed to go on living. He knows that without people around him he would soon succumb to the loneliness and silence.

## 9

Reidar and Veronica open the doors to the dining room and the throbbing music hits them in the chest. There's a crowd of people dancing round the table in the darkness. Some of them are still eating the saddle of venison and roasted vegetables.

The actor Wille Strandberg has unbuttoned his shirt. It's impossible to hear what he's saying as he dances his way through the crowd towards Reidar and Veronica.

'Take it off!' Veronica cries.

Wille laughs and pulls off his shirt, throws it at her and dances in front of her with his hands behind his neck. His bulging, middle-aged stomach bounces in time to his quick movements.

Reidar empties another glass of wine, then dances up to Wille with his hips rolling.

The music goes into a quieter, gentler phase and Reidar's old publisher David Sylwan takes hold of his arm and gasps something, his face sweaty and happy.

'What?'

'There's been no contest today,' David repeats.

'Stud poker?' Reidar asks. 'Shooting, wrestling . . .'

'Shooting!' several people cry.

'Get the pistol and a few bottles of champagne,' Reidar says with a smile.

The thudding beat returns, drowning out any further conversation. Reidar gets an oil painting down from the wall and carries it out through the door. It's a portrait of him, painted by Peter Dahl.

'I like that picture,' Veronica says, trying to stop him.

Reidar shakes her hand from his arm and carries on towards the hall. Almost all of the guests follow him outside into the ice-cold park. Fresh snow has settled smoothly on the ground. There are still flakes swirling round beneath the dark sky.

Reidar strides through the snow and hangs the portrait on an apple tree, its branches laden with snow. Wille Strandberg follows, carrying a flare he found in a box in the cleaning cupboard. He tears the plastic cover off, then pulls the string. There's a pop and the flare starts to burn, giving off an intense light. Laughing, he stumbles over and puts the flare in the snow beneath the tree. The white light makes the trunk and naked branches glow.

Now they can all see the painting of Reidar holding a silvery pen in his hand.

Berzelius, a translator, has brought three bottles of champagne, and David Sylwan holds up Reidar's old Colt with a grin.

'This isn't funny,' Veronica says in a serious voice.

David goes and stands next to Reidar, the Colt in his hand. He feeds six bullets into the barrel, then spins the cylinder.

Wille Strandberg is still shirtless, but he's so drunk he doesn't feel the cold.

'If you win, you can choose a horse from the stables,' Reidar mumbles, taking the revolver from David.

'Please, be careful,' Veronica says.

Reidar moves aside, raises his arm and fires, but hits nothing, the blast echoing between the buildings.

A few guests applaud politely, as if he were playing golf.

'My turn,' David laughs.

Veronica stands in the snow, shivering. Her feet are burning with cold in her thin sandals.

'I like that portrait,' she says again.

'Me too,' Reidar says, firing another shot.

The bullet hits the top corner of the canvas, there's a puff of dust as the gold frame gets dislodged and hangs askew.

David pulls the revolver from his hand with a chuckle, stumbles and falls, and fires a shot up at the sky, then another as he tries to stand up.

A couple of guests clap, and others laugh and raise their glasses in a toast.

Reidar takes the revolver back and brushes the snow off it.

'It's all down to the last shot,' he says.

Veronica goes over and kisses him on the lips.

'How are you doing?'

'Fine,' he says. 'I've never been happier.'

Veronica looks at him and brushes the hair from his forehead. The group on the stone steps whistles and laughs.

'I found a better target,' cries a red-haired woman whose name he can't remember.

She's dragging a huge doll through the snow. Suddenly she loses her grip of the doll and falls to her knees, then gets back on her feet again. Her leopard-skin-print dress is flecked with damp.

'I saw it yesterday, it was under a dirty tarpaulin in the garage,' she exclaims jubilantly.

Berzelius hurries over to help her carry it. The doll is solid plastic, and has been painted to look like Spiderman. It's as tall as Berzelius.

'Well done, Marie!' David cries.

'Shoot Spiderman,' one of the women behind them calls.

Reidar looks up, sees the big doll, and lets the gun fall to the snow.

'I have to sleep,' he says abruptly.

He pushes aside the glass of champagne Wille is holding out to him and walks back to the house on unsteady legs.

# 10

Veronica goes with Marie as she searches the house for Reidar. They walk through rooms and halls. His jacket is lying on the stairs to the first floor and they go up. It's dark, but they can see flickering firelight further off. In a large room they find Reidar sitting on a sofa in front of the fireplace. His cufflinks are gone and his sleeves are dangling over his hands. On the low bookcase beside him there are four bottles of Château Cheval Blanc.

'I just wanted to say sorry,' Marie says, leaning against the door.

'Oh, don't mind me,' Reidar mutters, still gazing into the fire.

'It was stupid of me to drag the doll out without asking first,' Marie goes on.

'As far as I'm concerned, you can burn all the old shit,' he replies.

Veronica goes over to him, kneels down and looks up at his face with a smile.

'Have you been introduced to Marie?' she asks. 'She's David's friend . . . I think.'

Reidar raises his glass towards the red-haired woman, then

takes a big gulp. Veronica takes the glass from him, tastes the wine, and sits down.

She pushes her shoes off, leans back and rests her bare feet in his lap.

Gently he caresses her calf, the bruise from the new stirrup leather of her saddle, then up the inside of her thigh towards her groin. She lets it happen, not bothered by the fact that Marie is still in the room.

The flames are rising high in the huge fireplace. The heat is pulsating and her face feels so hot it's almost burning.

Marie comes cautiously closer. Reidar looks at her. Her red hair has started to curl in the heat of the room. Her leopard-skin dress is creased and stained.

'An admirer,' Veronica says, holding the glass away from Reidar when he tries to reach it.

'I love your books,' Marie says.

'Which books?' he asks brusquely.

He gets up and fetches a fresh glass from the dresser and pours some wine. Marie misunderstands the gesture and holds out her hand to take it.

'I presume you go to the toilet yourself when you want to have a piss,' Reidar says, drinking the wine.

'There's no need—'

'If you want wine, then drink some fucking wine,' he interrupts in a loud voice.

Marie blushes and takes a deep breath. With her hand trembling she takes the bottle and pours herself a glass. Reidar sighs deeply, then says in a gentler tone of voice:

'I think this vintage is one of the better years.'

Taking the bottle with him, he goes back to his seat.

Smiling, he watches as Marie sits down beside him, swirls the wine in her glass and tastes it.

Reidar laughs and refills her glass, looks her in the eye, then turns serious and kisses her on the lips.

'What are you doing?' she asks.

Reidar kisses Marie softly again. She moves her head away, but can't help smiling. She drinks some wine, looks him in the eye, then leans over and kisses him.

He strokes the nape of her neck, under her hair, then moves his hand over her right shoulder and feels how the narrow strap of her dress has sunk into her skin.

She puts her glass down, kisses him again, and thinks that she's mad as she lets him caress one of her breasts.

Reidar suppresses the urge to burst into tears, making his throat hurt, as he strokes her thigh under her dress, feeling her nicotine patch, and moves his hand round to her backside.

Marie pats his hand away when he tries to pull her underwear down, then stands up and wipes her mouth.

'Maybe we should go back down and join the party again,' she says, trying to sound neutral.

'Yes,' he says.

Veronica is sitting motionless on the sofa and doesn't meet her enquiring gaze.

'Are you both coming?'

Reidar shakes his head.

'OK,' Marie whispers and walks towards the door.

Her dress shimmers as she leaves the room. Reidar stares through the open doorway. The darkness looks like dirty velvet.

Veronica gets up and takes her glass from the table, and drinks. She has sweat patches under the arms of her dress.

'You're a bastard,' she says.

'I'm just trying to get the most out of life,' he says quietly.

He catches her hand and presses it to his cheek, holding it there and looking into her sorrowful eyes.

## 11

The fire has gone out and the room is freezing cold when Reidar wakes up on the sofa. His eyes are stinging, and he thinks about his wife's story about the Sandman. The man who throws sand in children's eyes so that they fall asleep and sleep right through the night.

'Shit,' Reidar whispers, and sits up.

He's naked, and has spilled wine over the leather uphol-stery. In the distance is the sound of an aeroplane. The morning light hits the dusty windows.

Reidar gets to his feet and sees Veronica lying curled up on the floor in front of the fireplace. She's wrapped herself in the tablecloth. Somewhere in the forest a deer is calling. The party downstairs is still going on, but is more subdued now. Reidar grabs the half-full bottle of wine and leaves the room unsteadily. A headache is throbbing inside his skull as he starts to climb the creaking oak stairs to his bedroom. He stops on the landing, sighs, and goes back down again. Carefully he picks Veronica up and lays her on the sofa, covers her, then retrieves her glasses from the floor and puts them on the table.

Reidar Frost is sixty-two years old and the author of three international bestsellers, the so-called Sanctum series.

He moved from his house in Tyresö eight years ago, when he bought Råcksta Manor, outside Norrtälje. Two hundred hectares of forest, fields, stables and a fine paddock where he occasionally trains his five horses. Thirteen years ago Reidar Frost ended up alone in a way that shouldn't happen to anyone. His son and daughter vanished without trace one night after they sneaked out to meet a friend. Mikael and Felicia's bicycles were found on a footpath near Badholmen. Apart from one detective with a Finnish accent, everyone thought the children had been playing too close to the water and had drowned in Erstaviken.

The police stopped looking, even though no bodies were ever found. Reidar's wife Roseanna couldn't deal with him and her own loss. She moved in temporarily with her sister, asked for a divorce and used the money from the settlement to move abroad. A couple of months later she was found in her bath in a Paris hotel. She'd committed suicide. On the floor was a drawing Felicia had given her on Mother's Day.

The children have been declared dead. Their names are engraved on a headstone that Reidar rarely visits. The same day they were declared dead, he invited his friends to a party, and ever since has taken care to keep going, the way you would keep a fire alight.

Reidar Frost is convinced he's going to drink himself to death, but at the same time he knows he'd kill himself if he was left alone.

# 12

A goods train is thundering through the nocturnal winter landscape. The Traxx train is pulling almost three hundred metres of wagons behind it.

In the driver's cab sits Erik Johnsson. His hand is resting on the control. The noise from the engine and the rails is rhythmic and monotonous.

The snow seems to be rushing out of a tunnel of light formed by the two headlights. The rest is darkness.

As the train emerges from the broad curve around Vårsta, Erik Johnsson increases speed again.

He's thinking that the snow is so bad that he's going to have to stop at Hallsberg, if not before, to check the braking distance.

Far off in the haze two deer scamper off the rails and away across the white fields. They move through the snow with magical ease, and disappear into the night.

As the train approaches the long Igelsta Bridge, Erik thinks back to when Sissela sometimes used to accompany him on journeys. They would kiss in each tunnel and on every bridge. These days she refuses to miss a single yoga lesson.

He brakes gently, passes Hall and heads out across the high

bridge. It feels like flying. The snow is swirling and twisting in the headlights, removing any sense of up and down.

The train is already in the middle of the bridge, high above the ice of Hallsfjärden, when Erik Johnsson sees a flickering shadow through the haze. There's someone on the track. Erik sounds the horn and sees the figure take a long step to the right, onto the other track.

The train is approaching very fast. For half a second the man is caught in the light of the headlamps. He blinks. A young man with a dead face. His clothes are trembling on his skinny frame, and then he's gone.

Erik isn't conscious of the fact that he's applied the brakes and that the whole train is slowing down. There's a rumbling sound and the screech of metal, and he isn't sure if he ran over the young man.

He's shaking, and can feel adrenalin coursing through his body as he calls SOS Alarm.

'I'm a train driver, I've just passed someone on the Igelsta Bridge . . . he was in the middle of the tracks, but I don't think I hit him . . .'

'Is anyone injured?' the operator asks.

'I don't think I hit him, I only saw him for a few seconds.'

'Where exactly did you see him?'

'In the middle of the Igelsta Bridge.'

'On the tracks?'

'There's nothing but tracks up here, it's a fucking railway bridge . . .'

'Was he standing still, or was he walking in a particular direction?'

'I don't know.'

'My colleague is just alerting the police and ambulance in Södertälje. We'll have to stop all rail traffic over the bridge.'

# 13

The emergency control room immediately dispatches police cars to both ends of the long bridge. Just nine minutes later the first car pulls off the Nyköping road with its lights flashing and makes its way up the narrow gravel track alongside Sydgatan. The road leads steeply upwards, and hasn't been ploughed, and loose snow swirls up over the bonnet and windscreen.

The policemen leave the car at the end of the bridge and set out along the tracks with their torches on. It isn't easy walking along the railway line. Cars are passing far below them on the motorway. The four railway tracks narrow to two, and stretch out across the industrial estates of Björkudden and the frozen inlet.

The first officer stops and points. Someone has clearly walked along the right-hand track ahead of them. The shaky beams of their torches illuminate some almost eradicated footprints and a few traces of blood.

They shine their torches into the distance, but there's no one on the bridge as far as they can see. The lights of the harbour below make the snow between the tracks look like smoke from a fire.

Now the second police car reaches the other end of the deep ravine, more than two kilometres away.

The tyres thunder as Police Constable Jasim Muhammed pulls up alongside the railway line. His partner, Fredrik Mosskin, has just contacted their colleagues on the bridge over the radio.

The wind is making so much noise in the microphone that it's almost impossible to hear the voice, but it's clear that someone was walking across the railway bridge very recently.

The car stops and the headlights illuminate a steep rock face. Fredrik ends the call and stares blankly ahead of him.

'What's happening?' Jasim asks.

'Looks like he's heading this way.'

'What did they say about blood? Was there much blood?'

'I didn't hear.'

'Let's go and look,' Jasim says, opening his door.

The blue lights play upon the snow-covered branches of the pine trees.

'The ambulance is on its way,' Fredrik says.

There's no crust on the snow and Jasim sinks in up to his knees. He pulls out his torch and shines it towards the tracks. Fredrik is slipping on the verge, but keeps climbing.

'What sort of animal has an extra arsehole in the middle of its back?' Jasim asks.

'I don't know,' Fredrik mutters.

There's so much snow in the air that they can't see the glow of their colleagues' torches on the other side of the bridge.

'A police horse,' Jasim says.

'What the . . .?'

'That's what my mother-in-law told the kids.' Jasim grins, and heads up onto the bridge.

There are no footprints in the snow. Either the man is still on the bridge, or he's jumped. The cables above them are whistling eerily. The ground beneath them falls away steeply.

The lights of Hall Prison are glowing through the haze, lit up like an underwater city.

Fredrik tries to contact their colleagues, but the radio just crackles.

They head slowly further out across the bridge. Fredrik is walking behind Jasim, a torch in his hand. Jasim can see his own shadow moving across the ground, swaying oddly from side to side.

It's strange that their colleagues from the other side of the bridge aren't visible.

When they are out above the frozen inlet the wind from the sea is bitter. Snow is blowing into their eyes. Their cheeks feel numb with cold.

Jasim screws up his eyes to look across the bridge. It disappears into swirling darkness. Suddenly he sees something at the edge of the light from the torch. A tall stick-figure with no head.

Jasim stumbles and reaches his hand out towards the low railing, and sees the snow fall fifty metres onto the ice.

His torch hits something and goes out.

His heart is beating hard and Jasim peers forward again, but can no longer see the figure.

Fredrik calls him back and he turns round. His partner is pointing at him, but it's impossible to hear what he's saying. He looks scared, and starts to fumble with the holster of his pistol, and Jasim realises that he's trying to warn him, that he was pointing at someone behind his back.

He turns round and gasps for breath.

Someone is crawling along the track straight towards him. Jasim backs away and tries to draw his pistol. The figure gets to its feet and sways. It's a young man. He's staring at the policemen with empty eyes. His bearded face is thin, his cheekbones sharp. He's swaying and seems to be having trouble breathing.

'Half of me is still underground,' he pants.

'Are you injured?'

'Who?'

The young man coughs and falls to his knees again.

'What's he saying?' Fredrik asks, with one hand on his holstered service weapon.

'Are you injured?' Jasim asks again.

'I don't know, I can't feel anything, I . . .'

'Please, come with me.'

Jasim helps him up and sees that his right hand is covered with red ice.

'I'm only half . . . The Sandman has taken . . . he's taken half . . .'

## 14

The doors of the ambulance bay of Södermalm Hospital close. A red-cheeked auxiliary nurse helps the paramedics remove the stretcher and wheel it towards the emergency room.

'We can't find anything to identify him by, nothing . . .'

The patient is handed over to the triage nurse and taken into one of the treatment rooms. After checking his vital signs the nurse identifies the patient as triage-level orange, the second highest level, extremely urgent.

Four minutes later Dr Irma Goodwin comes into the treatment room and the nurse gives her a quick briefing:

'Airways free, no acute trauma . . . but he's got poor saturation, fever, signs of concussion and weak circulation.'

The doctor looks at the charts and goes over to the skinny man. His clothes have been cut open. His bony ribcage rises and falls with his rapid breathing.

'Still no name?'

'No.'

'Give him oxygen.'

The young man lies with his eyelids closed and trembling as the nurse puts an oxygen mask on him.

He looks strangely malnourished, but there are no visible needle marks on his body. Irma has never seen anyone so white. The nurse checks his temperature from his ear again.

'Thirty-nine point nine.'

Irma Goodwin ticks the tests she wants taken from the patient, then looks at him again. His chest rattles as he coughs weakly and opens his eyes briefly.

'I don't want to, I don't want to,' he whispers frantically. 'I've got to go home, I've got to, I've got to . . .'

'Where do you live? Can you tell me where you live?'

'Which . . . which one of us?' he asks, and gulps hard.

'He's delirious,' the nurse says quietly.

'Have you got any pain?'

'Yes,' he replies with a confused smile.

'Can you tell me . . .'

'No, no, no, no, she's screaming inside me, I can't bear it, I can't, I . . .'

His eyes roll back, he coughs, and mutters something about porcelain fingers, then lies there gasping for breath.

Irma Goodwin decides to give the patient a Neurobion injection, antipyretics and an intravenous antibiotic, Benzylpenicillin, until the test results come back.

She leaves the treatment room and walks down the corridor, rubbing the place where her wedding ring sat for eighteen years until she flushed it down the toilet. Her husband had betrayed her for far too long for her to forgive him. It no longer hurts, but it still feels like a shame, a waste of their shared future. She wonders about phoning her daughter even though it's late. Since the divorce she's been much more anxious than before, and calls Mia far too often.

Through the door ahead of her she can hear the staff nurse talking on the phone. An ambulance is on its way in from a priority call. A serious RTA. The staff nurse is putting together an emergency team and calling a surgeon.

Irma Goodwin stops and goes back to the room containing the unidentified patient. The red-cheeked auxiliary nurse is helping the other nurse to clean a bleeding wound in the man's thigh. It looks like the young man had run straight into a sharp branch.

Irma Goodwin stops in the doorway.

'Add some Macrolide to the antibiotics,' she says decisively. 'One gram of Erythromycin, intravenous.'

The nurse looks up.

'You think he's got Legionnaires' disease?' she asks in surprise.

'Let's see what the test—'

Irma Goodwin falls silent as the patient's body starts to jerk. She looks at his white face and sees him slowly open his eyes.

'I've got to get home,' he whispers. 'My name is Mikael Kohler-Frost, and I've got to get home . . .'

'Mikael Kohler-Frost,' Irma says. 'You're in Södermalm Hospital, and—'

'She's screaming, all the time!'

Irma leaves the treatment room and half-runs to her office. She closes the door behind her, puts on her reading glasses, sits down at her computer and logs in. She can't find him in the health service database and tries the national population register instead.

She finds him there.

Irma Goodwin unconsciously rubs the empty place on her ring finger and rereads the information about the patient in the emergency room.

Mikael Kohler-Frost has been dead for seven years, and is buried in Malsta cemetery, in the parish of Norrtälje.

# 15

Detective Inspector Joona Linna is in a small room whose walls and floor are made of bare concrete. He is on his knees while a man in camouflage is aiming a pistol at his head, a black SIG Sauer. The door is being guarded by a man who keeps his Belgian assault rifle trained on Joona the whole time.

On the floor next to the wall is a bottle of Coca-Cola. The light is coming from a ceiling lamp with a buckled aluminium shade.

A mobile phone buzzes. Before the man with the pistol answers he yells at Joona to lower his head.

The other man puts his finger on the trigger and moves a step closer.

The man with the pistol talks into the mobile phone, then listens, without taking his eyes off Joona. Grit crunches under his boots. He nods, says something else, then listens again.

After a while the man with the assault rifle sighs and sits down on the chair just inside the door.

Joona kneels there completely still. He is wearing jogging trousers and a white T-shirt that's wet with sweat. The sleeves are tight across the muscles of his upper arms. He raises his head slightly. His eyes are as grey as polished granite.

The man with the pistol is talking excitedly into the phone, then he ends the call and seems to think for a few seconds before taking four quick steps forward and pressing the barrel of the pistol to Joona's forehead.

'I'm about to overpower you,' Joona says amiably.

'What?'

'I had to wait,' he explains. 'Until I got the chance of direct physical contact.'

'I've just received orders to execute you.'

'Yes, the situation's fairly acute, seeing as I have to get the pistol away from my face, and ideally use it within five seconds.'

'How?' the man by the door asks.

'In order to catch him by surprise, I mustn't react to any of his movements,' Joona explains. 'That's why I've let him walk up, stop and take precisely two breaths. So I wait until he breathes out the second time before I—'

'Why?' the man with the pistol asks.

'I gain a few hundredths of a second, because it's practically impossible to do anything without first breathing in.'

'But why the second breath in particular?'

'Because it's unexpectedly early and right at the middle of the most common countdown in the world: one, two, three . . .'

'I get it.' The man smiles, revealing a brown front tooth.

'The first thing that's going to move is my left hand,' Joona explains to the surveillance camera up by the ceiling. 'It'll move up towards the barrel of the pistol and away from my face in one fluid movement. I need to grasp it, twist upwards and get to my feet, using his body as a shield. In a single movement. My hands need to prioritise the gun, but at the same time I need to observe the man with the assault rifle. Because as soon as I've got control of the pistol he's the primary threat. I use my elbow against his chin and neck as many times as it takes to get control of the pistol, then I fire three shots and spin round and fire another three shots.'

The men in the room start again. The situation repeats. The man with the pistol gets his orders over the phone, hesitates, then walks up to Joona and pushes the barrel to his forehead. The man breathes out a second time and is just about to breathe in again to say something when Joona grabs the barrel of the pistol with his left hand.

The whole thing is remarkably surprising and quick, even though it was expected.

Joona knocks the gun aside, twisting it towards the ceiling in the same movement, and getting to his feet. He jabs his elbow into the man's neck four times, takes the pistol and shoots the other man in the torso.

The three blank shots echo off the walls.

The first opponent is still staggering backwards when Joona spins round and shoots him in the chest.

He falls against the wall.

Joona walks over to the door, grabs the assault rifle and extra cartridge, then leaves the room.

## 16

The door hits the concrete wall hard and bounces back. Joona is changing the cartridge as he marches in. The eight people in the next room all take their eyes off the large screen and look at him.

'Six and a half seconds to the first shot,' one of them says.

'That's far too slow,' Joona says.

'But Markus would have let go of the pistol sooner if your elbow had actually hit him,' a tall man with a shaved head says.

'Yes, you would have won some time there,' a female officer adds with a smile.

The scene is already repeating on the screen. Joona's taut shoulder, the fluid movement forward, his eye lining up with the sights as the trigger is pulled.

'Pretty damn impressive,' the group commander says, setting his palms down on the table.

'For a cop,' Joona concludes.

They laugh, lean back, and the group commander scratches the tip of his nose as he blushes.

Joona Linna accepts a glass of water. He doesn't yet know that what he fears most is about to flare up like a firestorm.

He doesn't yet have any idea of the little spark drifting towards the great lagoon of petrol.

Joona Linna is at Karlsborg Fortress to instruct the Special Operations Group in close combat. Not because he's a trained instructor, but because he has more practical experience of the techniques they need to learn than just about anyone else in Sweden. When Joona was eighteen he did his military service at Karlsborg as a paratrooper, and was immediately recruited after basic training to a special unit for operations that couldn't be solved by conventional forces or weaponry.

Although a long time has passed since he left the military to study at the Police Academy, he still has dreams about his time as a paratrooper. He's back on the transport plane, listening to the deafening roar and staring out through the hydraulic hatch. The shadow of the plane moves over the pale water far below like a grey cross. In his dream he runs down the ramp and jumps out into the cold air, hears the whine of the cords, feels his harness jerk as his limbs are thrown forward when the parachute opens. The water approaches at great speed. The black inflatable boat is foaming against the waves far below.

Joona was trained in the Netherlands for effective close combat with knives, bayonets and pistols. He was taught to exploit changing situations and to use innovative techniques. These goal-orientated techniques were a specialised version of a system of close combat known by its Hebrew name, Krav Maga.

'OK, we'll take this situation as our starting point, and make it progressively harder as the day goes on,' Joona says.

'Like hitting two people with one bullet?' The tall man with the shaved head grins.

'Impossible,' Joona says.

'We heard that you did it,' the woman says curiously.

'Oh no.' Joona smiles, running his hand through his untidy blond hair.

His phone rings in his inside pocket. He sees on the screen that it's Nathan Pollock from the National Criminal Investigation Department. Nathan knows where Joona is, and would only call if it was important.

'Excuse me,' Joona says, then takes the call.

He drinks from the glass of water, and listens with a smile that slowly fades. Suddenly all the colour drains from his face.

'Is Jurek Walter still locked up?' he asks.

His hand is shaking so much that he has to put the glass down on the table.

## 17

Snow is swirling through the air as Joona runs out to his car and gets in. He drives straight across the large exercise yard where he trained as a teenager, takes the corner with the tyres crunching, and leaves the garrison.

His heart is beating hard and he's still having trouble believing what Nathan told him. Beads of sweat have appeared on his forehead, and his hands won't stop shaking.

He overtakes a convoy of articulated lorries on the E20 motorway just before Arboga. He has to hold the wheel with both hands because the drag from the lorries makes his car shake.

The whole time he can't stop thinking about the phone call he received in the middle of his training session with the Special Operations Group.

Nathan Pollock's voice was quite calm as he explained that Mikael Kohler-Frost was still alive.

Joona had been convinced that the boy and his younger sister were two of Jurek Walter's many victims. Now Nathan was telling him that Mikael had been found by the police on a railway bridge in Södertälje, and had been taken to Södermalm Hospital.

Pollock had said that Mikael's condition was serious, but not life-threatening. He hadn't yet been questioned.

'Is Jurek Walter still locked up?' was Joona's first question.

'Yes, he's still in solitary confinement,' Pollock had replied.

'You're sure?'

'Yes.'

'What about the boy? How do you know it's Mikael Kohler-Frost?' Joona had asked.

'Apparently he's said his name several times. That's as much as we know . . . and he's the right age,' Pollock had said. 'Naturally, we've sent a saliva sample to the National Forensics Lab—'

'But you haven't informed his father?'

'We have to try to get a DNA match before we do that, I mean, we can't get this wrong . . .'

'I'm on my way.'

## 18

The car sucks up the black, slushy road, and Joona Linna has to force himself not to speed up as his mind conjures up images of what happened so many years before.

Mikael Kohler-Frost, he thinks.

Mikael Kohler-Frost has been found alive after all these years.

The name Frost alone is enough for Joona to relive the whole thing.

He overtakes a dirty white car and barely notices the child waving a stuffed toy at him through the window. He is immersed in his memories, and is sitting in his colleague Samuel Mendel's comfortably messy living room.

Samuel leans over the table, making his curly black hair fall over his forehead as he repeats what Joona has just said.

'A serial killer?'

Thirteen years ago Joona embarked on a preliminary investigation that would change his life entirely. Together with his colleague Samuel Mendel, he began to investigate the case of two people who had been reported missing in Sollentuna.

The first case was a fifty-five-year-old woman who went missing when she was out walking one evening. Her dog had been found in a passageway behind the ICA Kvantum super-market, dragging its leash behind it. Just two days later the woman's mother-in-law vanished as she was walking the short distance between her sheltered housing and the bingo hall.

It turned out that the woman's brother had gone missing in Bangkok five years before. Interpol and the Foreign Ministry had been called in, but he had never been found.

There are no comprehensive figures for the number of people who go missing around the world each year, but everyone knows the total is a disturbingly large number. In the USA almost one hundred thousand go missing each year, and in Sweden around seven thousand.

Most of them show up, but there's still an alarming number who remain missing.

Only a very small proportion of the ones who are never found have been kidnapped or murdered.

Joona and Samuel were both relatively new at the National Criminal Investigation Department when they started to look into the case of the two missing women from Sollentuna. Certain aspects were reminiscent of two people who went missing in Örebro four years earlier.

On that occasion it was a forty-year-old man and his son. They had been on their way to a football match in Glanshammar, but never got there. Their car was found abandoned on a small forest road that was nowhere near the football ground.

At first it was just an idea, a random suggestion.

What if there was a direct link between the cases, in spite of the differences in time and location?

In which case, it wasn't impossible that more missing people could be connected to these four.

The preliminary investigation consisted of the most common sort of police work, the sort that happens at a desk, in front of the computer. Joona and Samuel gathered and organised information about everyone who had gone missing in Sweden and not been traced over the previous ten years.

The idea was to find out if any of those missing people had anything in common beyond the bounds of coincidence.

They laid the various cases on top of each other, as if they were on transparent paper – and slowly something resembling an astronomical map began to appear out of the vague motif of connected points.

The unexpected pattern that emerged was that in many of the cases more than one member of the same family had disappeared.

Joona could remember the silence that had descended upon the room when they stepped back and looked at the result. Forty-five missing people matched that particular criterion. Many of those could probably be dismissed over the following days, but forty-five was still thirty-five more than could reasonably be explained by coincidence.

## 19

One wall of Samuel's office in the National Criminal Investigation Department was covered with a large map of Sweden, dotted with pins to indicate the missing persons.

Obviously they couldn't assume that all forty-five had been murdered, but for the time being they couldn't rule any of them out.

Because no known perpetrator could be linked to the times of the disappearances, they started looking for motives and a modus operandi. There were no similarities with cases that had been solved. The murderer they were dealing with this time left no trace of violence, and he hid his victims' bodies very well.

The choice of victim usually divides serial killers into two groups: organised killers, who always seek out the ideal victim who matches their fantasies as closely as possible. These killers focus on a particular type of person, exclusively seeking out pre-pubertal blond boys, for example.

The other group comprises the disorganised killers – here it is the availability of the victim that counts. The victim primarily fills a role in the murderer's fantasies, and it doesn't particularly matter who they really are, or what they look like.

But the serial killer that Joona and Samuel were starting to envisage didn't seem to fit either of these categories. On the one hand he was disorganised, because the victims were so varied, but on the other hand none of them was especially easy to get hold of.

They were looking for a serial killer who was practically invisible. He didn't follow a pattern, and left no evidence, no intentional signature.

Days went by without the missing women from Sollentuna being found.

Joona and Samuel had no concrete proof of a serial killer that they could present to their boss. They merely repeated that there couldn't be any other explanation for all these missing people. Two days later the preliminary investigation was downgraded and the resources for further work reallocated.

But Joona and Samuel couldn't let it go, and started to devote their free time during the evenings and weekends to the search.

They concentrated on the pattern that suggested that if two people had gone missing from the same family, there was an increased risk of a further family member going missing within the near future.

While they were keeping an eye on the family of the women who had vanished from Sollentuna, two children were reported missing from Tyresö. Mikael and Felicia Kohler-Frost. The children of the well-known author, Reidar Frost.

## 20

Joona looks at the petrol gauge as he passes the Statoil filling station and a snow-covered lay-by.

He remembers talking to Reidar Frost and his wife Roseanna Kohler three days after their two children went missing. He didn't mention his suspicions to them – that they had been murdered by a serial killer whom the police had stopped looking for, a murderer whose existence they had only managed to identify in theory.

Joona just asked his questions, and let the parents cling onto the idea that the children had drowned.

The family lived on Varvsvägen, in a beautiful house facing a sandy beach and the water. There had been several mild weeks and a lot of the snow had thawed. The streets and footpaths were dark and wet. There was barely any ice along the shoreline, and what remained was grey slush.

Joona remembers walking through the house, passing a large kitchen and sitting down at a huge white table next to a window. But Roseanna had closed all the curtains, and although her voice was calm her head was shaking the whole time.

The search for the children was fruitless. There had been countless helicopter searches, divers had been called in, and the water had been dragged for bodies. The surroundings had been searched by chain gangs of both volunteers and specialist dog units.

But no one had seen or heard anything.

Reidar Frost looked like a captured animal.

He just wanted to keep on searching.

Joona had sat opposite the two parents, asking routine questions about whether they had received any threats, if anyone had behaved oddly or differently, if they had felt they were being followed.

'Everyone thinks they fell in the water,' the wife had said, her head starting to shake again.

'You mentioned that they sometimes climb out of the window after their bedtime prayers,' Joona went on calmly.

'Obviously, they're not supposed to,' Reidar said.

'But you know that they sometimes creep out and cycle off to see a friend?'

'Rikard.'

'Rikard van Horn, number 7 Björnbärsvägen,' Joona said.

'We've tried talking to Micke and Felicia about it, but . . . well, they're children, and I suppose we didn't think it was that harmful,' Reidar replied, gently laying his hand over his wife's.

'What do they do at Rikard's?'

'They never stay for long, just play a bit of Diablo.'

'They all do,' Roseanna whispered, pulling her hand away.

'But on Saturday they didn't cycle to Rikard's, but went to Badholmen instead,' Joona went on. 'Do they often go there in the evening?'

'We don't think so,' Roseanna said, getting up restlessly from the table, as if she could no longer keep her internal trembling in check.

Joona nodded.

He knew that the boy, Mikael, had answered the phone

just before he and his younger sister had left the house, but the number had been impossible to trace.

It had been unbearable, sitting there opposite the children's parents. Joona said nothing, but was feeling more and more convinced that the children were victims of the serial killer. He listened, and asked his questions, but he couldn't tell them what he suspected.

## 21

If the two children were victims of this serial killer, and they were correct in thinking that he would soon try to kill one of the parents as well, they had to make a choice.

Joona and Samuel decided to concentrate their efforts on Roseanna Kohler.

She had moved out to live with her sister in Gärdet, in north-east Stockholm.

The sister lived with her four-year-old daughter in a white apartment block at 25 Lanforsvägen, close to Lill-Jan's Forest.

Joona and Samuel took turns keeping watch on the building at night. For a week, one of them would sit in their car a bit further along the road until it got light.

On the eighth day Joona was leaning back in his seat, watching the building's inhabitants get ready for night as usual. The lights went off in a pattern that he was starting to recognise.

A woman in a silver-coloured padded jacket went for her usual walk with her golden retriever, then the last windows went dark.

Joona's car was parked in the shadows on Porjusvägen, between a dirty white pickup and a red Toyota.

In the rear-view mirror he could see snow-covered bushes and a tall fence surrounding an electricity substation.

The residential area in front of him was completely quiet. Through the windscreen he watched the static glow of the streetlamps, the pavements and unlit windows of the buildings.

He suddenly started to smile to himself when he thought about the dinner he had eaten with his wife and little daughter before he drove out there. Lumi had been in a hurry to finish so she could carry on examining Joona.

'I'd like to finish eating first,' he suggested.

But Lumi had adopted her serious expression and talked to her mother over his head, asking if he was brushing his teeth himself yet.

'He's very good,' Summa replied.

She explained with a smile that all of Joona's teeth had come through, as she carried on eating. Lumi put a piece of kitchen roll under his chin and tried to stick a finger in his mouth, telling him to open wide.

His thoughts of Lumi vanished as a light suddenly went on in the sister's flat. Joona saw Roseanna standing there in a flannel nightdress, talking on the phone.

The light went out again.

An hour passed, but the area remained deserted.

It was starting to get cold inside the car when Joona caught sight of a figure in the rear-view mirror. Someone hunched over, approaching down the empty street.

## 22

Joona slumped down slightly in his seat and followed the figure's progress in the rear-view mirror, trying to catch a glimpse of its face.

The branches of a rowan tree swayed as he passed.

In the grey lights from the substation Joona saw that it was Samuel.

His colleague was almost half an hour early.

He opened the car door and sat down in the passenger seat, pushed the seat back, stretched out his legs and sighed.

'OK, so you're tall and blond, Joona . . . and it's really lovely being in the car and everything. But I still think I'd rather spend the night with Rebecka . . . I want to help the boys with their homework.'

'You can help me with my homework,' Joona said.

'Thanks,' Samuel laughed.

Joona looked out at the road, at the building with its closed doors, the rusting balconies, the windows that shone blackly.

'We'll give it three more days,' he said.

Samuel pulled out the silver-coloured flask of yoich, as he called his chicken soup.

'I don't know, I've been doing a lot of thinking,' he said seriously. 'Nothing about this case makes sense . . . we're trying to find a serial killer who may not actually exist.'

'He exists,' Joona replied stubbornly.

'But he doesn't fit with what we've found out, he doesn't fit with any aspect of the investigation, and—'

'That's why . . . that's why no one has seen him,' Joona said. 'He's only visible because he casts a shadow over the statistics.'

They sat beside each other in silence. Samuel blew on his soup, and beads of sweat broke out on his forehead. Joona hummed a tango and let his eyes wander from Roseanna's bedroom window to the icicles hanging from the guttering, then up at the snow-covered chimneys and vents.

'There's someone behind the building,' Samuel suddenly whispered. 'I'm sure I saw movement.'

Samuel pointed, but everything was in a state of dreamlike peace.

A moment later Joona saw some snow fall from a bush close to the house. Someone had just brushed past it.

Carefully they opened the car doors and crept out.

The sleepy residential area was quiet. All they could hear were their own footsteps and the electric hum from the substation.

There had been a thaw for a couple of weeks, then it had started to snow again.

They approached the windowless gable-end of the building, walking quietly along the strip of grass, past a wallpaper shop on the ground floor.

The glow from the nearest streetlamp reached out across the smooth snow to the open space behind the houses. They stopped at the corner, hunched over, trying to check the trees as they got denser towards the Royal Tennis Club and Lill-Jan's Forest.

At first Joona couldn't see anything in the darkness between the crooked old trees.

He was about to give Samuel the signal to proceed when he saw the figure.

There was a man standing among the trees. He was as still as the snow-covered branches.

Joona's heart began to beat faster.

The slim man was staring like a ghost up at the window where Roseanna Kohler was sleeping.

The man showed no sign of urgency, had no obvious purpose.

Joona was filled with an icy conviction that the man in the garden was the serial killer whose existence they had speculated about.

The shadowy figure was thin and crumpled.

He was just standing there, as if the sight of the house gave him a sense of calm satisfaction, as if he already had his victim in a trap.

They drew their weapons, but were unsure of what to do. They hadn't discussed this in advance. Even though they had been keeping watch on Roseanna for days, they had never talked about what they would do if it transpired that they were right.

They couldn't just rush over and arrest a man who was simply standing there looking at a dark window. They may find out who he was, but they might well be forced to release him.

## 23

Joona stared at the motionless figure between the tree trunks. He could feel the weight of his semi-automatic pistol and the chill of the night air on his fingers. He could hear Samuel's breathing beside him.

The situation was beginning to seem slightly absurd when, without warning, the man took a step forward.

They could see he was holding a bag in one hand.

Afterwards it was hard to know what it was that convinced them both that they had found the man they were looking for.

The man just smiled up at the window of Roseanna's bedroom, then vanished into the bushes.

The snow covering the grass crunched faintly beneath their feet as they crept after him. They followed the fresh footprints through the dormant forest until they eventually reached an old railway line.

Far off to the right they could see the figure on the track. He passed below an electricity pylon, crossing the tangle of shadows thrown by its frame.

The railway was still used for goods traffic, and ran from Värta Harbour right through Lill-Jan's Forest.

Joona and Samuel followed, sticking to the deep snow beside the tracks to avoid being seen.

The railway line carried on beneath a viaduct and into the expanse of forest. Suddenly everything got much quieter and darker again.

The black trees stood close together with their snow-covered branches.

Joona and Samuel silently speeded up so as not to lose sight of him.

When they emerged from the curve around Uggleviken marsh they could see that the railway line stretching out ahead of them was empty.

The man had left the track somewhere and gone into the forest.

They climbed up onto the rails and looked out into the white forest, then started to walk back. It had been snowing over recent days and the snow was largely untouched.

Then they found a set of footprints they had missed earlier. The skinny man had left the rails and headed off into the forest. The ground beneath the snow was wet and the prints left by his shoes had darkened. Ten minutes before they had been white and impossible to see in the weak light, but now they were dark as lead.

They followed the tracks into the forest, towards the large reservoir. It was almost pitch-black among the trees.

The murderer's footprints were crossed three times by the lighter tracks of a hare.

At one point it was so dark that they lost his trail again. They stopped, then spotted the tracks again and hurried on.

Suddenly they could hear high-pitched whimpering sounds. It was like an animal crying, like nothing Joona and Samuel had ever heard before. They followed the footprints and drew closer to the source of the sounds.

What they saw between the tree trunks was like something out of some grotesque medieval story. The man they had followed was standing in front of a shallow grave. The ground around him was covered with freshly dug earth. An emaciated, filthy woman was trying to get out of the coffin, crying and struggling to clamber up over the edge. But each time she was on her way up, the man pushed her down again.

For a couple of seconds Joona and Samuel could only stand there, staring, before taking the safety catches off their weapons and rushing in.

The man wasn't armed, and Joona knew he ought to aim at the man's legs, but he couldn't help aiming at his heart.

They ran over the dirty snow, forced the man onto his stomach and cuffed both his wrists and feet.

Samuel stood panting, pointing his pistol at the man as he called emergency control.

Joona could hear the sob in his voice.

They had caught a previously unknown serial killer.

His name was Jurek Walter.

Joona carefully helped the woman up out of the coffin, and tried to calm her down. She just lay on the ground gasping. When Joona explained that help was on the way, he caught a glimpse of movement through the trees. Something large was running away, a branch snapped, fir trees swayed and snow fell softly like cloth.

Perhaps it was a deer.

Joona realised later that it must have been Jurek Walter's accomplice, but right then all they could think about was saving the woman and getting the man into custody in Kronoberg.

It turned out that the woman had been in the coffin for almost two years. Jurek Walter had regularly supplied her with food and water, then covered the grave over again.

The woman had gone blind, and was severely undernourished, her muscles had atrophied and compression sores had left her deformed, and her hands and feet had suffered frostbite.

At first it was assumed that she was merely traumatised, but as time passed it became clear that she had incurred severe brain damage.

## 24

Joona locked the door very carefully when he got home at half past four that morning. His heart thudding with trepidation, he moved Lumi's warm, sweaty body closer to the middle of the bed before putting his arm round both her and Summa. He realised he wasn't going to be able to sleep, but just needed to lie down with his family.

He was back in Lill-Jan's Forest by seven o'clock. The area had been cordoned off and was under guard, but the snow around the grave was already so churned up by the police, dogs and paramedics that there was no point trying to find any tracks of a potential accomplice.

Before ten o'clock a police dog unit had identified a location close to the Uggleviken reservoir, just two hundred metres from the woman's grave. A team of forensics experts and crime-scene analysts was called in, and a couple of hours later the remains of a middle-aged man and a boy of about fifteen had been exhumed. They were both squashed into a blue plastic barrel, and forensic examination indicated that they'd been buried almost four years before. They hadn't survived many hours in the barrel even though there was a tube supplying them with air.

Jurek Walter was registered as living on Björnövägen, part of a large housing estate built in the early 1970s, in the Hovsjö district of Södertälje. It was the only address in his name. According to the records, he hadn't lived anywhere else since he arrived in Sweden from Poland in 1994 and was granted a work permit.

He had taken a job as a mechanic for a small company, Menge's Engineering Workshop, where he repaired train gearboxes and renovated diesel engines.

All the evidence suggested that he lived a lonely, peaceful life.

Joona and Samuel and the two forensics officers didn't know what they might find in Jurek Walter's flat. A torture chamber or trophy cabinet, jars of formaldehyde, freezers containing body parts, shelves bulging with photographic documentation?

The police had cordoned off the immediate vicinity of the block of flats, and the whole of the second floor.

They put on protective clothing, opened the door and started to set out boards to walk on, so that they wouldn't ruin any evidence.

Jurek Walter lived in a two-room flat measuring thirty-three square metres.

There was a pile of junk mail below the letterbox. The hall was completely empty. There were no shoes or clothes in the wardrobe beside the front door.

They moved further in.

Joona was prepared for someone to be hiding inside, but everything was perfectly still, as if time had abandoned the place.

The blinds were drawn. The flat smelled of sunshine and dust.

There was no furniture in the kitchen. The fridge was open and switched off. There was nothing to suggest it had ever been used. The hotplates on the cooker had rusted slightly. Inside the oven the operating instructions were still taped to the side. The only food they found in the cupboards was two tins of sliced pineapple.

In the bedroom was a narrow bed with no bedclothes, and inside the wardrobe one clean shirt hung from a metal hanger.

That was all.

Joona tried to work out what the empty flat signified. It was obvious that Jurek Walter didn't live there.

Perhaps he only used it as a postal address.

There was nothing in the flat to lead them anywhere else. The only fingerprints belonged to Jurek himself.

He had no criminal record, had never been suspected of any crime, he wasn't on any registers held by social services. Jurek Walter had no private insurance, had never taken out a loan, his tax was deducted directly from his wages, and he had never claimed any tax credits.

There were so many different registers. More than three hundred of them, all covered by the Personal Records Act. Jurek Walter was only listed in the ones that no citizen could avoid.

Otherwise he was invisible.

He had never been off sick, had never sought help from a doctor or dentist.

He wasn't in the firearms register, the vehicle register, there were no school records, no registered political or religious affiliations.

It was as if he had lived his life with the express intention of being as invisible as possible.

There was nothing that could lead them any further.

The few people he had been in contact with at his workplace knew nothing about him. They could only report that he never said much, but he was a very good mechanic.

When the National Criminal Investigation Department received a response from the Policja, their Polish counterparts, it turned out that Jurek Walter had been dead for many years. Because this Jurek Walter had been found murdered in a public toilet at the central station, Kraków Główny, they were able to supply both photographs and fingerprints.

Neither pictures nor prints matched the Swedish serial killer.

Presumably he had stolen the identity of the real Jurek Walter.

The man they had captured in Lill-Jan's Forest was looking more and more like a frightening enigma.

They went on combing the forest for another three months, but after the man and boy in the barrel no more of Jurek Walter's victims had been found.

Not until Mikael Kohler-Frost turned up, walking across a bridge, heading for Stockholm.

# 25

A prosecutor took over responsibility for the preliminary investigation, but Joona and Samuel led the interviews, from the custody proceedings to the principal interrogation. Jurek Walter didn't confess to anything, but he didn't deny any crimes either. Instead he philosophised about death and the human condition. Because of the relative lack of supporting evidence, it was the circumstances surrounding his arrest, his failure to offer an explanation and the forensic psychiatrist's evaluation that led to his conviction in Stockholm Courthouse. His lawyer appealed against the conviction and while they were waiting for the case to be heard in the Court of Appeal, more interviews were held in Kronoberg Prison.

The staff at the prison were used to most things, but Jurek Walter's presence troubled them. He made them feel uneasy. Wherever he was, conflicts would suddenly flare up; on one occasion two warders started fighting, with one of them ending up in hospital.

A crisis meeting was held, and new security procedures agreed. Jurek Walter would no longer be allowed to come into contact with other inmates, or use the exercise yard.

When Samuel called in sick, Joona found himself walking

alone down the corridor, past the row of white thermos flasks, one outside each of the green doors. The shiny linoleum floor had long, black marks on it.

The door to Jurek Walter's cell was open. The walls were bare and the window barred. The morning light reflected off the worn plastic-covered mattress on the fixed bunk and the stainless-steel basin.

Further along the corridor a policeman in a dark-blue sweater was talking to a Syrian Orthodox priest.

'They've taken him to interview room two,' the officer called to Joona.

A guard was waiting outside the interview room, and through the window Joona could see Jurek Walter sitting on a chair, looking down at the floor. In front of him stood his legal representative and two guards.

'I'm here to listen,' Joona said when he went in.

There was a short silence, then Jurek Walter exchanged a few words with his lawyer. He spoke in a low voice and didn't look up as he asked the lawyer to leave.

'You can wait in the corridor,' Joona told the guards.

When he was on his own with Jurek Walter in the interview room he moved a chair and put it so close that he could smell the man's sweat.

Jurek Walter sat still on his chair, his head drooping forward.

'Your defence lawyer claims that you were in Lill-Jan's Forest to free the woman,' Joona said in a neutral voice.

Jurek went on staring at the floor for another couple of minutes, then, without the slightest movement, said:

'I talk too much.'

'The truth will do,' Joona said.

'But it really doesn't matter to me if I'm found guilty of something I didn't do,' Walter said.

'You'll be locked up.'

Jurek looked up at Joona and said thoughtfully:

'The life went out of me a long time ago. I'm not scared of anything. Not pain . . . not loneliness or boredom.'

'But I'm looking for the truth,' Joona said, intentionally naïve.

'You don't have to look for it. It's the same with justice, or gods. You make a choice to fit your own requirements.'

'But you don't choose the lies,' Joona said.

Jurek's pupils contracted.

'In the Court of Appeal the prosecutor's description of my actions will be regarded as proven beyond all reasonable doubt,' he said, without the slightest hint of a plea in his voice.

'You're saying that's wrong?'

'I'm not going to get hung up on technicalities, because there isn't really any difference between digging a grave and refilling it.'

When Joona left the interview room that day, he was more convinced than ever that Jurek Walter was an extremely dangerous man, but at the same time he couldn't stop thinking about the possibility that Jurek had been trying to say that he was being punished for someone else's crimes. Of course he understood that it had been Jurek Walter's intention to sow a seed of doubt, but he couldn't ignore the fact that there was actually a flaw in the prosecution's case.

## 26

The day before the appeal, Joona, Summa and Lumi went to dinner with Samuel and his family. The sun had been shining through the linen curtains when they started eating, but it was now evening. Rebecka lit a candle on the table and blew out the match. The light quivered over her luminous eyes, and her one strange pupil. She had once explained that it was a condition called dyscoria, and that it wasn't a problem, she could see just as well with that eye as the other.

The relaxed meal concluded with dark honey cake. Joona borrowed a kippah for the prayer, Birkat Hamazon.

That was the last time he saw Samuel's family.

The boys played quietly for a while with little Lumi before Joshua immersed himself in a video game and Reuben disappeared into his room to practise his clarinet.

Rebecka went outside for a cigarette, and Summa kept her company with her glass of wine.

Joona and Samuel cleared the table, and as soon as they were alone started talking about work and the following day's appeal.

'I'm not going to be there,' Samuel said seriously. 'I don't know, it's not that I'm frightened, but it feels like my soul gets dirty . . . that it gets dirtier for every second I spend in his vicinity.'

'I'm sure he's guilty,' Joona said.

'But . . .?'

'I think he's got an accomplice.'

Samuel sighed and put the dishes in the sink.

'We've stopped a serial killer,' he said. 'A lone lunatic who—'

'He wasn't alone at the grave when we got there,' Joona interrupted.

'Yes, he was.' Samuel started to rinse the dishes.

'It's not unusual for serial killers to work with other people,' Joona objected.

'No, but there's nothing that suggests that Jurek Walter belongs to that category,' Samuel said brightly. 'We've done our job, we're finished, but now you want to stick a finger in the air and say ודילמא איפכא.'

'I do?' Joona said with a smile. 'What does that mean?'

'Perhaps the opposite is the case.'

'You can always say that.' Joona nodded.

## 27

The sun was shining in through the mottled glass in the windows of the Wrangelska Palace. Jurek Walter's legal representative explained that his client had been so badly affected by the trial that he couldn't bear to explain the reason why he was at the crime scene when he was arrested.

Joona was called as a witness, and described their surveillance work and the arrest. Then the defence lawyer asked if Joona could see any reason at all to suspect that the prosecutor's account of events was based on a false assumption.

'Could my client have been found guilty of a crime that someone else committed?'

Joona met the lawyer's anxious gaze, and in his mind's eye saw Jurek Walter calmly pushing the woman back into the coffin every time she tried to get out.

'I'm asking you, because you were there,' the defence lawyer went on. 'Could Jurek Walter actually have been trying to rescue the woman in the grave?'

'No,' Joona replied.

After deliberating for two hours, the Chair of the Court declared that the verdict of Stockholm Courthouse was upheld. Jurek Walter's face didn't move a muscle as the more rigorous sentence was announced. He was to be held in a secure psychiatric clinic with extraordinary conditions applied to any eventual parole proceedings.

Seeing as he was closely connected to numerous ongoing investigations, he was also subject to unusually extensive restrictions.

When the Chair of the Court had finished, Jurek Walter turned towards Joona. His face was covered with fine wrinkles, and his pale eyes looked straight into Joona's.

'Now Samuel Mendel's two sons are going to disappear,' Jurek said in a measured voice. 'And Samuel's wife Rebecka will disappear. But . . . No, listen to me, Joona Linna. The police will look for them, and when the police give up Samuel will go on looking, but when he eventually realises that he'll never see his family again, he'll kill himself.'

Joona stood up to leave the courtroom.

'And your little daughter,' Jurek Walter went on, looking down at his fingernails.

'Be careful,' Joona said.

'Lumi will disappear,' Jurek whispered. 'And Summa will disappear. And when you realise that you're never going to find them . . . You're going to hang yourself.'

He looked up and stared directly into Joona's eyes. His face was quite calm, as if things had already been settled the way he wanted.

Ordinarily the convict is taken back to a holding cell until their destination and transportation to the facility have been organised. But the staff at Kronoberg were so keen to be rid of Jurek Walter that they had arranged transport directly from the Wrangelska Palace to the secure criminal psychology unit twenty kilometres north of Stockholm.

\*

Jurek Walter was to be held in strict isolation in Sweden's most secure facility for an indeterminate amount of time. Samuel Mendel had regarded Jurek's threat as empty words from a defeated man, but Joona had been unable to avoid the thought that the threat had been presented as a truth, a fact.

The investigation was downgraded when no further bodies were found.

Although it wasn't dropped altogether, it went cold.

Joona refused to give up, but there were too few pieces of the puzzle, and what lines of inquiry they had turned out to be dead ends. Even though Jurek Walter had been stopped and convicted, they didn't really know any more about him than before.

He was still a mystery.

One Friday afternoon, two months after the appeal, Joona was sitting with Samuel at Il Caffè close to police headquarters, drinking a double espresso. They were busy with other cases now, but still met up regularly to discuss Jurek Walter. They had been through all the material about him many times, but had found nothing to suggest that he had an accomplice. The whole thing was on the verge of becoming an in-joke, with the two of them weighing up innocent passers-by as possible suspects. And then something terrible happened.

## 28

Samuel's phone buzzed on the café table next to his espresso cup. The screen showed a picture of his wife Rebecka. Joona listened idly to the conversation as he picked the crystallised sugar from his cinnamon bun. Evidently Rebecka and the boys were heading out to Dalarö earlier than planned, and Samuel agreed to pick up some food on the way. He told her to drive carefully, and ended the call with lots of kisses.

'The carpenter who's been repairing our veranda wants us to take a look at the carving as soon as possible,' Samuel explained. 'The painter can start this weekend if it's ready.'

Joona and Samuel returned to their offices in the National Criminal Investigation Department and didn't see each other again for the rest of the day.

Five hours later Joona was eating dinner with his family when Samuel called. He was panting and talking so fast that it was difficult to make out what he was saying, but apparently Rebecka and the boys weren't at the house in Dalarö. They hadn't been there, and weren't answering the phone.

'There's bound to be an explanation,' Joona said.

'I've called the police, and all the hospitals, and—'

'Where are you now?' Joona asked.

'I'm out on the Dalarö road, but I'm heading back to the house again.'

'What do you want me to do?' Joona asked.

He had already thought the thought, but the hairs on the back of his neck still stood up when Samuel said:

'Make sure Jurek Walter hasn't escaped.'

Joona checked with the secure criminal psychology unit of the Löwenströmska Hospital at once, and spoke to Senior Consultant Brolin. He was told that nothing unusual had occurred in the secure unit. Jurek Walter was in his cell, and had been in total isolation all day.

When Joona called Samuel back, his friend's voice sounded different, shrill and hunted.

'I'm out in the forest,' Samuel almost shouted. 'I've found Rebecka's car, it's in the middle of the little road leading to the headland, but there's no one here, there's no one here!'

'I'm on my way,' Joona said at once.

The police searched intensively for Samuel's family. All traces of Rebecka and the boys vanished on the gravel road five metres from the abandoned car. The dogs couldn't pick up any scent, just walked up and down, sniffing and circling, but they couldn't find anything. The forests, roads, houses and waterways were searched for two months. After the police had withdrawn, Samuel and Joona carried on looking on their own. They searched with a determination and a fear that grew until it was on the brink of being unbearable. Not once did they mention what this was all about. Both refused to voice their fears about what had happened to Joshua, Reuben and Rebecka. They had witnessed Jurek Walter's cruelty.

## 29

Throughout this period Joona suffered such terrible anxiety that he couldn't sleep. He watched over his family, following them everywhere, picking them up and dropping them off, making special arrangements with Lumi's preschool, but he was forced to accept that this wouldn't be enough in the long term.

Joona had to confront his worst horror.

He couldn't talk to Samuel, but he could no longer deny the truth to himself.

Jurek Walter hadn't committed his crimes alone. Everything about Jurek Walter's understated grandiosity suggested that he was the leader. But after Samuel's family was abducted, there could be no doubt that Jurek Walter had an accomplice.

This accomplice had been ordered to take Samuel's family, and he had done so without leaving a single piece of evidence.

Joona realised that his family was next. It was probably only good fortune that had spared him this far.

Jurek Walter showed no mercy to anyone.

Joona raised this with Summa on numerous occasions, but she refused to take the threat as seriously as he did. She humoured him, accepting his concern and precautionary measures, but she assumed that his fears would subside over time.

He had hoped that the intensive police operation that followed the disappearance of Samuel Mendel's family would lead to the capture of the accomplice. When the search first got under way, Joona saw himself as the hunter, but as the weeks went by the dynamic changed.

He knew that he and his family were the prey, and the calm he tried to demonstrate to Summa and Lumi was merely a façade.

It was half past ten in the evening, and he and Summa were lying in bed reading when a noise from the ground floor made Joona's heart suddenly begin to beat faster. The washing machine hadn't finished its programme yet and it sounded like a zip rattling against the drum, nevertheless he couldn't help getting up and checking that all the windows downstairs were in one piece, and that the outside doors were locked.

When he returned, Summa had switched off her lamp and was lying there watching him.

'What did you do?' she asked gently.

He forced himself to smile and was about to say something when they heard little footsteps. Joona turned and saw his daughter come into the bedroom. Her hair was sticking up and her pyjama trousers had twisted round her waist.

'Lumi, you're supposed to be asleep,' he sighed.

'We forgot to say goodnight to the cat,' she said.

Every evening Joona would read Lumi a story, and before he tucked her in for the night they always had to look out of the window and wave to the grey cat that slept in their neighbours' kitchen window.

'Go back to bed now,' Summa said.

'I'll come and see you,' Joona promised.

Lumi mumbled something and shook her head.

'Do you want me to carry you?' he asked, and picked her up.

She clung onto him and he suddenly noticed her heart beating fast.

'What is it? Did you have a dream?'

'I only wanted to wave to the cat,' she whispered. 'But there was a skeleton out there.'

'In the window?'

'No, he was standing on the ground,' she replied. 'Right where we found the dead hedgehog . . . he was looking at me . . .'

Joona quickly put her in bed with Summa.

'Stay here,' he said.

He ran downstairs silently, not bothering to get his pistol from the gun cabinet, not bothering to put shoes on, and just opened the kitchen door and rushed outside into the cold night air.

There was no one there.

He ran behind the house, climbed over the neighbours' fence and carried on into the next garden. The whole area was quiet and still. He returned to the tree in the garden where he and Lumi had found a dead hedgehog in the summer.

There was no doubt that someone had been standing in the tall grass, just inside their fence. From there you could see very clearly in through Lumi's window.

Joona went inside, locked the door behind him, fetched his pistol, and searched the whole house before going back to bed. Lumi fell asleep almost instantly between him and Summa, and a little while later his wife was asleep beside him.

## 30

Joona had already tried to talk to Summa about taking off and starting a new life, but she had never encountered Jurek Walter, she didn't know the extent of what he had done, and she simply didn't believe that he was behind Rebecka's, Joshua's and Reuben's disappearance.

With fevered concentration, Joona began to confront the inevitable. A chill focus consumed him as he started to examine every detail, every aspect of it, and draw up a plan.

A plan that would save all three of them.

The National Criminal Investigation Department knew almost nothing about Jurek Walter. The disappearance of Samuel Mendel's family after his arrest provided strong support for the theory that he had an accomplice.

But this accomplice hadn't left a single shred of evidence. He was a shadow of a shadow.

His colleagues said it was hopeless, but Joona wouldn't give up. Naturally he understood it wasn't going to be easy to find this invisible accomplice. It might take several years, and there was only one of Joona. He couldn't search and protect Summa and Lumi at the same time, not every second.

If he hired two bodyguards to accompany them everywhere, the family's savings would be exhausted in six months.

Jurek's accomplice had waited months before seizing Samuel's family. Clearly this was a man who was in no hurry, patiently biding his time until he was ready to strike.

Joona tried to find a way they could stay together. They could move, get new jobs and change identities, and live quietly somewhere.

Nothing mattered more than being with Summa and Lumi.

But as a police officer, he knew that protected identities aren't secure. They just give a breathing space. The further away you got, the more breaths you would manage to take, but in the file of Jurek Walter's suspected victims was a man who went missing in Bangkok, disappearing without trace from the lift in the Sukhothai Hotel.

There was no escape.

Eventually Joona was forced to accept that there was something that mattered more than him being together with Summa and Lumi.

Their lives mattered more.

If he ran away or disappeared with them, it would be a direct challenge to Jurek to try to track them down.

And Joona knew that once you start looking, sooner or later you are going to find your quarry, no matter how hard they might try to hide.

Jurek Walter mustn't look, he thought. That's the only way not to be found.

There was only one solution. Jurek and his shadow had to believe that Summa and Lumi were dead.

## 31

By the time Joona reaches the outskirts of Stockholm the traffic has built up. Snowflakes are swirling about before vanishing on the damp asphalt of the motorway.

He can't bear to think about how he arranged Summa and Lumi's deaths in order to give them a different life. Nils Åhlén helped him, but didn't like it. He understood that they were doing the right thing, assuming the accomplice really did exist. But if Joona was wrong, this would be a mistake of incomprehensible proportions.

Over the years this doubt has settled over the pathologist's slender figure as a great sorrow.

The railings of the Northern Cemetery flicker past the car and Joona remembers the day Summa and Lumi's urns were lowered into the ground. The rain was falling on the silk ribbons on their wreaths, and pattering on the black umbrellas.

Both Joona and Samuel carried on looking, but not together; they were no longer in touch with each other. Their different fates had made them strangers to one another. Eleven months after his family disappeared, Samuel gave up searching and returned to duty. He lasted three weeks after abandoning hope. Early in the morning of a glorious March day, Samuel went to his summer house. He walked down to the beautiful beach where his boys used to swim, took out his service pistol, fed a bullet into the chamber and shot himself in the head.

When Joona got the call from his boss telling him that Samuel was dead, he felt a deep, unsettling numbness.

Two hours later he made his way, shivering, to the old clockmaker's on Roslagsgatan. It was long past closing time, but the aged clockmaker with the magnifying glass over his left eye was still working amidst a sea of different clocks. Joona tapped on the glass window in the door and was let in.

When he left the clockmaker's two weeks later he weighed seven kilos less. He was pale, and so weak he had to stop and rest every ten metres. He threw up in the park that would subsequently be renamed in honour of the singer Monica Zetterlund, then stumbled on to Odengatan.

Joona had never thought that he would be losing his family for ever. He had imagined being obliged to abstain from meeting them, seeing them, touching them for a while. He realised that it might take years, possibly several years, but he had always been convinced that he would find Jurek Walter's accomplice and arrest him. He had assumed that one day he would uncover their crimes, let in the light on their deeds and calmly examine every detail, but after ten years he had progressed no further than he had done in the first ten days. There was nothing that led anywhere. The only concrete proof that the accomplice actually existed was the fact that Jurek's prophecy for Samuel had been realised.

Officially there was no connection between the disappearance of Samuel's family and Jurek Walter. It was regarded as an accident. Joona was the only person who still believed that Jurek Walter's accomplice had taken them.

Joona was convinced that he was right, but had started to

accept the impasse. He wasn't going to find the accomplice, but his family was still alive.

He stopped talking about the case, but because it was impossible to ignore the likelihood that he was being watched, he was pretty much condemned to loneliness.

The years passed, and the fabricated deaths came to seem more and more real.

He truly had lost his wife and daughter.


Joona pulls up behind a taxi outside the main entrance of Södermalm Hospital, gets out and walks through the falling snow towards the revolving glass door.

## 32

Mikael Kohler-Frost has been moved from the emergency room of Södermalm Hospital to Ward 66, which specialises in acute and chronic cases of infection.

A doctor with tired eyes and a kind face introduces herself as Irma Goodwin, and is now walking across the shiny vinyl floor with Joona Linna. A light flickers above a framed print.

'His general condition is very poor,' she explains as they walk. 'He's malnourished, and he's got pneumonia. The lab found the antigens for Legionnaires' in his urine, and . . .'

'Legionnaires' disease?'

Joona stops in the corridor and runs his hand through his tousled hair. The doctor notices that his eyes have turned an intense grey, almost like burnished silver, and she hurriedly assures him that the disease isn't contagious.

'It's linked to specific locations with—'

'I know,' Joona replies, and carries on walking.

He remembers that the man who was found dead in the plastic barrel had been suffering from Legionnaires' disease. To contract the disease, you had to have been somewhere with infected water. Cases of infection in Sweden are extremely rare. The Legionella bacteria grow in pools, water tanks and pipes, but cannot survive if the temperature is too low.

'Is he going to be OK?' Joona asks.

'I think so, I gave him Macrolide at once,' she replies, trying to keep up with the tall detective.

'And that's helping?'

'It'll take a few days – he's still got a high fever and there's a risk of septic embolisms,' she says, opening a door and ushering him through before following him into the patient's room.

Daylight is passing through the bag on the drip-stand, making it glow. A thin, very pale man is lying on the bed with his eyes closed, muttering manically:

'No, no, no . . . no, no, no, no . . .'

His chin is trembling and the beads of sweat on his brow merge and trickle down his face. A nurse is sitting beside him, holding his left hand and carefully removing tiny splinters of glass from a wound.

'Has he said anything?' Joona asks.

'He's been delirious, and it isn't easy to understand what he's saying,' the nurse replies, taping a compress over the wound on his hand.

She leaves the room and Joona carefully approaches the patient. He looks at his emaciated features, and has no difficulty discerning the child's face he has studied in photographs so many times. The neat mouth with the pouting top lip, the long, dark eyelashes. Joona thinks back to the most recent picture of Mikael. He was ten years old, sitting in front of a computer with his fringe over his eyes, an amused smile on his lips.

The young man in the hospital bed coughs tiredly, takes a few irregular breaths with his eyes closed, then whispers to himself:

'No, no, no . . .'

There's no doubt that the man lying in the bed in front of him is Mikael Kohler-Frost.

'You're safe now, Mikael,' Joona says.

Irma Goodwin is standing silently behind him, looking at the emaciated man in the bed.

'I don't want to, I don't want to.'

He shakes his head and jerks, tensing every muscle in his body. The liquid in the drip-bag turns the colour of blood. He's trembling, and starts to whimper quietly to himself.

'My name is Joona Linna, I'm a detective inspector, and I was one of the people who looked for you when you didn't come home.'

Mikael opens his eyes a little, but doesn't seem to see anything at first, then he blinks a few times and squints at Joona.

'You think I'm alive . . .'

He coughs, then lies back panting and looks at Joona.

'Where have you been, Mikael?'

'I don't know, I just don't know, I don't know anything, I don't know where I am, I don't know anything . . .'

'You're in Södermalm Hospital in Stockholm,' Joona says.

'Is the door locked? Is it?'

'Mikael, I need to find out where you've been.'

'I don't understand what you're saying,' he whispers.

'I need to find out—'

'What the hell are you doing with me?' he asks in a despairing voice, and starts to cry.

'I'm going to give him a sedative,' the doctor says, and leaves the room.

'You're safe now,' Joona explains. 'Everyone here is trying to help you, and—'

'I don't want to, I don't want to, I can't bear it . . .'

He shakes his head and tries to pull the drip from his arm with tired fingers.

'Where have you been all this time, Mikael? Where have you been living? Were you hiding? Were you locked up, or—'

'I don't know, I don't understand what you're saying.'

'You're tired, and you've got a fever,' Joona says gently. 'But you have to try to think.'

# 33

Mikael Kohler-Frost is lying in his hospital bed, panting like a hare that's been hit by a car. He's talking quietly to himself, moistening his mouth and looking up at Joona with big, questioning eyes.

'Can you be locked up in nothing?'

'No, you can't,' Joona replies calmly.

'Can't you? I don't get it, I don't know, it's so hard to think,' the young man whispers quickly. 'There's nothing to remember, it's just dark . . . it's all a big nothing, and I get mixed up . . . I mix up what was before and how it was in the beginning, I can't think, there's too much sand, I don't even know what's dreams and . . .'

He coughs, leans his head back and closes his eyes.

'You said something about how it was in the beginning,' Joona says. 'Can you try—'

'Don't touch me, I don't want you to touch me,' he interrupts.

'I'm not going to.'

'I don't want to, I don't want to, I can't, I don't want to . . .'

His eyes roll back and he tilts his head in an odd, crooked way, then shuts his eyes and his body trembles.

'There's no danger,' Joona repeats.

After a while Mikael's body relaxes again, and he coughs and looks up.

'Can you tell me anything about how it was in the beginning?' Joona repeats gently.

'When I was little . . . we were huddled together on the floor,' he says, almost soundlessly.

'So there were several of you at the start?' Joona asks, a shiver running up his spine and making the hairs on the back of his neck stand on end.

'Everyone was frightened . . . I was calling for Mum and Dad . . . and there was a grown-up woman and an old man on the floor . . . they were sitting on the floor behind the sofa . . . She tried to calm me down, but . . . but I could hear her crying the whole time.'

'What did she say?' Joona asks.

'I don't remember, I don't remember anything, maybe I dreamed the whole thing . . .'

'You just mentioned an old man and a woman.'

'No.'

'Behind the sofa,' Joona says.

'No,' Mikael whispers.

'Do you remember any names?'

He coughs and shakes his head.

'Everyone was just crying and screaming, and the woman with the eye kept asking about two boys,' he says, his eyes focused inwardly.

'Do you remember any names?'

'What?'

'Do you remember the names of—'

'I don't want to, I don't want to . . .'

'I'm not trying to upset you, but—'

'They all disappeared, they just disappeared,' Mikael says, his voice getting louder. 'They all disappeared, they all . . .'

Mikael's voice cracks, and it's no longer possible to make out what he's saying.

Joona repeats that everything is going to be all right. Mikael looks him in the eye, but he's shaking so much he can't speak.

'You're safe here,' Joona says. 'I'm a police officer, and I'll make sure that nothing happens to you.'

Dr Irma Goodwin comes into the room with a nurse. They walk over to the patient and gently put his oxygen mask back on. The nurse injects the sedative solution into the drip while calmly explaining what she's doing.

'He needs to rest now,' the doctor says to Joona.

'I need to know what he saw.'

She tilts her head and rubs her ring finger.

'Is it very urgent?'

'No,' Joona replies. 'Not really.'

'Come back tomorrow, then,' Irma says. 'Because I think—'

Her mobile rings and she has a short conversation, then hurries out of the room. Joona is left standing by the bed as he hears her vanish down the corridor.

'Mikael, what did you mean about the eye? You mentioned the woman with the eye – what did you mean?' he asks slowly.

'It was like . . . like a black teardrop . . .'

'Her pupil?'

'Yes,' Mikael whispers, then shuts his eyes.

Joona looks at the young man in the bed, feeling his pulse roar in his temples, and his voice is brittle and metallic as he asks:

'Was her name Rebecka?'

## 34

Mikael is crying as the sedative enters his bloodstream. His body relaxes, his sobbing grows more weary, then subsides completely seconds before he drifts off to sleep.

Joona feels oddly empty inside as he leaves the patient's room and pulls out his phone. He stops, pauses for breath, then calls Åhlén, who carried out the extensive forensic autopsies on the bodies found in Lill-Jan's Forest.

'Nils Åhlén,' he says as he takes the call.

'Are you sitting at your computer?'

'Joona Linna, how nice to hear from you,' Åhlén says in his nasal voice. 'I was just sitting here in front of the screen with my eyes closed, enjoying its warmth. I was fantasising that I'd bought a facial solarium.'

'Elaborate daydream.'

'Well, if you look after the pennies . . .'

'Would you like to look up some old files?'

'Talk to Frippe, he'll help you.'

'No can do.'

'He knows as much as—'

'It's about Jurek Walter,' Joona interrupts.

A long silence follows.

'I've told you, I don't want to talk about that again,' Åhlén says calmly.

'One of his victims has turned up alive.'

'Don't say that.'

'Mikael Kohler-Frost . . . He's got Legionnaires' disease, but it looks as though he's going to pull through.'

'What are the files you're interested in?' Åhlén asks with nervous intensity in his voice.

'The man in the barrel had Legionnaires' disease,' Joona goes on. 'But did the boy who was found with him show any signs of the disease?'

'Why are you wondering that?'

'If there's a connection, it ought to be possible to put together a list of places where the bacteria might be present. And then—'

'We're talking about millions of places,' Åhlén interrupts.

'OK . . .'

'Joona. You have to realise, even if Legionella was mentioned in the other reports, that doesn't mean that Mikael was one of Jurek Walter's victims.'

'So there were Legionella bacteria?'

'Yes, I found antibodies against the bacteria in the boy's blood, so he'd probably had Pontiac fever,' Åhlén says with a sigh. 'I know you want to be right, Joona, but nothing you've said is enough to—'

'Mikael Kohler-Frost says he met Rebecka,' Joona interrupts.

'Rebecka Mendel?' Åhlén asks with a tremble in his voice.

'They were held captive together,' Joona confirms.

There is a long silence, then: 'So . . . so you were right about everything, Joona,' Åhlén says, sounding as if he's about to start crying. 'You've no idea how relieved I am to hear that.'

He gulps hard down the phone, and whispers that they did the right thing after all.

'Yes,' Joona says, in a lonely voice.

He and Åhlén had done the right thing when they arranged the car-crash for Joona's wife and daughter.

Two dead bodies were cremated and buried in place of Lumi and Summa. Using fake dental records, Åhlén had identified the bodies. He believed Joona, and trusted him, but it had been such a big decision, so momentous, that he has never stopped worrying about it.


Joona daren't leave the hospital until two uniformed officers arrive to guard Mikael's room. On his way out along the corridor he calls Nathan Pollock and says they need to send someone to pick up the man's father.

'I'm sure it's Mikael,' he says. 'And I'm sure he's been held captive by Jurek Walter all these years.'

He gets in the car and slowly drives away from the hospital as the windscreen wipers clear the snow aside.

Mikael Kohler-Frost was ten years old when he disappeared – and he was twenty-three when he managed to escape.

Sometimes prisoners manage to escape, like Elisabeth Fritzl in Austria, who escaped after twenty-four years as a sex-slave in her father's cellar. Or Natascha Kampusch, who fled her kidnapper after eight years.

Joona can't help thinking that, like Elisabeth Fritzl and Natascha Kampusch, Mikael must have seen the man holding him captive. Suddenly a conclusion to all this seems possible. In just a few days, as soon as he is well enough, Mikael ought to be able to show the way to the place where he was held captive for so long.

The car's tyres rumble as Joona crosses the ridge of snow in the middle of the road to overtake a bus. As he drives past the Palace of Nobility the city opens up in front of him once more, with heavy snow falling between the dark sky and the swirling black water below the bridge.

Obviously the accomplice must know that Mikael has escaped and can identify him, Joona thinks. Presumably he has already tried to cover his tracks and switch to a new hiding place, but if Mikael can lead them to where he was held captive, Forensics would be able to find some sort of evidence and the hunt would be on again.

There's a long way to go, but Joona's heart is already beating faster in his chest.

The thought is so overwhelming that he has to pull over to the side of Vasa Bridge and stop the car. Another driver blows his horn irritably. Joona gets out of his car and steps up onto the pavement, breathing the cold air deep into his lungs.

A sudden burst of migraine makes him stumble and he grabs the railing for support. He closes his eyes for a moment, waits, and feels the pain ebb away before he opens his eyes again.

Millions and millions of white snowflakes are flying through the air, vanishing on the dark water as if they had never existed.

It's too early to dare to think the thought, but he is well aware of what this means. His body feels weighed down by the realisation. If he manages to catch the accomplice, there will no longer be any threat to Summa and Lumi.

## 35

It's too hot to talk in the sauna. Gold-coloured light is shining on their naked bodies and the pale sandalwood. It's 97 degrees now and the air burns Reidar Frost's lungs when he breathes in. Drops of sweat are falling from his nose onto the white hair on his chest.

The Japanese journalist, Mizuho, is sitting on the bench next to Veronica. Their bodies are both flushed and shiny. Sweat is running between their breasts, over their stomachs and down into their pubic hair.

Mizuho is looking seriously at Reidar. She has come all the way from Tokyo to interview him. He told her good-naturedly that he never gives interviews, but that she was very welcome to attend the party. She was probably hoping he would say something about the Sanctum series being turned into a manga film. She has been here four days now.

Veronica sighs and closes her eyes for a while.

Mizuho didn't take off her gold necklace before entering the sauna, and Reidar can see that it's starting to burn. Marie only lasted five minutes before she went off to the shower, and now the Japanese journalist leaves the sauna as well.

Veronica leans forward and rests her elbows on her knees,

breathing through her half-open mouth as sweat drips from her nipples.

Reidar feels a sort of brittle tenderness towards her. But he doesn't know how to explain the desolate landscape inside him, and that everything he does now, everything he throws himself into, is just random fumbling for something to help him survive the next minute.

'Marie's very beautiful,' Veronica says.

'Yes.'

'Big breasts.'

'Stop it,' Reidar mutters.

She looks at him with a serious expression as she goes on: 'Why can't I just get a divorce . . .?'

'Because that would be the end for us,' Reidar says.

Veronica's eyes fill with tears and she is about to say something else when Marie comes back in and sits down next to Reidar with a little giggle.

'God, it's hot,' she gasps. 'How can you sit here?'

Veronica throws a scoop of water onto the stones. There's a loud hiss and hot clouds of steam rise up and surround them for a few seconds. Then the heat becomes dry and static again.

Reidar is hanging forward over his knees. The hair on his head is so hot he almost scalds himself when he runs his hand through it.

'No, that's enough,' he gasps, and climbs down.

The two women follow him out into the soft snow. Dusk is spreading its darkness across the snow, which is already glowing pale blue.

Heavy snowflakes drift down as the three naked people pound through the deep snow.

David, Wille and Berzelius are eating dinner with the other members of the Sanctum scholarship committee, and the drinking songs can be heard all the way out to the back of the garden.

Reidar turns and looks at Veronica and Marie. Steam is rising from their flushed bodies, they're enveloped in veils of mist as the snow falls around them. He is about to say something when Veronica bends over and throws an armful of snow up at him. He backs away, laughing, and falls onto his back, vanishing under the loose snow.

He lies there on his back, listening to their laughter.

The snow feels liberating. His body is still scorching hot. Reidar looks straight up at the sky, the hypnotic snow falling from the centre of creation, an eternity of drifting white.

A memory takes him by surprise. He is peeling off the children's snowsuits. Taking off hats with snow caught in the wool. He can remember their cold cheeks and sweaty hair. The smell of the drying cupboard and wet boots.

He misses the children so much that his longing feels purely physical in its intensity.

Right now he wishes he was alone, so he could lie in the snow until he lost consciousness. Die, surrounded by his memories of Felicia and Mikael. Of how they had once been his.

He gets to his feet with an effort and gazes out across the white fields. Marie and Veronica are laughing, making angels in the snow and rolling around a short distance away.

'How long have these parties been going on?' Marie calls to him.

'I don't want to talk about it,' Reidar mumbles.

He is about to walk off, drink until he's drunk, then tie a noose round his neck, but Marie is standing in front of him, legs akimbo.

'You never want to talk. I don't know anything,' she says with a laugh. 'I don't even know if you've got children, or—'

'Just leave me the fuck alone!' Reidar shouts, and pushes past. 'What is it you want?'

'Sorry, I . . .'

'Leave me the fuck alone,' he snaps, and disappears into the house.

The two women walk shivering back into the sauna. The steam on their bodies runs off as the heat closes round them again, as if it had never been gone.

'What's his problem?' Marie asks.

'He's pretending to be alive, but feels dead,' Veronica replies simply.

# 36

Reidar Frost is wearing a new pair of trousers with a double stripe, and an open shirt. The back of his hair is damp. He is clutching a bottle of Château Mouton Rothschild in each hand.

That morning he had been on his way to the room upstairs to remove the rope from the beam, but when he reached the door he had been filled instead with an aching sense of longing. He stood with his hand on the door handle and forced himself to turn round, go downstairs and wake his friends. They poured spiced schnapps into crystal glasses and rustled up some boiled eggs with Russian caviar.

Reidar is walking barefoot along a corridor lined with dark portraits.

The snow outside is casting an indirect light, like a pale darkness.

In the reading room with its shiny leather furniture he stops and looks out of the huge window. The view is like a fairytale. As if the king of winter had blown snow across a landscape of apple trees and fields.

Suddenly he sees flickering lights on the long avenue leading from the gates to the front of the house. The branches of the trees look like embroidered lace in the glow. A car approaching. The snow swirling into the air behind it is coloured red by its rear-lights.

Reidar can't recall inviting anyone else to join them.

He is just thinking that Veronica will have to take care of the new arrivals when he sees that it's a police car.

Reidar stops and puts the bottles down on a chest, then goes back downstairs and pulls on the felt-lined winter boots beside the door. He heads out into the cold air to meet the car as it arrives in the broad turning circle.

'Reidar Frost?' a woman in plain clothes says as she gets out of the car.

'Yes,' he replies.

'Can we go inside?'

'Here will do,' he says.

'Would you like to sit in the car?'

'Does it look like it?'

'We've found your son,' the woman says, taking a couple of steps towards him.

'I see,' he sighs, holding up a hand to silence the police officer.

He is breathing, feeling the smell of the snow, of water that has frozen to ice high up in the sky. Reidar composes himself, then slowly lowers his hand.

'So where did you find Mikael?' he says in a voice that has become strangely calm.

'He was walking over a bridge—'

'What?! What the hell are you saying, woman?' Reidar roars.

The woman flinches. She's tall, and has a long ponytail down her back.

'I'm trying to tell you that he's alive,' she says.

'What is this?' Reidar asks uncomprehendingly.

'He's been taken into Södermalm Hospital for observation.'

'Not my son, he died many years—'

'There's no doubt whatsoever that it's him.'

Reidar is staring at her with eyes that have turned completely black.

'Mikael's alive?'

'He's come back.'

'My son?'

'I appreciate that it's strange, but—'

'I thought . . .'

Reidar's chin trembles as the policewoman explains that his DNA is a one hundred per cent match. The ground beneath him feels soft, rolling like a wave, and he fumbles in the air for support.

'Sweet God in heaven,' he whispers. 'Dear God, thank you . . .'

His face cracks into a broad smile and he looks completely broken, and he stares up at the falling snow as his legs give way beneath him. The policewoman tries to catch him, but one of his knees hits the ground and he falls to the side, putting his hand out to break his fall.

The police officer helps him to his feet, and he is holding her arm as he sees Veronica come running down the steps barefoot, wrapped in his thick winter coat.

'You're sure it's him?' he says, staring into the police-woman's eyes.

She nods.

'We've just had a one hundred per cent match,' she repeats. 'It's Mikael Kohler-Frost, and he's alive.'

Veronica has reached him. He takes her arm as he follows the policewoman back to the car.

'What's going on, Reidar?' she asks, sounding worried.

He looks at her. His face is confused and he suddenly seems much older.

'My little boy,' he says simply.

## 37

From a distance the white blocks of Södermalm Hospital look like gravestones looming out of the thick snow.

Moving like a sleepwalker, Reidar Frost buttoned his shirt on the way to Stockholm and tucked it into his trousers. He's heard the police say that the patient who has been identified as Mikael Kohler-Frost has been moved from intensive care to a private room, but it all feels as if it's happening in a parallel reality.

In Sweden, when there are grounds to believe someone is dead, the relatives can apply for a death certificate after one year even though there is no body. Reidar had waited six years for his children's bodies to be found before he applied for death certificates. The Tax Office authorised his request, the decision was taken, and the declarations became legally binding six months later.

Now Reidar is walking beside the plain-clothed officer down a long corridor. He doesn't remember which ward they're on their way towards, he just follows her, staring at the floor and interwoven tracks left by the wheels of countless beds.

Reidar tries to tell himself not to hope too much, that the police might have made a mistake.

Thirteen years ago his children disappeared, Felicia and Mikael, when they were out playing late one evening.

Divers searched the waters, and the whole of the Lilla Värtan inlet was dragged, from Lindskär to Björndalen. Search parties had been organised and a helicopter spent several days searching the area.

Reidar provided photographs, fingerprints, dental records and DNA samples of both children to assist in the search.

Known offenders were questioned, but the conclusion of the police investigation was that one of the siblings had fallen into the cold March water, and the other had been dragged in while trying to help the first one out.

Reidar secretly commissioned a private detective agency to investigate other possible leads, primarily everyone in the children's vicinity: all their teachers, football coaches, neighbours, postmen, bus drivers, gardeners, shop assistants, café staff, and anyone the children had come into contact with by phone or on the internet. Their classmates' parents were checked, and even Reidar's own relatives.

Long after the police had stopped looking, and when everyone with even the faintest connection to the children had been investigated, Reidar began to realise that it was over. But for several years after that he carried on walking along the shore every day, expecting his children to be washed ashore.


Reidar and the plain-clothes officer with the blonde ponytail down her back wait while a bed containing an old woman is wheeled into the lift. They head over to the doors to the ward and pull on pale blue shoe-covers.

Reidar staggers and leans against the wall. He has wondered several times if he's dreaming, and daren't let his thoughts get carried away.

They carry on into the ward, passing nurses in white

uniforms. Reidar feels composed, he's clenched tight inside, but he can't help walking faster.

Somewhere he can hear the noise of other people, but inside him there is nothing but an immense silence.

At the far end of the corridor, on the right, is room number four. He bumps into a food trolley, sending a pile of cups to the floor.

It's as if he's become detached from reality as he enters the room and sees the young man lying in bed. He has a drip attached to the crook of his arm, and oxygen is being fed into his nose. An infusion bag is hanging from the drip-stand, next to a white pulse-monitor attached to his left index finger.

Reidar stops and wipes his mouth with his hand, and feels himself lose control of his face. Reality returns like a deafening torrent of emotions.

'Mikael,' Reidar says gently.

The young man slowly opens his eyes and Reidar can see how much he resembles his mother. He carefully puts his hand against Mikael's cheek, and his own mouth is trembling so much that he can hardly speak.

'Where have you been?' Reidar asks, and realises that he's crying.

'Dad,' Mikael whispers.

His face is frighteningly pale and his eyes incredibly tired. Thirteen years have passed, and the child's face that Reidar has hidden in his memory has become a man's face, but he's so skinny that he looks like he did when he was newborn, wrapped in a blanket.

'Now I can be happy again,' Reidar whispers, stroking his son's head.

## 38

Disa is finally back in Stockholm again. She's waiting in his flat, on the top floor of number 31 Wallingatan. Joona is on his way home from buying some turbot that he's planning to fry and serve with remoulade sauce.

Alongside the railings the snow is piled about twenty centimetres deep. All the lights of the city look like misty lanterns.

As he passes Kammakargatan he hears agitated voices up ahead. This is a dark part of the city. Heaps of snow and rows of parked cars throw shadows. Dull buildings, streaked with melt-water.

'I want my money,' a man with a gruff voice is shouting.

There are two figures in the distance. They're moving slowly along the railings towards the Dala steps. Joona carries on walking.

Two panting men are staring at each other, hunched, drunk and angry. One is wearing a chequered coat and a fur hat. In his hand is a small, shiny knife.

'Fucking bastard,' he rattles. 'Fucking little—'

The other one has a full beard and a black overcoat with a tear on one shoulder, and is waving an empty wine-bottle in front of him.

'I want my money back, with interest,' the bearded man repeats.

'*Kiskoa korkoa*,' the other man replies, spitting blood on the snow.

A thickset woman in her sixties is leaning against a blue box of sand for the steps. The tip of her cigarette glows, lighting up her puffy face.

The man with the bottle backs in beneath the snow-covered branches of the big tree. The other man stumbles after him. The knife blade flashes as he stabs with it. The bearded man moves backwards, waving the bottle and hitting the other man in the head. The bottle breaks and green glass flies around the fur hat. Joona has an impulse to reach for his pistol, even though he knows it's locked away in the gun cabinet.

The man with the knife stumbles but manages to stay on his feet. The other is holding the jagged remains of the bottle.

There's a scream. Joona jumps over the piled-up snow and ice from the gutters.

The bearded man slips on something and falls flat on his back. He's fumbling with his hand on the railings at the top of the steps.

'My money,' he repeats with a cough.

Joona sweeps some snow off a parked car and presses it to make a snowball.

The man in the chequered coat sways as he approaches the prone man with the knife.

'I'll cut you open and stuff you with your money—'

Joona throws the snowball and hits the man holding the knife in the back of the neck. There's a dull thud as the snow breaks up and flies in all directions.

'*Perkele*,' the man says, confused, as he turns round.

'Snowball fight, lads!' Joona shouts, forming a new ball.

The man with the knife looks at him and a spark appears in his clouded eyes.

Joona throws again and hits the man on the ground in the middle of the chest, spraying snow in his bearded face.

The man with the knife looks down at him, then laughs unkindly:

'*Lumiukko.*'

The man on the ground throws some loose snow up at him. He backs off, putting the knife away and forming a snowball. The bearded man rises unsteadily, clinging to the railing.

'I'm good at this,' he mutters as he forms a snowball.

The man in the chequered jacket takes aim at the other man, but abruptly turns round instead and throws a ball that hits Joona on the shoulder.

For several minutes snowballs fly in all directions. Joona slips and falls. The bearded man loses his hat and the other man rushes over and fills it with snow.

The woman claps her hands, and is rewarded with a snowball to her forehead which sits there like a white bump. The bearded man bursts out laughing and falls backwards into a pile of old Christmas trees. The man in the chequered jacket kicks some snow over him, but gives up. He's panting as he turns to look at Joona.

'And where the hell did you come from?' he asks.

'National Criminal Police,' Joona replies, brushing the snow from his clothes.

'The police?'

'You took my child,' the woman mutters.

Joona picks up the fur hat and shakes the snow off it before handing it to the man in the jacket.

'Thanks.'

'I saw the wishing star,' the drunken woman goes on,

looking Joona in the eye. 'I saw it when I was seven . . . and I wish you'd burn in the fires of hell and scream like—'

'You shut your mouth,' the man in the chequered jacket shouts. 'I'm glad I didn't stab you, little brother, and—'

'I want my money,' the other man calls with a smile.

## 39

There's a light on in the bathroom when Joona gets home. He opens the door slightly and sees Disa lying in the bath with her eyes closed. She's surrounded by bubbles and is humming to herself. Her muddy clothes are in a big heap on the bathroom floor.

'I thought they'd locked you up in prison,' Disa says. 'I was all prepared to take over your flat.'

Over the winter Joona has been under investigation by the Prosecution Authority's national unit for internal investigations, accused of wrecking a long-term surveillance operation and exposing the Security Police rapid-response unit to danger.

'Apparently I'm guilty,' he replies, picking her clothes up and putting them in the washing machine.

'I said that right at the start.'

'Yes, well . . .'

Joona's eyes are suddenly grey as a rainy sky.

'Is it something else?'

'A long day,' he replies, and goes out into the kitchen.

'Don't go.'

When he doesn't come back she climbs out of the bath,

dries herself and puts on a thin dressing gown. The beige silk clings to her warm body.

Joona is standing in the kitchen, frying some baby potatoes golden brown when she comes in.

'What's happened?'

Joona glances at her.

'One of Jurek Walter's victims has come back . . . he's been held captive all this time.'

'So you were right – there was an accomplice.'

'Yes,' he sighs.

Disa takes a few steps towards him, then gently rests her palm flat against the small of his back.

'Can you catch him?'

'I hope so,' Joona says seriously. 'I haven't had the chance to question the boy properly, he's in a bad way. But he should be able to lead us there.'

Joona takes the frying pan off the heat, then turns and looks at her.

'What is it?' she asks, suddenly looking worried.

'Disa, you have to say yes to the research project in Brazil.'

'I've told you, I don't want to go,' she says quickly, then realises what he means. 'You can't think like that. I don't give a damn about Jurek Walter. I'm not scared, I won't be governed by fear.'

He gently brushes aside the wet hair that has fallen over her face.

'Only for a little while,' he says. 'Until I get this sorted out.'

She leans against his chest and hears the muffled double beat of his heart.

'There's never been anyone but you,' she says simply. 'When you stayed with me after your family's accident, well, that was . . . you know, that was when I . . . lost my heart, as they say . . . but it's true.'

'I'm just worried about you.'

She strokes his arm and whispers that she doesn't want to go. When her voice breaks, he pulls her to him and kisses her.

'But we've seen each other all the way through,' Disa says, looking up into his face. 'I mean, if there is an accomplice who's a threat to us, why hasn't anything happened? It doesn't make sense . . .'

'I know, I agree, but . . . I have to do this. I'm going after him, and now is when it's all happening.'

Disa can feel a sob rising in her throat. She fights it back down and turns her face away. Once she had been Summa's friend. That was how they met. And when his life fell apart, she was there.

He moved in and stayed with her for a while when things were at their very worst for him.

At night he would sleep on her sofa, and she would hear him moving about, and knew that he knew she was lying awake in the next room. That he was looking at the door to her bedroom and thinking about her lying in there, more and more confused and hurt by how distant he was being, how cold. Until one night he got up, got dressed and left her flat.

'I'm staying,' Disa whispers, wiping the tears from her face.

'You have to go.'

'Why?'

'Because I love you,' he says. 'You must know that . . .'

'Do you really think I'd go now?' she asks with a broad smile.

## 40

Jurek Walter is visible on one of the nine squares of the huge monitor. Like a caged beast he is pacing the dayroom, walking round the sofa, then turning left and going past the television. He goes round the running machine, turns left again and goes back into his room.

Anders Rönn watches him from above on another of the screens, as well as on the other monitor.

Jurek washes his face, then sits down on the plastic chair without drying himself. He stares at the door to the corridor as the water drips onto his shirt and dries.

My is sitting in the operator's chair. She checks the time, waits another thirty seconds, looks at Jurek, makes a note of the zone on the computer, and locks the door to the dayroom.

'He's getting faggots this evening . . . he likes that,' she says.

'He does?'

Anders Rönn already thinks that the routines surrounding this one patient are so repetitive and static that it would be hard to tell the days apart if it weren't for the daily meeting up on Ward 30. The other doctors talk about their patients and care plans. No one even expects him to repeat that the situation in the secure unit is unchanged.

'Have you ever tried talking to the patient?' Anders asks.

'With Jurek? We're not allowed to,' she replies, and scratches her tattooed arm. 'It's because . . . well, he says things you can't forget.'

Anders hasn't spoken to Jurek Walter since that first day. He just makes sure that the patient gets his regular injection of neuroleptic drugs.

'Do you know how the computer system works?' Anders asks. 'I couldn't work out how to sign out of the medical records.'

'In that case you're not allowed to go home,' she says.

'But I . . .'

'I'm joking,' she laughs. 'The computers down here are always getting snarled up.'

She gets up, grabs her bottle of Fanta from the desk and goes out into the corridor. Anders sees that Jurek is still sitting completely motionless with his eyes open.

It might not be that much fun doing his specialist service deep underground, behind security doors and airlocks, but for him it's fantastic to work so close to home, and to be able to spend time with Agnes each evening, he tells himself as he goes after My. She is walking along the dimly lit corridor at a relaxed stroll. When she reaches the brightly lit office he notices that her red underwear is visible through the white fabric of her nurse's trousers.

'Now let's see,' she mutters, sitting in his chair and rousing the computer from standby mode. With a contented grin she forces the program to close and logs in again.

Anders thanks her, asks who's working that night, and asks her to restock the medication trolley if she has time.

'Don't forget to sign the requisition orders afterwards,' he says, then leaves.

He walks round the corner into the other corridor and into the changing room. The ward is completely silent. He doesn't know what drives him to do it, but he opens My's locker and starts to search through her gym bag with trembling hands. Carefully he unfolds a damp T-shirt and a pair of pale grey jogging pants, and finds a pair of sweaty knickers. He takes them out, lifts them to his face and breathes in her scent. Suddenly he realises that My might see him on the monitor the moment she returns to the control room.

# 41

When Anders gets home the house is quiet and the light is off in Agnes's room. He locks the door behind him and goes into the kitchen. Petra is standing at the sink rinsing the glass cylinder from the blender.

She's wearing baggy stay-at-home clothes: a Chicago White Sox T-shirt that's too big for her, and yellow leggings that she's pulled up to her knees. Anders goes up behind her and puts his arms round her, smelling her hair and fresh deodorant. She's about to pull away when he moves his hands up to cup her heavy breasts.

'How's Agnes?' he asks, letting go of her.

'She's got a new best friend at preschool,' Petra says with a big smile. 'A little boy who started last week, apparently he's in love with her . . . I don't how reciprocated his feelings are, but she let him give her some bits of Lego.'

'Sounds like love,' he says, sitting down.

'Tired?'

'I fancy a glass of wine – do you want one?' he asks.

'Want one?'

She looks him in the eye, smiling more broadly than she's done for a very long time.

'What do you mean by that?' he asks.

'Does what I want matter?' she whispers.

He shakes his head and she looks at him with twinkling eyes. They leave the kitchen and go silently into the bedroom. Anders locks the door to the corridor and watches as Petra opens the mirrored wardrobe door and pulls out a drawer. She removes a bundle of underwear and gets out a carrier bag.

'So that's where you hid everything?'

'You're not to make me feel embarrassed now,' she says.

He pulls the duvet aside and Petra empties the contents of the bag, all the things they bought after she'd read *Fifty Shades of Grey*. He picks up the soft rope and ties her hands, loops it through the slatted headboard, then tightens it, making her fall onto her back with her hands above her head. He ties the rope to the bottom of the bed with two half-hitch knots. She parts her legs and squirms as he pulls off her leggings and underwear.

He loosens the rope again, loops it round her left ankle and ties it to the bedpost, then pulls it round the other post and ties her right ankle.

He pulls the rope gently, making her legs slowly spread open.

She's looking at him, her cheeks flushed.

He suddenly pulls harder and forces her thighs apart as far as they'll go.

'Careful,' she says quickly.

'Keep quiet,' he tells her sternly, and sees her smile happily to herself.

He fastens the rope, then moves up the bed and pulls her T-shirt over her face so she can no longer see him. Her breasts sway as she tries to get the fabric off her face.

There's no way she can get loose – she's entirely helpless in this position, with her arms over her head and her legs pulled so far apart that her inner thighs must be aching.

Anders just stands there, watching her shake her head, and feels his heart beat faster, harder. Slowly he undoes his trousers as he sees her crotch start to glisten with moisture.

## 42

Joona enters the patient's room and sees an older man sitting by the boy's bed. It takes him a few seconds to realise that it's Reidar Frost. It's been years since he last saw him, but he's aged considerably more than that. The young man is asleep, but Reidar is sitting there holding his left hand in both of his.

'You never believed my children had drowned,' the father says in a muted voice.

'No,' Joona replies.

Reidar's gaze rests on Mikael's sleeping face, then he turns to Joona and says:

'Thank you for not telling me about the murderer.'

The suspicion that Mikael and Felicia Kohler-Frost had been among Jurek Walter's victims had been strengthened by the fact it was via the children that he had been tracked down and arrested, and that he had first been spotted by Joona and Samuel below their mother's window.

Joona looks at the young man's thin face, his straggly beard, his sunken cheeks and the beads of sweat on his forehead.

When Mikael had talked about the way things were at the start, when there were more of them and he met Rebecka

Mendel, he had been talking about the first few weeks of Jurek Walter's isolation, Joona thinks.

Since then more than a decade of imprisonment has gone by.

But Mikael managed to escape – it must be possible to find out where from.

'I never stopped looking,' Joona says quietly to Reidar.

Reidar looks at his son and his face cracks into an uncontrollable smile. He has been sitting like that for hours, and still can't get enough of just gazing at his child.

'They're saying he's going to be fine. They've promised, they've promised there's nothing wrong with him,' he says in a rough voice.

'Have you talked to him?' Joona asks.

'He's been given a lot of painkillers, so he's mostly been asleep, but they say that's good, it's what he needs.'

'I'm sure it is,' Joona agrees.

'He's going to be fine . . . mentally, I mean. It will just take a bit of time.'

'Has he said anything at all?'

'He's whispered things to me, but not so that I can hear them,' Reidar says. 'It just sounds confused. But he recognised me.'

Joona knows it's important to start talking about things right from the outset. Remembering is an important part of the healing process. Mikael needs time, but he mustn't be left to himself. As time goes by the questions can gradually probe deeper, but there's always a risk that a traumatised person will shut off entirely.

And there's no real rush, Joona reminds himself.

It could take months to map out everything that's happened, but he does need to ask the most important question today.

I need to find out if Mikael knows who the accomplice is, he thinks, feeling his heart beating faster again.

If he can just get a name or a decent description, this nightmare could be over.

'I have to talk to him as soon as he wakes up,' Joona says. 'I just need to ask him a few very specific questions, but he might find it a bit difficult.'

'As long as it doesn't frighten him,' Reidar says. 'I can't let that happen . . .'

He falls silent when a nurse comes in. She says hello quietly, then checks Mikael's pulse and oxygen levels.

'His hands have gone cold,' Reidar tells her.

'I'm going to give him some antipyretics soon,' the nurse assures him.

'He is getting antibiotics, isn't he?'

'Yes, but it can take a couple of days before those start to work,' the nurse says with a reassuring smile as she hangs a new infusion bag on the drip-stand.

Reidar helps her, standing up and holding the tube out of the way to make it easier for her, then walks to the door with her.

'I want to talk to the doctor,' he says.

Mikael sighs and whispers something to himself. Reidar stops and turns round. Joona leans forward and tries to hear what he's saying.

## 43

Mikael's breathing has speeded up, and he's tossing his head, whispering something. He opens his eyes and stares at Joona with a haunted expression.

'You've got to help me, I can't lie here,' he says. 'I can't bear it, I can't bear it, my sister's waiting for me, I can feel her the whole time, I can feel . . .'

Reidar hurries over and takes his hand, holds it to his cheek.

'Mikael, I know,' he whispers, then gulps hard.

'Dad . . .'

'I know, Mikael, I think about her all the time . . .'

'Dad,' Mikael cries with an anguished voice. 'I can't bear it, I can't, I . . .'

'Calm down,' Reidar reassures him.

'She's alive, Felicia's alive,' he cries. 'I can't lie here, I've got to . . .'

He lets out a long, rattling cough. Reidar holds his head up and tries to help him. He keeps saying soothing things to his son, but Mikael's eyes are burning with boundless panic.

He sinks back onto the pillow, gasping and whispering inaudibly to himself as tears run down his cheeks.

'What were you saying about Felicia?' Reidar asks calmly.

'I don't want to,' Mikael gasps. 'I can't just lie here . . .'

'Mikael,' Reidar interrupts. 'You need to be clearer.'

'I can't bear it . . .'

'You said that Felicia is alive,' Reidar repeats. 'Why did you say that?'

'I left her, I left her behind,' Mikael sobs. 'I ran, and I left her behind.'

'Are you saying that Felicia is still alive?' Reidar asks, for the third time.

'Yes, Dad,' Mikael whispers, tears streaming down his cheeks.

'Dear God in heaven,' his father whispers, stroking his son's head with a trembling hand. 'Dear God in heaven.'

Mikael coughs violently, a cloud of blood billows into the tube and he gasps for air, then coughs again and lies there panting.

'We were together the whole time, Dad. In the darkness, on the floor . . . but I left her.'

Mikael falls silent, as though every last drop of strength has been exhausted. His eyes suddenly seem clouded and tired.

Reidar looks at his son with a face that has lost all trace of stability and abandoned any attempt at a façade.

'You have to tell us . . .'

His voice cracks, he takes a deep breath and then goes on:

'Mikael, you know you have to tell us where she is so I can go and get her . . .'

'She's still there . . . Felicia's still there,' Mikael says weakly. 'She's still there. I can feel her, she's scared . . .'

'Mikael,' Reidar pleads.

'She's scared, because she's on her own . . . She can't bear it, she always wakes up at night crying until she realises I'm there . . .'

Reidar feels his chest tighten. Big patches of sweat have formed under the arms of his shirt.

## 44

Reidar can hear what Mikael's saying, but he's still having trouble absorbing the significance. He stands beside his son's bed, looking at him and speaking in a soothing voice.

But his thoughts are going round in circles, around one single idea. He has to find Felicia. She mustn't be left on her own.

He stares into the middle distance, then walks heavily over to the window. Far below some sparrows are sitting in the bare rose bushes. Some dogs have pissed in the snow under a lamppost. Over at the bus stop a glove is lying beneath the bench.

Somewhere behind him he hears Joona Linna try to find out more from Mikael. His deep voice merges with the heavy thud of Reidar's heartbeat.

You only see your mistakes in hindsight, and some of them are so painful that you can hardly live with yourself.

Reidar knows that he was an unfair father. That was never his intention, it just turned out that way.

Everyone always says that they love their children equally, he thinks. Yet we still treat them differently.

Mikael was his favourite.

Felicia always irritated him, and sometimes made him so

angry that he frightened her. In hindsight it seemed incomprehensible. After all, he was an adult and she was just a child.

I shouldn't have shouted at her, he thinks, staring out at the overcast sky and feeling that his left armpit is starting to really hurt now.

'I can feel her the whole time,' Mikael is telling Joona. 'Now she's just lying there on the floor . . . she's so terrified.'

Reidar lets out a groan as he feels a burst of pain in his chest. Sweat is running down his neck. Joona rushes over to him, grabs the top of his arm and says something.

'It's nothing,' Reidar says.

'Does your chest hurt?' Joona asks.

'I'm just tired,' he replies quickly.

'You seem—'

'I have to find Felicia,' he says.

A burning pain shoots through his jaw and he feels another stab in his chest. He falls, hitting his cheek against the radiator, but all he can think is how he shouted at Felicia and told her she was useless the day she disappeared.

He gets to his knees and is trying to crawl as he hears Joona come back into the room with a doctor.

# 45

Joona talks to Reidar's doctor, then returns to Mikael's room, hangs his jacket on the hook behind the door, pulls up the only chair and sits down.

If it's true that Felicia is still alive, then all of a sudden it really is urgent. Maybe there are even more captives? He has to get Mikael to talk about his memories.

An hour later Mikael wakes up. He opens his eyes slowly, squinting against the light. As Joona repeats that his father's not in any danger, he shuts his eyes again.

'I need to ask you a question,' Joona says seriously.

'My sister,' he whispers.

Joona puts his mobile on the bedside table and starts to record.

'Mikael, I have to ask you . . . Do you know who was holding you captive?'

'It wasn't like that . . .'

'Like what?'

The boy's breathing speeds up.

'He just wanted us to sleep, that was all, we had to sleep . . .'

'Who?'

'The Sandman,' Mikael whispers.

'What did you say?'

'Nothing, I can't go on . . .'

Joona looks down at his phone and checks that it's recording the conversation.

'I thought you mentioned the Sandman?' he goes on. 'You mean like Wee Willie Winkie, putting the children to sleep?'

Mikael looks him in the eye.

'He's real,' he whispers. 'He smells of sand, he sells barometers during the day.'

'What does he look like?'

'It's always dark when he comes . . .'

'You must have seen something, surely?'

Mikael shakes his head, sobbing silently as tears run down his cheeks and onto the pillow under his head.

'Does the Sandman have another name?' Joona asks.

'I don't know, he never says a word, he never spoke to us the whole time.'

'Can you describe him?'

'I've only heard him in the darkness . . . his fingertips are made of porcelain and when he takes the sand out of the bag they tinkle against each other . . . and . . .'

Mikael's mouth is moving, but no sound is coming out.

'I can't hear what you're saying,' Joona says quietly.

'He throws sand in children's faces . . . and a moment later they're asleep.'

'How do you know it's a man?' Joona asks.

'I've heard him cough,' Mikael replies seriously.

'But you never saw him?'

'No.'

## 46

A very beautiful woman with Indian features is standing looking down at Reidar when he comes round. She explains that he's had a coronary spasm.

'I thought I was having a heart attack,' he mutters.

'Naturally we're considering X-raying the coronary arteries, and—'

'Yes,' he sighs, sitting up.

'You need to rest.'

'I found out . . . that my . . .' he says, but his mouth starts to tremble so much that he can't finish the sentence.

She puts her hand against his cheek and smiles as if he were an unhappy child.

'I have to see my son,' he explains in a slightly steadier voice.

'You understand that you can't leave the hospital before we've investigated your symptoms,' she says.

She gives him a small pink bottle of nitroglycerine for him to spray under his tongue at the first sign of pain in his chest.

Reidar walks to Ward 66, but before he reaches Mikael's room he stops in the corridor, leans against the wall.

When he enters the room, Joona stands up and offers him the chair. His phone is still next to the bed.

'Mikael, you have to help me find her,' he says as he sits down.

'Dad, how are you?' his son asks in a steady voice.

'It was nothing,' Reidar replies, trying to smile.

'What have they said, what does the doctor think?' Mikael asks.

'She says I have a bit of a problem with my arteries, but I don't believe that. Anyway it doesn't matter, we've got to find Felicia.'

'She was convinced you wouldn't care that she was missing. I said that wasn't true, but she was sure you'd only be looking for me.'

Reidar sits motionless. He knows what Mikael means, because he's never forgotten what happened on that last day. His son puts his bony hand on his arm and their eyes meet once more.

'You were walking from Södertälje – is that where I should start looking?' Reidar asks. 'Is that where she might be?'

'I don't know,' Mikael says quietly.

'But you must remember something,' Reidar goes on in a subdued voice.

'I don't remember anything,' his son says. 'It's just that there's nothing to remember.'

Joona is leaning on the end of the bed. Mikael's eyes are half-open and he's still clutching his father's hand tightly.

'You said before that you and Felicia were together, on the floor in the darkness,' Joona begins.

'Yes,' Mikael whispers.

'How long was it just the two of you? When did the others disappear?'

'I don't know,' he replies. 'I can't say, time doesn't work the way you think.'

'Describe the room.'

Mikael looks into Joona's grey eyes with a tortured expression.

'I never saw the room,' he says. 'Apart from at the start, when I was little . . . there was a bright light that was sometimes switched on, when we could look at each other. But I don't remember what the room looked like, I was just scared . . .'

'But you do remember something?'

'The darkness, there was almost nothing but darkness.'

'There must have been a floor,' Joona says.

'Yes,' Mikael whispers.

'Go on,' Reidar says softly.

Mikael looks away from the two men. He stares into space as he starts to talk about the place where he was held captive so long:

'The floor . . . it was hard, and cold. Six paces one way . . . four paces the other . . . And the walls were made of solid concrete, there was no echo when you hit them.'

## 47

Reidar squeezes his hand without saying anything. Mikael closes his eyes and lets the images and memories guide his words.

'There's a sofa, and a mattress that we pull away from the drain when we need to use the tap,' he says, gulping hard.

'The tap,' Joona repeats.

'And the door . . . it's made of iron, or steel. It's never open. I've never seen it open, there's no lock on the inside, no handle . . . and next to the door there's a hole in the wall, that's where the bucket of food appears. It's only a little hole, but if you stick your arm in and reach up, you can feel a metal hatch with your fingertips . . .'

Reidar is sobbing gently as he listens to Mikael telling them what he remembers of the room.

'We try to save the food,' he says. 'But sometimes it runs out . . . sometimes it would take so long that we'd just lie there listening for the hatch, and when we did get something we ended up being sick . . . and sometimes there was no water in the tap, we got thirsty and the drain started to smell . . .'

'What sort of food was it?' Joona asks calmly.

'Leftovers, mainly . . . bits of sausage, potato, carrot, onions . . . macaroni.'

'The person who gave you the food . . . he never said anything?'

'At the start we shouted out the moment the hatch opened, but then it just slammed shut and we went without food . . . after that we tried talking to whoever opened it, but we never got any answer . . . We always listened hard . . . we could hear breathing, shoes on a concrete floor . . . the same shoes every time . . .'

Joona checks that the recording is still working. He can't help thinking about the extreme isolation that the siblings have endured. Most serial killers avoid contact with their victims, not speaking to them so they can continue to regard them as objects. But at some point they always have to visit their victims, they have to see the horror and helplessness in their faces.

'You heard him moving about,' Joona says. 'Did you ever hear anything else from outside?'

'How do you mean?'

'Think about it,' Joona says seriously. 'Birds, dogs barking, cars, trains, voices, aeroplanes, television, laughter, shouting, sirens . . . anything at all.'

'Just the smell of sand . . .'

The sky outside the hospital window is dark now, and hailstones are falling against the glass.

'What did you do when you were awake?'

'Nothing . . . To start with, when we were still fairly little, I managed to pull a loose screw out of the bottom of the sofa . . . We used it to scratch a hole in the wall. The screw got so hot it almost burned our fingers. We kept going for ages . . . there was nothing but cement, then, after five centimetres or so, we hit some metal mesh. We kept going through one of the gaps, but a short distance further on we hit more mesh, it was impossible . . . It's impossible to escape from the capsule.'

'Why do you call the room "the capsule"?'

Mikael smiles wearily, in a way that makes him look incredibly lonely.

'It was Felicia who started that . . . she imagined we were out in space, that we were on a mission . . . That was back at the start, before we stopped talking, but I went on thinking of the room as the capsule.'

'Why did you stop talking?'

'I don't know, we just did, there was nothing left to say . . .'

Reidar raises a trembling hand to his mouth. It looks as though he's struggling not to cry.

'You say it's impossible to escape . . . yet that's precisely what you did,' Joona says.

# 48

Carlos Eliasson, chief of the National Police, is walking through a light shower of snow from a meeting in Rådhuset, and talking to his wife on the phone. Right now police headquarters looks like a summer palace in a wintery park. The hand holding the phone is so cold that his fingers are aching.

'I'm going to be deploying a lot of resources.'

'Are you sure Mikael's going to get well?'

'Yes.'

Carlos stamps the snow from his shoes when he reaches the pavement.

'That's fantastic,' she mutters.

He hears her sigh as she sits down on a chair.

'I can't tell you,' he says after a brief pause. 'I just can't, can I?'

'No,' she replies.

'What if it turned out to be crucial to the investigation?' he asks.

'You can't tell me,' she says gravely.

Carlos carries on up Kungsholmsgatan and glances at his watch; he hears his wife whisper that she's got to go.

'See you tonight,' she says quietly.

Over the years, police headquarters has been extended, one piece at a time. The various sections reflect changes in fashion. The most recent part is up by Kronoberg Park. That's where the National Criminal Investigation Department is based.

Carlos goes through two different security doors, carries on past the covered inner courtyard and takes the lift up to the eighth floor. There's a worried expression on his face as he removes his outdoor coat and walks past the row of closed doors. A newspaper cutting on a noticeboard flutters in his wake. It's been there since the painful evening when the police choir was voted off *Sweden's Got Talent*.

There are already five other officers in the meeting room. On the pine table are glasses and bottles of water. The yellow curtains have been drawn back and snow-covered treetops are visible through the row of low windows. Everyone is doing their best to appear calm, but beneath the surface they are all thinking dark thoughts. The meeting that Joona has called is due to start in two minutes. Benny Rubin has already taken off his shoes and is telling Magdalena Ronander what he thinks of the new security evaluation forms.

Carlos shakes hands with Nathan Pollock and Tommy Kofoed from the National Murder Squad. As usual, Nathan is wearing a dark-grey jacket and his grey ponytail is hanging down his back. Beside the two men sits Anja Larsson in a silver-coloured blouse and pale-blue skirt.

'Anja's been trying to modernise us . . . we're supposed to learn how to use the Analyst's Notebook.' Nathan smiles. 'But we're too old for that.'

'Speak for yourself,' Tommy mutters sullenly.

'I reckon you've all been round the block a few times,' Anja says.

Carlos stands at the end of the table and the sombre look on his face makes even Benny shut up.

'Welcome, all of you,' Carlos says, without a hint of his usual smile. 'As you may have heard, some new information has come to light concerning Jurek Walter and . . . well, the preliminary investigation can no longer be regarded as concluded . . .'

'What did I tell you?' a quiet voice with a Finnish accent says.

## 49

Carlos turns round quickly and sees Joona Linna standing in the doorway. The tall detective's black coat is sparkling with snow.

'Joona isn't always right, of course,' Carlos says. 'But I have to admit . . . this time . . .'

'So Joona was the only person who thought Jurek Walter had an accomplice?' Nathan Pollock asks.

'Well, yes . . .'

'And a lot of people got very upset when he said Samuel Mendel's family were among the victims,' Anja says quietly.

'True.' Carlos nods. 'Joona did some excellent work, no question . . . I'd only recently been appointed back then, and perhaps I didn't listen to the right people, but now we know . . . and now we can go on to . . .'

He falls silent and looks at Joona, who steps into the room.

'I've just come from Södermalm Hospital,' he says curtly.

'Have I said something wrong?' Carlos asks.

'No.'

'Perhaps you think I should say something else?' Carlos asks, looking embarrassed as he glances at the others. 'Joona, it was thirteen years ago, a lot of water's passed under the bridge since then . . .'

'Yes.'

'And you were absolutely right back then, as I just said.'

'What was I right about?' Joona asks in a quiet voice, looking at his boss.

'What you were right about?' Carlos repeats shrilly. 'Everything, Joona. You were right about everything. Is that enough now? I think that's probably enough . . .'

Joona smiles briefly and Carlos sits down with a sigh.

'Mikael Kohler-Frost's general condition is already much better, and I've questioned him a couple of times . . . Naturally, I was hoping that Mikael would be able to identify the accomplice.'

'Maybe it's too soon,' Nathan says thoughtfully.

'No . . . Mikael can't give us a name, or a description . . . he can't even give us a voice, but—'

'Is he traumatised?' Magdalena Ronander asks.

'He's simply never seen him,' Joona says, meeting her gaze.

'So we've got nothing at all to go on?' Carlos whispers.

Joona steps forward and his shadow falls across the table and the room.

'Mikael calls his kidnapper the Sandman . . . I asked Reidar Frost about it, and he explained that the name comes from a bedtime story the children's mother used to tell them . . . The Sandman is some sort of personification of sleep; he throws sand in children's eyes to get them to fall asleep.'

'That's right,' Magdalena says with a smile. 'And the proof that the Sandman has been there is the little gritty deposits at the corners of your eyes when you wake up.'

'The Sandman,' Pollock says thoughtfully, and jots something down in his black notebook.

Anja takes Joona's phone and starts to connect it to the wireless sound system.

'Mikael and Felicia Kohler-Frost are half-German. Roseanna Kohler moved to Sweden from Schwabach when she was eight years old,' Joona explains.

'That's south of Nuremburg,' Carlos adds.

'The Sandman is their version of Wee Willie Winkie,' Joona goes on. 'And every evening before the children said their prayers she would tell them a bit more about him . . . Over the years she mixed up the story from her own childhood with a load of things she made up herself, and with fragments about E. T. A. Hoffmann's barometer salesman and mechanical girls . . . Mikael and Felicia were only ten and eight years old, and they thought it was the Sandman who had taken them.'

The men and women seated round the table watch Anja prepare the recording of Mikael's account. Their faces are sombre. For the first time they're about to hear Jurek Walter's only surviving victim talk about what happened.

'In other words, we can't identify the accomplice,' Joona says. 'Which leaves the location . . . If Mikael can lead us back there, then . . .'

## 50

There's a hiss from the loudspeakers and certain sounds are emphasised, like the rustle of paper, while others are barely audible. At times Reidar's sobbing can be heard, such as when his son talks about Felicia's space-capsule fantasy.

As they listen, Nathan Pollock makes notes and Magdalena Ronander types non-stop on her laptop.

'You say it's impossible to escape,' they hear Joona say seriously. 'Yet that's precisely what you did.'

'It *is* impossible, it wasn't like that,' Mikael Kohler-Frost replies quickly.

'How was it, then?'

'The Sandman blew his dust over us and when I woke up I realised I wasn't in the capsule any more,' Mikael says. 'It was completely dark, but I could hear that the room was different, and could tell that Felicia wasn't there. I felt my way forward until I came to a door with a handle . . . and I opened it and found myself in a corridor . . . I don't think I was aware that I was escaping, I just knew I had to keep moving forward . . . I came to a locked door and thought I'd ended up in a trap, because obviously I realised that the Sandman might come back any second . . . I panicked and broke the glass with my hand, and reached through to unlock it . . . I ran through a storeroom full of boxes and bags of cement . . . and then I saw that the wall to the right was nothing more than a plastic sheet stapled in place . . . I was having trouble breathing, and I could feel my fingers bleeding as I tried to pull the plastic down. I knew I'd hurt myself on the glass, but I didn't care, I just carried on across a big concrete floor . . . the room wasn't finished, and I kept going until I found myself walking on snow . . . the sky wasn't completely dark by then . . . I ran past a digger with a blue star on it and carried on into the forest, and started to realise that I was free. I ran through trees and undergrowth and got covered in snow, I never looked back, just kept on going, across a field and up into a clump of trees, and suddenly I couldn't go any further. A broken branch had jabbed straight into my thigh, I was completely stuck, I couldn't move. Blood was running down into the snow and it hurt badly. I tried to pull free, but I was stuck fast . . . I thought I might be able to break the branch, but I was too weak, I just couldn't do it. So I stood there. I was sure I could hear the Sandman's porcelain fingers clicking. When I turned to look behind me I slipped and the branch came out. I don't know if I passed out . . . I was much slower now, but I got to my feet and carried on up a slope, I was stumbling and kept thinking I couldn't go any further, then I was crawling, and I found myself on a railway track. I've no idea how long I walked, I was freezing, but I kept going, occasionally I could see houses in the distance but I was so exhausted that I stuck to the tracks . . . It was snowing more and more, but it was like I was walking in a trance, it never occurred to me to stop, I just wanted to get further away . . .'

## 51

When Mikael has stopped talking and the hissing noise from the speakers has ceased, there's total silence in the meeting room. Carlos stands up. He's biting one of his thumbnails as he stares blankly into space.

'We abandoned two children,' he eventually says in a quiet voice. 'They were missing, but we said they were dead and just went on with our lives.'

'We were actually convinced that was true, though,' Benny says gently.

'Joona wanted to carry on,' murmurs Anja.

'But in the end even I didn't believe they were still alive,' says Joona.

'And there was nothing left to go on,' Pollock points out. 'No evidence, no witnesses . . .'

Carlos's cheeks are pale as he puts a hand to his neck and tries to undo the top button of his shirt.

'But they were alive,' he says, almost in a whisper.

'Yes,' Joona replies.

'I've seen a lot, but this . . .' Carlos says, tugging at his collar again. 'I just can't understand why. I mean, why the hell? I don't get it, I just . . .'

'There's nothing to get,' Anja says kindly. 'You need a drink of water.'

'Why would anyone keep two children locked up for all those years?' he goes on, his voice raised. 'Making sure that they survived, but nothing more, no blackmail, no violence, no abuse . . .'

Anja tries to lead him from the room, but he resists and grabs Nathan Pollock's arm.

'Find the girl,' he says. 'Whatever you do, find her today!'

'I'm not sure—'

'Find her!' Carlos cuts in, then leaves the meeting room.

Anja returns shortly afterwards. The members of the group mutter and look through their papers. Tommy Kofoed is smiling a strained smile to himself. Benny is sitting with his mouth open, absentmindedly poking at Magdalena's sports bag with his toes.

'What's wrong with you all?' Anja asks sharply. 'Didn't you hear what the boss said?'

The group quickly agrees that Magdalena and Kofoed should put together a response team and a forensics unit while Joona tries to identify a preliminary search area to the south of Södertälje Syd station.

Joona studies a printout of the last picture that was taken of Felicia. He doesn't know how many times he's looked at it. Her eyes are big and dark, her long black hair is draped over her shoulder in a loose plait. She's holding a riding hat and smiling shrewdly at the camera.

'Mikael Kohler-Frost says he started walking just before it got dark,' Joona begins, gazing at the large-scale map on the wall. 'When exactly did the train driver raise the alarm?'

Benny checks his laptop.

'At three twenty-two,' he replies.

'They found Mikael here,' Joona says, drawing a circle round the northern end of the Igelsta Bridge. 'It's hard to imagine he could have been walking any faster than five kilometres an hour, if he was wounded and suffering from Legionnaires' disease.'

Anja uses a ruler to measure the furthest distance he could have walked from the south, at that speed and on a map of that scale, then draws a circle using a large pairs of compasses. Twenty minutes later they've managed to identify five current construction projects that could match Mikael's description.

A two-metre plasma screen is now showing a hybrid of a map and a satellite picture. Benny is still laboriously adding information to the computer which is connected to the plasma screen. Beside him Anja is sitting with two telephones, gathering supplementary information, while Nathan and Joona discuss the various building sites.

Five red circles on the map mark the ongoing construction projects within the preliminary search area. Three of them are in built-up areas.

Joona is standing in front of the map, his eyes following the railway line, then he points at one of the two other circles, in the forest close to Älgberget.

'This is the one,' he says.

Benny clicks the circle and brings up the coordinates, and Anja reads out a short description of the building works: NCC are building a new server farm for Facebook, but work has been at a standstill for the past month because of environmental objections.

'Do you want me to get hold of the plans?' Anja asks.

'We'll set off at once,' Joona says.

## 52

The snow is lying undisturbed on the bumpy track through the forest. A large area has been cleared. Pipes and cable-runs are in place, and the drains have been installed. Forty thousand square metres of concrete foundations have been laid, and several ancillary buildings are more or less complete, while others are just shells. There's a thick layer of snow on the diggers and dumper trucks.

During the drive to Älgberget, Joona received detailed plans on his mobile. Anja had got hold of them from the local planning department.

Magdalena Ronander examines the map with the rapid-response unit before they leave their vehicles and approach the site from three directions.

They're creeping through the edge of the forest. It's dark in among the tree trunks, and the snow is uneven. They quickly take up their positions, approaching cautiously as they observe the open area.

There's a strange, somnolent atmosphere over the whole place. A large digger is parked in front of a gaping shaft.

Marita Jakobsson runs over and crouches down beside a pile of blast mats. She's a middle-aged superintendent with plenty of experience. She carefully scans the buildings through her binoculars before waving the rest of the group forward.

Joona draws his pistol and heads towards a low building with the others. Snow is blowing off the roof and drifting through the air, sparkling.

They're all wearing bulletproof vests and helmets, and two of them are carrying Heckler & Koch assault rifles.

They pass an unfinished wall and head up onto the bare concrete foundations.

Joona points towards a sheet of protective plastic that's flapping in the wind. It's hanging loose between two struts.

The group follows Marita through a storeroom and over to a door whose window has been smashed. There are black bloodstains on the floor and sill of the door.

There's no doubt that this is the place Mikael escaped from.

The glass crunches beneath their boots. They carry on into the corridor, opening door after door and securing each room in turn.

Everywhere is empty.

In one room is a crate of empty bottles, but otherwise there's nothing.

So far it's impossible to tell which room Mikael was in when he woke up, but everything suggests that it was one of the rooms along this corridor.

The rapid-response units sweep efficiently through the industrial units and search each room before withdrawing to their vehicles.

Now Forensics can get to work.

Then the forest needs to be searched with dog patrols.

Joona is standing with his helmet in his hand, looking at the snow as it sparkles on the ground.

If I'm honest, I knew we weren't going to find Felicia here, he thinks. The room that Mikael called the capsule had thick, reinforced walls, a water tap and a hatch for food. It was constructed to hold people captive.

Joona has read Mikael's medical records, and knows that the doctors found traces of the anaesthetic drug Sevoflurane in his soft tissues. Now he's thinking that Mikael must have been drugged and moved here while he was unconscious. That matches his description of just waking up to find himself in a different room. He fell asleep in the capsule and woke up here.

For some reason, Mikael was moved here after all those years.

Was it finally time for him to end up in a coffin when he managed to escape?

The temperature is falling even lower as Joona watches the police officers return to their vehicles. Marita Jakobsson's careworn face is tense, and she looks sad.

If Mikael was drugged, then there is no way he can lead them to the capsule.

He never saw anything.

Nathan Pollock waves to Joona, to let him know it's time to leave. Joona starts to raise his hand, but gives up.

It mustn't end like this. It can't be over, he thinks, running his hand through his hair.

What is left to be done?

As Joona walks back towards the cars, he already knows the terrifying answer to his own question.

## 53

Joona turns gently into the Q-Park garage, takes a ticket, then drives down the ramp and parks. He remains seated in the car as a man from the carpet warehouse above gathers up shopping trolleys.

When he can't see anyone else in the car park, Joona gets out of the car and goes over to a shiny black van with tinted windows, opens the side door and climbs in.

The door closes silently behind him and Joona says a muted hello to Carlos Eliasson, chief of the National Police, and the head of the Security Police, Verner Zandén.

'Felicia Kohler-Frost is being held in a dark room,' Carlos begins. 'She's been there more than ten years, together with her older brother. Now she's entirely alone. Are we going to abandon her? Say she's dead and leave her there? If she's not ill, she could live another twenty years or so.'

'Carlos,' Verner says in a soothing voice.

'I know, I've lost all detachment.' He smiles, raising his hands apologetically. 'But I really do want us to do absolutely everything we can this time.'

'I need a large team,' Joona says. 'If I can have fifty people we can try to pick up all the old threads, every missing-person case. It might not lead to anything, but it's our only chance. Mikael never saw the accomplice, and he was drugged before he was moved. He can't tell us where the capsule is. Obviously we're going to carry on talking to him, but I simply don't believe he knows where he's been kept for the past thirteen years.'

'But if Felicia is alive, then she's probably still in the capsule,' Verner says in his deep voice.

'Yes,' Joona agrees.

'How the hell are we going to find her? It's impossible,' Carlos says. 'No one knows where the capsule is.'

'No one apart from Jurek Walter,' Joona says.

'Who can't be questioned,' Verner says.

'No,' Joona replies.

'He's utterly psychotic, and—'

'No, he was never that,' Joona interrupts.

'All I know is what it says in the forensic medical report,' Verner says. 'They wrote that he was schizophrenic, psychotic, prone to chaotic thinking and extremely violent.'

'Only because that's what Jurek wanted it to say,' Joona replies calmly.

'So you think he's healthy? Is that what you mean, that there's nothing wrong with him?' Verner asks. 'What the hell is this? Why wasn't he interrogated, then?'

'He was sentenced to solitary confinement,' Carlos says. 'In the verdict of the Supreme Court—'

'It must be possible to get round the terms of the sentence,' Verner sighs, stretching out his long legs.

'Maybe,' Carlos says.

'And I've got some very skilled people who've interrogated people suspected of terrorist—'

'Joona's the best,' Carlos interrupts.

'No, I'm not,' Joona responds.

'It was you who tracked down and apprehended Jurek,

and you're actually the only person he spoke to before his trial.'

Joona shakes his head and looks out at the deserted garage through the tinted window.

'I've tried,' he says slowly. 'But it's impossible to fool Jurek. He isn't like other people, he isn't unhappy, he doesn't need sympathy, he won't say anything.'

'Do you want to try?' Verner asks.

'No, I can't,' says Joona.

'Why not?'

'Because I'm frightened,' he replies simply.

Carlos looks at him uncertainly.

'I know you're only joking,' he says nervously.

Joona turns to face him. His eyes are hard, and as grey as wet slate.

'Surely we've no reason to be scared of an old man who's already locked up,' Verner says, scratching his head slightly nervously. 'He ought to be scared of us. For God's sake, we could rush in, pin him down on the floor and scare the shit out of him. I mean, seriously fucking tough.'

'It won't work,' Joona says.

'There are methods that always work,' Verner goes on. 'I've got a secret group who were involved in Guantanamo.'

'Obviously, this meeting has never taken place,' Carlos says hurriedly.

'I very rarely have meetings that have,' Verner says in his deep voice, then leans forward. 'My group knows all about waterboarding and electric shocks.'

Joona shakes his head. 'Jurek isn't scared of pain.'

'So we just give up?'

'No,' Joona says, leaning back and making his seat creak.

'So what do you think we should do?' Verner asks.

'If we go in and talk to Jurek, the only thing we can be sure of is that he'll be lying. He'll steer the conversation and once he's found out what we want with him, he'll get us to start bargaining, and we'll end up giving him something we'll only regret.'

Carlos looks down and scratches his knee irritably.

'So what does that leave us with?' Verner asks quietly.

'I don't know if it's even possible,' Joona says. 'But if you could place an agent as a patient in the same secure psychiatric unit as—'

'I don't want to hear any more,' Carlos interrupts.

'It would have to be someone so convincing that Jurek would want to talk to them,' Joona goes on.

'Bloody hell,' Verner mutters.

'A patient,' Carlos whispers.

'Because it would be enough to have someone who might be useful to him, someone he could exploit,' Joona says.

'What are you saying?'

'We need to find an agent who's so exceptional that they can make Jurek Walter curious.'

## 54

The punchbag lets out a sigh and the chain rattles. Saga Bauer moves nimbly to one side, follows the movement of the bag with her body and strikes again. Two blows, then an echo that rumbles off the walls of the empty boxing gym.

She's practising a combination of two quick left hooks, one high, one low, followed by a hard right hook.

The black punchbag sways, and the hook creaks. Its shadow crosses Saga's face and she punches again. Three rapid blows. She rolls her shoulders, moves backwards, glides round the punchbag and strikes once more.

Her long blonde hair flies out with the rapid movement of her hips, flicking across her face.

Saga loses track of time when she's training, and all thoughts vanish from her head. She's been on her own in the gym for the past two hours. The last of the others left while she was doing her skipping. The lamps above the boxing ring are switched off, but the bright glow from the drinks machine is shining through the doorway. There's snow swirling outside the windows, around the dry cleaners' sign and along the pavement.

From the corner of her eye Saga sees a car stop in the

street outside the boxing club, but she carries on with the same combination of blows, trying to increase their power the whole time. Drops of sweat hit the floor next to a smaller punchbag that has come off its support.

Stefan walks in. He stamps the snow from his feet, then stands quietly for a moment. His coat is undone, showing the pale suit and white shirt beneath.

She goes on punching as she sees him take off his shoes and come closer.

The only sounds are the thump of the bag and the rattle of the chain.

Saga wants to go on training, she's not ready to break her concentration yet. She lowers her brow and attacks the bag with a rapid series of punches even though Stefan is standing right behind it.

'Harder,' he says, holding the bag in place.

She throws a straight right, so hard that he has to take a step back. She can't help laughing, and before he's managed to regain his balance she punches again.

'Give me some resistance,' she says, with a hint of impatience in her voice.

'We need to leave.'

Her face is closed and hot as she fires off another salvo of punches. She finds it so easy to succumb to desperate rage. Rage makes her feel weak, but it's also what makes her keep fighting, long after others have given up.

The heavy blows make the punchbag tremble and the chain rattle. She slows herself down, even though she could carry on for ages yet.

Panting, she takes a couple of easy steps backwards. The bag continues to swing. A light shower of concrete dust falls from the catch in the ceiling.

'OK, I'm happy now.' She smiles at him, pulling off her boxing gloves with her teeth.

He follows her into the women's changing room and helps her remove the strapping from her hands.

'You've hurt yourself,' he whispers.

'No problem,' she says, looking at her hand.

Her washed-out gym clothes are wet with sweat. Her nipples are showing through her damp bra, and her muscles are swollen and pumped with blood.

Saga Bauer is an inspector with the Security Police, and she's worked with Joona Linna of the National Criminal Investigation Department on two big cases. She's not just an elite-level boxer, but a very good sniper, and has been specially trained in advanced interrogation techniques.

She's twenty-seven years old, her eyes are blue as a summer sky, she has colourful ribbons plaited into her long, blonde hair, and is almost improbably beautiful. Most people who see her are filled with a strange, helpless sense of longing. Just seeing her is enough to make people fall helplessly in love.

The hot shower creates steam that mists up the mirrors. Saga stands solidly with her legs apart and her arms hanging by her sides as the water washes over her. A large bruise is forming on one thigh, and the knuckles of her right hand are bleeding.

She looks up, wipes the water from her face and sees Stefan standing there watching her with a perfectly neutral expression.

'What are you thinking?' Saga asks.

'That it was raining the first time we had sex,' he says quietly.

She remembers that afternoon very well. They had been to a matinee at the cinema, and when they emerged onto Medborgarplatsen it was pouring with rain. They ran down Sankt Paulsgatan to his studio, but still got drenched. Stefan has often talked about the unembarrassed way she got undressed and hung her clothes over the radiator, then stood there picking out notes on his piano. He said he knew he shouldn't stare, but that she lit up the room like a ball of molten glass in a dark hut.

'Get in the shower,' Saga says.

'There isn't time.'

She looks at him with a little frown between her eyebrows.

'Am I alone?' she suddenly asks.

He smiles uncertainly. 'What do you mean?'

'Am I alone?'

Stefan holds out a towel and says calmly:

'Come on, now.'

## 55

It's snowing as they get out of the taxi at the Glenn Miller Café. Saga turns her face towards the sky, shuts her eyes and feels the snow fall on her warm skin.

The cramped premises are already full, but they're in luck and find a free table. Candles flicker in frosted lanterns and the snow slides wetly down the windows facing Brunnsgatan.

Stefan hangs his coat on the back of a chair and goes over to the bar to order.

Saga's hair is still wet and she shivers as she takes off her green parka, its back dark with damp. The people nearby keep looking round and she's worried they've taken someone's seats.

Stefan puts two vodka martinis and a bowl of pistachio nuts on the table. They sit opposite each other and drink a silent toast. Saga is about to say how hungry she is when a thin man in glasses comes over.

'Jacky,' Stefan says, surprised.

'I thought I could smell cat-piss.' Jacky grins.

'This is my girl,' Stefan says.

Jacky glances at Saga but doesn't bother to say hello, just whispers something to Stefan instead and laughs.

'No, seriously, you've got to play with us,' he says. 'Mini's here as well.'

He points to a thickset man who's making his way towards the corner where an almost black contrabass and a half-acoustic Gibson guitar stand ready.

Saga can't hear what they're saying; they're talking about some legendary gig, a contract that's the best so far, and a cleverly put-together quartet. She lets her eyes roam round the bar as she waits. Stefan says something to her as Jacky starts pulling him to his feet.

'Are you going to play?' Saga asks.

'Just one song,' Stefan calls with a smile.

She waves him off. The noise in the bar subsides as Jacky takes the microphone and introduces his guest. Stefan sits down at the piano.

'"April in Paris",' he says simply, and starts to play.

## 56

Saga watches Stefan half-close his eyes and her skin breaks out in goosebumps as the music takes over and shrinks the room, making the subdued lighting soft and shimmering.

Jacky starts to play gently ornate harmonies, and then the bass joins in.

Saga knows that Stefan loves this, but at the same time she can't forget the fact that they'd arranged to sit and talk, just for once.

She's been looking forward to this all week.

Slowly she eats the pistachio nuts, gathering a heap of empty shells and waiting.

A peculiar angst at his walking away from her like that makes her feel suddenly chill; she has no idea where the feeling has come from. She knows that she's being irrational, and keeps telling herself not to be childish.

When her drink is finished she moves on to Stefan's. It's no longer cold, but she drinks it anyway.

She looks over at the door just as a red-cheeked man takes a picture of her with his phone. She's tired, and is considering going home to sleep, but she'd really like to talk to Stefan first.

Saga has lost track of how many numbers they've played.

John Scofield, Mike Stern, Charles Mingus, Dave Holland, Lars Gullin, and a long version of a song she doesn't know the name of, from that record with Bill Evans and Monica Zetterlund.

Saga looks at the heap of pale nutshells, the toothpicks in the martini glasses and the empty chair opposite her. She goes over to the bar and gets a bottle of Grolsch, and when she's finished it she heads to the bathroom.

Some women are adjusting their make-up in front of the mirror, the toilets are all occupied and she has to queue for a while. When one of the cubicles is finally free she goes in, locks the door, sits down and just stares at the white door.

An old memory makes her feel suddenly impotent. She remembers her mother lying in bed, her face marked by sickness, staring at the white door. Saga was only seven years old and was trying to comfort her, trying to say everything would soon be all right, but her mum didn't want to hold her hand.

'Stop it,' Saga whispers to herself as she sits on the toilet, but the memory won't let go.

Her mum got worse and Saga had to find her medication, help her take her tablets and hold the glass of water.

Saga sat on the floor beside her mother's bed looking up at her, fetching a blanket when she was cold, trying to call her dad each time her mum asked her to.

When her mum finally fell asleep Saga can remember switching off the little lamp, curling up on top of the bed and wrapping her mother's arms round her.

She doesn't usually think of it. She usually manages to keep her distance from the memory, but this time it was just there, and her heart is beating hard in her chest as she leaves the toilet.

Their table is still empty, the empty glasses are still there, and Stefan is still playing. He's maintaining eye contact with

Jacky, and they're responding playfully to each other's improvisations.

Maybe it's the drink or her memories affecting her judgment. She forces her way through to the musicians. Stefan is in the middle of a long, meandering improvisation when she puts a hand on his shoulder.

He starts, looks at her, then shakes his head irritably. She grabs his arm and tries to get him to stop playing.

'Come, now,' she says.

'Get your girl under control,' Jacky hisses.

'I'm playing,' Stefan says through gritted teeth.

'But the two of us . . . We'd agreed . . .' she tries, feeling to her own surprise that tears are rising to her eyes.

'Get lost,' she hears Jacky snarl at her.

'Can't we go home soon?' she asks, patting the back of Stefan's neck.

'For God's sake,' he whispers sharply.

Saga backs away and manages to knock over a glass of beer on top of one of the amplifiers, and it falls to the floor and shatters.

Beers splashes up onto Stefan's clothes.

She stands still, but his eyes are focused solely on the keys of the piano, and the hands racing across them as sweat runs down his cheeks.

She waits a moment, then returns to their table. Some men have sat down in their chairs. Her green parka is lying on the floor. She picks it up with trembling hands, and hurries out into the heavy snow.

## 57

Saga Bauer spends the whole of the following morning in one of the Security Police's generously proportioned meeting rooms with four other agents, three analysts and two people from admin. Most of them have laptops or tablets in front of them, and a grey screen is currently showing a diagram illustrating the extent of non-wireless communication traffic across the country's borders during the past week.

Under discussion are the analytical database of the Signals Intelligence Unit, new search methods and the apparently rapid radicalisation of thirty or so Islamists who are in favour of violence.

'Mind you, even if al-Shabaab have made extensive use of the al-Qimmah network,' Saga is saying, brushing her long hair back over her shoulders, 'I don't think it will give us much. Obviously we need to carry on, but I still say we should be trying to infiltrate the group of women on their periphery . . . as I mentioned before, and—'

The door opens and the head of the Security Police, Verner Zandén, comes in, raising his hand apologetically.

'I really don't want to interrupt,' he says in his rumbling voice as he catches Saga's eye. 'But I was just thinking of going for a little stroll, and would very much appreciate your company.'

She nods and logs out, but leaves her laptop on the table as she exits the meeting room with Verner.

Shimmering snow is falling from the sky as they emerge onto Polhemsgatan. It's extremely cold and the tiny crystals in the air are lit up by the hazy sunlight. Verner walks with long strides and Saga hurries along beside him like a child.

They pass Fleminggatan in silence, walk through the gate to the health centre, across the circular park surrounding the chapel and down the steps towards the ice of Barnhusviken.

The situation is feeling more and more peculiar, but Saga refrains from asking any questions.

Verner makes a little gesture with his hands and turns left onto a cycle path.

Some small rabbits scamper for cover under the bushes as they approach. The snow-covered park benches are soft shapes in the white landscape.

After walking a bit further they turn in between two of the tall buildings lining Kungsholms Strand and go up to a door. Verner taps in a code, opens the door and leads her into the lift.

In the scratched mirror Saga can see snowflakes covering her hair. They're melting, forming glistening drops of water.

When the creaking lift stops, Verner takes out a key with a plastic card attached, unlocks a door that bears the telltale signs of attempted burglaries, then nods to her to follow him inside.

They walk into an entirely empty flat. Someone has recently moved out. The walls are full of holes where pictures and shelves have been removed. There are large dustballs on the floor and a forgotten Ikea Allen key.

The toilet flushes and Carlos Eliasson, chief of the National Criminal Investigation Department, comes out. He wipes his hands on his trousers and then shakes hands with Saga and Verner.

'Let's go into the kitchen,' Carlos says. 'Can I offer you something to drink?'

He gets out a pack of plastic cups and fills them with tap-water, then offers them to Saga and Verner.

'Perhaps you were expecting lunch?' Carlos says as he sees the mystified look on her face.

'No, but . . .'

'I've got some throat sweets,' he says quickly, pulling out a little box of Läkerol.

Saga shakes her head, but Verner takes the box from Carlos, taps out a couple of pastilles and pops them in his mouth.

'Quite a party.'

'Saga, as you've no doubt realised, this is an extremely unofficial meeting,' Carlos says, then clears his throat.

'What's happened?' Saga asks.

'Have you heard of Jurek Walter?'

'No.'

'Not many people have . . . and that's just as well,' Verner says.

## 58

A ray of sunlight is twinkling on the dirty kitchen window as Carlos Eliasson hands Saga Bauer a dossier. She opens the folder and finds herself staring directly into Jurek Walter's pale eyes. She moves the photograph and starts to read the thirteen-year-old report. Her face turns white and she sits down on the floor with her back against the radiator, still reading, looking at the pictures, glancing through post-mortem reports and reading about his sentence and where it was being served.

When she closes the file Carlos tells her how Mikael Kohler-Frost was found wandering across the Igelsta Bridge after being missing for thirteen years.

Verner gets out his mobile and plays the recording of the young man describing his captivity and escape. Saga listens to his anguished voice, and when she hears him talk about his sister her face goes red and her heart starts beating hard. She looks at the photograph in the folder. The little girl is standing with her loose plait and riding hat, smiling as if she were planning something naughty.

When Mikael's voice falls silent she stands up and

paces the empty kitchen before stopping in front of the window.

'National Crime have got nothing more to go on than they had thirteen years ago,' Verner says.

'We don't know anything . . . but Jurek Walter knows, he knows where Felicia is, and he knows who his accomplice is . . .'

Verner explains that it's impossible to get the truth out of Jurek Walter in a conventional interrogation, or by using psychologists or priests.

'Not even torture would work,' Carlos says, trying to sit down on the windowsill.

'What the hell, why don't we do what we usually do, then?' Saga asks. 'Surely all we have to do is recruit just one damn informant, that's pretty much the only thing our organisation does these days apart from—'

'Joona says . . . sorry to interrupt,' Verner cuts in. 'But Joona says that Jurek would break down any informer who tried—'

'So what the hell do we do, then?'

'Our only option is to install a trained agent as a patient in the same institution,' he replies.

'Why would he talk to a patient?' Saga asks sceptically.

'Joona reckons we need to find an agent who's so exceptional that Jurek Walter ends up curious enough to want to know more.'

'Curious how?'

'Curious about them as a person . . . not just in the possibility of getting out,' Carlos replies.

'Did Joona mention me?' she asks in a serious voice.

'No, but you're our first choice,' Verner says firmly.

'Who's your second choice?'

'There isn't one,' Carlos replies.

'So how would this be arranged, in purely practical terms?' she asks in a neutral tone of voice.

'The bureaucratic machinery is already hard at work,' Verner says. 'One decision leads to another, and if you accept the mission you just have to climb on board . . .'

'Tempting,' she mutters.

'We'll arrange for you to be sentenced to secure psychiatric care in the Court of Appeal, and transferred at once to Karsudden Hospital.'

Verner goes over to the tap and refills his plastic cup.

'We spotted something that might work to our advantage, a formulation in the original county council permit . . . the one that was granted when the psychiatric unit at Löwenströmska Hospital was first set up.'

'It states very clearly that the ward is designed to offer treatment to three patients,' Carlos adds. 'But for the past thirteen years they've had just one patient, Jurek Walter.'

Verner drinks noisily, then crumples up his cup and tosses it in the sink.

'The hospital managers have always tried to fend off other patients,' Carlos goes on. 'But they're perfectly aware that they have to accept more if they receive a direct request.'

'Which is precisely what's happening now . . . The Prison Service Committee has called an extraordinary meeting, where the decision will be taken to transfer one patient from the secure psychiatric unit at Säter to Löwenströmska, and another from Karsudden Hospital.'

'In other words, you would be the patient from Karsudden,' Carlos says.

'So if I agree to this, I'd be admitted as a dangerous patient?' she asks.

'Yes.'

'Are you going to give me a criminal record?'

'A decision from the National Judiciary Administration will probably be sufficient,' Verner replies. 'But we need to create an entire identity, with guilty court verdicts and psychiatric evaluations.'

## 59

Saga is standing in the empty flat together with the two police chiefs. Her heart is beating hard and every fibre of her being is screaming at her to say no.

'Is this illegal?' she asks, and feels that her mouth has gone dry.

'Yes, of course . . . and it's extremely confidential,' Carlos replies seriously.

'Extremely?' she replies, the corner of her mouth curling into a smile.

'At National Crime we'll be declaring it confidential, so that the Security Police can't see the file.'

'And I'll make sure that it's declared confidential by the Security Police so National Crime can't see it,' Verner goes on.

'No one will know about this unless there's a direct request from the government,' Carlos says.

The sun is shining through the dirty window, and Saga looks out at the panelled façade of the neighbouring building. A chimney vent is glinting at her and she turns back towards the two men.

'Why are you doing this?' she asks.

'To save the girl,' Carlos says with a smile, but the smile doesn't reach his eyes.

'And I'm supposed to believe that the heads of National Crime and the Security Police are working together to—'

'I knew Roseanna Kohler,' Carlos interrupts.

'The mother?'

'We were in the same class at Adolf Fredrik School, we were very close . . . we . . . it's been very tough, very . . .'

'So this is personal?' Saga asks, taking a step back.

'No, it's . . . it's the only right thing to do, you can see that for yourself,' he replies, gesturing towards the folder.

When Saga's expression doesn't change, he goes on:

'But if you want me to be honest . . . Obviously it's hypothetical, but I'm not sure we would have had a meeting quite like this if it wasn't personal.'

He starts fiddling with the mixer tap on the sink. Saga watches him, and gets the strong impression that he's not telling her the whole truth.

'In what way is it personal?' she asks.

'It's not important,' he replies quickly.

'You're sure?'

'What's important is . . . that we actually do this, it's the right thing to do, the only right thing . . . because we believe the girl can still be saved.'

'So we're sending in an agent as quickly as we possibly can – that's all, no large-scale operation,' Verner says.

'Obviously we don't know if Jurek Walter's going to say anything, but there's a chance . . . and everything suggests that it's our only chance.'

Saga stands perfectly still with her eyes closed for a long while.

'What happens if I say no?' she asks. 'Will you let the girl die in that damn capsule?'

'We'll find another agent,' Verner says simply.

'Go ahead, then,' Saga says, and begins to walk towards the hall.

'Do you want to think about it?' Carlos calls.

She stops with her back to the two police chiefs and shakes her head. Light filters through her thick hair with the interwoven ribbons.

'No,' she replies, and walks out of the flat.

## 60

Saga takes the underground to Slussen, then walks the short distance to Stefan's studio on Sankt Paulsgatan. At Södermalmstorg she buys a bunch of red roses, wondering if Stefan might have bought roses for her.

She feels relieved to have declined the difficult task of infiltrating Jurek Walter and the secure psychiatric unit.

She strides up the steps and unlocks the door, she can hear the sound of the piano and smiles to herself. She goes in, sees Stefan sitting at the piano and stops. His blue shirt is unbuttoned. He has a bottle of beer beside him and the room smells of cigarette smoke.

'Darling,' she says after a brief pause. 'I'm sorry . . . I need you to know how sorry I am about what happened yesterday . . .'

He goes on playing, softly, radiantly.

'Forgive me,' she says seriously.

Stefan's face is turned away, but she has no trouble hearing what he says:

'I don't want to talk to you right now.'

Saga holds out the bouquet towards him and tries to smile.

'Sorry,' she repeats. 'I know I'm difficult, but I—'

'I'm playing,' he interrupts.

'But we need to talk about what happened.'

'Just go,' he says loudly.

'I'm sorry I—'

'And close the fucking door behind you.'

He stands up and points towards the hall. Saga drops the flowers on the floor, goes up to him and pushes him in the chest, so hard that he has to take a step back, knocks over the piano stool and pulls his score down. She follows him, ready to hit him again if he hits back, but Stefan just stands there with his hands by his side, looking her straight in the eye.

'This isn't working,' he says simply.

'I'm a bit off balance right now, that's all,' she says.

He picks the piano stool up and gathers his music together. Fear rises within her and she takes a step back.

'I don't want you to be upset,' he says with an emptiness in his voice that transforms her fear into panic.

'What is it?' she asks, suddenly feeling sick.

'This isn't working, we can't be together, we . . .'

He falls silent and she tries to smile, tries to function, but her forehead has broken out in a cold sweat and she feels giddy.

'Because I was difficult last night?' she manages to say.

Stefan glances up at her unwillingly.

'You're the most beautiful woman I've ever seen, the most beautiful woman in the world . . . and you're smart and funny and I ought to be the happiest man alive . . . I'm probably going to regret this for the rest of my life, but I think we should break up.'

'I still don't understand,' she whispers. 'Because I got angry . . . because I disturbed you when you were playing?'

'No, it's . . .'

He sits down again and shakes his head.

'I can change,' she says, and looks at him for a moment before going on. 'But it's already too late, isn't it?'

When he nods she turns and leaves the room. She goes out into the hall, picks up the old stool from Dalarna and throws it at the mirror. The splinters fall to the floor, shattering again as they hit the hard tiles. She shoves the front door open and runs down the stairs, straight out into the radiant blue winter light.

Saga runs along the pavement, between the buildings and the bank of snow lining the road. She breathes in the icy air so deeply that it hurts her lungs. She crosses the road, runs across Mariatorget, then stops on the other side of Hornsgatan and gets some snow from a car roof and presses it to her hot, stinging eyes, then runs the rest of the way home.

Her hands are shaking as she unlocks the door. She lets out a lonely whimper as she steps into the hall and closes the door behind her.

Saga lets the keys fall to the floor, kicks off her shoes and walks straight through the flat to her bedroom.

She picks up the phone, dials the number, then stands and waits. After six rings she is put through to Stefan's voicemail. She doesn't listen to his message, just throws the phone at the wall as hard as she can.

She staggers, leans forward and grabs the chest of drawers.

Still fully dressed, she lies down on the double bed and curls up like a foetus. She knows all too well when she last felt like this. When she was little and woke up in her dead mother's arms.

Saga Bauer can no longer remember how old she was

when her mother got ill. But when she was five she realised that her mum had a serious brain tumour. The illness changed her mum in terrible ways. The poisoned cells made her distant and increasingly irritable.

Her dad was hardly ever home. She can't bear to think about how he let them down. As an adult she's tried to tell herself he was only human, he couldn't help being weak. She repeats it like a mantra, but her fury at him won't subside. It's quite incomprehensible that he kept out of the way and handed the burden to his young daughter. She doesn't want to think about it, never talks about it, it just makes her angry.

The night the illness finally claimed her mother she was so tired she needed help taking her medication. Saga gave her pill after pill, and ran to get more water.

'I can't take any more,' her mum whispered.

'You have to.'

'Just call Daddy and tell him I need him.'

Saga did as her mum asked, and told her dad that he had to come home now.

'Mummy knows I can't,' he replied.

'But you have to, she can't take any more . . .'

Later that evening her mum was very weak, she didn't eat anything but her medication and shouted at Saga when she knocked over the bottle of pills on the rug. Her mum was in terrible pain, and Saga tried to comfort her.

Her mum just asked Saga to call her dad and tell him she'd be dead before morning.

Saga cried and said she mustn't die, that she didn't want to live if her mum died. Her tears were trickling into her mouth as she called her dad once more. She sat on the floor, listening to the sound of her own crying and her dad's answerphone message.

'Call . . . call Daddy,' her mum whispered.

'I'm trying,' Saga sobbed.

When her mum finally fell asleep, Saga turned out the little lamp and stood by the bed for a while. Her mum's lips were shiny and she was breathing heavily. Saga curled up in her warm embrace and fell asleep, exhausted. She slept beside her mum until she woke up early next morning, frozen.

Saga gets out of bed, looks at the remnants of the broken phone, takes off her coat and lets it fall to the floor, then goes to the kitchen and gets a pair of scissors, and heads for the bathroom. She studies herself in the mirror, sees John Bauer's pretty princess, and thinks about how she could save a lonely girl. Maybe I'm the only person who can save Felicia, she thinks, looking sternly at her own reflection.

## 62

A meeting was arranged just two hours after Saga Bauer told her boss that she'd changed her mind and was going to accept the job.

Now Carlos Eliasson, Verner Zandén, Nathan Pollock and Joona Linna are waiting in a flat on the top floor of Tantogatan 71, with a view of the snow-covered ice in Årstaviken and the rainbow arch of the railway bridge.

The flat is furnished in a modern style, with white furniture and inset lamps. On the large dining table in the living room are plates of sandwiches from Non Solo Bar. Carlos stops abruptly and just stares as Saga walks in. Verner breaks off mid-sentence and looks almost scared, and Nathan Pollock slumps down at the table with a sad look on his face.

Saga has shaved off her long hair. She has several grazes on her scalp.

Her eyes are swollen with crying.

Her pale, beautiful head is still graceful, though, with its small ears and long, narrow neck.

Joona Linna walks over and gives her a hug. She holds him hard for a while, pressing her cheek to his chest and listening to the beat of his heart.

'You don't have to do this,' he says against her head.

'I want to save the girl,' she replies quietly.

She holds on for a few more seconds, then goes into the kitchen.

'You know everyone here,' Verner says, pulling out a chair for her.

'Yes,' Saga nods.

She drops her dark green parka on the floor and sits down. She's wearing her usual clothes, a pair of black jeans and a tracksuit top from the boxing club.

'If you really are prepared to go undercover in the same unit as Jurek Walter, we need to act at once,' Carlos says, unable to hide his enthusiasm.

'I looked through your contract with us and there are a few things that could be improved,' Verner adds quickly.

'Good,' she mutters.

'We may have a little scope to increase your salary, and—'

'I don't really give a shit about that right now,' she interrupts.

'You're aware that there are certain risks associated with this mission?' Carlos asks cautiously.

'I want to do this,' she says firmly.

Verner pulls a grey phone from his bag, puts it on the table next to his usual mobile, writes a short text message, then looks up at her.

'Shall we set things in motion, then?' he asks.

When she nods he sends the message, which vanishes with a small whooshing sound.

'We've got a few hours now to prepare you for what you'll be faced with,' Joona says.

'Get going,' she says calmly.

The men quickly take out folders, open laptops, spread out their papers. Saga feels a shiver run through her arms when she sees how extensive the preparations are.

The table is covered by big maps of the area around Löwenströmska Hospital, the drains, and a detailed plan of the secure psychiatric unit.

'You're going to get a conviction from Uppsala District Court, and you'll be sent to the women's section of Kronoberg Prison first thing tomorrow morning,' Verner explains. 'In the afternoon you'll be driven to Karsudden Hospital in Katrineholm. That'll take an hour or so. By then the Prison Service Committee will be evaluating the proposal to transfer you to Löwenströmska.'

'I've started sketching out a diagnosis that you'll need to look at,' Nathan Pollock says, giving Saga a careful smile. 'You'll be given a credible medical history, with a juvenile psychiatric record, emergency treatment, placements, diagnoses and all sorts of medication, leading up to the present.'

'I understand,' she says.

'Do you have any allergies or illnesses we ought to know about?'

'No.'

'No problems with your liver or heart?'

## 63

Wet snow has started to fall outside the borrowed flat on Tantogatan. As the flakes hit the windows they make a clicking sound. On the pale wooden bookshelf there's a framed photograph of a family in a pool. The dad's nose is red with sunburn and the two children are laughing as they hold up inflatable crocodiles.

'To start with, we've got very little time indeed,' Nathan Pollock says.

'We don't even know if Felicia is alive,' Carlos says, and starts tapping the table with his pen. 'But if she is, it's extremely likely that she's suffering from Legionnaires' disease.'

'So we may have a week or so,' Pollock says.

'But the worst-case scenario is that she's already been abandoned,' Joona says, unable to conceal the anxiety in his voice.

'What do you mean?' Saga asks. 'She's survived more than ten years, and—'

'Yes,' Verner interrupts, 'but one possible explanation for why Mikael was able to escape is that Jurek's accomplice is ill, or—'

'He could have died, or he might just have taken off,' Carlos says.

'We aren't going to make it in time,' Saga whispers.

'We have to,' Carlos says quickly.

'If Felicia doesn't have access to water, there's nothing we can do, she'll die today or tomorrow,' Pollock says. 'If she's as ill as Mikael, she probably won't survive more than another week, but at least that gives us a chance . . . there's a hypothetical possibility, even if the odds are very low.'

'If she's only having to go without food, we may have three or four weeks,' Verner says.

'We've so little to go on,' Joona says. 'We don't know if the accomplice is carrying on as if nothing's happened, or if he's buried Felicia alive.'

'He may be thinking of keeping her in the capsule for another twenty years,' Carlos says in an unsteady voice.

'All we know is that she was still alive when Mikael escaped,' Joona goes on.

'I can't bear this,' Carlos says, getting to his feet. 'I just want to scream when I think—'

'We haven't got time for tears at the moment,' Verner interrupts.

'All I'm trying to say is—'

'I know, I feel the same,' Verner says, raising his voice. 'But in just over an hour the Prison Service Committee will hold an extraordinary meeting to take the formal decision to move patients to the secure unit at Löwenströmska, so—'

'I don't even know what I'm supposed to be doing,' Saga says.

'By then we need to have your new identity finished,' Verner goes on, holding a calming hand towards Saga. 'We need to have your medical history sorted, and the forensic psychology report; the District Court judgment will have to be added to the National Judiciary Administration database, and your temporary transfer to Karsudden needs to be organised.'

'We'd better get a move on,' Pollock says.

'But Saga wants to know what the mission is,' Joona says.

'It's just that it's bloody difficult for me to . . . I mean, how can I have an opinion about what you're discussing if I don't even know what's expected of me?' Saga says.

Pollock holds a plastic folder up to her.

'On your first day you need to place a tiny microphone in the dayroom, with a fibre-optic receiver and transmitter,' Verner says.

Pollock gives her the folder containing the microphone.

'Smuggled in up my backside?' she asks.

'No, they're bound to carry out a full body-cavity search,' Verner replies.

'You need to swallow it, then vomit it back up before it reaches your duodenum . . . and then swallow it again,' Pollock explains.

'Never leave it longer than four hours,' Verner says.

'And I carry on doing this until I manage to place it in the dayroom,' Saga says.

'We're going to have people positioned in a van who'll be listening to everything in real time,' Pollock says.

'OK, I get that bit,' Saga says. 'But giving me a District Court conviction, a whole load of psychiatric evaluations and all that—'

'We need that because—'

'Let me finish,' she interrupts. 'I get it . . . I'll have a coherent background, I'll be in the right place, and I'll plant the microphone, but . . .'

The look in her eyes is hard and her lips are pale as she looks at each of them in turn:

'But why the hell . . . Why would Jurek Walter tell me anything?'

## 64

Nathan is standing up, Carlos has both hands over his face, and Verner is fiddling with his mobile.

'I don't understand why Jurek Walter would talk to me,' Saga repeats.

'Obviously, we're taking a chance,' Joona says.

'In the unit there are three separate secure rooms, with a shared dayroom containing a running machine and a television concealed behind reinforced glass,' Verner explains. 'Jurek Walter has been held in isolation for thirteen years, so I don't know how much the dayroom has been used.'

Nathan Pollock pushes the plan of the secure unit over and points out Jurek's room and the dayroom next to it.

'If we're really unlucky, the staff won't allow the patients to see each other . . . we have no influence over that,' Carlos admits.

'I understand,' Saga says calmly. 'But I'm thinking more about the fact that I have no idea . . . not a fucking clue about how I might approach Jurek Walter.'

'You could try asking to see a representative from the administrative court, and demand to have a fresh risk assessment,' Carlos says.

'Who do I say that to?' she asks.

'Senior Consultant Roland Brolin,' Verner replies, putting a photograph in front of her.

'Jurek himself is hemmed in by restrictions,' Pollock says. 'So he'll be watching you closely, and will probably ask questions, seeing as your visits will be a sort of window on the world.'

'What should I expect from him? What does he want?' Saga says.

'He wants to escape,' Joona replies sternly.

'Escape?' Carlos repeats incredulously, tapping a pile of reports. 'He hasn't made a single attempt to escape in all the time he's—'

'He won't try if he knows he won't succeed,' Joona says.

'And you think he might say something in these circumstances that could lead you to the capsule?' Saga asks, without even trying to hide her scepticism.

'We now know that Jurek has an accomplice . . . which means that he has the capacity to trust other people,' Joona says.

'So he's not paranoid,' Pollock says.

Saga smiles. 'That makes things a whole lot easier.'

'None of us imagines that Jurek's going to confess just like that,' Joona says. 'But if you can persuade him to talk, sooner or later he'll say something that can get us closer to Felicia.'

'You've spoken to him,' Saga says to Joona.

'Yes, he talked to me because he was hoping I'd change my testimony . . . but in all that time he didn't go anywhere close to anything personal.'

'So why would he with me?'

'Because you're exceptional,' Joona replies, looking her straight in the eye.

## 65

Saga gets up, wraps her arms around herself and stands quite still, looking at the sleet through the window.

'The most difficult thing right now is having to justify the transfer to the secure unit at Löwenströmska, whilst simultaneously finding a crime and a diagnosis that won't lead to heavy medication,' Verner says.

'The whole mission will probably fail if you're put in a straitjacket or given electroconvulsive treatment,' Pollock says bluntly.

'Shit,' she whispers, and turns to face them again.

'Jurek Walter's an intelligent man,' Joona says. 'It's not easy to manipulate him, and it will be very dangerous lying to him.'

'We need to create a perfect identity,' Verner says, his eyes fixed on Saga.

'I've been giving this some thought, and I think it makes sense to give you a schizophrenic personality disorder,' Pollock says, peering at her through his narrow black eyes.

'Will that be enough?' Carlos asks.

'If we throw in recurrent psychotic attacks with violent outbursts . . .'

'OK,' Saga nods, as her cheeks start to blush red.

'You're kept calm with eight milligrams of Trilafon three times a day,' he says.

'Just how dangerous is this mission?' Verner eventually asks, seeing as Saga hasn't put the question.

'Jurek is extremely dangerous, the other patient who's going to be arriving at the same time as Saga is also dangerous, and we have no control over her treatment once she's there,' Pollock replies honestly.

'So you can't give any guarantees about the safety of my agent?' Verner says.

'No,' Carlos replies.

'You're aware of this, Saga?' Verner asks.

'Yes.'

'Only a very select group will know about the existence of this mission, and we won't have any overview of what's going on inside the secure unit,' Pollock says. 'So if for some reason we don't hear you over the microphone, we'll break off the mission after twenty-seven hours – but until then you'll have to take care of yourself.'

Joona puts the detailed plan of the secure unit in front of Saga and points at the dayroom with his pen.

'As you can see, there are airlocks here . . . and three automated doors there,' Joona says. 'It's not easy, but in an emergency you could try to barricade yourself in here, possibly also here or here . . . And if you're outside the airlock, the operations room and this storeroom are clearly the best options.'

'Is it possible to get past this passageway?' she asks, pointing.

'Yes, but not here,' he says, crossing off the doors that can't be forced without cards and codes.

'Lock yourself in and wait for help.'

Carlos starts to leaf through the papers on the table.

'But if something goes wrong at a later point, I want to show you—'

'Hang on a minute,' Joona interrupts. 'Have you memorised the plan?'

'Yes,' Saga says.

Carlos pulls out the large map of the area surrounding the hospital.

'In the first instance, we'll be sending emergency vehicles in this way,' he says, indicating the road behind the hospital. 'We'll stop here, at the side of the big exercise yard . . . But if you can't make it there, carry on up into the forest till you get here.'

'Good,' she says.

'The response units will probably go in here . . . and through the drains, depending on the nature of the alarm.'

'As long as you don't blow your cover, we can get you out and put things back to normal,' Verner says. 'Nothing will have happened, we change the National Judiciary Administration records back the way they were before, you'll have no criminal conviction and have never received treatment anywhere.'

A sudden silence fills the room. It's as if the impossibility of the task has suddenly become abundantly and unpleasantly apparent.

'How many of you think my mission is actually going to succeed?' Saga asks quietly.

Carlos nods uncertainly and mutters something.

Joona just shakes his head.

'Maybe,' Pollock says. 'But it's difficult, and dangerous.'

'Do your best,' Verner says, putting his hand on her shoulder for a moment.

## 66

Saga takes Nathan Pollock's comprehensive character profile into a pink bedroom with pictures of Bella Thorne and Zendaya on the walls. Fifteen minutes later she returns to the kitchen. She walks slowly, and stops in the middle of the floor. The shadows of her long eyelashes dance on her cheeks. The men fall silent and turn their heads to look at the slender figure with the shaved head.

'My name is Natalie Andersson, and I've got a schizophrenic personality disorder, which makes me a bit introverted,' she says, sitting down on a chair. 'But I've also had recurrent psychotic episodes, with some extremely violent outbursts. That's why I've been prescribed Trilafon. I'm OK at the moment with eight milligrams, three times a day. The pills are small and white . . . and they make my breasts so sore I can't sleep on my front. I also take Cipramil, thirty milligrams . . . or Seroxat, twenty milligrams.'

While she's been speaking she has secretly pulled the tiny microphone out of the lining of her trousers.

'When I was really bad I used to get injected with Risperdal . . . and Oxascand for the side effects . . .'

Under the cover of the tabletop she removes the protective

plastic from the glue and sticks the microphone under the table.

'Before Karsudden and the verdict from Uppsala District Court, I escaped from a non-secure ward at Bålsta psychiatric unit and killed a man in the playground behind Gredelby School in Knivsta, then, ten minutes later, a man in the drive of his house in Daggvägen . . .'

The little microphone comes loose from the table and falls to the floor.

'After I was arrested I was put in the acute psychiatric unit of the University Hospital in Uppsala, I was given twenty milligrams of Stesolid and one hundred milligrams of cisordinol injected into my backside, I was kept strapped up for eleven hours and then I was given a solution of Heminevrin . . . it was really cold . . . and I got all bunged up and had a really bad headache.'

Nathan Pollock claps his hands. Joona bends down and picks the microphone up from the floor.

He smiles as he holds it out to her. 'The glue needs four seconds to firm up.'

Saga takes the microphone and looks at it as she turns it over in her hand.

'Are we agreed about this identity?' Verner asks. 'In seven minutes I've got to enter it on the National Judiciary Administration database.'

'I think it sounds good,' Pollock says. 'But this evening you need to memorise the rules at Bålsta, and learn the name and physical characteristics of the staff and other patients.'

Verner nods in agreement to Pollock, then stands up. In a deep voice he declares that an infiltrator needs to know every detail about their background off by heart in order not to be uncovered.

'You have to become one with your new identity, so that

you don't have to think before reeling off phone numbers and imaginary family members, birthdays, past addresses, dead pets, ID numbers, schools, teachers, workplaces, colleagues, their personal habits, and—'

'I'm not sure that's the right line to take,' Joona interrupts.

Verner falls silent with his mouth open and turns to look at Joona. Carlos nervously sweeps up some crumbs on the table with his hand. Nathan Pollock leans back and smiles expectantly.

'I can learn all that,' Saga says.

Joona nods calmly and looks her in the eye. His eyes are dark as lead now.

'Seeing as Samuel Mendel is no longer alive,' Joona says, 'I can say that he had remarkable knowledge of long-term infiltration techniques . . . serious undercover work.'

'Samuel?' Carlos says sceptically.

'I can't explain how, but he knew what he was talking about,' Joona says.

'Was he Mossad?' Verner asks.

'I can only say that . . . when he told me about his method, I realised he was right, and that's why I've remembered what he said,' Joona said.

'We're already aware of all the methods,' Verner says, sounding stressed.

'When you're working undercover, you speak as little as possible and only in short sentences,' Joona says.

'Why short sentences?'

'To sound authentic,' Joona goes on, addressing Saga directly. 'Never pretend to feel things, never pretend to be angry or happy, and always mean what you say.'

'OK,' Saga says warily.

'And the most important thing,' Joona continues. 'Never say anything but the truth.'

'The truth,' Saga repeats.

'We'll make sure that you've got your diagnoses,' Joona explains. 'But you need to claim that you're healthy.'

'Because it's true,' Verner whispers.

'You don't even need to know about what crimes you committed – you need to claim that it's all lies.'

'Because that wouldn't be a lie,' Saga says.

'Bloody hell,' Verner says. 'Bloody hell.'

Saga's face flushes as she realises what Joona is saying. She gulps, then says slowly:

'So if Jurek Walter asks me where I live, I just tell him that I live on Tavastgatan on Södermalm?'

'That way you'll remember your answer if he asks more than once.'

'And if he asks about Stefan I tell the truth?'

'That's the only way you're going to sound genuine, and remember what you've said.'

'What if he asks what my job is?' she laughs. 'Shall I say I'm a superintendent with the Security Police?'

'In a secure psychiatric unit, that would probably work.' Joona grins. 'But otherwise . . . if you're asked a question that really would give you away, you can always ignore it . . . seeing as that would be a perfectly honest reaction – you don't want to answer.'

Verner smiles as he scratches his head. The atmosphere in the room is suddenly buoyant.

'I'm starting to believe in this now,' Pollock says to Saga. 'We'll give you your psychological evaluations and criminal record, but you just answer any questions honestly.'

Saga gets up from the table and her face is quite calm as she says:

'My name is Saga Bauer, and I'm perfectly healthy, and completely innocent.'

## 67

Nathan Pollock is sitting next to Verner Zandén as he logs into the National Judiciary Administration database and types in the twelve-digit code. Together they add the dates when charges were laid, when the application to go to trial was filed, and the main hearing. They classify the crimes, formulate the forensic psychiatric report and the fact that Uppsala District Court found the accused guilty of two unusually violent cases of premeditated manslaughter. At the same time Carlos is adding Saga Bauer's crimes, sentence and sanctions in the criminal records register of the National Police Authority.

Verner moves on to the National Board of Forensic Medicine's database, adds a copy of the forensic psychiatric report, enters the examination in the journal, then smiles to himself.

'How are we doing in terms of time?' Saga asks.

'Fairly well, I think,' Verner says, glancing at his watch. 'In precisely two minutes the Prison Service Committee will be gathering for their extraordinary meeting . . . and then they'll check what it says in the National Judiciary

Administration database . . . and take the decision to transfer two patients to the secure psychiatric unit at Löwenströmska Hospital.'

'You never explained why there have to be two new patients,' Saga says.

'To make you less exposed,' Pollock replies.

'We imagined that Jurek Walter would get suspicious if a new patient suddenly appeared after so many years,' Carlos explains. 'But if a patient from the secure unit at Säter shows up first . . . followed a day or so later by one from Karsudden, with a bit of luck you won't attract quite as much scrutiny.'

'You're being moved because you're dangerous and liable to try to escape . . . and the other patient has himself requested a transfer,' Pollock says.

'Time to let Saga go now,' Verner says.

'Tomorrow night you'll be sleeping in Karsudden Hospital,' Pollock says.

'You'll have to tell your family you're on a secret mission abroad,' Verner begins. 'You'll need someone to look after bills, pets, houseplants—'

'I'll sort it out,' she interrupts.

Joona picks up her parka from where she dropped it on the floor and holds it up for her to put on.

'Do you remember the rules?' he asks quietly.

'Say little, talk in short sentences, mean what I say and stick to the truth.'

'I've got one more rule,' Joona says. 'It probably varies from person to person, but Samuel said you should avoid talking about your parents.'

She shrugs her shoulders.

'OK.'

'I don't know why he thought that was so important.'

'It seems wise to listen to Samuel's advice,' Verner agrees quietly.

'Yes, I'd say so.'

Carlos puts two sandwiches in a bag and gives them to Saga.

'I ought to remind you than in there you'll be a patient, nothing more . . . you won't have access to any police information or rights,' he says seriously.

Saga looks him in the eye:

'I know.'

'It's important that you understand that if we're to be able to protect you afterwards,' Verner says.

'I'm going to go home and get some rest,' Saga says quietly, and walks towards the hall.

As she's sitting on a stool tying her boots, Joona comes out to her. He squats down beside her.

'It'll soon be too late to change your mind,' he whispers.

'I want to do this, Joona.' She smiles, meeting his gaze.

'I know,' Joona says. 'It'll be fine, as long as you don't forget how dangerous Jurek is. He affects people, changes them, rips their souls out like—'

'I'm not going to let Jurek get into my head,' she says confidently, then stands up and begins to fasten her coat.

'He's like—'

'I'm a big girl,' she interrupts.

'I know.'

Joona holds the door open for her and goes out onto the landing with her. He hesitates and she leans against the wall.

'What is it you want to say?' she asks gently.

A few seconds of silence follow. The lift is standing motionless on their floor. A car races past outside, sirens blaring.

'Jurek will do anything he can to escape,' Joona says in his sombre voice. 'You mustn't let that happen. You're like a sister to me, Saga, but it would be better that you died than he got out.'

## 68

Anders Rönn is sitting at the big conference table, waiting. It's already half past five. The pale, impersonal room is full of the usual members of the hospital committee, two representatives from general psychiatry, Senior Consultant Roland Brolin and head of security, Sven Hoffman.

The hospital manager, Rikard Nagler, is still talking on the phone as he is given a glass of iced tea by his secretary.

Snow is falling slowly from the low sky.

All conversation in the room ceases as the hospital manager puts his empty glass down on the table, wipes his mouth and opens the meeting.

'It's good that you could all come,' he says. 'I had a call from the Prison Service Committee an hour ago.'

Silence falls as people sit and wait for him to go on.

'They've decided that the secure unit is going to have to admit two new patients at short notice,' he continues. 'Obviously we've been very spoiled, with just one patient . . . and an old, quiet one at that.'

'Because he's biding his time,' Brolin says gravely.

'I called this meeting to hear your opinions about what

this means in terms of security and the general medical situation,' the manager goes on without taking any notice of Brolin's comment.

'What sort of patients are they thinking of sending?' Anders asks.

'Naturally they're both high risk,' the manager replies. 'One is in the secure unit at Säter, and the other is in the psychiatric unit at Karsudden after—'

'It's not going to work,' Brolin says.

'Our secure unit was actually built to house three patients,' the hospital manager says patiently. 'Times have changed, we can't—'

'Yes, but Jurek is . . .'

Brolin falls silent.

'What were you going to say?'

'It's impossible for us to handle any more patients,' Brolin says.

'Even though we have a direct obligation to accept them.'

'Find some excuse.'

The manager laughs wearily and shakes his head.

'You've always seen him as a monster, but he—'

'I'm not scared of monsters,' Brolin interrupts. 'But I'm smart enough to be scared of Jurek Walter.'

The manager smiles at Brolin and then whispers something to his secretary.

'I'm still fairly new here,' Anders says. 'But has Jurek Walter ever caused any direct problems?'

'He made Susanne Hjälm disappear,' Brolin replies.

Silence descends on the room. One of the doctors from general psychiatry takes his glasses off, then puts them back on at once.

'I was told that she was on leave of absence . . . for a research project, I think it was?' Anders says slowly.

'We're calling it a leave of absence,' Brolin says.

'I'd very much like to hear what happened,' Anders says, feeling a vague anxiety growing inside him.

'Susanne smuggled out a letter from Jurek Walter, but regretted it,' Brolin explains, with his eyes closed. 'She called me and told me everything. She was completely, I don't know . . . she was just crying and promising that she'd burned the letter . . . And I believe that she had, because she was frightened, and kept saying she wasn't going to go in to see Jurek again.'

'She's taken a leave of absence,' the hospital manager says, shuffling his papers.

A few people laugh, while others look troubled. Sven Hoffman, head of security, projects an image of the secure unit on the white screen.

'In terms of security, we have no problem accepting more patients,' he says sternly. 'But we'll maintain a higher level of alert to start with.'

'Jurek Walter mustn't meet other people,' Brolin persists.

'Well, he's going to have to now . . . You'll just need to ensure that security isn't compromised,' the manager says, looking at the others.

'It won't work . . . and I want it in the minutes that I'm abdicating responsibility for the secure unit. It will have to come under the umbrella of general psychiatry, or become a separate—'

'Don't you think you're exaggerating now?'

'This is exactly what Jurek Walter has been waiting all these years for,' Brolin says, his voice breathless with agitation.

He gets up and leaves the room without another word. Shadows of falling snowflakes drift slowly down the wall holding the whiteboard.

'I'm sure I could take care of three patients, regardless of their diagnoses,' Anders says calmly, leaning back in his chair.

The others look at him in surprise, and the hospital manager puts his pen down and smiles amiably.

'I don't actually understand the problem,' he continues, glancing at the door through which Brolin disappeared.

'Go on,' the manager nods.

'It's merely a matter of medication,' Anders says.

'We can't just keep them sedated,' Hoffman laughs.

'Of course we can, if it's absolutely necessary,' Anders says with a boyish smile. 'Take St Sigfrid's, for instance . . . we were so stretched that there wasn't the capacity to deal with lots of incidents.'

He sees the intent look on the hospital manager's face, raises his eyebrows and throws out his hands, then says lightly:

'We know that heavy medication is perhaps . . . uncomfortable for the patient, but if I was responsible for the secure unit, I wouldn't want to take any risks.'

## 69

Agnes is sitting on the floor in her blue pyjamas with bees on. She's clutching her little white hairbrush and feeling each bristle with her fingertip, one by one, as if she were counting them. Anders is sitting on the floor in front of her, holding her Barbie doll and waiting.

'Brush the doll's hair,' he says.

Agnes doesn't look up at him, she just goes on picking at each individual bristle, one row after the other, slowly and intently.

He knows she doesn't play spontaneously like other children, but she plays in her own way. She has trouble understanding what other people see and think. She's never given her Barbie dolls personalities, she just tests their mechanics, bending their arms and legs and twisting their heads round.

But he has learned from courses organised by the Autism and Asperger Association that she can be trained to play if the games are divided up sequentially.

'Agnes? Brush the doll's hair,' he repeats.

She stops fiddling with the brush, holds it out and pulls it through the doll's blonde hair, then repeats the movement twice more.

'She looks lovely now,' Anders says.

Agnes starts picking at the brush again.

'Have you seen how lovely she looks?' he asks.

'Yes,' she says, without looking.

Anders gets out a Sindy doll and before he even has time to say anything Agnes reaches forward and brushes its hair with a smile.

When Agnes is asleep three hours later Anders settles down on the sofa in front of the television and watches *Sex and the City*. In front of the house heavy snowflakes are falling through the yellow glow of the outside lights. Petra's at a staff party. Victoria picked her up at five o'clock. She said she wasn't going to be late, but it's almost eleven now.

Anders drinks a sip of cold tea and sends Petra a text to tell her about Agnes brushing her dolls' hair.

He's tired, but he'd like to tell her about the meeting at the hospital, and how he's assumed responsibility for the secure unit and has a guarantee of permanent work.

In the advert break Anders goes to turn out the light in Agnes's room. The nightlight is shaped like a life-size hare. It gives off a lovely pink light, casting a soft glow on the sheets and Agnes's relaxed face.

The floor is littered with pieces of Lego, dolls, dolls' furniture, plastic food, pens, princess's tiaras and a whole porcelain tea set.

Anders can't understand how it's got into such a mess.

He has to shuffle forward so as not to stand on anything. The toys rattle slightly as they slide about the wooden floor. As he's reaching for the light switch he imagines he can see a knife on the floor beside the bed.

The big Barbie house is in the way, but he can make out the glint of steel through the little doorway.

Anders tiptoes closer, leans over and his heart starts to beat faster when he sees that the knife looks like the one he found in the secure cell.

He can't understand it, he gave the knife to Brolin.

Agnes begins to whimper anxiously and whisper in her sleep.

Anders crawls over the floor and sticks his hand through the ground floor of the dolls' house, opens the little door wide and reaches for the knife.

The floor creaks and Agnes is coughing slightly as she breathes.

Something is glinting in the darkness under the bed. It could be the shiny eyes of a teddy bear. It's difficult to tell through the tiny leaded windows of the dolls' house.

'Ow,' Agnes whispers in her sleep. 'Ow, ow . . .'

Anders has just managed to touch the knife with his fingertips when he sees the twinkling eyes of a wrinkled face under the bed.

It's Jurek Walter – and he moves fast as lightning, grabbing his hand and pulling.

Anders wakes up as he snatches his hand back. He's gasping as he realises he's fallen asleep on the sofa in front of the television. He switches it off, and sits there with his heart pounding.

Car headlights shine in through the window. A taxi turns round and disappears. Then the front door opens carefully.

It's Petra.

He hears her go to the bathroom and pee, then take her make-up off. He walks slowly closer, towards the light of the bathroom spilling into the corridor.

## 70

Anders stands in the dark watching Petra in the mirror above the basin. She brushes her teeth, spits, cups her hand to lift some water to her mouth, then spits again.

When she sees him she looks scared for a few seconds.

'Are you awake?'

'I was waiting for you,' Anders said in a strange voice.

'That's sweet of you.'

She turns the light out and he follows her into the bedroom. She sits down on the edge of the bed and rubs cream into her hands and elbows.

'Did you have a good time?'

'It was OK . . . Lena's got a new job.'

Anders grabs her left hand and holds her tightly by the wrist. She looks into his eyes.

'You know we've got to be up early tomorrow.'

'Shut up,' he says.

She tries to pull free, but he grabs her other hand and pushes her down onto the bed.

'Ow—'

'Just shut up!'

He forces one knee between her thighs and she tries

to twist aside, then lies there quite still and looks at him.

'I mean it: red light . . . I have to get some sleep,' she says gently.

'I've been waiting for you.'

She looks at him for a moment, then nods.

'Lock the door.'

He gets off the bed, listens out for any sounds from the corridor, but the house is quiet, so he shuts and locks the door. Petra has taken off her nightdress and is opening the box. With a smile she gets out the soft rope and the carrier bag with the whip, the vibrator and the big dildo, but he pushes her onto the bed.

She tells him to stop, but he roughly pulls off her underwear, leaving red marks on her hips.

'Anders, I—'

'Don't look at me,' he interrupts.

'Sorry . . .'

She doesn't resist as he ties her tightly, a bit too tightly. It's possible that the drink has made her less sensitive than usual. He ties the rope round one of the bedposts, and forces her thighs apart.

'Ow,' she whimpers.

He fetches the blindfold and she shakes her head as he pulls it down over her face. She tries to pull loose, tugging at the ropes so hard that her heavy breasts swing.

'You're so beautiful,' he whispers.

It's four o'clock by the time they finish and he loosens the ropes. Petra is silent, her body trembling as she massages her sore wrists. Her hair is sweaty, her cheeks streaked with tears, and the blindfold has slipped down round her neck. He had stuffed the remnants of her underwear in her mouth when she wanted to stop, didn't want to go on.

## 71

Saga abandons any attempt to sleep at five o'clock. Ninety minutes left. Then they're coming to get her. Her body feels heavy as she pulls on her jogging outfit and leaves the flat.

She jogs a couple of blocks, then speeds up down towards Söder Mälarstrand.

There's no traffic this early.

She runs along the silent streets. The fresh snow is so airy she can barely feel it under her feet.

She knows she can still change her mind, but today's the day she's going to give up her freedom.

Södermalm is asleep. The sky is black above the glow of the streetlamps.

Saga runs quickly, thinking about the fact that she hasn't been given an assumed identity, that she's being admitted under her name and doesn't have to remember anything but her medication. Intramuscular injections of Risperdal, she repeats silently to herself. Oxascand for the side effects, Stesolid and Heminevrin.

Pollock had explained that it didn't matter what her diagnosis was: 'You still know exactly what medication you're on,' he said. 'It's a matter of life or death; the medication is what helps you survive.'

An empty bus swings into the deserted, well-lit terminal for the Finland ferries.

'Trilafon, eight milligrams three times a day,' she whispers as she runs. 'Cipramil thirty milligrams, Seroxat twenty milligrams . . .'

Just before she reaches the Photography Museum, Saga changes direction and carries on up the steep steps leading away from Stadsgårdsleden. She stops at the highest point of Katarinavägen and looks out across Stockholm as she goes through Joona's rules once more.

I have to keep to myself, say little, and only in short sentences. I have to mean what I say and only tell the truth.

That's all, she thinks, and keeps on running towards Hornsgatan.

Over the last kilometre she speeds up again and tries to sprint the last stretch along Tavastgatan to her building.

Saga runs up the stairs, kicks her shoes off on the hall mat and goes straight into the bathroom for a shower.

It feels strange to be able to dry herself so quickly afterwards without all that long hair. All she has to do is rub a towel over her head.

She pulls on the most basic underwear she owns. A white sport bra and a pair of pants she only wears when she's got her period. A pair of jeans, a black T-shirt and a washed-out tracksuit top.

She doesn't usually feel worried, but all of a sudden she has butterflies in her stomach.

It's almost twenty past six. They're picking her up in eleven minutes. She puts her watch back on the bedside table, next to her glass of water. Where she's going, time is dead.

First she'll be going to Kronoberg Prison, but she'll only be there a couple of hours before she's transported to

Katrineholm. Then she'll spend a day or so at Karsudden Hospital before the decision to transfer her to the secure psychiatric unit at Löwenströmska Hospital is put into action.

She walks slowly through the flat, switching off lights and pulling out a few plugs, before going into the hall and putting on her green parka.

It's not such a difficult mission, she thinks once more.

Jurek Walter is an elderly man, probably heavily medicated and not really with it.

She knows he's guilty of terrible things, but all she has to do is stay calm, wait for him to approach her, wait for him to say something that could be useful.

Either it will work, or it won't.

It's time to leave now.

Saga turns off the lamp in the hall and goes out into the stairwell.

She's thrown out all the perishable goods from the fridge, but she hasn't asked anyone to look after the flat, water the flowers and take care of the post.

## 72

Saga double-locks the door, then goes downstairs to the main entrance. She feels a flutter of anxiety as she sees the Prison Service van waiting in the dark street.

She opens the door and gets in beside Nathan Pollock.

'It's dangerous to pick up hitch-hikers,' she says, trying to smile.

'Did you get any sleep?'

'A bit,' she replies, and fastens her seat belt.

'I know you already know this,' Pollock says, glancing at her. 'But I'm still going to remind you not to try to manipulate him into revealing any information.'

He puts the van in gear and it pulls out into the silent street.

'That's almost the hardest thing,' Saga says. 'What if he only wants to talk about football? What if he doesn't talk at all?'

'That will just be how it is, there'll be nothing you can do about it.'

'But Felicia might only survive a few more days . . .'

'That's not your responsibility,' Pollock replies. 'This infiltration is a gamble, we all know that, we're agreed on that . . . we can't second-guess the results. What you're doing is entirely separate from the ongoing preliminary investigation. We're going to carry on talking to Mikael Kohler-Frost, follow up all the old lines of inquiry, and—'

'But no one believes . . . no one believes we'll be able to save Felicia unless Jurek starts talking to me.'

'You mustn't think like that,' Pollock says.

'OK, I'll stop now.' She smiles.

'Good.

She starts tapping her feet, and raises her arm to shield a sudden sneeze. Her pale-blue eyes are still glassy, as if part of her had taken a step back to observe the situation from a distance.

Dark buildings flit past as they drive on.

Saga puts her keys, wallet and other loose possessions in a Prison Service personal effects bag.

Before they reach Kronoberg Prison, Pollock hands her the fibre-optic microphone inside a silicon capsule and a small portion of butter.

'Digestion of fatty foods takes longer,' he says. 'But I still don't think you should ever wait more than four hours.'

She opens the pack of butter, swallows the contents, then examines the microphone in the soft capsule. It looks like an insect in amber. She straightens up, pops the capsule in her mouth, tips her head back and swallows. It hurts her throat and she can feel herself breaking out into a sweat as it slowly slips down.

## 73

The morning is still black as midnight and all the lights are on in the women's section of Kronoberg Prison.

Saga takes two steps forward and stops when they tell her to. She tries to shut herself off from the world around her and not look at anyone.

The radiators are ticking with the heat.

Nathan Pollock puts her bag of personal effects on the counter and hands over Saga's papers. He is given a written receipt and then disappears.

From now on she will have to cope on her own, no matter what happens.

The automated gates whirr briefly, then fall abruptly silent.

No one looks at her, but she can't help noticing the way the atmosphere gets more tense when the guards realise that she's got the highest security classification.

She is to be kept in strict isolation until her transfer.

Saga stands still, eyes fixed on the yellow vinyl floor, not answering any questions.

She is patted down before being led along a corridor for the full-body search.

Two thickset women are discussing a new television series

as they lead her through a door with no window in it. The room looks like a small medical examination room, with a narrow bunk covered with rustling paper and locked cabinets along one wall.

'Remove all your clothes,' one of the women says in a blank voice as she pulls on a pair of latex gloves.

Saga does as she is told and drops her clothes in a heap on the floor. When she is naked she just stands there under the bare fluorescent light with her arms hanging by her sides.

Her pale body is girlishly slender, toned and athletic.

The warder with the gloves breaks off mid-sentence and just stares at Saga.

'OK,' one of them sighs after a few seconds.

'What?'

'Let's try to do what we've got to do.'

Carefully they set about examining Saga, shining a light in her mouth, nose and ears. They tick each thing off from a list, then ask her to lie on the bunk.

'Lie on your side and pull one knee up as far as you can,' the woman with the gloves says.

Saga obeys, unhurriedly, and the woman moves between the bunk and the wall behind her back. She shivers, and feels her skin break out in goosebumps.

The dry paper rustles against her cheek as she turns her head. She shuts her eyes tight as lubricant is squeezed from a bottle.

'This is going to feel a bit cold now,' the woman says, sticking two fingers as far up Saga's vagina as she can.

It doesn't hurt, but it's extremely unpleasant. Saga tries to breathe evenly, but can't help gasping as the woman sticks a finger in her anus.

The examination is over in a matter of seconds, and the woman quickly pulls the gloves off and throws them away.

She hands Saga a piece of paper to wipe herself with, and explains that she'll be given new clothes while she's there.

Dressed in a baggy green outfit and a pair of white gym shoes, she is taken to her cell in Ward 8:4.

Before they close and lock the door behind her they ask amiably if she'd like a cheese sandwich and a cup of coffee.

Saga just shakes her head.

Once the women have gone, Saga stands completely still in her cell for a moment.

It's hard to know what the time is, but before it's too late she goes over to the sink and fills her hands with water, drinks some, then sticks her fingers down her throat. She coughs and her stomach clenches. After a couple of hard, painful cramps, the microphone comes back up.

She can't help her eyes watering as she washes the capsule and then rinses her face.

She lies on the bunk and waits, holding the microphone hidden in her hand.

The corridor outside is silent.

Saga can smell the toilet and drain in the floor as she lies staring at the ceiling and reads the messages and names that have been carved into the walls over the years.

Rectangles of sunlight have moved left towards the floor by the time Saga hears footsteps outside. She quickly pops the capsule in her mouth, stands up and swallows as the lock clicks and the door is opened.

It's time for her to be taken to Karsudden Hospital.

The uniformed guard signs her out, along with her possessions and transfer documents. Saga stands still as they cuff her hands and ankles, then sign the forms.

The police team consists of thirty-two people in total, civilian staff and officers from the surveillance and detection units of the National Criminal Investigation Department and the National Murder Squad.

In one of the big workrooms on the fifth floor the walls are covered with maps marking the locations of the disappearances and finds in the Jurek Walter case. Colour copies of photographs of the missing people are surrounded by constellations of their families, colleagues and friends.

Old interviews with the relatives of victims are examined again, and new interviews conducted. Medical and forensic reports are checked, and anyone who knew any of the victims is spoken to, no matter how peripheral the relationship.

Joona Linna and his team are standing in the winter light by the window reading the printout of the latest interview with Mikael Kohler-Frost. As they read, a sombre mood settles over the group. There's nothing in Mikael's account that can take the investigation forward.

Once the analysts have discounted the expressions of

regret and despair from his statements, there's very little left.

'Nothing,' Petter Näslund mutters, rolling the printout up.

'He says he can feel his sister's movements, that she tries to find him every time she wakes up in the darkness,' Benny says with a sorrowful expression on his face. 'He can feel how much she hopes he might have returned—'

'I don't believe any of that,' Petter interrupts.

'We have to assume that Mikael is telling the truth, at least in some form or other,' Joona says.

'But this business with the Sandman,' Petter says with a grin. 'I mean . . .'

'The same thing with the Sandman,' Joona replies.

'He's talking about a character in a fairytale,' Petter says. 'Are we going to question everyone who sells barometers, or—'

'As a matter of fact I've already compiled lists of manufacturers and dealers,' Joona replies with a smile.

'What the hell?'

'I'm aware that there's a barometer salesman in E. T. A. Hoffmann's story about the Sandman,' Joona goes on. 'And I know Mikael's mother used to tell them a bedtime story about the Sandman. But none of that precludes the possibility that he might actually exist in real life.'

'We haven't got a fucking thing, we might as well admit it,' Petter says, tossing his rolled-up printout on the desk.

'Almost nothing,' Joona gently corrects him.

'Mikael was sedated when he was moved to the capsule, and sedated when he was removed from it,' Benny sighs, rubbing a hand over his bald head. 'It's impossible even to start identifying a location. In all likelihood, Felicia is in Sweden – but even that isn't certain.'

Magdalena goes over to the whiteboard and lists what little

information they have about the capsule: concrete, electricity, water, Legionella bacteria.

Because Mikael has never seen the accomplice, or heard him speak, they know nothing beyond the fact that it is a man. That's all. Mikael was sure that the coughs he heard came from a man.

Everything else in the description can be traced back to childhood fantasies about the Sandman.

Joona leaves the room, takes the lift down, walks out of police headquarters and carries on up Fleminggatan, across the Sankt Erik bridge and into Birkastan.

The attic flat of Rörstrandsgatan 19 is where Athena Promacho is based.

When the goddess Pallas Athena is depicted as a beautiful girl with a lance and a shield, she is known as Athena Promacho, the goddess of war.

Athena Promacho is also the name of a secret investigative group that has been put together to analyse the material that Saga Bauer is expected to provide while she is undercover. The group doesn't exist in any official records, and has no budget from either the National Criminal Investigation Department or the Swedish Security Police.

Athena Promacho consists of Joona Linna from National Crime, Nathan Pollock from the National Murder Squad, Corinne Meilleroux from the Security Police, and forensic officer Johan Jönson.

As soon as Saga is transferred to the secure unit at Löwenströmska Hospital they'll be there twenty-four hours a day to receive, collate and analyse the surveillance recordings.

Athena Promacho has another three officers attached to it. They'll be responsible for recording the transmissions from the fibre-optic microphone in a minibus belonging to the local council's parks department that's been left in the hospital grounds. All the material will be saved on hard disks, encrypted and sent to Athena Promacho's computers with a delay of no more than a tenth of a second.

## 75

Anders Rönn looks at the time again. The new patient from the secure unit at Säter Prison is on his way to the isolation unit at Löwenströmska. Prison Service transport have called to warn him that the man is anxious and aggressive. They've given him ten milligrams of Stesolid en route, and Anders Rönn has prepared a syringe with another ten milligrams. An older warder named Leif Rajama throws the packaging of the syringe in the bin, then stands and waits, legs spread.

'I don't think he'll need more than that,' Anders says, not quite managing to summon up his carefree smile.

'It normally depends on how much the search upsets them,' Leif says. 'I try to tell myself that my job is to help people who are having a hard time . . . even if they may not actually want help.'

The guard on the other side of the reinforced glass gets a message that the transport is on its way down. There's a metallic clang from the walls, then a muffled cry.

'This is only the second patient,' Anders says. 'We won't know how things are going to be until all three are in place.'

'It'll be fine,' Leif smiles.

Anders looks at a monitor showing a view of the staircase

from the side. Two security guards are supporting a patient who's unable to walk unaided, a thickset man with a fair moustache and glasses that have slid down his narrow nose. His eyes are closed and sweat is running down his cheeks. His legs are bowed, but the guards are holding him up.

Anders glances quickly at Leif. They can hear the blond patient babbling nonsensically. Something about dead slaves and the fact that he's wet himself.

'I'm standing in piss, right up to my knees, and . . .'

'Hold still,' the guards order, and lay him down on the floor.

'Ow, it hurts,' he whimpers.

The guard behind the glass is standing up now, and takes the transfer documents from the senior transport officer.

The patient is lying on the floor with his eyes shut, gasping. Anders tells Leif calmly that they aren't going to need any more Stesolid, then pulls his pass card through the reader.

## 76

Jurek Walter is walking monotonously on the running machine. His face is turned away, but his back is moving with focused determination.

Anders Rönn and head of security Sven Hoffman are standing in the hospital's security control room looking at a monitor showing the dayroom.

'You know how to sound the alarm, and how to switch it off,' Hoffman says. 'You know someone with a pass card must accompany the guards when they come into contact with the patients.'

'Yes,' Anders says, with a hint of impatience in his voice. 'And the security door behind you has to be locked before you open the next one.'

Sven Hoffman nods.

'Guards will show up within five minutes of the alarm being sounded.'

'We won't be sounding any alarms,' Anders says, watching the monitor as the new patient comes into the dayroom.

They watch the patient as he sits down on the brown sofa, holding one hand over his mouth as though trying not to be sick. Anders thinks about the handwritten notes from Säter, detailing aggression, recurrent psychosis, narcissism and an antisocial personality disorder.

'We'll have to conduct our own evaluation,' Anders says. 'And I'll increase his medication if there's the slightest reason to . . .'

The large computer screen in front of him is divided into nine squares, for the nine cameras in the unit. Airlocks, security doors, corridors, dayroom and patients' rooms are all filmed. There aren't enough staff to monitor the cameras round the clock, but there always has to be someone with operational responsibility for the system on duty in the unit.

'You'll be spending a lot of time in the office, but it's good if everyone knows how these things work,' Sven Hoffman says, gesturing towards the monitors.

'We'll have to muck in together when we've got more patients.'

'The basic principle is that the staff should always know where all the patients are.'

Sven clicks one of the squares, and the image immediately fills the monitor alongside, and suddenly Anders can see psychiatric nurse My taking off her wet coat.

The changing room is reflected on the screen with unexpected clarity, five yellow metal lockers, a shower, and doors to the toilet and corridor.

The outline of My's breasts can clearly be seen beneath her black T-shirt bearing an image of an angel of death. She must have been in a rush to get there, because her cheeks are flushed. She has melted snow in her hair. She gets out her uniform, lays it on the bench, then puts a pair of Birkenstock sandals on the floor.

Sven clicks away from the changing room and enlarges the image from the dayroom instead. Anders forces himself not to look at the smaller square as My starts to unbutton her black jeans.

He sits down and tries to sound unconcerned as he asks if recordings are stored.

'We haven't got permission to do that . . . not even in exceptional circumstances.' Hoffman winks at him.

'Shame,' Anders says, running a hand over his short brown hair.

Sven Hoffman starts to go through the cameras covering the rooms. Then Anders tries clicking his way through the monitor, checking the corridors and airlocks.

'We cover everything where—'

A door opens in the distance, they hear the hum of the coffee machine, then My walks into the security control room.

'What are you doing huddled up in here?' she asks with a grin.

'Sven's going through the security system with me,' Anders replies.

'And there was me thinking you were watching while I took my clothes off,' she jokes with a sigh.

## 77

They fall silent and watch the screen covering the dayroom. Jurek Walter is walking on the running machine with even strides, and Bernie Larsson gradually slips down until he is lying with his neck against the low back of the sofa. His shirt slides up and his fat stomach moves as he breathes. His face is sweaty, one of his legs is bouncing nervously and he seems to be talking to the ceiling.

'What's he doing?' My asks, looking at the others. 'What's he saying?'

Anders shrugs. 'No idea.'

The only sound audible in the security control room is the ticking of a golden, solar-powered Chinese cat waving its paw.

Anders thinks back to Bernie Larsson's medical notes from Säter. Twenty-one years ago he was sentenced to secure psychiatric care for what was described as a bestial series of rapes.

Now he's slumped on the sofa, yelling up at the ceiling. Saliva is spraying from his mouth. He's making aggressive slicing gestures with his hands, and throws the cushion beside him onto the floor.

Jurek Walter does what he has always done. With long strides he walks his nine kilometres on the running machine, then stops it, gets off and heads in the direction of his room.

Bernie shouts something at him as he leaves. Jurek stops in the doorway and turns back towards the dayroom again.

'What's happening now?' Anders asks anxiously.

Sven quickly picks up his radio and calls two colleagues, then hurries out. Anders leans forward and watches Sven as he appears on one of the monitors. He's walking along the corridor, talking to the other guards, then he stops outside the airlock, evaluating the situation.

Nothing happens.

Jurek is standing in the doorway, between the rooms, precisely where his face is in shadow. He's not moving, but both Anders and My can see that he's talking. Bernie is slumped in the sofa, eyes closed as he listens. After a while his bottom lip starts to quiver. The whole scenario plays out in little more than a minute, then Jurek turns and disappears into his room.

'Back to your lair,' My mutters.

One of the other monitors shows Jurek from above. Slowly he walks into his room, sits down on the plastic chair directly beneath the CCTV camera, and stares at the wall.

After a while Bernie Larsson gets up from the sofa in the dayroom. He wipes his mouth a few times before shuffling off to his room.

Another monitor shows Bernie Larsson going over to the sink, leaning forward and rinsing his face. He stands there as water runs over his face, then he walks to the door to the dayroom, presses his thumb against the inside of the frame and slams the door shut as hard as he can. The door bounces back and Bernie sinks to his knees, shrieking out loud.

## 78

It's ten o'clock in the morning and sharp winter light is shining on Magdalena Ronander as she returns to police headquarters from her yoga session. Petter Näslund is standing in front of a large-scale map of the residential area where the two Kohler-Frost children disappeared. He frowns as he pins up photographs from the old investigation. Magdalena says a quick hello, throws her bag onto her chair, and goes over to the whiteboard. She quickly strikes through the lines of inquiry they managed to follow up yesterday. Benny Rubin, Johnny Isaksson and Fredrik Weyler are sitting round the conference table making notes.

'We need to take another look at everyone who was employed at Menge's Engineering Workshop at the same time as Jurek Walter,' she says.

'I've compiled the interviews with Richard van Horn from yesterday,' Johnny says. He's blond and thin, and sports the same haircut that Rod Stewart had in the 1980s.

'Who's calling Reidar Frost today?' Petter asks, twirling a pen between his fingers.

'I can take care of that,' Magdalena replies calmly.

'Wonder if they want us to carry on looking for Wee Willie Winkie,' Benny says.

'Joona wants us all to take the whole Sandman thing seriously,' Petter reminds him.

'I found a great clip on YouTube,' Benny says, searching his mobile.

'Do we have to?' Magdalena sighs, picking up a heavy file from the table.

'But have you seen that clown who hides from stupid cops?' Benny asks, putting his phone down.

'No,' Petter replies.

'No, because I'm probably the only person in the room who's actually managed to catch sight of him,' Benny laughs.

Magdalena is smiling as she opens the file.

'Who's going to help me find the last people connected to Agneta Magnusson?' she asks.

She's the woman who was found alive in the grave in Lill-Jan's Forest when Jurek Walter was caught. The two bodies in the plastic barrel that was buried nearby belonged to her brother and nephew.

'Her mother vanished years ago, and her dad disappeared just after she was found.'

'Didn't they all disappear?' Fredrik Weyler asks.

'Not her husband,' Magdalena says, glancing at the file.

'This whole thing's so sick,' Fredrik whispers.

'But her husband is still alive, and—'

'Does yoga make you more flexible?' Benny asks, slapping both hands down on the table with a bang.

'Why did you do that?' Magdalena asks gravely.

## 79

Magdalena Ronander says hello to the large woman who's just opened the door. She has fine laughter lines at the corners of her eyes, and the name Sonja tattooed on her shoulder.

Everyone with any connection to Agneta Magnusson was questioned by the police thirteen years ago. All their houses and flats were searched by forensics officers, as well as summer houses, shacks, sheds, children's dens, caravans, boats and cars.

'I called earlier,' Magdalena says, showing her police ID.

'Oh, yes,' the woman nods. 'Bror's waiting for you in the living room.'

Magdalena follows the woman through the little 1950s house. There's a smell of fried steak and onions from the kitchen. A man in a wheelchair is sitting in a living room with dark curtains.

'Is that the police?' he asks in a dry voice.

'Yes, it's the police,' Magdalena says, pulling the piano stool over and sitting down in front of the man.

'Haven't we talked enough?'

It's been thirteen years since anyone questioned Bror

Engström about what happened in Lill-Jan's Forest, and in that time he's got old, she thinks.

'I need to know more,' Magdalena says gently.

Bror Engström shakes his head.

'There's nothing left to say. Everyone vanished. In just a few years they were all gone. My Agneta and . . . her brother and nephew . . . and then Jeremy, my father-in-law . . . He stopped talking when . . . when they went missing, his children and grandson.'

'Jeremy Magnusson,' Magdalena says.

'I liked him a lot . . . But he missed his children so terribly.'

'Yes,' Magdalena says quietly.

Bror Engström's clouded eyes close at the memory.

'One day he was just gone, him too. Then I got my Agneta back. But she was never herself again.'

'No,' Magdalena says.

'No,' he whispers.

She knows that Joona made countless visits to see the woman in the long-stay ward where she was being looked after. She never regained the power of speech, and died four years ago. The brain damage was too severe for anyone ever to reach her again.

'I suppose I should sell off Jeremy's forests,' the man says. 'But I can't do it. They meant everything to him. He was always trying to get me to go up to the hunting cabin with him, but it never quite happened . . . and now it's too late.'

'Where's the cabin?' she asks, taking out her phone.

'Way up in Dalarna, beyond Tranuberget, not far from the Norwegian border . . . I've got the maps from the Land Registry somewhere, if Sonja can find them.'

The hunting cabin isn't on the list of locations searched by forensics. It's probably nothing, but Joona has said that they mustn't leave any stone unturned.

## 80

A police officer and a forensics expert are making their way across the deep snow between the dark trunks of the pine trees on snowmobiles. In some places they can go faster and cover longer distances by using cleared boundary lines and foresters' tracks, leaving a cloud of smoke and snow behind them.

Stockholm wanted them to get out to a hunting cabin beyond Tranuberget. Apparently it had been owned by a Jeremy Magnusson, who disappeared thirteen years ago. The National Criminal Investigation Department have asked them to conduct a thorough forensic examination of the place, and to take video footage and photographs. Anything there is to be seized and packed up, and any potential evidence and biological matter is to be secured.

The two men on the snowmobiles know that the Stockholm Police are hoping to find something that might throw light on the disappearance of Magnusson and other members of his family. Obviously it should have been searched thirteen years ago, but at the time the police hadn't been aware of the hunting cabin's existence.

Roger Hysén and Gunnar Ehn are driving side by side

down a slope at the edge of the forest in blinding light. They emerge onto a sunlit bog where everything is glistening white, completely untouched, and continue at speed across the ice before swinging north into denser forest once more.

The forest has grown so wild on the southern side of Tranuberget that they almost miss the building entirely. The low timber shack is completely covered in snow. It's piled up higher than the windows, and is at least a metre thick on the roof.

All that's visible are a few silver-grey timber planks.

They get off their snowmobiles and begin to dig the cabin out.

The small windows are covered by faded curtains inside.

The sun is going down, nudging the treetops as it sinks towards the great expanse of bog.

When the door is finally uncovered they're sweating, and forensics expert Gunnar Ehn can feel his scalp itching under his hat.

A tree is rubbing against another in the wind, making a desolate creaking sound.

In silence the two men roll out a sheet of plastic in front of the door and get out their boxes, unpacking boards to walk on. They pull on protective outfits and gloves.

The door is locked and there's no key on the hook under the eaves.

'The daughter was found buried alive in Stockholm,' Roger Hysén says, glancing briefly at his colleague.

'I've heard the talk,' Gunnar says. 'It doesn't bother me.'

Roger inserts a crowbar into the crack next to the lock and pushes. The frame creaks. He pushes it further in and shoves harder. The frame splinters and Roger gives the door a tentative tug, then pulls as hard as he can. It swings open and bounces back.

'Shit,' Roger whispers behind his mask.

The draught from the unexpected movement has made all the dust that's settled inside the house fly up into the air. Gunnar mutters that it doesn't matter. He reaches into the dark cabin and puts two boards on the floor.

Roger unpacks the video camera and hands it over. Gunnar bends down beneath the low lintel, steps inside the cabin and stops on the first board.

It's so dark inside that he can't see anything at first. The air is dry from the swirling dust.

Gunnar sets the camera to record, but the light won't switch on. He tries recording the room anyway, but all he manages to get are vague outlines.

The whole cabin resembles a murky aquarium.

There's an odd-looking shadow in the middle of the room, like a large grandfather clock.

'What's happening?' Roger calls from outside.

'Give me the other camera.'

Gunnar passes the video camera out and is given the ordinary camera in its place. He checks the viewscreen. Unable to see anything but black, he snaps a picture at random. The flash fills the room with a white glow.

Gunnar screams when he sees the long, thin figure right in front of him. He takes a step back, loses his footing, drops the camera, puts out an arm to regain his balance and knocks over a coat stand.

'What the fuck was that . . .?'

He backs out, hitting his head on the lintel and cutting himself on the loose splinters sticking out from the frame.

'What's happening, what's going on?' Roger asks.

'Someone's in there,' Gunnar says, grinning nervously.

Roger switches on the light on the video camera, opens the door cautiously, bends down and slowly makes his way inside. The floor creaks beneath the boards. The light from the camera searches through the dust and over the furniture.

A branch scratches against the window. It sounds like someone knocking anxiously.

'OK,' he gasps.

In the dim light from the camera he sees that a man has hanged himself from the beam in the roof. A very long time ago. The body is thin and the skin has dried out and is stretched across the face. The mouth is wide open and black. His leather boots are lying on the floor.

The door behind the police officer creaks as Gunnar comes back in.

The sun has gone down behind the treetops and the windows are black. Carefully they spread out a body bag beneath the corpse.

The branch hits the window again, and slides over the glass with a scrape.

Roger reaches over to hold the body while Gunnar cuts the rope, but just as he touches the swaying corpse its head comes lose from the neck. The body collapses at their feet. The skull thuds on the wooden floor, dust swirls up around the room once more, and the old noose swings noiselessly.

## 81

Saga is sitting quite still inside the van, gazing out of the window. The chains attached to her handcuffs rattle in time with the motion of the vehicle.

She hasn't wanted to think about Jurek Walter. She's actually managed to keep her distance from what she knows about his murders since she accepted the mission.

But that's no longer possible. After three days of monotony at Karsudden Hospital, the Prison Service decision to transfer her is being put into practice. She's on her way to the secure unit of Löwenströmska Hospital.

Her encounter with Jurek is drawing closer.

In her mind's eye she can clearly see the photograph that was at the front of his file: his wrinkled face and those clear, pale eyes.

Jurek worked as a mechanic and lived a solitary and withdrawn life until his arrest. There was nothing in his flat that could be linked to his crimes, yet he was still caught red-handed.

Saga had been drenched with sweat by the time she finished reading the reports and looking at the photographs of the crime scenes. One large colour picture showed the forensics team's numbered signs in the clearing, as well as a heap of damp soil, a grave and an open coffin.

Nils Åhlén had produced a thorough forensic record of the woman's injuries, after she'd been buried alive for two years.

Saga feels travel-sick and looks out at the road and trees flitting past. She thinks about how malnourished the woman was, and about her pressure sores, frostbite and lost teeth. Joona had described how the weak, emaciated woman had tried to climb out of the coffin time after time, but how Jurek kept pushing her back down.

Saga knows she shouldn't be thinking about this.

A shudder of anxiety slowly spreads out from her stomach.

She tells herself that under no circumstances must she let herself feel afraid. She's in control of the situation.

The van brakes and the handcuffs rattle.

The plastic barrel and the coffin had both been equipped with air tubes leading up above ground.

Why couldn't he have just killed them outright?

It's incomprehensible.

Saga moves on to considering what Mikael Kohler-Frost had said about his captivity in the capsule, and her heart beats faster as she thinks of Felicia alone there, the little girl with the loose plait and riding hat.

It has stopped snowing, but there's no sign of the sun. The sky remains overcast and blind. The van leaves the old main road and slowly turns right as it enters the hospital grounds.

A woman in her forties is sitting in the bus shelter with two shopping bags in her hands, taking deep drags on a cigarette.

Government approval is required to establish a secure unit, but Saga knows that the legislation allows plenty of leeway for the institutions to conduct their own evaluations.

Ordinary laws and rights cease to apply inside those locked doors. There's no real scrutiny or supervision. The staff are lords of their own Hades, as long as none of their patients escape.

## 82

Saga's hands and ankles are still cuffed as she is led down an empty corridor by two armed guards. They're both walking fast and holding her upper arms tightly.

It's too late to change her mind now – she's on her way to meet Jurek Walter.

The textured wallpaper is scratched and the skirting boards scuffed. On the ivory-coloured floor is a box of old shoe-covers. The closed doors they pass on the way have small plastic signs with numbers on them.

Saga has a stomach ache and tries to stop, but is pushed onward.

'Keep going,' one of the guards says.

The isolation unit at Löwenströmska Hospital has a very high security level, way above the requirements for level one. That means that the building itself is basically impossible to break in or out of. The rooms have fireproof steel doors, fixed inner ceilings and walls that have been reinforced with thirty-five-millimetre-thick metal plate.

A heavy gate clangs shut behind them as they head down the stairs towards level zero.

The guard at the airlock leading to the secure unit takes the bag of Saga's possessions, checks the documentation and signs Saga in on the computer. An older man with a baton hanging from his belt is visible on the other side of the airlock. He's wearing big glasses and has wavy hair. Saga looks at him through the scratched reinforced glass.

The man with the baton takes Saga's papers, leafs through them, peers at her for a moment, then carries on reading her notes.

Saga's stomach is aching so much that she could do with lying down. She tries to breathe calmly, but she gets a sudden cramp and leans forward.

'Stand still,' the guard says in a neutral voice.

A younger man in a doctor's coat appears beyond the airlock. He pulls a pass card through the reader, taps in a code and comes out.

'OK, my name is Anders Rönn, I'm acting Senior Consultant here,' he says drily.

After a superficial search, Saga follows the doctor and the guard with the wavy hair through the doors of the airlock. She can smell their body odour in the confined space before the second door opens.

Saga recognises every detail of the ward from the plans she memorised.

They walk round a corner in silence and over to the unit's cramped security control room. A woman with pierced cheeks is sitting at the monitors of the alarm system. She blushes when she sees Saga, but says a friendly hello before looking down and writing something in her logbook.

'My, would you remove the cuffs from the patient's ankles?' the young doctor asks.

The woman nods, gets down on her knees and unlocks

the cuffs. The hair on her head rises up from the static electricity in Saga's clothes.

The young doctor and the guard go through the door with her, wait until it bleeps, then carry on to one of the three doors in the corridor.

'Unlock the door,' the doctor orders the man with the baton.

The guard takes out a key, unlocks the door, then tells her to go in and stand on the red cross on the floor with her back to the door.

She does as he asks and hears the lock click as the key is turned again.

In front of her is another metal door, and she knows this one is locked, and leads straight out into the dayroom.

The room is furnished with no thought to anything but security and function. All it contains is a bed fixed to the wall, a plastic chair, a plastic table and a toilet, with no seat or lid.

'Turn round, but stay on the cross.'

She does as she's told and sees that the little hatch in the door is open.

'Come slowly over here and hold out your hands.'

Saga walks over to the door, clasps her hands tightly together and puts them through the narrow opening. The cuffs are removed and she backs away from the door again.

She sits down on the bed while the guard informs her of the unit's rules and routines.

'You can watch television and socialise with the other patients in the dayroom between one o'clock and four o'clock,' he concludes, then looks at her for a few moments before closing and bolting the hatch.

Saga remains seated and thinks that she is in position now, that her mission has started. The seriousness of the moment make her stomach tingle, and the feeling spreads through her arms and legs. She knows she's a closely guarded patient in the secure unit of Löwenströmska Hospital, and she knows that serial killer Jurek Walter is very close.

She curls up on her side, then rolls over onto her back and stares straight up at the CCTV camera in the ceiling. It's hemispherical in shape, black and shiny as a cow's eye.

It's been a long time since she swallowed the microphone and she daren't leave it any longer. She can't let the microphone slip into her duodenum. When she goes over to the tap and drinks some water her stomach ache kicks in again.

Breathing slowly, Saga kneels down by the drain in the floor, turns away from the camera and sticks two fingers down her throat. She vomits the water back up, then sticks her fingers in deeper and eventually manages to retrieve the little capsule containing the microphone and quickly hides it in her hand.

## 83

The secret investigative team, Athena Promacho, has been sitting listening to the sounds of Saga Bauer's stomach for two hours since she arrived at Löwenströmska Hospital.

'If anyone walked in now they'd think we were some sort of new-age sect,' Corinne says with a smile.

'It's actually quite beautiful,' Johan Jönson says.

'Relaxing,' Pollock grins.

The whole team is sitting with their eyes half-closed, listening to the gently bubbling, fizzing sounds.

Suddenly there's a roar that almost breaks the big loud-speakers as Saga vomits up the microphone. Johan Jönson knocks over his can of Coca-Cola and Nathan Pollock starts shaking.

'Well, at least we're awake now,' laughs Corinne, and her jade bracelet jangles pleasantly as she runs an index finger over one eyebrow.

'I'll call Joona,' Nathan says.

'Good.'

Corinne Meilleroux opens her laptop and notes the time in the logbook. Corinne is fifty-four years old, with a

French-Caribbean background. She's slim, and always wears tailored suits with silk tops under her jacket. Her face looks stern, with pronounced cheekbones and narrow temples. She wears her grey-streaked black hair tied with a clasp at the back of her neck.

Corinne Meilleroux worked for Europol for twenty years, and has been with the Security Police in Stockholm for seven years.

Joona is standing in Mikael Kohler-Frost's hospital room. Reidar is sitting on a chair holding his son's hand. The three of them have been talking for four hours, trying to identify any fresh details that could help pinpoint the place where Mikael was held captive with his sister.

Nothing new has emerged, and Mikael looks very tired.

'You need to get some sleep,' Joona tells him.

'No,' Mikael says.

'Just for a while.' The detective smiles as he switches off the recording.

Mikael's breathing is already heavy and even as Joona pulls the newspaper out of his coat-pocket and sets it down in front of Reidar.

'I know you asked me not to,' Reidar says, meeting his gaze without wavering. 'But how could I live with myself if I don't do absolutely everything I can?'

'I understand,' Joona says. 'But it could cause problems, and you have to be prepared for that.'

One whole page of the paper is covered with a digital image of how Felicia might look today.

A young woman bearing a strong resemblance to Mikael, with high cheekbones and dark eyes. Her black hair is shown hanging loose around her pale, serious face.

Large lettering announces that Reidar is offering a reward of twenty million kronor to anyone who can provide information that leads to Felicia being found.

'We're already getting loads of e-mails and calls,' Joona explains. 'We're trying to follow them all up, but . . . I'm sure most of them mean well, they believe they've seen something, but there are still plenty just hoping to get rich.'

Reidar slowly folds the newspaper, whispers to himself, then looks up.

'Joona, I'm doing whatever I can, I . . . my daughter's been held captive for so long, and she might die without ever . . .'

His voice cracks and he looks away for a moment.

'Do you have children?' he asks, his voice barely audible.

Before Joona has time to lie, his phone rings in his jacket. He apologises, answers it, and hears Pollock's soft voice explaining that Athena Promacho is hooked up.

## 84

Saga lies down on the bed with her back to the camera in the ceiling and carefully peels the silicon covering from the fibre-optic microphone. Barely moving at all, she slips it into the lining of her trousers.

Suddenly there's an electronic buzz from the door to the dayroom – and then the lock clicks. It's open. Saga sits up, her heart beating hard.

The microphone needs to be installed in a good position right away. She might only get one chance. She mustn't miss it. She'll be found out if she gets searched.

She doesn't know what the dayroom looks like, if the other patients are in there, or if there are cameras or guards.

Maybe the room is nothing but a trap where Jurek Walter is waiting for her.

No, there's no way he could possibly know about her mission.

Saga throws the pieces of silicon in the toilet and flushes them away, then goes over to the door, opens it a crack and hears a rhythmic throbbing sound, cheerful voices from the television and a whining, hissing noise.

She remembers Joona's advice and forces herself to go back to her bed and sit down.

Never show any urgency, she thinks. Never do anything unless you have a valid reason for doing it, a justification.

Through the crack in the door she can hear music from the television, the hissing sound of the running machine, and heavy footsteps.

A man with a sharp, stressed voice speaks occasionally, but never gets any response.

Both patients are out there.

Saga knows she has to go in and install the microphone.

She gets up and goes over to the door again, and stands there for a while, trying to breathe slowly.

A smell of aftershave hits her.

She grasps the door handle, takes a deep breath, opens the door wide. She can hear the rhythmic thuds more clearly as she takes a couple of steps into the dayroom with her head lowered. She doesn't know if she's being watched, but decides to let them get used to the sight of her before looking up.

A man with a bandaged hand is sitting on the sofa in front of the television, and another is walking with long strides on the running machine. The man on the machine is facing away from her, but although she can only see his back and neck, she's sure it's Jurek Walter.

He's marching along, and the sound of his rhythmic steps fills the room.

The man on the sofa belches and swallows several times, wipes the sweat from his cheeks and one of his legs starts to bounce nervously. He's overweight, in his forties, with thin hair, a blond moustache and glasses.

'Obrahiim,' he mutters, staring at the television.

His leg bounces as he suddenly points at the screen.

'There he is,' he says loudly. 'I'd turn him into my slave,

my skeleton slave. Fucking hell . . . Look at those lips . . . I'd—'

He falls silent abruptly as Saga walks across the room, stops in one corner and watches the television. It's a repeat of the European ice-skating championship in Sheffield. The sound and picture alike are made worse by the reinforced glass. She can feel the man on the sofa looking at her, but doesn't meet his gaze.

'I'd whip him first,' he goes on, still facing Saga. 'I'd make him really scared, like a whore . . . I mean, fucking hell . . .'

He coughs, leans back, closes his eyes as if waiting for pain to pass, feels his neck with his hand, then lies there panting.

Jurek Walter is still striding along on the running machine. He looks bigger and stronger than she had imagined. There's an artificial palm in a pot next to the machine, and its dusty leaves sway as he walks.

Saga looks round for somewhere to hide the microphone, preferably away from the television so as not to interfere with its reception of other voices. The back of the sofa would make sense, but she can't really imagine Jurek is the sort to sit and watch television.

The man on the sofa tries to get up, and looks as though he's about to throw up from the effort. He cups his hand over his mouth and swallows a few times before turning back to watch television again.

'Start with the legs,' he says. 'Cut everything off, peel the skin away, muscles, sinew . . . he can keep his feet so he can walk quietly . . .'

## 85

Jurek stops the running machine and leaves the room without giving either of them so much as a glance. The other patient slowly gets up.

'Zyprexa makes you feel like shit . . . and Stemetil doesn't work on me, it just fucks my insides up . . .'

Saga stays where she is for a little while, facing the television, watching as the figure skater speeds up and hearing the sound of skates cutting across the ice. She can feel the other patient's staring eyes as he slowly approaches.

'My name's Bernie Larsson,' he says in an intimate voice. 'They don't think I can fuck with all the bastard Suprefact in my system, but they don't know a fucking thing . . .'

He jabs his finger in her face, but she stands her ground, her heart pounding.

'They don't know a fucking thing,' he repeats. 'They're so fucking brain-damaged . . .'

He falls silent, staggers aside and burps loudly. Saga is thinking that she might be able to place the microphone in the artificial palm next to the running machine.

'What's your name?' Bernie asks, panting.

She doesn't answer, just stands there with her eyes lowered, looking towards the television, thinking that her time is running out. Bernie walks behind her back and quickly sticks his hand round and pinches her hard on the nipple. She pushes his hand away and feels anger start to bubble up inside her.

'Little Snow White,' he smiles with his sweaty face. 'What's the matter with you? Can I feel your head? It looks so fucking soft. Like a shaved cunt . . .'

From the little she's seen of Jurek Walter, the running machine is what he's most interested in inside the dayroom. He was on it for at least an hour, then he went straight back into his room.

Saga walks slowly over to the running machine and steps up onto it. Bernie follows her, biting a fingernail and pulling off a sharp fragment. Sweat is dripping from his face onto the dirty vinyl floor.

'Do you shave your cunt? You have to do that, yeah?'

Saga turns and stares at him intently. His eyelids are heavy, his eyes have a drugged look about them, his blond moustache hides the scar left by a cleft palate.

'You never touch me again,' she replies.

'I can kill you,' he says, scratching her neck with his sharpened nail.

She feels the wound sting as a loud voice echoes from the loudspeaker:

'Bernie Larsson, step back.'

He tries to touch her between the legs as the doors open and a guard with a baton comes in. Bernie moves away from Saga and holds his hands up in a gesture of surrender.

'No touching,' the guard says sternly.

'OK, I know, fucking hell.'

Bernie feels his way wearily over the armrest of the sofa and sits down heavily, then shuts his eyes and belches.

Saga gets off the running machine and turns to the guard.

'I want to see a legal ombudsman,' she says.

'Stay where you are,' the guard says, glancing at her.

'Can you pass on the message?'

Without replying, the guard goes over to the airlock and is let out. It's as if she hadn't said anything, as if her words had stopped mid-air before reaching him.

Saga turns away and slowly approaches the artificial palm. She sits down on the edge of the running machine, right beside it, and looks at one of its lower leaves. The underneath isn't too dirty and the glue on the microphone will firm up in four seconds.

Bernie is staring up at the ceiling, licking his lips, then he shuts his eyes again. Saga watches him as she slides a finger into the lining of her trousers, gets the microphone out and hides it in her hand. She pulls off one of her shoes and leans forward to adjust its tongue, thereby shielding the palm from the camera. She shifts position slightly, and is just reaching out to the leaf to attach the microphone as the sofa creaks.

'I've got my eye you, Snow White,' Bernie says in a weary voice.

She calmly withdraws her hand, puts her foot back in her shoe, and sees Bernie sitting there watching her as she sticks the velcro down.

## 86

Saga starts to walk on the running machine, thinking that she'll have to wait for him to go into his room before she positions the microphone. Bernie gets up from the sofa, takes a couple of steps towards her, and reaches out to steady himself against the wall.

'I come from Säter,' he whispers with a smile.

She doesn't look at him, but is aware of him coming closer. Sweat is dripping from his face onto the floor.

'Where were you before you got moved here?' he asks.

He waits a moment, then punches the wall hard before looking at her again.

'Karsudden,' he replies in a squeaky voice. 'I was at Karsudden, but I moved here because I wanted to be with Bernie . . .'

Saga turns away and just catches a shadow cross the third doorway as someone pulls back from it. She realises that Jurek Walter is standing there listening to them.

'You must have met Yekaterina Ståhl at Karsudden,' Bernie says in his normal voice.

She shakes her head, she can't remember anyone with that name, she doesn't even know if he's talking about a patient or a guard.

'No,' she replies honestly.

'Because she was at St Sigfrid,' he grins, and spits on the floor. 'So who did you meet?'

'No one.'

He mutters something about skeleton slaves, then stands in front of the running machine and watches her.

'I can feel from your cunt if you're lying,' he says, scratching his moustache. 'Is that what you want?'

She stops the machine, stands there for a moment, and thinks about the fact that she has to stick to the truth. She was actually at Karsudden.

'What about Micke Lund, then? You must have seen Micke Lund if you were there,' he says with a flash of a smile. 'Tall bloke, one metre ninety . . . scar across his forehead.'

She nods, unsure what to say, considers leaving it at that, but still replies:

'No.'

'Fucking weird.'

'I sat in my room watching television.'

'There aren't any televisions in the rooms there, you're fucking lying, you're a—'

'There are in isolation,' she interrupts.

She can't tell whether he knew that. He's breathing hard and staring at her, grinning all the while. Then he licks his lips and comes closer.

'You're my slave,' he says slowly. 'Fucking hell, that's brilliant . . . you lie there, sucking my toes . . .'

Saga gets off the running machine and returns to her cell. She lies on her bunk and hears Bernie standing by her door for a while, calling for her, before he settles back down on the sofa.

'Shit,' she whispers.

She'll have to be quick out tomorrow, sit down on the edge of the running machine, adjust her shoes and attach the microphone. She'll walk on the machine with long strides, she won't look at anyone, and when Jurek comes out she'll simply get off the machine and leave the dayroom.

Saga thinks about the sofa and the angle of the wall adjacent to the reinforced glass covering the television. The camera's view must be partially obscured by the protruding section. She'll have to watch out for that blind spot. That's where she was standing when Bernie pinched her nipple. That was why the staff didn't react.

She has been in the Löwenströmska unit for just over five hours, and already she's exhausted.

The metal-walled room feels more enclosed now. She shuts her eyes and thinks about why she's here. In her mind's eye she can see the girl in the photograph. All of this is for her sake, for Felicia.

## 87

The Athena group sit completely still and listen to the broad-cast from the dayroom in real time. The sound quality is bad, muffled and distorted by loud scraping noises.

'Is it going to sound like this the whole time?' Pollock asks.

'She hasn't positioned the microphone yet. Maybe it's in her pocket,' Johan Jönson replies.

'As long as she doesn't get searched . . .'

They listen to the recording again. They can hear the rasping of Saga's trousers, her shallow breathing, the sound of steps on the running machine and the drone of the televi-sion. Like a group of blind people, the members of Athena Promacho are being guided through the closed world of the secure unit with the help of hearing alone.

'Obrahiim,' a slurred voice says.

The entire group are suddenly very focused. Johan Jönson raises the volume slightly and adds a filter to reduce the hissing.

'There he is,' the man continues. 'I'd turn him into my slave, my skeleton slave.'

'I thought that was Jurek to start with,' says Corinne.

'Fucking hell,' the voice goes on. 'Look at those lips . . . I'd . . .'

They listen in silence to the other patient's aggressive torrent of words, and hear a guard come in and break up the confrontation. After the intervention there's a short period of silence. Then the patient starts to interrogate Saga about Karsudden in a very thorough, suspicious way.

'She's handling it well,' Pollock says through clenched teeth.

Eventually they hear Saga leave the dayroom without having managed to position the microphone.

She swears quietly to herself.

She's surrounded by silence until the electronic lock on the door clicks shut.

'Well, at least we know that the technology seems to work,' Pollock says.

'Poor Saga,' Corinne whispers.

'She should have positioned the microphone,' Johan Jönson mutters.

'It must have been impossible.'

'But if she gets found out, then . . .'

'She won't be,' Corinne says.

She smiles, then throws out her arms, spreading the pleasant scent of her perfume through the room.

'No Jurek so far,' Pollock says, glancing over at Joona.

'What if he's being held in total isolation? All this will have been in vain,' Jönson sighs.

Joona says nothing, but he's thinking that something was being conveyed by the recording. For several minutes it was as if he could feel the almost physical presence of Jurek. As if Jurek were in the dayroom even though he hadn't said anything.

'Let's listen to it one more time,' he says, looking at the clock.

'Are you going somewhere?' Corinne asks, raising her neat black eyebrows.

'I'm meeting someone,' Joona says, returning her smile.

'Finally, a bit of romance . . .'

## 88

Joona walks into a white-tiled room with a long wash basin along one wall. Water is running from an orange hose into a drain on the floor. The body from the hunting cabin in Dalarna is lying on a plastic-covered autopsy table. Its sunken brown chest has been sawn open and yellow liquid is trickling slowly down into the stainless-steel trough.

'Tra la la la laa – we'd catch the rainbow,' Nils Åhlén sings to himself. 'Tra la la la laa – to the sun . . .'

He pulls out a pair of latex gloves and is just blowing into them when he sees Joona standing in the doorway.

'You ought to record a forensic album,' Joona smiles.

'Frippe's a very good bassist,' Åhlén replies.

The light from the powerful lamps in the ceiling reflects off his pilot's glasses. He's wearing a white polo-neck under his doctor's coat.

They hear rustling footsteps from the corridor, and moments later Carlos Eliasson comes in, with pale-blue shoe covers on his feet.

'Have you managed to identify the dead man?' he asks, stopping abruptly when he catches sight of the corpse on the table.

The raised edges make the autopsy table look like a draining board where someone's left a piece of dried meat, or some strange, blackened root. The corpse is desiccated and distorted, its severed head placed above the neck.

'There's no doubt that it's Jeremy Magnusson,' Åhlén replies. 'Our forensic dentist – who plays the guitar, by the way – has compared the body's oral characteristics with Magnusson's dental records.'

Åhlén leans over, takes the head in his hands and opens the wrinkled black hole that was Jeremy Magnusson's mouth.

'He had an impacted wisdom tooth, and—'

'Please,' Carlos says, beads of sweat glinting on his forehead.

'The palate has gone,' Åhlén says, forcing the mouth open a bit further. 'But if you feel with your finger—'

'Fascinating,' Carlos interrupts, then looks at the time. 'Do we have any idea how long he was hanging there?'

'The drying process would probably have been impeded slightly by the low temperatures,' Åhlén replies. 'But if you look at the eyes, the conjunctiva dried out very quickly, as did the undersides of the eyelids. The parchment-like texture of the skin is uniform, apart from round the neck where it was in contact with the rope.'

'Which means . . .?' Carlos says.

'The post-mortal process forms a sort of diary, an ongoing life after death, as the body changes . . . And I would estimate that Jeremy Magnusson hanged himself . . .'

'Thirteen years, one month and five days ago,' Joona says.

'Good guess,' Åhlén says.

'I just got a scan of his farewell note from Forensics,' Joona says, taking out his mobile.

'Suicide,' Carlos says.

'Everything points to that, even if Jurek Walter could feasibly have been there at the time,' Åhlén replies.

'Jeremy Magnusson was on the list of Jurek's most likely

victims,' Carlos says slowly. 'And if we can write off his death as suicide . . .'

An indefinable thought is flitting through Joona's mind. It's as if there were some sort of hidden association tucked away in this conversation – one he can't quite grasp.

'What did he say in the note?' Carlos asks.

'He hanged himself just three weeks before Samuel and I found his daughter Agneta in Lill-Jan's Forest,' Joona says, bringing up the image of the dated note that Forensics had sent him.

*I don't know why I've lost everyone, my children, my grandson and my wife.*
*I'm like Job, but with no restitution.*
*I have waited, and that waiting must end.*

He took his life in the belief that everyone he loved had been taken from him. If he had only put up with loneliness for a little longer, he would have got his daughter back. Agneta Magnusson lived on for several more years before her heart finally stopped. She was cared for in a long-stay ward at Huddinge Hospital, under constant supervision.

## 89

Reidar Frost has ordered food from Noodle House, and had it delivered to the foyer of Södermalm Hospital. Steam is rising from mince and coriander dim sum, spring rolls that smell of ginger, rice noodles with chopped vegetables and chilli, fried pork fillet and chicken soup.

Because he doesn't know what Mikael likes, he's ordered eight different dishes.

Just as he emerges from the lift and starts walking along the corridor, his phone rings.

Reidar puts the bags down by his feet, sees that the caller has withheld their number, and hurries to answer:

'Reidar Frost.'

The phone is silent, nothing but a crackling sound.

'Who is this?' he asks.

Someone groans in the background.

'Hello?'

He's on the point of ending the call when someone whispers:

'Daddy?'

'Hello?' he repeats. 'Who is this?'

'Daddy, it's me,' a strange, high voice whispers. 'It's Felicia.'

The floor starts to spin under Reidar's feet.

'Felicia?'

It's almost impossible to hear her voice now.

'Daddy . . . I'm so scared, Daddy . . .'

'Where are you? Please, darling . . .?'

Suddenly he hears giggling, and he feels a shiver run through his whole body.

'Darling Daddy, give me twenty million kronor . . .'

It's obvious now that it's a man disguising his voice and trying to make it sound higher.

'Give me twenty million and I'll sit in your lap and—'

'Do you know anything about my daughter?' Reidar asks.

'You're such a bad writer it makes me sick.'

'Yes, I am . . . but if you know anything about—'

The call ends and Reidar's hands are shaking so much that he can't tap in the number for the police. He tries to pull himself together, and tells himself that he's going to report the call, even though it won't lead anywhere, even though they're bound to think he has only himself to blame.

## 90

Anders Rönn is still at the hospital, even though it's evening now. He wants to check up on the third patient, the young woman.

She's come direct from Karsudden Hospital, and shows no sign of wanting to communicate with the staff. Her medication is extremely conservative, considering the findings of the psychiatric evaluation.

Leif has gone home and a well-built woman named Pia Madsen is working the evening shift. She doesn't say much, mostly sits there reading thrillers and yawning.

Anders finds himself staring at the new patient on the screen again.

She's astonishingly beautiful. Earlier in the day he stared at her for so long that his eyes started to dry out.

She is regarded as dangerous and an escape risk, and the crimes she was convicted of in the District Court were deeply unpleasant.

As Anders watches her, he can't believe it's true, even though he knows it must be.

She's as slight as a ballet dancer, and her shaved head makes her look fragile.

Maybe she was only prescribed Trilafon and Stesolid at Karsudden Hospital because she's so beautiful.

After his meeting with hospital management, Anders almost has a senior consultant's authority over the secure unit.

For the foreseeable future he makes the decisions about the patients.

He has consulted Dr Maria Gomez in Ward 30. Usually an initial period of observation would be advisable, but he could go in and give her an intramuscular injection of Haldol now. The thought makes him tingle, and he is filled with a heavy, remarkable sense of anticipation.

Pia Madsen returns from the toilet. Her eyelids are half-closed. A bit of toilet paper has got stuck to one of her shoes and is trailing after her. She's approaching along the corridor with shuffling steps, her face lethargic.

'I'm not that tired,' she laughs, meeting his gaze.

She removes the toilet paper and throws it in the bin, then sits down at the control desk next to him and looks at the time.

'Shall we sing a lullaby?' she asks, before logging on to the computer and switching out the lights in the patients' rooms.

The image of the three patients stays on Anders's retina for a while. Just before everything went dark Jurek was already lying on his back in bed, Bernie was sitting on the floor holding his bandaged hand to his chest, and Saga was sitting on the edge of her bed, looking angry and vulnerable in roughly equal measure.

'They're already part of the family,' Pia yawns, then opens her book.

## 91

At nine o'clock the staff turn out the ceiling light. Saga is sitting on the edge of her bed. She's got the microphone tucked into the lining of her trousers again. It seems safest to keep it close until she's able to put it in position. Without the microphone, the whole mission will be pointless. She waits, and a short while later a grey rectangle becomes visible through the darkness. It's the thick glass window in the door. Shortly after that the shapes of the room appear as a foggy landscape. Saga gets up and goes over to the darkest corner, lies down on the cold floor and starts doing sit-ups. After three hundred she rolls over, slowly stretches her stomach muscles and starts doing push-ups.

Suddenly she gets the feeling that she's being watched. Something's different. She stops and looks up. The glass window is darker, shaded. Hurriedly she sticks her fingers in the lining of her trousers, takes the microphone out, but drops it on the floor.

She hears steps and movement, then a metallic scraping sound against the door.

Saga sweeps her hands quickly over the floor, finds the microphone and puts it in her mouth just as the lamp in the ceiling comes on.

'Stand on the cross,' a woman says in a stern voice.

Saga is still on all fours with the microphone in her mouth. Slowly she gets to her feet as she tries to gather saliva.

'Hurry up.'

She takes her time walking towards the cross, looks up at the ceiling, then down at the floor again. She stops on the cross, turns her back nonchalantly towards the door, raises her eyes to the ceiling and swallows. Her throat hurts badly as the microphone slowly slips down.

'We met earlier,' a man says in a drawling voice. 'I'm the Senior Consultant here, and I'm responsible for your medication.'

'I want to see a lawyer,' Saga says.

'Take your top off and walk slowly over to the door,' the first voice says.

She takes her blouse off, lets it fall to the floor, turns and walks towards the door in her washed-out bra.

'Stop and hold both your hands up, turn your arms round and open your mouth wide.'

The metal hatch opens and she holds out her hand to take the little cup with her pills.

'I've changed your medication, by the way,' the Senior Consultant with the drawling voice says.

Saga suddenly grasps the full significance of being in these people's power as she sees the doctor fill a syringe with a milky-white emulsion.

'Stick your left arm through the hatch,' the woman says.

She realises she can't refuse, but her pulse quickens as she obeys. A hand grabs her arm and the doctor rubs his thumb over the muscle. A panicked desire to fight her way free bubbles up inside her.

'I understand that you've been getting Trilafon,' the doctor says, giving her a look that she can't read. 'Eight milligrams, three times a day, but I was thinking of trying—'

'I don't want to,' she says.

She tries to pull her arm back, but the guard is holding it tight, she's capable of breaking it. The guard is heavy and forces her arm down, making her stand on tiptoe.

Saga forces herself to breathe calmly. What are they going to give her? A clouded drop is hanging from the point of the needle. She tries to pull her arm back again. A finger strokes the thin skin over the muscle. There's a prick and the needle slides in. She can't move her arm. A chill spreads through her body. She sees the doctor's hands as the needle is withdrawn and a small compress stops the bleeding. Then they let go of her. She pulls her arm free and retreats from the door and the two figures behind the glass.

'Now go and sit on the bed,' the guard says in a hard voice.

Her arm stings where the needle went in, as if it had burned her. An immense weariness spreads through her body. She hasn't got the energy to pick up her blouse from the floor, just stumbles and takes a step towards the bed.

'I've given you Stesolid to help you relax,' the doctor says.

The room lurches and she fumbles for support, but can't reach the wall with her hand.

'Shit,' Saga gasps.

Tiredness sweeps over her, and, just as she's thinking that she'd better lie down on the bed, her legs give way. She collapses and hits the floor, the jolt running through her body and jarring her neck.

'I'm going to be coming in shortly,' the doctor goes on. 'I was thinking we might try a neuroleptic drug that sometimes works very well, Haldol depot.'

'I don't want to,' she says quietly, trying to roll onto her side.

She opens her eyes and tries to overcome the dizziness.

One hip hurts after the fall. A tingling sensation rises from her feet, making her more and more drowsy. She attempts to get up, but doesn't have the energy. Her thoughts are getting slower. She tries again, but is completely impotent.

## 92

Her eyelids are heavy, but she forces herself to look. The light from the lamp in the ceiling is strangely clouded. The metal door opens and a man in a white coat comes in. It's the young doctor. He's got something in his slender hands. The door closes behind him and the lock clicks. She blinks her dry eyes and sees the doctor put two ampoules of yellow oil on the table. Carefully he opens the plastic packaging of a syringe. Saga tries to crawl under the bed, but she's too slow. The doctor grabs hold of one of her ankles and starts to pull her out. She tries to cling on, and rolls over onto her back. Her bra slides up, uncovering her breasts as he drags her out onto the floor.

'You look like a princess,' she hears him whisper.

'What?'

She looks up and sees his moist gaze, and tries to cover her breasts, but her hands are too weak.

She shuts her eyes again and just lies there waiting.

Suddenly the doctor rolls her over onto her stomach. He pulls her trousers and pants down. She dozes off and is woken by a sharp prick in the top of her right buttock, then another slightly lower down.

*

Saga wakes up in the darkness on the cold floor and realises that she's got the blanket on top of her. Her head aches
and she has almost no feeling in her hands. She sits up,
adjusts her bra and thinks about the microphone in her
stomach.

There's very little time.

She could have been asleep for hours.

She crawls over to the drain in the floor, sticks two fingers
down her throat and throws up some acrid liquid. She gulps
hard and tries again, her stomach cramps, but nothing comes
up.

'Shit . . .'

She has to have the microphone tomorrow, so she can
put it in position in the dayroom. It mustn't disappear into
her duodenum. She gets up on wobbly legs and drinks some
water from the tap in the basin, then kneels down again,
leans forward and sticks two fingers down her throat. The
water comes back up, but she keeps her fingers where they
are. The meagre contents of her stomach trickle down her
lower arm. Gasping for breath, she sticks her fingers in
deeper, setting off the gag reflex again. She throws up some
bile, and her mouth is filled with the bitter taste. She coughs
and sticks her fingers down once more, and this time she
finally feels the microphone come up through her throat
and into her mouth. She catches it in her hand and hides
it, even though the room is dark, then stands up, washes it
under the tap and tucks it into the lining of her trousers
again. She spits out a mixture of bile and slime, rinses her
mouth and face, spits again, drinks some water and goes
back to the bed.

Her feet and fingertips are cold and numb. She has a vague
itch in her toes. As Saga lies down on the bed and adjusts
her trousers she realises that her pants are inside out. She
isn't sure if she put them on wrong herself, or if something

else has happened. She curls up under the blanket and carefully puts one hand down to her crotch. It isn't sore or hurt, but it feels strangely numb.

## 93

Mikael Kohler-Frost is sitting at a table in the dining room of his hospital ward. He has one hand wrapped round a cup of warm tea as he speaks to Magdalena Ronander of the National Criminal Investigation Department. Reidar is too agitated to sit, but he stands by the door and watches his son for a while before going down to the entrance to meet Veronica Klimt.

Magdalena smiles at Mikael, then gets out the bulky interview protocols and puts them on the table. They fill four spiral-bound folders. She leafs through to the marker, then asks if he's ready to continue.

'I only ever saw the inside of the capsule,' Mikael explains, as he's done so many times before.

'Can you describe the door again?' she asks.

'It's made of metal, and is completely smooth . . . at the start you could pick little flakes of paint off it with your fingernails . . . there's no keyhole, no handle . . .'

'What colour is it?'

'Grey . . .'

'And there was a hatch which—'

She breaks off when she sees him swipe the tears from his cheeks and turn his face away.

'I can't tell Dad,' he says, his lips trembling. 'But if Felicia doesn't come back . . .'

Magdalena gets up and goes round the table, hugs him and repeats that everything is going to be OK.

'I know,' he says, 'I know I'd kill myself.'


Reidar Frost has barely left Södermalm Hospital since Mikael came back. He's been renting a room at the hospital, on the same floor as Mikael, so he can be with his son the whole time.

Even though Reidar knows it wouldn't do any good, it's all he can do to stop himself running out to join the search for Felicia. He's paid for adverts in the national press every day, pleading for information and promising a reward. He's employed a team of the country's best private detectives to look for her, but her absence is tearing at him, stopping him sleeping, forcing him to roam the corridors hour after hour.

The only thing that makes him feel calm is watching Mikael get better and stronger with each passing day. Inspector Joona Linna says it's a huge help if he can stay with his son, letting him talk at his own pace, listening and writing down every memory, every detail.

When Reidar gets down to the entrance Veronica is already waiting for him inside the glass doors that lead to the snow-covered car park.

'Isn't it a bit early to be sending Micke home?' she asks, handing over the bags.

'They say it's fine,' Reidar smiles.

'I bought a pair of jeans and some softer trousers, shirts, T-shirts, a thick jumper and a few other—'

'How are things at home?' Reidar asks.

'Lots of snow,' says Veronica, laughing, then she tells him about the last few guests leaving.

'What, even my cavaliers?' Reidar asks.

'No, they're still there . . . you'll see.'

'What do you mean?'

Veronica just shakes her head and smiles.

'I told Berzelius that they're not allowed to come here, but they're very keen to meet Mikael,' she replies.

'Are you coming up?' Reidar asks, smiling and adjusting her collar.

'Another time,' Veronica replies, looking him in the eye.

## 94

As Reidar drives, Mikael sits there in his new clothes, changing stations on the radio. Suddenly he stops. Satie's ballet music fills the car like warm summer rain.

'Dad, isn't it a bit over the top to live in a manor?' Mikael smiles.

'Yes.'

He actually bought the run-down estate because he could no longer bear the neighbours in Tyresö.

Snow-covered fields spread out before them. They turn into the long avenue where Reidar's three friends have lit torches all along the drive. When they stop and get out of the car, Wille Strandberg, Berzelius and David Sylwan come out onto the steps.

Berzelius takes a step forward, and for a moment it looks as though he doesn't know whether to embrace or shake hands with the young man. Then he mumbles something and hugs Mikael hard.

Wille wipes some tears away behind his glasses.

'You're all grown up, Micke,' he says. 'I've—'

'Let's go inside,' Reidar interrupts, coming to his son's rescue. 'We need to eat.'

David blushes and shrugs his shoulders apologetically:

'We've organised a backwards party.'

'What's one of those?' Reidar asks.

'You start with dessert and conclude with the starter.' Sylwan smiles, slightly embarrassed.

Mikael is first through the imposing doorway. The broad oak tiles in the hallway smell as if they've recently been scrubbed.

There are balloons hanging from the ceiling of the dining room, and on the table is a large cake decorated with a figure of Spiderman made out of coloured marzipan.

'We know you're grown up, but you used to love Spiderman, so we thought . . .'

'We got it wrong,' Wille concludes.

'I'd love to try some,' Mikael says kindly.

'That's the spirit!' David laughs.

'Then there's pizza . . . and alphabet soup to finish up with,' Berzelius says.

They sit down at the huge oval table.

'I remember one time when you said you had to keep an eye on a cake in the kitchen until the guests arrived,' Berzelius says, cutting Mikael a large slice. 'It was completely hollow by the time we came to light the candles . . .'

Reidar excuses himself, gets up and leaves the table. He tries to smile at the others, but his heart is pounding with angst. He's missing his daughter so much it hurts, enough to make him want to scream. Seeing Mikael sitting there with that childish cake. As if resurrected from the dead. He takes a few deep breaths and goes out into the hall, remembering the day he buried the children's empty caskets next to Roseanna's ashes. Then he went home. Invited everyone to a party, and was never properly sober again.

He stands in the hall, looking back into the dining room where Mikael is eating cake while Reidar's friends try to make conversation and cajole him into laughing. Reidar knows he shouldn't keep doing it, but he gets out his phone and calls Joona Linna.

'It's Reidar Frost,' he says, feeling a faint pressure in his chest.

'I heard that Mikael was discharged,' the detective says.

'But Felicia, I have to know . . . she's, she's so . . .'

'I know, Reidar,' Joona says gently.

'You're doing what you can,' Reidar whispers, feeling that he has to sit down.

He hears the detective ask something, but he still ends the call in the middle of a sentence.

## 95

Reidar swallows hard, time after time, leans against the wall and feels the texture of the wallpaper under his hand, and notices some dead flies on the dusty base of the standard lamp.

Mikael said that Felicia didn't think he'd look for her, that she was sure he didn't care about her going missing.

He was an unfair father, he knew that, but he couldn't help it.

It wasn't that he loved the children differently, just that . . .

The pressure in his chest increases.

Reidar glances towards the corridor where he threw down his coat with the little nitroglycerine spray.

He tries to breathe calmly, takes a few steps, stops and thinks that he ought to turn and face his memories and let himself be overwhelmed by guilt.

Felicia had turned eight that January. There had been a slight thaw in March, but it was about to get colder again.

Mikael was always so sharp and aware, he would look at you attentively and do whatever was expected of him.

Felicia was different.

Reidar had a lot to do back then, he would write all day, answering letters from his readers, giving interviews, having his picture taken, travelling to other countries for book launches. He never had enough time and he hated it when people kept him waiting.

Felicia was always late.

And that day, when the unimaginable happened, the day when the stars were in terrible alignment, the day that God abandoned Reidar, that morning was a perfectly ordinary morning and the sun was shining.

The children started school early. Because Felicia was always slow and unfocused, Roseanna had already put some clothes out for her, but it was Reidar's job to see that the children got to school on time. Roseanna had left early, she used to drive into Stockholm before the rush-hour traffic made the journey take five times as long.

Mikael was ready to go by the time Felicia sat down at the kitchen table. Reidar buttered toast for her, poured her some cereal, and put out the chocolate powder, milk and a glass. She sat and read the back of a cereal packet, tore off the corner of her toast and rolled it into a buttery lump.

'We're in a bit of a rush again,' Reidar said in a measured tone of voice.

Looking down, she spooned some chocolate powder from the packet without moving it closer to the glass, and managed to spill most of it on the table. Leaning forward on her elbows she started to draw in the spilled powder with her fingers. Reidar told her to wipe the table, but she didn't answer, just licked the finger she'd been poking at the chocolate powder with.

'You know we have to be out of the door by ten past eight if we're to get there on time?'

'Stop nagging,' she muttered, then got up from the table.

'Brush your teeth,' Reidar said. 'Mum's laid your clothes out in your room.'

He decided against telling her off for not putting her glass away or wiping the table.


Reidar stumbles and the standard lamp hits the floor and goes out. His chest feels horribly tight now. Pain is coursing down his arm and he can barely breathe. Mikael and David Sylwan are suddenly there beside him. He tries to tell them to leave him be. Berzelius runs over with his coat, and they hunt through the pockets for his medication.

He takes the bottle and sprays some under his tongue, then lets go of it on the floor as the pressure in his chest eases. In the distance he hears them wondering if they should call an ambulance. Reidar shakes his head and notices that the nitroglycerine spray has triggered a growing headache.

'Go and eat now,' he tells them. 'I'm fine, I just . . . I need to be alone for a while.'

## 96

Reidar is sitting on the floor with his back against the wall. He wipes his mouth with a trembling hand, and forces himself to confront his memories again. It was eight o'clock when he went into Felicia's room. She was sitting on the floor reading. Her hair was a mess and she had chocolate round her mouth and smeared across one cheek. To make herself more comfortable she had crumpled up her freshly ironed blouse and skirt to form a cushion to sit on. She had one leg in her woolly tights and was still sucking her sticky fingers.

'You need to be on your bicycle in nine minutes,' he told her. 'Your teacher has said you mustn't be late any more this term.'

'I know,' she said in a monotone, without looking up from her book.

'And wash your face, it's filthy.'

'Stop nagging,' she muttered.

'I'm not nagging,' he tried to say. 'I just don't want you to be late. Can't you understand that?'

'You're nagging so much it's making me sick,' she said to the book.

He must have felt stressed by his writing and the journalists who wouldn't leave him alone, because he suddenly exploded. He'd had enough. He grabbed her arm hard and dragged her into the bathroom, turned the tap on and scrubbed her face roughly.

'What's wrong with you, Felicia? Why can't you ever do anything properly?' he yelled. 'Your brother's ready, he's waiting for you, he's going to be late because of you. But you don't get it, you're just a filthy little monster, not fit to be in a nice, tidy home . . .'

She started to cry, which only made him more angry.

'What's wrong with you?' he went on, grabbing hold of a brush. 'You're completely useless.'

'Stop it!' she sobbed. 'You're horrid, Daddy!'

'I'm horrid? You're behaving like an idiot! Are you an idiot?'

He started tugging at her hair, his hands rough with rage. She screamed and swore at him, and he stopped.

'What did you say?'

'Nothing,' she muttered.

'It sounded like something.'

'Maybe there's something wrong with your ears,' she whispered.

He dragged her out of the bathroom, opened the front door and shoved her out so hard that she fell over on the path.

Mikael was standing by the garage door, waiting with both bicycles. Reidar realised that he had refused to ride off without his sister.


Reidar is sitting on the floor in the hall of the manor, his hands over his face. Felicia had been just a child, and had been acting like a child. Timing and messy hair really hadn't mattered to her.

He remembers the way Felicia had stood in the drive in her underwear. Her right knee was bleeding, her eyes were red and wet from crying, and she still had a bit of chocolate powder on her neck. Reidar was shaking with anger. He went back inside and got her blouse, skirt and jacket, and threw them on the ground in front of her.

'What have I done?' she sobbed.

'You're ruining this family,' he said.

'But I . . .'

'Say you're sorry, say you're sorry this instant.'

'Sorry,' she wept. 'I'm sorry.'

She looked at him with tears streaming down her cheeks and dripping off her chin.

'Just make sure you change,' he replied.

He watched her get dressed, shoulders heaving as she cried, he watched as she wiped the tears from her cheeks and climbed on her bicycle, blouse half tucked in and coat open. He stood there as his rage subsided and heard his little daughter cry as she cycled off to school.

He wrote all day, and felt pleased. He hadn't bothered to get dressed, just sat in front of the computer in his dressing gown, he hadn't brushed his teeth or shaved, he hadn't even made the beds or cleared away the breakfast things. He thought he'd say all this to Felicia, and explain that he was just like her, but he never got the chance.

He was out late, having dinner with his German publisher, and by the time he got home that evening the children had already gone to bed. It was the following morning when they discovered their empty beds. There's nothing in his life that he regrets more than the unfair way he treated Felicia.

It's unbearable to think of her sitting alone in that terrible room, believing that he doesn't care about her, and that he'd only bother to look for Mikael.

## 97

Saga is woken the next morning when the light in the ceiling comes on. Her head feels heavy and she can't focus properly. She's still lying under the blanket, and feels with her numb fingertips to make sure the microphone is safe in her trousers.

The woman with the pierced cheeks is standing outside the door shouting that it's time for breakfast.

Saga gets up, takes the narrow tray through the hatch and sits down on the bed. Slowly she forces herself to eat the sandwiches while she thinks to herself that the situation is becoming intolerable.

She won't be able to handle this much longer.

Cautiously she touches the microphone and wonders about asking to break off the mission.

After lunch she goes over to the sink on unsteady legs, brushes her teeth and washes her face with ice-cold water.

I can't abandon Felicia, she thinks.

Saga sits back down on the bed and stares at the door until the lock starts to whirr between her cell and the dayroom. It clicks and opens. She counts to five, stands up and goes and gets a drink of water from the tap so she doesn't look too eager. With a weary gesture she wipes her mouth with the back of her hand, then walks straight out into the dayroom.

She's the first one there, but the television is on behind the reinforced glass as if it's never been switched off. She can hear angry shouting from Bernie Larsson's room. It sounds like he's trying to destroy his table. She hears his food tray hit the floor. He's screaming as he throws the plastic chair at the wall.

Saga gets on to the running machine, switches it on, takes a few steps, then stops it and sits down on the edge, close to the palm, and pulls off one shoe, pretending there's something wrong with the inner sole. Her fingers are cold and the numbness still hasn't gone. She knows she has to hurry, but she mustn't move too quickly. She blocks the camera's view with her body and tugs the microphone from her trousers, trembling as she does so.

'Fucking whores!' Bernie shouts.

Saga removes the protective wrapping from the tiny microphone. The little object slips between her numb fingers. She catches it against her thigh and turns it the right way up in her hand. She can hear footsteps on the floor. Saga leans forward and presses the microphone to the underneath of one of the leaves. She holds it for a short while, then waits a few extra seconds before letting go.

Bernie pulls open his door and comes out into the dayroom. The palm-leaf is still swaying from her touch, but the microphone is finally in position.

'Obrahiim,' he whispers, and stops abruptly when he sees her.

Saga remains seated, tugs at her sock, smoothing out a crease, then pulls her shoe back on.

'Fucking hell,' he says, and coughs.

She doesn't look at the artificial palm at all. Her legs are trembling beneath her and her heart is beating much harder than usual.

'They took my pictures,' Bernie says, panting as he sits down on the sofa. 'I hate those fucking . . .'

Saga's whole body feels oddly exhausted, sweat is trickling down her back, and her pulse is throbbing in her ears. It must be because of the medication. She slows the pace of the running machine, but still has trouble keeping up.

Bernie is sitting on the sofa with his eyes closed, one leg bouncing restlessly.

'Shit!' he suddenly exclaims loudly.

He gets up, sways, then goes over to the running machine and stands in front of Saga, very close to her.

'I was top of the class,' he says, spraying saliva in Saga's face. 'My teacher used to feed me raisins during breaks.'

'Bernie Larsson, step back,' a voice says over the loud-speaker.

He stumbles to the side and leans against the wall, coughs and takes a step back, straight into the palm with the microphone hanging from its bottom leaf.

## 98

Bernie almost falls, kicks the palm, walks round the running machine and approaches Saga again.

'They're so fucking terrified of me that they pump me full of Suprefact . . . Because I'm a real fucking machine, a big fucking stud . . .'

Saga looks at the camera and realises that she was right. Its view is blocked by the reinforced glass protruding in front of the television. There's a narrow blind strip that the camera can't reach, no more than a metre at most.

Bernie walks round the palm, almost toppling it, then carries on round the running machine and stops behind Saga. She ignores him, just goes on walking as she hears his breathing close behind her.

'Snow White, you're sweating between your buttocks,' he says. 'Your cunt's probably pretty sweaty now. I can get you some tissues . . .'

On the television a man dressed as a chef is drawling something as he puts a load of little crabs on a barbecue.

The far door opens and Jurek comes into the dayroom. Saga catches a glimpse of his furrowed face and immediately stops the machine. She steps down onto the floor, panting from the exertion, and walks towards the sofa. Jurek shows no sign of having noticed. He just gets up onto the running machine, switches it on and begins walking with long strides.

His heavy steps echo around the dayroom once again.

Saga looks at the chef, who is frying red onion rings in a braising pan. Bernie comes closer, wiping sweat from his neck and walking round her, very close.

'You can keep your cunt when you're my skeleton slave,' he says, moving behind her. 'I'll cut off all the rest of your flesh and —'

'Quiet,' Jurek says.

Bernie falls silent instantly and looks at her, forming the word 'whore' with his mouth, then licks his fingers and grabs her breast. She reacts immediately, seizing his hand and taking a step back, pulling him into the camera's blind spot. She punches him hard on the nose. The cartilage cracks and his nose breaks. She spins round, gaining momentum from the movement and hitting Bernie over the ear with a lightning-fast right hook. He's on the point of lurching into range of the camera, but she stops him with her left hand. He's staring at her through his crooked glasses. A copious amount of blood is trickling through his moustache and over his mouth.

Saga is still consumed by rage, holding him in the blind spot and hitting him with another right hook. The blow is extremely hard. His head is knocked aside, his cheeks flap and his glasses fly off to his left.

Bernie sinks to his knees, his head hanging as blood drips onto the floor in front of him.

Saga pulls his head up, sees that he's on the point of losing consciousness and punches him on the nose once more.

'I warned you,' she whispers, letting go of him.

Bernie falls forward, puts his arms out to stop himself, then stays like that, with blood dripping from his face, through his hands onto the vinyl floor.

Saga is breathing hard, and steps away. Jurek Walter has got down from the running machine and is standing there watching her with his pale eyes. His face is motionless and his body strangely relaxed.

Saga has time to think that she's ruined everything as she walks past Jurek towards her own room.

## 99

The fan in the computer whirrs as Anders logs in. The second hand is moving jerkily on the clock with Bart Simpson's weary face on it. Anders reminds himself that has to leave early today because he's attending a class on Socratic conversations at the Autism Education Centre.

A post-it note next to the keyboard says it's recycling week. He has no idea what that means.

Once the secure unit's journal program opens up, he types in his user ID and password.

He checks the log, then taps in Saga Bauer's ID number to make a note about her medication.

Twenty-five milligrams of Haldol depot, he writes. Two intramuscular injections in the outer top quadrant of the gluteal region.

It was the right decision, he thinks, and in his mind's eye he can see her writhing slowly on the floor with her breasts exposed.

Her pale nipples had stiffened, her mouth had been afraid.

If that doesn't help her, he can try Cisordinol, although that can sometimes have serious side effects. Possibly extrapyramidal symptoms, combined with problems with vision, balance, and orgasm.

Anders closes his eyes and thinks of how he pulled the patient's underwear down in the cell.

'I don't want to,' she had said, several times.

But he didn't have to listen to her. He did what he had to do. Pia Madsen had supervised the intervention.

He gave her two injections in the buttock, and stared between her legs at her blonde pubic hair and pink, closed vagina.

Anders goes to the surveillance room. My is already sitting at the control desk. She gives him a friendly glance as he walks in.

'They're in the dayroom,' she says.

Anders leans over her and looks at the screen. Jurek Walter is walking on the running machine with monotonously even paces. Saga is standing and watching television. She seems fairly unaffected by the new medication. Bernie goes over to her, says something and stands behind her.

'What's he doing now?' Anders asks in a light tone of voice.

'Bernie seems unsettled,' My says, frowning.

'I would really have liked to have increased his dosage yesterday, maybe I should have . . .'

'He keeps following the new patient, chattering manically—'

'Bloody hell,' Anders says, sounding stressed.

'Leif and I are ready to go in,' My reassures him.

'But you shouldn't have to,' he says. 'That means the medication is wrong. I'm raising his fortnightly dose this evening from two hundred to four hundred milligrams . . .'

Anders falls silent and watches as Bernie circles Saga Bauer in front of the television.

The other cameras are showing rooms, security doors, corridors and the empty patients' rooms. In one square Sven

Hoffman has a mug of coffee in his hand outside the airlock leading to the dayroom. He's standing with his legs apart, talking to two of the guards.

'Bloody hell,' My suddenly yells, and sets off the emergency alarm.

## 100

A harsh, pulsing alarm begins to sound. Anders is staring at the screen showing the dayroom. The light in the ceiling is reflecting off the dusty glass. He leans forward. To begin with he can only see two patients. Jurek is standing still beside the television, and Saga is on her way to her room.

'What's going on?' he asks.

My has got to her feet and is shouting something into the emergency radio unit. The desk lamp topples over and her office chair rolls backwards into the filing cabinet behind her. She's yelling that Bernie Larsson is injured, and that the response unit has to go in immediately.

Only now does Anders notice that Bernie is hidden behind the protruding section of wall.

All he can see is a bloody hand on the floor.

He must be right in front of Jurek Walter.

'You've got to go in,' My repeats into the radio unit several times, then rushes out.

Anders remains seated, and watches as Jurek leans over and drags Bernie out by his hair, into the middle of the floor where he lets go of him.

A trail of blood shimmers on the floor.

He watches on the screen as Leif gives instructions to two guards outside the airlock, and sees My running to join them.

The alarm is still ringing.

Bernie's face is covered in blood. His eyes are twitching spasmodically, and his arms are flailing in the air.

Anders locks the door to patient room number 3, then talks to Sven over the radio. A group of guards is being sent down from Ward 30.

Someone switches the alarm off.

Anders's radio bleeps and he can hear someone breathing hard.

'I'm opening the door now, repeat, opening the door,' My calls.

Jurek's expressionless face is visible on the screen showing the dayroom. He's standing still, watching Bernie's shocked movements, as he coughs and sprays blood across the floor.

There's a flash of a baton. Guards and carers are entering the airlock. Their faces look tense.

The outer door locks and there's a rumbling sound.

Jurek says something to Bernie, sinks down on one knee and hits him hard across the mouth.

'Christ,' Anders gasps.

The emergency team enter the dayroom and fan out. Jurek straightens his back, shakes the blood from his hand, takes a step back and waits.

'Give him forty milligrams of Stesolid,' Anders tells My.

'Four ampoules of Stesolid,' My repeats over the radio.

Three guards are approaching from different directions with their batons drawn. They shout at Jurek to move away and lie down on the floor.

Jurek looks at them, slowly sinks to his knees and closes his eyes. Leif takes a few quick steps and hits Jurek on the back of the neck with his baton. It's a hard blow. Jurek's head jerks forward, and his body follows. He falls to the floor and just lies there.

The second guard holds him down with a knee on his spine, as he grabs Jurek's arms and holds them behind his back. My is unwrapping a syringe. Anders can see her hands shaking.

Jurek is lying on his stomach. Two guards are holding him down now, and they cuff his wrists and pull his trousers down so that My can give him the injection straight into his muscle.

## 101

Anders looks into the emergency doctor's brown eyes and thanks her quietly. Her white coat is flecked with Bernie's blood.

'His nose bone has been reset. I've stitched up his eyebrow, but tape was fine everywhere else . . . He's probably got concussion, so you'll need to keep him under close supervision.'

'We always do,' Anders replies, glancing at Bernie on the monitor.

He's lying on his bed, his face obscured by bandages. His mouth is half-open and his bulging stomach is moving in time with his breathing.

'He says some really revolting things,' the doctor says, then walks out.

Leif Rajama opens the security door for her. One camera shows him waving, and another how the doctor's coat flaps as she heads up the stairs.

Leif comes back to the surveillance room, runs his hand through his wavy hair and says that he really hadn't been expecting this.

'I've read the journals,' Anders says. 'This is the first time in thirteen years that Jurek Walter has done anything violent.'

'Perhaps he doesn't like company,' Leif suggests.

'Jurek's an old man and he's used to having things his way, but he has to understand that that's not going to work from now on.'

'How're we supposed to make him understand that?' Leif smiles.

Anders pulls his card through the reader and lets Leif in ahead of him. They go past patient rooms 3 and 2, and stop outside the last one, Jurek Walter's cell.

Anders looks into the room. Jurek is lying on the bed, strapped down. The blood from his nose has congealed and his nostrils look strangely black now.

Leif takes a pair of earplugs out of his pocket and offers them to Anders, but he shakes his head.

'Lock the door once I'm inside, and be ready to sound the alarm.'

'Just go in and do what you need to, don't talk to him, and pretend you can't hear what he's saying,' Leif says, then unlocks the door.

Anders goes in and hears Leif quickly lock the door behind him. Jurek's wrists and ankles are fastened to the edges of the bed. Thick fabric straps are stretched across his thighs, hips and torso. His eyes are still tired after the emergency tranquiliser, and a trickle of blood has dribbled out of one ear.

'We've decided to change your medication in light of what happened in the dayroom,' Anders says drily.

'Yes . . . I was expecting a punishment,' Jurek Walter says hoarsely.

'I'm sorry you choose to see it like that, but as acting Senior Consultant, it's my responsibility to prevent violence in this ward.'

## 102

Anders lines up the ampoules of yellow liquid for the injection on the table. Jurek is lying strapped to his bed, watching him with weary eyes.

'I've got no feeling in my fingers,' he says, trying to free his right hand.

'You know we have to apply emergency measures sometimes,' Anders says.

'The first time we met you looked scared . . . now you're looking for fear in my eyes,' Jurek says.

'Why do you think that?' Anders asks.

Jurek takes several breaths, then moistens his mouth and looks Anders in the eye.

'I can see that you're preparing three hundred milligrams of Cisordinol, even though you know that's too much . . . and that the combination of that with my normal medication is risky.'

'I've reached a different conclusion,' Anders says, feeling his cheeks blush.

'Yet you'll write in my notes that you've merely tried fifty milligrams.'

Anders doesn't reply, just prepares the syringe and makes sure that the needle is completely dry.

'You know that the intoxication can be fatal,' Jurek goes on. 'But I'm strong, so I'll probably be OK . . . I'll scream, I'll suffer terrible clonic cramps, and I'll lose consciousness.'

'There's always a risk of side effects,' Anders replies laconically.

'Pain doesn't bother me.'

Anders feels his face glowing as he squeezes a couple of drops from the needle. One drop runs down the syringe. It smells a bit like sesame oil.

'We've noticed that the other patients have unsettled you,' Anders says, without looking at Jurek.

'You don't have to make excuses to me,' Jurek says.

Anders presses the needle into Jurek's thigh, injects three hundred milligrams of Cisordinol, then waits.

Jurek gasps, his lips quiver and his pupils contract to pinpricks. Saliva dribbles from his mouth, down his cheek and neck.

His body twitches and jerks, then suddenly goes completely rigid, his head straining backwards, his back bowed off the bed, the straps over his body straining.

He remains in that position, without breathing.

The frame of the bed creaks.

Anders is staring at him open-mouthed. He's having a protracted, unbearable cramp attack.

Suddenly the tonic state ends and Jurek's body begins to spasm instead. He's jerking uncontrollably, biting his tongue and emitting guttural roars of pain.

Anders tries to tighten the straps across his body. Jurek's arms are flailing and pulling so hard that his wrists start to bleed.

He sinks back, whimpering and panting, as all the blood drains from his face.

Anders steps away, and can't help smiling as he sees tears trickling down Jurek's cheeks.

'It'll soon feel better,' he lies softly.

'Not for you,' Jurek gasps.

'What did you say?'

'You'll just look surprised when I chop your head off and throw it in—'

Jurek is interrupted by a fresh attack of cramps. He screams as his head twists to one side; a fan of veins stand out on his throat as the bones in his neck crack, then his whole body starts to shake again, making the bed rattle.

## 103

Saga lets ice-cold water run over her hands. Her swollen knuckles are sore and she's got three small wounds on them.

Everything has gone wrong.

She lost control, beat Bernie up, and Jurek got the blame.

Through the door she heard the guards shouting about four ampoules of Stesolid before they dragged him into his cell.

They thought he was the one who had attacked Bernie.

Saga turns the tap off, lets her hands drip on the floor and sits down on the bed.

The adrenalin has left a drowsiness, a quivering heaviness in her muscles.

An emergency doctor was called in to take care of Bernie. She heard him chattering manically until the door closed.

Saga is so frustrated she's almost in tears. She has ruined everything with her wretched anger. Her complete inability to control her damn emotions. Why couldn't she just keep out of the way? How could she possibly have let herself be provoked into fighting?

She shudders and clenches her jaw. It's quite possible that Jurek Walter will want to get his own back for the fact that he got blamed.

The security doors clatter and she can hear rapid steps in the corridor, but no one comes to her cell.

Silence.

Saga sits on the bed with her eyes closed as the noises start to reverberate through the walls. Her heart is beating faster. Suddenly Jurek Walter lets out a guttural howl and screams with pain. She thinks she can hear someone kicking their bare heels against the reinforced steel. It sounds a bit like a fist hitting a punchbag.

Saga stares at the door, thinking about electric shocks and lobotomies.

Jurek is still screaming, his voice cracking, then she hears some heavy thuds.

Then silence again.

All she can hear now is the gentle clicking of the water pipes in the wall. Saga gets up and stares through the thick glass of the window in the door. The young doctor walks past. He stops and looks at her with a blank expression on his face.

She sits on the bed until the light in the ceiling goes out.

Life in the secure unit is much harder to bear than she had imagined. Instead of crying, she goes through her mission in her head, thinking about the rules for long-term infiltration and the purpose of the entire operation.

Felicia Kohler-Frost is completely alone in a locked room. She could be starving, and may well have Legionnaires' disease.

Time is running out.

Saga knows that Joona is looking for the girl, but without any information from Jurek Walter the chances of making any kind of breakthrough aren't very high.

Saga has to stick it out, she has to try to bear this for a while longer.

As the light goes out she shuts her eyes and feels them pricking.

She ponders the fact that the life she left behind had already left her first. Stefan is gone. She has no family.

## 104

Joona Linna is in one of the large offices in the headquarters of National Crime, along with part of the investigating team. The walls are covered with maps, photographs and printouts of the tip-offs that are currently being prioritised. On a large-scale map of Lill-Jan's Forest, the sites of the various finds are clearly marked.

With a yellow pen, Joona traces the railway line from the harbour through the forest, then turns to the group.

'One of the things Jurek Walter used to work on was train gearboxes,' he says. 'It's possible that the victims were buried in Lill-Jan's Forest because of this railway line.'

'Like Ángel Reséndiz,' Benny Rubin says, smiling for no reason.

'So why the hell don't we just go in and interrogate Jurek Walter?' Petter Näslund demands, far too loudly.

'It wouldn't work,' Joona says patiently.

'Petter, I presume you've read the psychiatric report?' Magdalena Ronander says. 'Is there really any point interrogating someone who's both schizophrenic and psychotic, and who—'

'We've got eighteen thousand kilometres of railway lines in Sweden,' he interrupts. 'We might as well get digging.'

'Sit on my Facebook,' Benny mutters.

Joona can't help thinking that Petter Näslund has a point. Jurek Walter is the only person who can lead them to Felicia before it's too late. They're checking every single line of inquiry from the old preliminary investigation, they are looking into all the tip-offs that have come in, but they're still not making any progress. Saga Bauer is their only real hope. Yesterday she beat up another patient and Jurek Walter got the blame. That isn't necessarily a bad thing, Joona thinks. It might even help bring them together.

It's getting dark outside, and sparse snowflakes hit Joona's face as he gets out of the car and hurries in to Södermalm Hospital. He finds out from the reception desk that Irma Goodwin is doing an extra shift in the emergency room. He spots her as soon as he walks in. The door to one of the examination rooms is open. A woman with a split lip and bleeding wound on her chin is sitting quietly while Irma Goodwin talks to her.

There's a smell of damp wool and the floor is damp with slush. A construction worker is sitting on one of the benches with one foot in a steamed-up plastic bag.

Joona waits until Irma Goodwin emerges from the room, then walks with her along the corridor towards another treatment room.

'This is the third time she's been here in as many months,' Irma says.

'You should refer her to a women's refuge,' Joona says.

'I already have. But what good will that do?'

'It does help,' Joona insists.

'What can I do for you, then?' she asks, stopping outside the door.

'I need to know about the progression of Legionnaires' disease for—'

'He's going to be fine,' she interrupts, opening the door.

'Yes, but what if he hadn't been treated?' Joona says.

'How do you mean?' she asks, looking into his grey eyes.

'We're trying to find his sister,' Joona says. 'And it seems likely that she was infected at the same time as Mikael . . .'

'In that case it's serious,' Irma says.

'How serious?'

'Without treatment . . . obviously it depends on her general condition, but she's probably got a high fever by now.'

'And then what?'

'She'll be coughing already, and having trouble breathing . . . it's impossible to say with any degree of accuracy, but by the end of the week I'd say she'll be at risk of brain damage and . . . well, you know that Legionnaires' disease can be fatal.'

## 105

The following morning Saga is even more worried about what happened in the dayroom. She has no appetite, and just sits on her bed until lunchtime.

Her mind won't let go of her failure.

Instead of building up trust she has once again managed to unleash conflict. She has beaten up another patient and Jurek Walter has been blamed.

He must hate her now, and is bound to want revenge for what he's been subjected to.

She isn't particularly scared, seeing as the security in the ward is so high.

But she'll have to be very careful.

Prepared for anything, while never betraying any sign of fear.

When the door whirrs and the lock clicks, she gets up and walks out into the dayroom without letting any other thoughts into her head. The television is already on, showing three people sitting in a cosy studio talking about winter gardens.

She's first into the dayroom, and gets up on the running machine at once.

Her legs feel clumsy, her fingertips numb, and with every step she takes the plastic leaves of the palm shake.

Bernie is shouting from inside his room, but soon falls silent.

Someone's cleared up the blood from the floor.

Suddenly Jurek's door opens. His entrance is preceded by a shadow. Saga forces herself not to look at him. With long strides he walks across the floor, heading straight for the running machine.

Saga stops the machine, gets off and steps aside to let him pass. She manages to see that he has black scabs on his lips, and his face is ashen and grey. He climbs heavily onto the machine, then just stands there.

'You got the blame for what I did,' she says.

'You think?' he asks without looking at her.

When he starts the machine she sees that his hands are shaking. The whining, swishing sound starts up once again. The whole machine moves with every step he takes. She can feel the vibrations through the floor. The palm containing the microphone is swaying and moving a tiny bit closer to the running machine with each step.

'Why didn't you kill him?' he asks, glancing at her.

'Because I didn't want to,' she replies honestly.

She looks into his pale eyes and feels the blood pumping round her body as the realisation that she's in direct contact with Jurek Walter catches up with her.

'It would have been interesting to watch you do it,' he says quietly.

She can feel him looking at her with unfeigned curiosity. Maybe she should go and sit on the sofa, but she decides to stay a while longer.

'You're here, which means you've probably killed people,' he says.

'Yes, I have,' she replies after a pause.

He nods. 'It's inevitable.'

'I don't want to talk about it,' Saga mumbles.

'Killing is neither good nor bad,' Jurek goes on calmly. 'But it feels strange the first few times . . . like eating something you didn't think was edible.'

Saga suddenly remembers the time when she killed another person. His blood squirted up over the trunk of a birch tree with a sort of jerky rapidity. Even though there was no need, she fired a second shot and watched through the telescopic sight as the bullet struck within a centimetre or so above the first.

'I did what I had to do,' she whispers.

'Just like yesterday.'

'Yes, but I didn't mean for you to get the blame.'

Jurek stops the machine and stands there looking at her.

'I've been waiting for this . . . quite a long time, I have to say,' he explains. 'Stopping the door from closing again was nothing but a pleasure.'

'I could hear your screams through the walls,' Saga says quietly.

'Yes, those screams,' he replies gloomily. 'They were the result of our new doctor giving me an overdose of Cisordinol . . . They're nature's reaction to pain . . . Something hurts, and the body screams, even though there's no point . . . and in this instance it actually felt like an indulgence . . . Because I knew that the door would have closed again otherwise . . .'

'What door?'

'I doubt they're ever going to let me see a lawyer, so that door is closed . . . but there might be others.'

He looks her in the eye. His gaze is strangely pale; she's reminded of metal.

'You think I can help you,' she whispers. 'That's why you took the blame for what I did.'

'I can't let the doctor become scared of you,' he explains.
'Why?'

'Anyone who ends up here is violent,' Jurek says. 'The staff know that you're dangerous, it says so in your medical notes, and in the forensic psychiatrist's report . . . But that's not what anyone sees when they look at you.'

'I'm not that dangerous.'

Even though she hasn't said anything she regrets – she's only told the truth, and hasn't revealed anything – she feels peculiarly exposed.

'Why are you here? What have you done?' he asks.

'Nothing,' she replies curtly.

'What did they say you'd done . . . in court?'

'Nothing.'

A flash of a smile flickers in his eyes.

'You're a real siren . . .'

## 106

In the attic flat, the members of Athena Promacho are eaves-dropping on the conversation in the dayroom as it happens.

Joona is standing next to the large speaker listening once again to Jurek Walter's voice, his choice of words, phrasing, the nuances in his voice, his breathing.

Corinne Meilleroux is sitting at the desk, transcribing the conversation onto her laptop so they can all see the words on the big screen. The regular clicking sound of her long fingernails is soothing.

Nathan Pollock's silver-streaked ponytail is hanging down over the waistcoat of his suit. He's making notes as Johan Jönson monitors the audio quality on his own computer.

The group is completely silent while the conversation in the dayroom is going on. The sun is pouring through the balcony doors that look out onto glistening, snow-topped roofs.

They hear Jurek Walter tell Saga she's a real siren, then he leaves the room.

After a few seconds of silence, Nathan leans back in his chair and claps his hands. Corinne is just shaking her head, impressed.

'Saga's brilliant,' Pollock mutters.

'Even if we haven't found out anything that could lead us closer to Felicia,' Joona says, turning to face the others, 'contact has been established, which is seriously good work . . . and I think she's made him curious.'

'I have to admit, I was a bit worried when she let herself be provoked by the other patient,' Corinne says, squeezing some lime into a glass of water and passing it to Pollock.

'But Jurek deliberately assumed responsibility for the attack,' Joona says slowly.

'Yes, why did he do that? He must have heard her yesterday, when she told the guard she wanted to see a lawyer,' Pollock says. 'That's why Jurek can't allow the doctor to become scared of her, because then she wouldn't be allowed any visits from—'

'He's new,' Joona interrupts. 'Jurek says the doctor's new.'

'So what?' Johan Jönson asks, open-mouthed.

'When I spoke to Brolin, the Senior Consultant . . . on Monday, he said there hadn't been any changes in the secure unit.'

'That's right,' Pollock says.

'It might be nothing,' Joona says. 'But why did Brolin tell me they had the same staff they'd always had?'

## 107

Joona Linna is driving north up the E4 motorway. A gentle Max Bruch violin sonata is playing on the radio. The shadows and falling snow in front of the cars merge with the music. As he's passing Norrviken, Corinne Meilleroux calls.

She quickly informs him that out of all the doctors that have been added to the payroll of Löwenströmska Hospital over the past two years, only one of them works in the field of psychiatry.

'His name's Anders Rönn, fairly recently qualified, although he had a temporary post at a psychiatric unit in Växjö.'

'Anders Rönn,' Joona repeats.

'Married to Petra Rönn, works in recreational administration for the council . . . they've got a daughter, mildly autistic, apparently. I'm not sure if that's at all useful, but you might as well know,' she laughs.

'Thanks, Corinne,' Joona says, turning off the motorway at Upplands Väsby. He drives past Solhagen, where his dad used to go for lunch when he was still alive.

The old road to Uppsala is lined on one side by black oaks. The snow-covered fields beyond the trees slope down towards a lake.

Joona parks the car outside the main entrance to the hospital and walks in, turning left and hurrying past the unmanned reception desk towards the department for general psychiatry.

Joona passes the secretary and heads straight for the Senior Consultant's closed door. He opens it and walks in. Roland Brolin looks up from his computer and takes off his bifocal glasses. Joona lowers his head slightly, but still manages to nudge the low ceiling lamp. He takes his time pulling out his police ID, holds it in front of Brolin for a minute or two, then starts to ask the same questions as before.

'How is the patient?'

'I'm afraid I'm busy right now, but—'

'Has Jurek Walter done anything unusual recently?' Joona interrupts in a harsh tone of voice.

'I've already answered that,' Brolin says, turning back towards his computer.

'And the security routines haven't changed?'

The thickset doctor sighs through his nose and looks at him wearily.

'What are you doing?'

'Is he still getting intramuscular Risperdal?' Joona asks.

'Yes,' Brolin sighs.

'And the staffing in the secure unit remains unchanged?'

'Yes, but I've already told—'

'Is the staff in the secure unit unchanged?' Joona interrupts.

'Yes,' Brolin says with a hesitant smile.

'Is there a new doctor called Anders Rönn working in the secure unit?' Joona asks in a voice hoarse with persistence.

'Well, yes—'

'So why are you saying the staff is unchanged?'

A slight blush appears below the doctor's tired eyes.

'He's only a temp,' Brolin explains slowly. 'Surely you understand that we have to bring in temps sometimes?'

'Who is he standing in for?'

'Susanne Hjälm, she's on leave of absence.'

'How long has she been gone?'

Brolin answers as he breathes out:

'Three months.'

'What's she doing?'

'I don't actually know – staff don't have to give reasons for leave of absence.'

'Is Anders Rönn working today?'

Brolin looks at his watch and says coldly:

'I'm afraid he's finished for the day.'

Joona gets his phone out and leaves the room. Anja Larsson answers just as he's walking past the secretary.

'I need addresses and phone numbers for both Anders Rönn and Susanne Hjälm,' he says curtly.

# 108

Joona has just pulled out of the hospital grounds and is accelerating along the old main road when Anja calls back.

'Baldersvägen 3, in Upplands Väsby,' she tells him. 'That's where Anders Rönn lives.'

'I'll find it,' he says, and puts his foot down as he heads south.

'Would you convert for my sake?'

'What do you mean?'

'When we get married . . . I was just thinking, if I happened to be Catholic or Muslim, or—'

'But you're not.'

'No, you're right . . . there's nothing stopping us, we could have a proper summer wedding.'

'I'm not sure I'm mature enough to take a step like that,' laughs Joona.

'Me neither, but I've got a feeling I might be getting there,' Anja whispers over the phone.

Then she clears her throat, changes tone and says coolly that she'll check out Susanne Hjälm.

Joona heads back to the Upplands Väsby junction on the

E4 and has just turned into Sandavägen to look for Anders Rönn's house when Anja calls again.

'This is a bit weird,' she says in a serious voice. 'Susanne Hjälm's phone is switched off. As is her husband's. He hasn't shown up at the insurance company where he works for the past three months, and their two children haven't been at school either. The girls are both off sick, with doctor's certificates, nevertheless the school has been in touch with Social Services . . .'

'Where do they live?'

'Biskop Nils väg 23, in Stäket, on the way to Kungsängen.'

Joona pulls over to the side of the road and lets the lorry behind him drive past. Snow is blowing off the back.

'Send a patrol to the address,' Joona says, then does a U-turn.

The front right wheel goes up on the kerb, the car's suspension lurches and the glove compartment pops open.

He's trying not to think too far ahead, but his speed is increasing the whole time. He ignores the red traffic lights, races through the junction and onto the roundabout. By the time he reaches the slip road to the motorway he's already going at a hundred and sixty kilometres an hour.

## 109

Route 267 is covered in snow, and the car leaves a great white cloud behind it. Joona overtakes an old Volvo and the tyres roll softly over the ridge of snow between the carriageways. He turns the headlights on full-beam and the deserted road becomes a tunnel with a black roof over a white floor. To begin with he drives through a landscape of fields, where the snow takes on a blue tone in the deepening darkness, then the road passes through thick forest until the lights of Stäket are flickering ahead of him and the landscape opens up towards Lake Mälaren.

What's happened to the psychiatrist's family?

Joona brakes and turns right, driving into a small residential area with snow-covered fruit trees and rabbit hutches on the lawns in front of the houses.

The weather's been getting worse, and the snow is blowing in from the lake, thick and slanting.

Biskop Nils väg 23 is one of the last houses; beyond it there's nothing but forest and rough ground.

Susanne Hjälm's home is a large white villa with pale-blue shutters at the windows and a red tiled roof.

All the windows are unlit, and the driveway is thick with untouched snow.

Joona stops just beyond the house and barely has time to put the handbrake on before the patrol car from Upplands-Bro police pulls up a short distance away.

Joona gets out of the car, grabbing his coat and scarf from the back seat, and walks over to his uniformed colleagues as he does his coat up.

'Joona Linna, National Crime,' he says, holding out his hand.

'Eliot Sörenstam.'

Eliot has a shaved head, a little vertical strip of beard on his chin, and melancholic brown eyes.

The other officer shakes his hand firmly and introduces herself as Marie Franzén. She has a cheerful, freckled face, blonde eyebrows and a ponytail high up at the back of her head.

'Nice to see you in real life,' she smiles.

'It's good that you could come so quickly,' Joona says.

'Only because I have to get home and plait Elsa's hair,' she says chattily. 'She's desperate to have curly hair for preschool tomorrow.'

'We'd better hurry up, then,' Joona says, and sets off towards the house.

'Only kidding, there's no rush . . . I've got some curling tongs as backup.'

'Marie's been on her own with her daughter for five years,' Eliot explains. 'But she's never had a day off sick, or left early.'

'That's a lovely thing to say – considering you're a Capricorn,' she adds with real warmth in her voice.

The forest behind the house shelters it from the wind blowing off the lake, and the snow seems to roll up above the trees and fall on the little residential area. There are lights in the windows of most houses on the road, but number 23 is ominously dark.

'There's probably a good explanation,' Joona tells the two

officers. 'But neither of the parents has been at work for the past few months, and the children are off school sick.'

The low hedge facing the road is covered with snow, and the green plastic mailbox next to the electricity meter is bursting with post and adverts.

'Are Social Services involved?' Marie asks seriously.

'They've been out here already, but say the family is away,' Joona replies. 'Let's try knocking, then we're probably going to have to ask the neighbours.'

'Do we suspect a crime?' Eliot asks, looking at the virgin snow on the drive.

Joona can't help thinking about Samuel Mendel. His whole family vanished. The Sandman took them, just as Jurek had predicted. But at the same time, it doesn't fit. Susanne Hjälm reported the children sick, and herself signed the doctor's note that was sent to the school.

## 110

The two police officers calmly follow Joona up to the house. The snow crunches under their boots.

No one's been here for weeks.

A loop of garden hose is sticking out of the snow next to the sandpit.

They go up the steps to the porch and ring the bell, wait for a while, then ring again.

They listen for any noises from the house. Clouds of breath rise from their mouths. The porch creaks beneath them.

Joona rings again.

He can't shake his bad feeling, but says nothing. There's no reason to worry his colleagues.

'What do we do now?' Eliot asks quietly.

Leaning on the little bench, Joona bends over and peers through the narrow hall window. He can see a brown stone floor and striped wallpaper. The glass prisms hanging from the wall lamps are motionless. He looks back at the floor. The dustballs by the wall are still. He's just thinking that the air inside the house doesn't seem to be moving when one of the dustballs rolls under the dresser. Joona leans closer to the glass, cupping his hands to the pane, and sees a shadowy figure in the hall.

Someone standing with their hands raised.

It takes Joona a moment to realise that he's seeing his own reflection in the hall mirror, but adrenalin is already coursing through his body.

He sees himself as a silhouette in the narrow hall window, he sees umbrellas in a stand, the inside of the door, the security chain and the red hall rug.

There's no sign of any shoes or outdoor clothing.

Joona knocks on the window, but nothing happens.

The prisms of the lamps are hanging motionless, everything is still inside the house.

'OK, let's go and have a word with the nearest neighbours,' he says.

But instead of going back to the road he starts to walk round the house. His colleagues stand on the drive, looking at him curiously.

Joona goes past a snow-covered trampoline, then stops. There are tracks from some animal leading through several of the gardens. Light from a window in the neighbouring house stretches out like a golden sheet across the snow.

Everything is completely silent.

Where the garden ends, the forest begins. Pine cones and needles have fallen on the thinner snow beneath the trees.

'Aren't we going to talk to the neighbours?' Eliot asks, bemused.

'I'm coming,' Joona replies quietly.

'What?'

'What did he say?'

'Wait a moment . . .'

Joona pads a bit further through the snow, his feet and ankles getting cold. A garden bird-feeder is swinging outside the dark kitchen window.

He carries on round the corner of the house, thinking that something isn't right.

Snow has drifted against the wall of the house.

Shimmering icicles are hanging off the sill below the window closest to the forest.

But why only that one? he asks himself.

As he gets closer he sees the neighbours' outside light reflected in the window.

There are four long icicles, and a series of smaller ones.

He's almost reached the window when he notices a dip in the snow, next to an air vent close to the ground. Which means that every now and then warm air comes out of the vent.

That's why there are icicles in that spot.

Joona leans forward and listens. All he can hear is the sound of wind moving slowly through the treetops.

The silence is broken by voices from the neighbouring house. Two children are shouting angrily at each other. A door slams, and the voices get quieter.

A faint scraping sound makes Joona bend down towards the vent again. He's holding his breath, and thinks he can hear a quick whisper from the vent, like a command.

Instinctively he draws back, uncertain whether he imagined the whisper, then turns round and sees the other officers standing in the driveway, the dark trees, the snow-crystals sparkling in the air, and suddenly he realises what he saw a little while ago.

When he looked through the narrow hall window and saw himself in the mirror, he was so surprised that he missed the most important detail.

The door's security chain was on, and to do that you had to be inside the house.

Joona runs through the deep snow, back round to the front. Loose snow flies up round his legs. He digs out his skeleton key from his inside pocket and goes up the steps to the porch.

'There's someone in there,' he says quietly.

His colleagues just look at him in astonishment as he picks the lock, opens the door carefully, closes it again and then pushes hard to break the security chain.

Joona gestures to them to keep behind him.

'Police!' he calls into the house. 'We're coming in!'

# 111

The three police officers go into the hall, and are struck at once by the acrid stench of old rubbish. The house is silent, and as cold as outside.

'Is anyone home?' Joona calls.

All they can hear are their own footsteps and movements. The sounds from the next house don't carry inside. Joona reaches out to switch on the light, but it doesn't work.

Marie turns on her torch behind him. Its light flits nervously in different directions. They move further into the house, and Joona sees his own shadow grow and slide across the closed blinds.

'Police,' he calls again. 'We only want to talk.'

They enter the kitchen, and see a mound of empty packets under the table – cornflakes, pasta, flour and sugar.

'What the hell is this?' Eliot whispers.

The fridge and freezer stand dark and empty, all the kitchen chairs are missing, and on the windowsills, next to the closed curtains, the houseplants have all withered.

It's only from the outside that it looks like the family has left.

They go on, into a television room with a corner sofa. Joona steps over the cushions that have been pulled off it.

Marie whispers something that he can't make out.

The thick curtains covering the windows reach all the way to the floor.

Through the door to the corridor they can see a staircase leading down to the cellar.

They stop when they see a dead dog with a plastic bag taped round its head. It's lying on the floor in front of the television stand.

Joona carries on towards the corridor and staircase. He can hear his colleagues' careful footsteps behind him.

Marie's breathing has speeded up.

The light from her torch is shaking.

Joona moves to the side so he can see into the unlit corridor. Further along it the bathroom door is ajar.

Joona gestures to the others to stop, but Marie is already beside him, pointing the torch towards the stairs. She takes a step closer and tries to see further down the corridor.

'What's that?' she whispers, unable to control the nervousness in her voice.

There's something lying on the floor by the bathroom door. She points the torch in that direction. It's a doll with long blonde hair.

The light hovers over its shiny plastic face.

Suddenly the doll is pulled in behind the door.

Marie smiles and takes a long stride forward, but at the same moment there's a stomach-churning bang.

The flare as the shotgun goes off fills the corridor like lightning.

It looks as if Marie is hit hard in the back, as some of the hail of shot cuts right through her neck.

Her head flies back and blood spurts out of the exit wound in her throat.

The torch hits the floor.

Marie is really already dead when she takes one last step

with her head hanging loose. She collapses in a heap with one leg folded beneath her, raising her hips at an odd angle.

Joona has drawn his pistol, released the safety catch and spun round. The corridor leading to the stairs is empty. There's no one there. Whoever fired the shot must have disappeared down into the cellar.

Blood is bubbling from Marie's neck, steaming in the chill air.

The torch is rolling slowly over the floor.

'Dear God, dear God,' Eliot whispers.

Their ears are ringing from the blast.

A child suddenly appears with the doll in its arms, slips on the blood, lands on its back and disappears into the darkness by the staircase. Footsteps thud down the stairs and disappear with a clatter.

## 112

Joona kneels down and takes a quick look at Marie. There's nothing to be done, the heavy charge hit her lungs and heart and ripped through her carotid artery.

Eliot Sörenstam is yelling and sobbing into his radio, calling for an ambulance and backup.

'Police,' Joona shouts down the stairs. 'Put the weapon down and—'

The shotgun goes off again from down in the cellar, and the shot hits the wood of the stairs, sending up a cascade of splinters.

Joona hears the metallic click as the gun snaps open. He rushes over, reaches the stairs as he hears the little sigh as the first empty cartridge is released.

Taking several steps at a time, Joona races down the dark stairs, pistol raised.

Eliot Sörenstam has picked up the torch to give him some light, and the beam reaches the bottom of the stairs just in time for Joona to stop himself before he's impaled.

At the foot of the stairs the kitchen chairs have been piled up to form a barricade. The protruding legs have been sharpened into spears, and kitchen knives have been fixed to them with duct tape.

Joona aims his Colt Combat over the barricade, into a room containing a billiard table.

There's no sign of anyone, everything's quiet again.

The adrenalin in his body makes him strangely calm, as if he were in a new, sharper version of reality.

Slowly he takes his finger off the trigger and loosens the rope that's tied to the end of the banister to help him get round the barricade.

'What the hell are we going to do?' Eliot whispers with panic in his voice as he comes down.

'Are you wearing a bulletproof vest?'

'Yes.'

'Shine the torch further into the cellar,' Joona says as he starts to move.

There are two empty shotgun cartridges on the floor, surrounded by broken glass and empty tins of food. Eliot is breathing too fast, holding the torch next to his pistol as he shines it into the corners. It's warmer down here, and there's a sharp smell of sweat and urine.

There's wire strung across the passageway at neck height, forcing them to duck down. Behind them the wires tap against each other.

Suddenly they hear whispering, and Joona stops and signals to Eliot. A ticking sound, followed by footsteps.

'Run, run,' someone whispers.

Cold air rushes in and Joona hurries forward, while the shaky light from Eliot Sörenstam's torch sweeps round the cellar. There is a boiler room to their left, and in the other direction some concrete steps lead up to an open cellar door.

Snow is blowing in over the steps.

Joona has already caught sight of the concealed figure as the light of the torch glints off the knife-blade.

He takes another step forward, and hears rapid breathing followed by a sudden whimper.

A tall woman with a dirty face rushes out with a knife in her hand, and Joona instinctively aims his pistol at her torso.

'Watch out!' Eliot cries.

It's a matter of no more than a second, but Joona still has time to decide not to shoot. Without thinking he moves towards her, stepping quickly aside as she lunges. He blocks her arm, grabs it and lets his shoulders carry on moving, hitting the left side of her neck with his lower right arm. The blow is so hard and sudden that it knocks her backwards.

Joona is holding the arm holding the knife. There's a cracking sound, like two stones knocking together underwater, as her elbow breaks. The woman falls to the floor, howling with pain.

The knife clatters to the ground. Joona kicks it away, then aims his pistol towards the boiler room.

A middle-aged man is half-lying over the geo-energy pump. He's been tied up with rope and duct tape, and there's a rag in his mouth.

Eliot Sörenstam cuffs the woman to a water pipe as Joona cautiously approaches the man, explains that he's a police officer, and removes the gag.

'The girls,' the man gasps. 'They ran out, you mustn't hurt the girls, they're—'

'Is there anyone else here?'

Eliot's already run up the concrete steps.

'Only the girls.'

'How many?'

'Two . . . Susanne gave them the shotgun, they're just scared, they've never used a gun, you mustn't hurt them,' the man pleads desperately. 'They're just scared . . .'

Joona runs up the steps and out into the back garden. Behind him the man calls out over and over again, telling them not to hurt the girls.

Footsteps lead across the garden and straight into the forest. A beam of light is flickering among the trees.

'Eliot,' Joona shouts. 'There's only children out here!'

He follows the tracks into the forest and feels the sweat on his face cooling.

'They're armed!' Joona calls.

He runs towards the light between the trees. Twigs snap beneath the snow under his weight. Ahead of him he can see Eliot pushing through the snow with his pistol and torch.

'Wait!' Joona shouts, but Eliot doesn't seem to hear.

Loose snow falls from a tree with soft thumps.

In the weak light he can make out the children's tracks among the trees, at different angles, then the straight line of Eliot's steps following them.

'They're just children!' Joona cries again, trying to gain on him by sliding down a steep slope.

He slips onto one hip, bringing down loose stones and pine cones, and scrapes his back on something, but gets to his feet again as he reaches the bottom.

Through the dense foliage he can make out the searching beam of the torch, and close by a skinny girl is standing next to a tree, holding the shotgun in both hands.

Joona runs straight through the thicket of dry twigs. He tries to shield his face, but his cheeks still get scratched. He sees Eliot's frame moving between the tree trunks, then the little girl behind the tree steps out and fires the gun at the policeman.

The cloud of shot hits the snow just a metre or so in front of the end of the barrel. The butt jerks back and the girl's thin frame is shaken by the recoil. She falls and Eliot spins round and aims his pistol at her.

'Wait!' Joona shouts, trying to force his way through the branches.

He ends up with snow all over him and inside his coat, but the branches give way and he emerges on the other side, and stops abruptly.

Eliot Sörenstam is sitting on the ground, with his arms round the sobbing girl. A few steps away her little sister is standing and staring at them.

Susanne Hjälm's arms are cuffed behind her back. Her broken elbow juts out at an odd angle. She's screaming hysterically and putting up fierce resistance as two uniformed police officers drag her up the cellar steps. The blue lights from the various emergency vehicles make the snowy landscape ripple like water. Neighbours are watching events from a distance, like silent ghosts.

Susanne stops screaming when she sees Joona and Eliot emerge from the forest. Joona is carrying the younger girl, and Eliot is holding the other one by the hand.

Susanne's eyes open wide and she breathes hard in the ice-cold winter night. Joona puts the girl on the ground so she can go over to her mother with her sister. They hug for a long time, and she tries to calm them.

'It's going to be all right now,' she says in a broken voice. 'Everything's going to be all right . . .'

An older female officer starts talking to the girls, trying to explain that their mother needs to go with the police.

The father is led out of the cellar by the paramedics, but he's so weak that he has to be put on a stretcher.

Joona follows as the officers lead Susanne through the

deep snow towards one of the police cars in the drive. They put her in the back seat while a senior officer talks to a prosecutor over the phone.

'She needs to go to hospital,' Joona says, stamping the snow from his shoes and trousers.

He walks over to Susanne Hjälm. She's sitting quietly in the car, her face turned towards the house as she tries to catch a glimpse of her daughters.

'Why did you do this?' Joona asks.

'You'd never understand,' she mumbles. 'No one could understand.'

'Maybe I could,' he says. 'I was the person who arrested Jurek Walter thirteen—'

'You should have killed him,' she interrupts, looking him in the eye for the first time.

'What happened? After so many years working as a psychiatrist in the secure unit . . .'

'I should never have spoken to him,' she says through gritted teeth. 'We're not supposed to, but I never imagined . . .'

She falls silent and looks up at the house again.

'What did he say?'

'He . . . demanded that I post a letter,' she whispers.

'A letter?'

'There are loads of restrictions limiting what he's allowed to do, so I couldn't . . . but I, I . . .'

'You couldn't send it? So where's the letter now?'

'Maybe I should talk to a lawyer,' she says.

'Have you still got the letter?'

'I burned it,' she says, then turns away again.

Tears start to trickle down her exhausted, filthy face.

'What did it say in the letter?'

'I want to see a lawyer before I answer any more questions,' she says resolutely.

'This is important, Susanne,' Joona persists. 'You're going

to get medical treatment now, and you can see a lawyer, but first I need to know where the letter was to be sent . . . Give me a name, an address.'

'I don't remember . . . it was a PO box.'

'Where?'

'I don't remember . . . there was a name,' she says, shaking her head.

Joona watches the eldest daughter being carried towards an ambulance on a stretcher. She looks scared, and is trying to undo the straps holding her on.

'Do you remember the name?'

'It wasn't Russian,' Susanne whispers. 'It was—'

The daughter suddenly panics in the ambulance and starts screaming.

'Ellen!' Susanne cries. 'I'm here, I'm here!'

Susanne tries to get out of the car, but Joona forces her to stay where she is.

'Leave me alone!'

She struggles to pull free and get out. The doors of the ambulance close and everything is quiet again.

'Ellen!' she calls.

The ambulance drives off and Susanne turns her head away with her eyes closed.

## 115

When Anders Rönn gets home from the parents' meeting organised by the Autism and Asperger Association, Petra is sitting at the computer paying bills. He goes over and kisses her on the back of the neck, but she shrugs him off. He tries to smile, and pats her cheek.

'Stop it,' she says.

'Can we try to be friends?'

'You went far too far,' she tells him wearily.

'I know, sorry, I thought you wanted—'

'Well, stop thinking it,' she interrupts.

Anders looks her in the eye, nods and then goes off to Agnes's room. She's sitting by her dolls' house with her back to him. He can see that she's got the hairbrush in her hand, she's brushed all the dolls and has piled them on top of each other in one of the beds in the dolls' house.

'You've made it very nice,' Anders says.

Agnes turns, shows him the brush and meets his gaze for a few seconds.

He sits down next to her and puts his arm around her thin shoulders. She pulls slowly away.

'Now they're all lying asleep together,' Anders says cheerily.

'No,' she says in her monotonous voice.

'What are they doing, then?'

'They're looking.'

She points at the dolls' painted eyes, wide open.

'You mean they can't sleep if they're looking? But you can pretend—'

'They're looking,' she interrupts, her head starting to move anxiously.

'I can see that,' he says in a soothing voice. 'But they're lying in bed, just like they should be, and that's really good—'

'Ow, ow, ow . . .'

Agnes is moving her head jerkily, then she quickly claps her hands three times. Anders holds her in his arms and kisses her head, and whispers that she's done really well with the dolls. In the end her body relaxes again and she starts lining up pieces of Lego along the floor.

The doorbell rings and Anders leaves the room, glancing at Agnes one last time before going to answer it.

The outside light shows a tall man in a suit, with wet trousers and a torn pocket. The man's hair is curly and messed up. His cheeks are dimpled, and his eyes look serious.

'Anders Rönn?' he says with a Finnish accent.

'Can I help you?' Anders says in a neutral tone of voice.

'I'm from the National Criminal Investigation Department,' he says, showing his police ID. 'Can I come in?'

## 116

Anders stares at the tall man outside the door. For a fleeting moment he feels chill with fear. He opens the door to let the man in, and as he asks whether his guest would like coffee, a thousand thoughts are going through his fevered mind.

Petra's called a women's helpline and talked.

Brolin has fabricated some sort of complaint against him.

They've worked out that he isn't really qualified to work in the secure unit.

The tall detective says his name is Joona Linna, and politely declines the offer of coffee. He goes into the living room and sits down on an armchair. He gives Anders a friendly, appraising look that makes him feel like a guest in his own home.

'You're standing in for Susanne Hjälm in the secure unit,' the detective inspector says.

'Yes,' Anders replies, trying to work out what the man is after.

'What's your opinion of Jurek Walter?'

Jurek Walter, Anders thinks. Is this just about Jurek Walter? He relaxes, and manages to bring a dry tone to his voice:

'I can't discuss individual patients,' he says sternly.

'Do you speak to him?' the man asks, with a sharp look in his grey eyes.

'We have no conversational therapy in the secure unit,' Anders says, running a hand through his short hair. 'But obviously, the patients talk . . .'

Joona Linna leans forward:

'You're aware that the Supreme Court applied specific restrictions to Jurek Walter because he's deemed to be extremely dangerous?'

'Yes,' Anders says. 'But everything becomes a matter of interpretation, and as a responsible doctor I'm always having to weigh restrictions and treatment against each other.'

The detective nods a couple of times, then says:

'He asked you to send a letter – didn't he?'

Anders loses his grip for a moment, then reminds himself that he's the one with the responsibility, the one who takes decisions regarding the patients.

'Yes, I posted a letter for him,' he replies. 'I considered it an important way of building up trust between us.'

'Did you read the letter before you sent it?'

'Yes, of course . . . he knew I would, it was nothing remarkable.'

The detective's grey eyes darken as his pupils expand.

'What did it say?'

Anders doesn't know if Petra's come in, but it feels like she's standing behind his back watching them.

'I don't remember exactly,' he says, uncomfortably aware that he's blushing. 'It was a formal letter to a legal firm . . . something I consider to be a human right.'

'Yes,' the detective says, without taking his eyes off him.

'Jurek Walter wanted a lawyer to come and see him in the unit, to help him understand the possibilities of getting a retrial in the Supreme Court . . . that was more or less what he wanted . . . and that he . . . if there was to be a retrial, wanted a private defence lawyer to represent him.'

The living room is silent.

'What address?' the detective inspector asks calmly.

'Rosenhane Legal Services . . . a PO box in Tensta.'

'Would you be able to reconstruct the exact wording of the letter?'

'I actually only read it once, and like I said, it was very formal and polite . . . even if there were a number of spelling mistakes.'

'Spelling mistakes?'

'More like dyslexic errors,' Anders explains.

'Did you discuss the letter with Roland Brolin?'

'No,' Anders replies. 'Why would I do that?'

## 117

Joona goes back to his car and sets off towards Stockholm. He calls Anja and asks her to check for Rosenhane Legal Services.

'Do you have any idea what time it is?'

'The time,' he repeats, suddenly thinking that it's only been a few hours since Marie Franzén was shot and killed. 'I . . . sorry, let's do it tomorrow.'

He realises that she's already ended the call. A couple of minutes pass before she calls him back.

'There's no Rosenhane,' she says. 'No law firm, and no solicitor either.'

'There was a PO box address,' Joona insists.

'Yes, in Tensta, I found that,' she replies gently. 'But it's been closed down and the lawyer who was renting it doesn't exist.'

'I see . . .'

'Rosenhane is the name of an extinct aristocratic family,' she says.

'Sorry I called so late.'

'I was joking, you can call me whenever you like. I mean, we'll soon be married and everything . . .'

The address is a trail that doesn't lead anywhere, Joona is thinking. No PO box, no law firm, no name.

It suddenly occurs to him how strange it was for Anders Rönn to call Jurek Walter dyslexic.

I've seen his writing, Joona thinks.

What Anders Rönn interpreted as dyslexia was probably just the result of long-term medication.

Once again his thoughts go to Marie Franzén, murdered by Susanne Hjälm. Now there's a child waiting for a parent who'll never be coming home.

She shouldn't have rushed forward, but he knows he could easily have made the same mistake if his operational training wasn't ingrained so deeply – and then he would have been killed, just like his own father.

Maybe Maria Franzén's daughter has been told the news by now. The world will never be the same again. When he was eleven his father was shot and killed with a shotgun. His father, also a police officer, had only gone to a flat where there had been reports of a domestic disturbance. Some time that day Joona remembers sitting in his classroom when the headmaster came in and got him. The world was never the same again.

## 118

It's morning, and Jurek is striding along on the running machine. Saga can hear his heavy, ponderous breathing. On the television a man is making his own rubber balls. Colourful spheres are floating in various glasses of water.

Saga is feeling a mixture of emotions. Her self-preservation instinct is telling her she ought to avoid all contact with Jurek, but every conversation she has with him increases her colleagues' chances of finding Felicia.

The man on television is warning viewers against using too much glitter, because it can spoil the ball's ability to bounce.

Slowly Saga walks over to Jurek. He steps off the running machine and gestures to her to take over.

She thanks him, gets up and starts walking. Jurek stands alongside watching her. Her legs are still tired and her joints sore. She tries to speed up, but is already breathing laboriously.

'Have you had your injection of Haldol?' Jurek asks.

'Had it the first day,' she replies.

'From the doctor?'

'Yes.'

'Did he come in and pull your trousers down?'

'I was given Stesolid first,' she replies quietly.

'Was he inappropriate?'

She shrugs her shoulders.

'Has he been in your room more times?'

Bernie comes into the dayroom and walks straight over to the running machine. His broken nose has been fixed up with white fabric tape. One eye is closed by a dark grey swelling. He stops in front of Saga, looks at her and coughs quietly.

'I'm your slave now . . . fucking hell . . . I'm here, and I shall follow you for all eternity, like the pope's butler . . . until death do us part . . .'

He wipes the sweat from his top lip and seems unsteady.

'I shall obey every—'

'Sit down on the sofa,' Saga interrupts without looking at him.

He burps and swallows several times.

'I shall lie on the floor and warm your feet . . . I am your dog,' he says, and sinks to his knees with a sigh. 'What do you want me to do?'

'Go and sit on the sofa,' Saga repeats.

She's walking slowly on the machine. The palm leaves are swaying. Bernie crawls over, tilts his head and looks up at her.

'Anything, I'll obey you,' he says. 'If your breasts are getting sweaty, I can wipe—'

'Go and sit on the sofa,' Jurek says in a detached voice.

Bernie crawls away instantly and lies down on the floor in front of the sofa. Saga has to lower the speed of the machine slightly. She forces herself not to look at the swaying palm leaf and tries not to think about the microphone and transmitter.

Jurek is standing motionless, watching her. He wipes his mouth, then rubs his hand through his short, metal-grey hair.

'We can get out of the hospital together,' he says calmly.

'I don't know if I want to,' she replies honestly.

'Why not?'

'I haven't really got anything left outside.'

'Left?' he repeats quietly. 'Going back is never an option . . . not to anything, but there are better places than this.'

'And probably some worse.'

He looks genuinely surprised and turns away with a sigh.

'What did you say?' she asks.

'I just sighed, because it occurred to me that I can actually remember a worse place,' he says, gazing at her with a dreamy look in his eyes. 'The air was filled with the hum from high-voltage electricity wires . . . the roads were wrecked by big diggers . . . and the tracks full of red, clayey water, up to your waist . . . but I could still open my mouth and breathe.'

'What do you mean?'

'That worse places might be preferable to better ones . . .'

'You're thinking about your childhood?'

'I suppose so,' he whispers.

Saga stops the running machine, leans forward and hangs over the handles. Her cheeks are flushed, as if she'd run ten kilometres. She knows she ought to continue the conversation, without seeming too eager, and get him to reveal more.

'So now . . . have you got a hiding place, or are you going to find a new one?' she asks, without looking at him.

The question is far too direct, she realises that at once, and forces her face upwards, forces herself to meet his gaze.

'I can give you an entire city if you like,' he replies seriously.

'Where?'

'Take your pick.'

Saga shakes her head with a smile, but suddenly remembers a place she hasn't thought of for many years.

'When I think about other places . . . I only ever think

357

about my grandfather's house,' she says. 'I had a swing in a tree . . . I don't know, but I still like swings.'

'Can't you go there?'

'No,' she replies, and gets off the running machine.

## 119

In the attic flat at Rörstrandsgatan 19, the members of Athena Promacho are listening to the conversation between Jurek Walter and Saga Bauer.

Johan Jönson is sitting at his computer in a grey tracksuit top. Corinne is at her desk, transcribing the whole conversation onto her laptop. Nathan Pollock has drawn ten flowers in the margin of his notebook, and has written down the words 'high-voltage electricity wires, big diggers, red clay'.

Joona is merely standing by the speaker, feeling a cold shiver run up his spine as Saga talks about her grandfather. She mustn't let Jurek inside her head, he thinks. Susanne Hjälm's image flits through his memory. Her dirty face and the terrified look in her eyes down there in the cellar.

'Why can't you go there if you want to?' he hears Jurek ask.

'It's my dad's house now,' Saga Bauer replies.

'And you haven't seen him for a while?'

'I haven't wanted to,' she says.

'If he's alive, he's waiting for you to give him another chance,' Jurek says.

'No,' she replies.

'Obviously that depends on what happened, but—'

'I was little, I don't remember much,' she explains. 'But I know I used to call him all the time, promising I'd never be a nuisance again if he'd come home . . . I'd sleep in my own bed and sit nicely at the table and . . . I don't want to talk about it.'

'I understand,' Jurek says, but his words are almost drowned out by a rattling sound.

There's a whining noise, then the rhythmic thud of the running machine.

## 120

Jurek is walking on the running machine. He looks stronger again. His strides are long and forceful, but his pale face is calm.

'You're disappointed in your father because he didn't come home,' he says.

'I remember all those times I called him . . . I mean, I needed him.'

'But your mother . . . where was she?'

Saga pauses, and thinks to herself that she's saying too much now, but at the same time she has to respond to his openness. It's an exchange, otherwise the conversation will become superficial again. It's time for her to say something personal, but as long as she sticks to the truth, she'll be on secure territory.

'Mum wasn't well when I was little . . . I only really remember the end,' Saga replies.

'She died?'

'Cancer . . . she had a malignant brain tumour.'

'I'm sorry.'

Saga remembers the tears trickling into her mouth, the smell of the phone, her hot ear, the light coming through the grimy kitchen window.

Maybe it's because of the medication, her nerves, or just Jurek's penetrating gaze. She hasn't talked about this for years. She doesn't really know why she's doing so now.

'It was just that Dad . . . he couldn't deal with her illness. He couldn't bear to be at home.'

'I can understand why you're angry.'

'I was far too little to look after Mum . . . I tried to help her with her medication, I tried to comfort her . . . she would get headaches in the evenings, and just lie in her bedroom crying.'

Bernie crawls over and tries to sniff between Saga's legs. She shoves him away and he rolls straight into the artificial palm.

'I want to escape too,' he says. 'I'll come with you, I can bite—'

'Shut up,' she interrupts.

Jurek turns round and looks at Bernie, who's sitting there grinning and peering up at Saga.

'Am I going to have to put you down?' Jurek asks him.

'Sorry, sorry,' Bernie whispers, and gets up from the floor.

Jurek starts walking on the machine again. Bernie goes and sits on the sofa and watches television.

'I'm going to need your help,' Jurek says.

Saga doesn't answer, but can't help thinking that she'd be lying if she says she wants to escape. She wants to stay here until Felicia has been found.

'I think human beings are more tied to their families than any other creature,' Jurek goes on. 'We do everything we can to stave off separation.'

'Maybe.'

'You were only a small child, but you took care of your mother . . .'

'Yes.'

'Could she even feed herself?'

'Most of the time . . . but towards the end she had no appetite,' Saga says, truthfully.

'Did she have an operation?'

'I think she only had chemotherapy.'

'In tablet form?'

'Yes, I used to help her every day . . .'

Bernie is sitting on the sofa, but keeps glancing at them. Every now and then he carefully touches the bandage over his nose.

'What did the pills look like?' Jurek asks, and speeds up slightly.

'Like normal pills,' she replies quickly.

She feels suddenly uneasy. Why is he asking about the drugs? There's no reason for it. Maybe he's testing her? Her pulse-rate increases as she repeats to herself that it isn't a problem, because she's only telling the truth.

'Can you describe them?' he goes on calmly.

Saga opens her mouth to say that it was far too long ago, but all of a sudden she remembers the white pills among the long, brown strands of the shag-pile rug. She had knocked the jar over and was crawling around next to the bed, picking the pills up.

The memory is quite vivid.

She had gathered the pills in her cupped hand, and blew the fluff from the rug off them. In her hand she had been holding something like ten little round pills. On one side they bore the impression of two letters in a square.

'White, round,' she says. 'With letters on one side . . . KO . . . I've no idea why I remember that.'

## 121

Jurek turns the running machine off, then stands there smiling to himself for a long while as he catches his breath.

'You say you gave your mother cytostatic medication, chemotherapy . . . But you didn't . . .'

'Yes I did,' she says.

'The medicine you describe is codeine phosphate,' he says.

'Painkillers?' she asks.

'Yes, you don't prescribe codeine for cancer, only strong opiates, like morphine and Ketogan.'

'But I can remember the pills exactly . . . there was a groove on one side . . .'

'Yes,' he says bluntly.

'Mum said . . .'

She falls silent and her heart is beating so hard she's scared it shows on her face. Joona warned me, she thinks. He told me not to talk about my parents.

She gulps and looks down at the worn floor.

It doesn't matter, she thinks, and walks off towards her room.

It just happened, she said a bit too much, but she stuck to the truth the whole time.

She hadn't had a choice. Not answering his questions would have been far too evasive. It was a necessary exchange, but she isn't going to say any more now.

'Wait,' Jurek says, very gently.

She stops, but doesn't turn round.

'For all these years I haven't had a single chance to escape,' he goes on. 'I've known that the decision to sentence me to secure psychiatric care would never be reviewed, and I've realised I'm never going to get parole . . . but now that you're here, I can finally leave this hospital.'

Saga turns round and looks directly at the thin face, into his pale eyes.

'What could I possibly do?' she asks.

'It will take a few days to prepare everything,' he replies. 'But if you can get hold of some sleeping pills . . . I need five Stesolid tablets.'

'How can I get hold of them?'

'You stay awake, say you can't sleep, ask for ten milligrams of Stesolid, hide the pill, then go to bed.'

'Why don't you do it yourself?'

A smile breaks out on Jurek's cracked lips.

'They'd never give me anything I ask for, they're too frightened of me. But you're a siren . . . everyone sees how beautiful you are, not how dangerous.'

Saga thinks that this could be what it takes to win Jurek's confidence. She'll do as he says, join in with his plan, as long as it doesn't get too risky.

'You took the punishment for what I did, so I'll try to help you,' she replies quietly.

'But you don't want to come?'

'I've got nowhere to go.'

'You will have.'

'Tell me,' she asks, venturing a smile.

'The dayroom's closing now,' he says, and walks out.

She feels strangely out of kilter, as if he already knows everything about her, even before she tells him.

Of course it wasn't chemotherapy medication. She just assumed it was, without really thinking. You don't administer chemotherapy drugs like that; they have to be taken at strict intervals. The cancer was probably far too advanced. All that was left was pain relief.

When she gets back into her cell, it feels as if she's been holding her breath all the way through her encounter with Jurek Walter.

She lies down on the bunk, completely exhausted.

Saga thinks that she'll stay passive from now on, and let Jurek reveal his plans to the police.

## 122

It's only five to eight in the morning, but all the members of the Athena group are in place in the attic flat. Nathan Pollock has washed the mugs and left them upside down on a chequered blue tea-towel.

After the dayroom doors were locked yesterday they sat there analysing the wealth of material until seven o'clock in the evening. They listened to the conversation between Jurek Walter and Saga Bauer, structuring and evaluating the information.

'I'm worried that Saga's being too personal,' Corinne says, smiling as Nathan hands her a cup of coffee. 'Obviously it's a tightrope, because without volunteering something of herself she can't build up any trust . . .'

'She's in control of the situation,' Pollock says, opening his black notebook.

'Let's hope so,' Joona mutters.

'Saga's brilliant,' Johan Jönson says. 'She's getting him to talk.'

'But we still don't know anything about Jurek Walter,' Pollock says, tapping the table with a pen. 'Apart from the fact that his real name is different . . .'

'And that he wants to escape,' Corinne says, raising her eyebrows.

'Yes,' Joona says.

'But what's he got in mind? What does he want five sleeping pills for? Who's he going to drug?' Corinne asks with a frown.

'He can't drug the staff . . . because they're not allowed to take anything from him,' Pollock says.

'Let's allow Saga to carry on the way she is,' Corinne says after a brief pause.

'I don't like it,' Joona says.

He stands up and goes over to the window. It has started snowing again.

'Breakfast's the most important meal of the day,' Johan Jönson says, taking out a Dime bar.

'Before we move on,' Joona says, turning to face the room, 'I'd like to hear the recording one more time . . . the bit where Saga says she might not want to leave the hospital.'

'We've only listened to it thirty-five times so far,' Corinne sighs.

'I know, but I've got a feeling we're missing something,' he explains, in a voice made sharp by conviction. 'We haven't talked about it, but what's actually going on? To begin with, Jurek sounds the same as usual when he says there are better places than the secure unit . . . but when Saga replies that there are probably worse places, she manages to get him off balance.'

'Maybe,' Corinne says, looking down.

'No maybe about it,' Joona insists. 'I've spent hours talking to Jurek, and I can hear that his voice changes, it becomes reflective, but only for a few moments, when he's describing the place with the red clay . . .'

'And the high-voltage electricity wires and big diggers,' Pollock says.

'I know there's something there,' Joona says. 'Not just the

fact that Jurek seems to surprise himself when he starts talking about a genuine fragment of memory . . .'

'But it doesn't go anywhere,' Corinne interrupts.

'I want to listen to the recording again,' Joona says, turning towards Johan Jönson.

## 123

Johan Jönson leans forward and moves the cursor on the screen across the sequence of sound-waves. The speakers crackle and hiss, then the rhythmic sound of footsteps on the running machine become audible.

'We can get out of the hospital together,' Jurek says.

There's a knocking, then a rustling noise that gets gradually louder.

'I don't know if I want to,' Saga replies.

'Why not?'

'I haven't really got anything left outside.'

They can hear laughter on the television in the background.

'Left? Going back is never an option . . . not to anything, but there are better places than this.'

'And probably some worse,' Saga says.

More knocking, then a sigh.

'What did you say?' she asks.

'I just sighed, because it occurred to me that I can actually remember a worse place . . .'

His voice is oddly soft and hesitant as he continues:

'The air was filled with the hum from high-voltage electricity wires . . . the roads were wrecked by big diggers . . . and the tracks full of red, clayey water, up to your waist . . . but I could still open my mouth and breathe.'

'What do you mean?' Saga says.

Applause and more laughter from the television.

'That worse places might be preferable to better ones,' Jurek replies, almost inaudibly.

The sound of breathing and heavy footsteps merge with a whining, hissing noise.

'You're thinking about your childhood?' Saga Bauer says.

'I suppose so,' Jurek whispers.

They sit in total silence as Johan Jönson stops the recording and looks at Joona with a frown.

'We're not going to get any further with this,' Pollock says.

'What if Jurek's saying something that we're not getting,' Joona persists, pointing at the screen. 'There's a gap here, isn't there? Just after Saga says there are worse places outside the hospital.'

'He sighs,' Pollock says.

'Jurek says he sighs, but are we sure that's what he does?' Joona asks.

Johan Jönson scratches his stomach, moves the cursor back, raises the volume and plays the segment again.

'I need a cigarette,' Corinne says, picking up her shiny handbag from the floor.

The speakers hiss, and there's a loud creaking sound followed by an exhaled sigh.

'What did I say?' Pollock says, smiling broadly.

'Try playing it slower,' Joona insists.

Pollock is drumming nervously on the table. The clip plays again at half-speed, and now the sigh sounds like a storm sweeping ashore.

'He's sighing,' Corinne says.

'Yes, but there's something about the pause, and the tone of his voice afterwards,' Joona says.

'Tell me what I should be looking for,' Johan Jönson says, frustrated.

'I don't know . . . I want you to imagine that he's actually saying something . . . even if it isn't audible,' Joona replies, smiling at his own answer.

'I can certainly try.'

'Isn't it possible to raise and lower the sound until we know for certain if there's anything in that silence or not?'

'If I increase the sound pressure and intensity a few hundred times, the footsteps on the running machine would burst our eardrums.'

'So get rid of the footsteps.'

Johan Jönson shrugs and makes a loop of that segment, stretches it out and then divides the sound into thirty different curves, ordered by hertz and decibels. Puffing his cheeks out, he highlights some of the curves and gets rid of them.

Each removed curve appears on a smaller screen instead.

Corinne and Pollock get up. They go outside onto the balcony and freeze for a while as they gaze out across the rooftops and the Philadelphia Church.

Joona remains seated and watches the painstaking work.

After thirty-five minutes Johan Jönson leans back and listens to the cleaned-up loop at various speeds, then removes another three curves and plays the result.

What's left sounds like a heavy stone being dragged across a concrete floor.

'Jurek Walter sighs,' Johan Jönson declares, and stops the playback.

'Shouldn't those be lined up as well?' Joona says, pointing to three of the removed curves on the smaller screen.

'No, that's just an echo that I removed,' Johan says, then looks suddenly thoughtful. 'But I could actually try to remove everything except the echo.'

'He could have been facing the wall,' Joona says quickly.

Johan Jönson highlights and moves the curves of the echo back again, multiplies the sound pressure and intensity by three hundred and replays the loop. Now the dragging sound resembles a shaky exhalation as it's repeated at just under normal speed.

'Isn't there something there?' Joona asks with renewed concentration.

'There could be,' Johan Jönson whispers.

'I can't hear it,' Corinne says.

'Well, it doesn't sound like a sigh now,' Johan Jönson admits. 'But we can't do any more to it, because at this level the longitudinal soundwaves start to blur with the transversal . . . and because they're running at different rates, they'll only cancel each other out.'

'Try anyway,' Joona says impatiently.

## 124

Johan Jönson presses his lips together in a way that makes him look like August Strindberg as he surveys the fifteen different curves.

'You're not really supposed to do this,' he mutters.

With fingertip precision he adjusts the timing of the curves and extends some of the peaks to longer plateaux.

He tries replaying the loop, and the room is filled with strange, underwater sounds. Corinne stands with her hand over her mouth as Jönson stops it, makes some more adjustments, pulls certain sections further apart, then plays it again.

Sweat has broken out on Nathan Pollock's forehead.

There's a deep rumble from within the loudspeakers, followed by a long exhalation divided into indistinct syllables.

'Listen,' Joona says.

What they can hear is a slow sigh that's been unconsciously formed out of a thought. Jurek Walter isn't using his larynx, just moving his lips and tongue as he breathes out.

Johan Jönson moves one of the curves slightly, then gets up from his chair with a grin as the loop of the whisper repeats over and over again.

'What's he saying?' Pollock says in a tense voice. 'It sounds a bit like Lenin?'

'Leninsk,' Corinne says, wide-eyed.

'What?' Pollock says, almost shouting.

'There's a city called Leninsk-Kuznetsky,' she says. 'But because he was just talking about red clay, I think he means the secret city.'

'A secret city?' Pollock mutters.

'The cosmodrome at Baikonur is well-known,' she explains. 'But fifty years ago the town was called Leninsk, and it was top secret.'

'Leninsk in Kazakhstan,' Joona says quietly. 'Jurek has a childhood memory from Leninsk . . .'

Corinne sits down at the table, her back straight, tucks her hair behind her ear and explains:

'Kazakhstan was part of the Soviet Union in those days . . . and it was so sparsely populated that they could build an entire town without the rest of the world noticing anything. There was an arms race going on, and they needed research bases and launch sites for rockets.'

'Kazakhstan is a member of Interpol,' Pollock says.

'If they can give us Jurek Walter's real name, we can start to uncover his background,' Joona says. 'Then the hunt would really be on . . .'

'It shouldn't be impossible,' Corinne says. 'I mean . . . now we have a location and an approximate time for his birth. We know he arrived in Sweden in 1994. We've got pictures of him, we've documented the scars on his body and . . .'

'We even have his DNA and blood type,' Pollock smiles.

'So either Jurek's family belonged to the local Kazakhstan population, or they were among the scientists, engineers and military who were sent there from Russia . . .'

'I'll put everything together,' Pollock says quickly.

'I'll try to get hold of the NSC in Kazakhstan,' Corinne says. 'Joona? Do you want me to . . .?'

She falls silent and gives him a quizzical look. Joona stands up slowly, meets her gaze and nods, picks up his coat from a chair and starts walking towards the hall.

'Where are you going?' Pollock asks.

'I need to talk to Susanne Hjälm,' Joona mutters, and keeps walking.

# 125

When Corinne was talking about the scientists who were sent to the test facility in Kazakhstan, Joona was suddenly reminded of his conversation with Susanne Hjälm in the police car. Just before her daughter started shouting from the ambulance, he had asked if Susanne could remember the address on Jurek's letter.

She had said it was a PO box address, and was trying to remember the name when she said it wasn't Russian.

Why had she said the name wasn't Russian?

Joona shows his ID to the guard and explains who he wants to see. They walk through the women's section of Kronoberg Prison together.

The well-built guard stops outside a thick metal door. Joona looks in through the window. Susanne Hjälm is sitting motionless, eyes closed. Her lips are moving, as if she is praying under her breath.

When the guard unlocks the door she starts and opens her eyes. She begins rocking her upper body when she sees Joona come in. Her broken arm has been fixed up, and the other is wrapped round her waist, as though she were trying to hug herself.

'I need to talk to you about—'

'Who's going to protect my girls?' she asks desperately.

'They're with their father now,' Joona tells her, looking into her anguished eyes.

'No, no . . . he doesn't understand, he doesn't know . . . no one knows, you have to do something, you can't just leave them.'

'Did you read the letter Jurek gave you?' Joona asks.

'Yes,' she whispers. 'I did.'

'Was it addressed to a lawyer?'

She looks at him, and starts to breathe more calmly.

'Yes.'

Joona sits down beside her on the bunk.

'Why didn't you post it?' he asks quietly.

'Because I didn't want him to get out,' she says, sounding distraught. 'I didn't want to give him the slightest chance. You could never understand, no one could.'

'It was me who arrested him, but—'

'Everyone hates me,' she goes on without listening. 'I hate myself, I couldn't see anything, I didn't mean to hurt that police officer, but you shouldn't have been there, you shouldn't have been trying to find me, you should—'

'Do you remember the address on the letter?' Joona interrupts.

'I burned it, I thought it would end if I did, I don't know what I thought.'

'Did he want it sent to a law firm?'

Susanne Hjälm's body is shaking violently, and her sweaty hair hits her forehead and cheeks.

'When can I see my children?' she wails. 'I have to tell them I did everything for them, even if they never understand, even if they hate me—'

'Rosenhane Legal Services?'

She looks at him, wild-eyed, as if she'd already forgotten he was there.

'Yes, that was it,' she slurs.

'When I asked you before, you said the name wasn't Russian,' Joona says. 'Why would it have been Russian?'

'Because Jurek spoke Russian to me once . . .'

'What did he say?'

'I can't bear it any more, I can't bear it . . .'

'Are you sure he was talking Russian?'

'He said such terrible things . . .'

## 126

Susanne stands up on the bed, beside herself, and turns to face the wall as she sobs, trying to hide her face with her one good hand.

'Please, sit down,' Joona says gently.

'He mustn't, he mustn't . . .'

'You shut your family away in your cellar because you were frightened of Jurek.'

Susanne looks at him, then starts pacing up and down on the bed again.

'No one would listen to me, but I know he speaks the truth . . . I've felt his fire on my face . . .'

'I would have done the same as you,' Joona says seriously. 'If I believed I could protect my family from Jurek that way, I would have done the same thing.'

She stops with a curious look in her eyes, and wipes her mouth.

'I was supposed to give Jurek an injection of Zypadhera. He'd been given a sedative and was lying on his bed . . . he couldn't move. Sven Hoffman opened the door, I went in and gave Jurek the injection in his buttock . . . As I was putting a plaster on it, I simply explained that I didn't want anything to do with his letter, I wasn't going to send it, I didn't say I'd already burned it, I just said . . .'

She falls silent and tries to pull herself together before continuing. She holds her hand to her mouth for a while, then lets it fall:

'Jurek opened his eyes and looked straight at me, and started to speak Russian . . . I don't know if he knew I could understand, I'd never told him I once lived in St Petersburg.'

She breaks off and lowers her head.

'What did he say?'

'He promised to cut Ellen and little Anja open . . . and let me choose which one would bleed to death,' she says, then smiles to stop herself going to pieces. 'Patients can say the most terrible things, you have to put up with all sorts of threats, but it was different with Jurek.'

'Are you sure he was speaking Russian, not Kazakh?'

'Jurek Walter spoke an unusually refined Russian, as if he were a professor at Lomonosov.'

'You told him you didn't want anything to do with his letter,' Joona says. 'Were there any other letters?'

'Only the one he replied to.'

'So he received a letter first?' Joona asks.

'It was addressed to me . . . from a lawyer who was offering to review his rights and options.'

'And you gave it to Jurek?'

'I don't know why, I suppose I was thinking that it was a human right, but he isn't . . .'

She starts crying and takes a few steps back on the soft mattress.

'Try to remember what—'

'I want my children, I can't bear it,' she whimpers, pacing on the bed again. 'He's going to hurt them.'

'You know that Jurek is locked up in the secure . . .'

'Only when he wants to be,' she interrupts, and stumbles. 'He fools everyone, he can get in and out . . .'

'That's not true, Susanne,' Joona says gently. 'Jurek Walter hasn't left the secure unit once in thirteen years.'

She looks at him, then says through white, cracked lips:

'You don't know anything.'

For a moment it looks as though she's going to start laughing.

'Do you?' she says. 'You really don't know anything.'

She blinks her dry eyes and her hand is shaking violently as she raises it to brush her hair from her face.

'I saw him in the car park in front of the hospital,' she says quietly. 'He was just standing there, looking at me.'

The bed creaks under her feet and she puts her hand out to steady herself against the wall. Joona tries to calm her down:

'I appreciate that his threats were—'

'You're so stupid,' she yells. 'I've seen your name written on the glass . . .'

She takes a step forward, slips off the bed, hits her neck on the edge of the bed and collapses in a heap on the floor.

## 127

Corinne Meilleroux puts her phone down on the table and shakes her head, sending a waft of expensive perfume all the way over to Pollock.

He's been sitting there waiting for her to conclude the call, and has been thinking of asking if she'd like to have dinner with him one evening.

'I'm not getting a sausage,' she says.

'A sausage,' he repeats with a wry smile.

'Isn't that what you say?'

'It's not too common these days, but . . .'

'I spoke to an Anton Takirov at Kazakhstan's security police, the NSC,' she says. 'It only took a second. He told me that Jurek Walter isn't a Kazakh citizen quicker than I can open my laptop. I was very polite and asked them to conduct a new search, but this Takirov just seemed insulted and said that they did actually have computers in Kazakhstan.'

'Maybe he's not good at talking to women.'

'When I tried to tell Mr Takirov that DNA matching can take a bit of time, he interrupted me and explained that they had the most modern system in the world.'

'So basically they don't want to help.'

'In contrast to the federal security service of the Russian Federation. We have a good relationship with them these days. Dmitry Urgov just called me back. They've got nothing that matches what I sent them, but he said he'd personally ask the national police to look through the pictures and check their DNA register . . .'

Corinne closes her eyes and massages her neck. Pollock looks at her, trying to suppress the urge to offer to help. He'd be more than happy to stand behind her, gently softening up the muscles in her back.

'I've got warm hands,' Pollock says just as Joona Linna comes in.

'Can I feel?' he asks in his deep Finnish accent.

'Kazakhstan aren't making things easy for us,' Corinne tells him. 'But I—'

'Jurek Walter comes from Russia,' Joona says, taking a handful of sweets from a bowl.

'Russia,' she repeats blankly.

'He speaks perfect Russian.'

'Would Dmitry Urgov have lied to me . . .? Sorry, but I know him, and I really don't believe that . . .'

'He probably doesn't know anything,' Joona says, putting the sweets in his pocket. 'Jurek Walter's so old that it must have been in the days of the KGB.'

## 128

Pollock, Joona and Corinne are leaning over the table, summarising the situation. Not long ago they didn't have anything. Now, thanks to Saga's infiltration, they have a location. Jurek Walter let slip something when he whispered 'Leninsk'. He grew up in Kazakhstan, but because Susanne Hjälm heard him talking educated Russian, it seems highly likely that his family came from Russia.

'But the security police there didn't know anything,' Corinne repeats.

Joona takes out his phone and starts looking for a contact he hasn't called for years. He can feel himself getting excited as he realises he might finally be on the trail of the mystery of Jurek Walter.

'What are you doing?' Corinne asks.

'I'm going to talk to an old acquaintance.'

'You're calling Nikita Karpin!' Pollock exclaims. 'Aren't you?'

Joona moves away, holding the mobile to his ear. The phone rings with a hissing echo, and a fair while later there's a crackle.

'Didn't I thank you for your help with Pichushkin?' Karpin asks abruptly.

'Yes, you sent some little bars of soap—'

'Isn't that enough?' he interrupts. 'You're the most persistent young man I ever met, so I might have guessed you'd phone and disturb me.'

'We're working on a very complex case here, which—'

'I never talk on the phone,' Nikita interrupts.

'What if I organise an encrypted line?'

'There's nothing we couldn't crack in twenty seconds,' the Russian laughs. 'But that's beside the point . . . I'm out of it now, I can't help you.'

'But you must have contacts?' Joona tries.

'There's no one left . . . and they don't know anything about Leninsk, and if they did they wouldn't say so.'

'You already knew what I was going to ask,' Joona sighs.

'Of course. It's a small country.'

'Who should I talk to if I need an answer?'

'Try the dear old FSB in a month or so . . . I'm sorry,' Karpin yawns. 'But I have to take Zean out for his walk, we usually go down the Klyazma, on the ice, as far as the bathing jetties.'

'I see,' Joona says.

He ends the call, and smiles at the old man's exaggerated caution. The former KGB agent doesn't seem to trust that Russia has changed. Maybe he's got a point. Maybe the rest of the world has simply been tricked into thinking that things are moving in the right direction.

It wasn't exactly a formal offer, but coming from Nikita Karpin it was almost a generous invitation.

Nikita's old Samoyed dog Zean died when Joona was visiting eight years ago. He had been invited to give three lectures on the work that led to Jurek Walter's capture. At the time the Moscow police were in the middle of the hunt for serial killer Alexander Pichushkin.

Nikita Karpin knows that Joona knows the dog is dead. And he knows that Joona knows where to find him if he goes for a walk on the ice on the Klyazma River.

## 129

It's ten to seven in the evening, and Joona Linna is sitting on the last flight to Moscow. By the time the plane lands in Russia it's gone midnight. The country is in the grip of a crisp chill, and the low temperature makes the snow quite dry.

Joona is being driven through the vast, monotonous suburbs in a taxi. It feels as though he's caught in a loop of sprawling municipal housing estates when the city finally changes. He manages to catch a glimpse of one of Stalin's seven sisters – the beautiful skyscrapers – before the taxi turns into a back street and stops outside the hotel.

His room is very basic and dimly lit. The ceiling is high, and the walls are yellow with cigarette smoke. On the desk is an electric brown plastic samovar. The fire-escape notice on the back of the door has a circular scorch-mark over the emergency exit.

As Joona stands at the only window looking down at the alley, he can feel the winter chill through the glass. He lies back on the rough brown bedspread, gazes up at the ceiling and can hear muffled voices laughing and talking in the next room. He thinks it's too late to call Disa and say goodnight.

Thoughts are swirling through his mind, and their images carry him into sleep. A girl waiting for her mother to plait her hair, Saga Bauer looking at him with her head covered in cuts, and Disa lying in his bath humming with her eyes half-closed.

At half past five in the morning Joona's mobile starts to vibrate on the bedside table. He slept in his clothes, with all the blankets and covers on top of him. The tip of his nose is frozen and he has to blow on his fingers before he can switch the alarm off.

Through the window the sky is still dark.

Joona goes down to the foyer and asks the young woman in reception to hire a car for him. He sits at one of the ornately laid tables, drinks tea and eats warm bread with melted butter and thick slices of cheese.

An hour later he is driving a brand-new BMW X3 on the M2 motorway out of Moscow. Shiny black tarmac rushes under the car. There's heavy traffic through Vidnoye and it's already eight o'clock when he leaves the motorway and turns off onto winding, white roads.

The trunks of the birch trees look like skinny young angels in the snow-covered landscape. Russia is so beautiful, it's almost frightening.

It's cold and clear, and Ljubimovka is bathed in wintery sunshine when Joona turns off and pulls up in a cleared yard in front of the house. He was once told the place used to be Russian theatre legend Stanislavsky's summer residence.

Nikita Karpin comes out onto the veranda.

'You remembered my grubby old dog,' he smiles, shaking hands with Joona.

Nikita Karpin is a short, stout man with an attractively

aged face, a steely gaze and a military haircut. When he was an agent, he was a frightening man.

Nikita Karpin is no longer formally a member of the security services, but he's still employed by the Ministry of Justice. Joona knows that if anyone can find out whether Jurek Walter has any connection to Russia, it's Karpin.

'We share an interest in serial killers,' Nikita says, showing Joona in. 'For my part, they can be seen as empty wells that can be filled with unsolved crimes . . . which of course is very practical. But on the other hand we have to arrest them so as not to appear incompetent, which makes the whole business much more complicated . . .'

Joona follows Karpin into a large, beautiful room whose interior seems to have remained untouched since the turn of the last century.

The old medallion wallpaper shimmers like thick cream. A framed portrait of Stanislavsky hangs above a black grand piano.

The agent pours a drink from a misty glass jug. On the table is a grey cardboard box.

'Elderflower cordial,' he says, patting his liver.

As Joona takes the glass and they sit down facing each other, Nikita's face changes. His friendly smile vanishes as though it had never existed.

'The last time we met . . . most things were still secret, but in those days I was in charge of a specially trained group that went by the name of the Little Stick, in direct translation,' Nikita says in a low voice. 'We were fairly heavy-handed . . . both my men and I . . .'

He leans back in his chair, making it creak.

'Maybe I'll burn in hell for that?' he says seriously. 'Unless there's an angel who protects people who defend the mother-land.'

Nikita's veined hands are lying on the table between the grey box and the jug of cordial.

'I wanted to come down harder on the Chechen terrorists,' he goes on gravely. 'I'm proud of our actions in Beslan, and in my opinion Anna Politkovskaya was a traitor.'

He puts his glass down and takes a deep breath.

'I've looked at the material that your Security Police sent to the FSB . . . you haven't managed to find out very much, Joona Linna.'

'No,' Joona says patiently.

'We used to call the young engineers and workmen who were sent to the cosmodrome in Leninsk rocket fuel.'

'Rocket fuel?'

'Everything surrounding the space programme had to be kept secret. All reports were carefully encrypted. The intention was that engineers would never come back from there. They were the best educated scientists of their day, but they were treated like cattle.'

The KGB agent falls silent. Joona raises his glass and drinks.

'My grandmother taught me how to make elderflower cordial.'

'It's very good.'

'You did the right thing, coming to me, of course, Joona Linna,' Nikita Karpin says, wiping his mouth. 'I've borrowed a file from the Little Stick's own archives.'

## 130

The old man pulls a grey file out of the equally grey cardboard box, opens it and puts a photograph on the table in front of Joona. It's a group picture of twenty-two men standing in front of some polished stone steps.

'This was taken in Leninsk in 1955,' Karpin says in a different tone of voice.

In the middle of the front row sits the legendary Sergei Korolev, smiling calmly on one of the benches, the chief engineer behind the first man in space and the world's first satellite.

'Look at the men at the back.'

Joona leans forward and looks along the row of faces. Half-hidden behind a man with tousled hair stands a skinny man with a thin face and pale eyes.

Joona jerks his head back as if he'd just smelled ammonia.

He's found Jurek Walter's father.

'I see him,' Joona says.

'Stalin's administration picked out the youngest and most talented engineers,' Nikita says calmly, tossing an old Soviet passport in front of Joona. 'And Vadim Levanov was without doubt one of the best.'

As he opens the passport, Joona feels his pulse quicken.

The black-and-white photograph features a man resembling Jurek Walter, but with warmer eyes and without all the wrinkles in his face. So, Jurek Walter's father's name was Vadim Levanov, Joona thinks.

His journey here hasn't been in vain. Now they can start to investigate Jurek Walter's past properly.

Nikita lays out a set of ten fingerprints, some small private photographs of Jurek's father's christening and schooldays, junior schoolbooks and a child's drawing of a car with a chimney on its roof.

'What do you want to know about him?' Karpin smiles. 'We've got most things . . . every address he ever lived at, names of girlfriends before his marriage to Elena Mishailova, letter home to his parents in Novosibirsk, the time when he was active in the party . . .'

'His son,' Joona whispers.

'His wife was also an engineer, but she died in childbirth when they'd been married two years,' Karpin goes on.

'The son,' Joona repeats.

Karpin stands up, opens the wooden cupboard, gets out a heavy case and puts it on the table. When he lifts the lid, Joona sees that it's a film-projector for 16-millimetre film.

Nikita Karpin asks Joona to close the curtains, then takes a reel of film from his grey box.

'This is a private film from Leninsk that I think you should see . . .'

The projector starts to click, and the image is projected directly onto the medallion wallpaper. Karpin adjusts the focus, then sits down again.

The saturation of the image varies, but otherwise it's fine. The camera must have been on a stand.

Joona realises that he's looking at a film taken by Jurek Walter's father during his time in Leninsk.

The image on the wall in front of him shows the back of a house and a verdant garden. Sunlight filters through the leaves and above the trees in the background he can make out an electricity pylon.

The image shakes a little, then Jurek's father comes into view. He puts a heavy case down in the long grass, opens it and gets out four camping chairs. A boy with neatly combed hair enters the frame from the left. He looks about seven years old and has chiselled features and big, pale eyes.

There's no doubt that it's Jurek, Joona thinks, hardly daring to breathe.

The boy says something, but all that can be heard is the clicking of the projector.

Father and son help each other unfold the metal legs of the case, which transforms into a wooden-topped table when they turn it over.

Young Jurek disappears from view, but returns with a jug of water from the opposite direction. It happens so quickly that Joona thinks there must have been some trick.

Jurek bites his lips and clasps his hands tight as his father speaks to him.

He disappears from view again, and his father strides after him.

The water in the jug sparkles in the sunlight.

A short while later Jurek returns with a white paper bag, and then his father comes back with another child on his shoulders.

The father is shaking his head and trotting like a horse.

Joona can't see the other child's face.

The child's head is out of frame, but Jurek waves up at it.

Feet with small shoes on kick at the father's chest.

Jurek calls out something.

And when his father puts the second child down on the grass in front of the table Joona sees that it too is Jurek.

The identical boy stares into the camera with a serious face. A shadow sweeps across the garden. The father takes the paper bag and disappears out of the picture.

'Identical twins,' the agent smiles, stopping the projector.

'Twins,' Joona repeats.

'That was why their mother died.'

## 131

Joona is staring straight at the medallion wallpaper, and repeating silently to himself that the Sandman is Jurek Walter's twin brother.

That's who's holding Felicia captive.

That was who Lumi saw in the garden when she was going to wave at the cat.

And that was why Susanne Hjälm was able to see Jurek Walter in the darkness of the car park outside the hospital.

The warm projector is making small clicking sounds.

Taking his glass with him, Joona gets to his feet and goes over to open the curtains, then stands at the window gazing out at the ice-covered surface of the Klyazma River.

'How were you able to find all this?' he asks when he's confident his voice won't crack. 'How many files and films did you have to go through? I mean, you must have material covering millions of people.'

'Yes, but we only had one defector from Leninsk to Sweden,' Karpin replies calmly.

'Their father fled to Sweden?'

'August 1957 was a difficult month in Leninsk,' Nikita replies cryptically, lighting a cigarette.

'What happened?'

'We made two attempts to launch Semyorka. The first time the auxiliary rocket caught fire and the missile crashed four hundred kilometres away. The second time – the same fiasco. I was sent down there to remove the people responsible. Give them a taste of the little stick. Don't forget that no less than five per cent of the entire GDP of the Soviet Union went to the installation at Leninsk. The third launch attempt succeeded and the engineers could breathe out, until the Nedelin disaster three years later.'

'I've read about that,' Joona says.

'Mitrofan Nedelin rushed the development of an intercontinental rocket,' Nikita says, looking at the glowing tip of his cigarette. 'It exploded in the middle of the cosmodrome, and more than a hundred people were burned to death. Vadim Levanov and the twins were unaccounted for. For months we thought they'd been killed along with everyone else.'

'But they hadn't,' Joona says.

'No,' Nikita says. 'He fled because he was afraid of reprisals, and he would certainly have ended up in the gulag, probably the Siblag work camp . . . but instead he turned up in Sweden.'

Nikita Karpin falls silent and slowly stubs his cigarette out on a small porcelain saucer.

'We kept Vadim Levanov and the twins under constant surveillance, and obviously we were prepared to liquidate him,' Karpin goes on quietly. 'But we didn't need to . . . because Sweden treated him like garbage, and arranged a special gulag for him . . . The only work he could get was as a manual labourer in a gravel quarry.'

Nikita Karpin's eyes flash cruelly.

'If you'd shown any interest in what he knew, Sweden could have been first into space,' he laughs.

'Maybe,' Joona replies calmly.

'Yes.'

'So Jurek and his brother arrived in Sweden at the age of ten or so?'

'But they only stayed a couple of years,' Nikita smiles.

'Why?'

'You don't become a serial killer for no reason.'

'Do you know what happened?' Joona asks.

'Yes.'

Nikita Karpin gazes out of the window and wets his lips. The low winter light is shining in through the uneven glass.

## 132

Today Saga is first into the dayroom, and immediately gets onto the running machine. She manages to run for four minutes, and has just lowered the speed and started to walk when Bernie comes in from his room.

'I'm going to start driving a taxi when I'm free . . . Bloody hell, like some fucking Fittipaldi . . . and you can ride for free, and I'll get to touch you between—'

'Just shut up,' she cuts him off.

He nods, looking wounded, then walks straight over to the palm leaf, turns it over and points at the microphone with a thin grin.

'Now you're my slave,' he laughs.

Saga jabs him hard, making him stumble back and sit down on the floor.

'I want to escape as well,' he hisses. 'I want to drive a taxi and—'

'Shut up,' Saga says, checking over her shoulder to see if the guards are on their way in through the airlock.

But no one seems to be watching them on the monitor in the security control room.

'You're going to take me with you when you escape, do you hear—'

'Shut up,' Jurek interrupts behind them.

'Sorry,' Bernie whispers quietly at the floor.

Saga didn't hear Jurek come into the dayroom. A shiver runs down her spine when she realises that he may have seen the microphone under the palm leaf.

Maybe her cover is already blown?

Maybe it's going to happen now, she thinks. The crisis she's been dreading is happening now. She feels adrenalin rushing through her, and tries to visualise the plan of the secure unit. In her thoughts she moves quickly through the marked doors, the different zones, the best places to take temporary shelter.

If Bernie blows her cover, she'll have to barricade herself in her room to start with. Ideally she needs to get hold of the microphone and shout for immediate backup, get them to come and rescue her.

Jurek stops in front of Bernie, who's lying on the floor whispering his apologies.

'You're to pull the lead off the running machine, then go to your room and hang yourself from the top of your door,' Jurek tells him.

Bernie looks up at Jurek with fear in his eyes.

'What? What the fuck . . .?'

'Tie the lead to the handle on the outside, throw it over the door and pull your plastic chair over,' Jurek explains curtly.

'I don't want to, I don't want to,' Bernie says, his lips trembling.

'We can't have you alive any longer,' Jurek says calmly.

'But . . . what the fuck, I was only joking, I know very well that I can't come with you . . . I know it's just your thing . . . just your thing . . .'

# 133

Nathan Pollock and Corinne Meilleroux both stand up from the table when the situation in the dayroom becomes more acute.

They realise that Jurek has decided to execute Bernie, and are hoping that Saga won't forget that she has no police responsibilities or rights.

'There's nothing we can do,' Corinne whispers.

Slow, thunderous rumbling sounds emerge from the speakers. Johan Jönson adjusts the sound levels and scratches his head anxiously.

'Give me a punishment instead,' Bernie whimpers. 'I deserve a punishment . . .'

'I can break both his legs,' Saga says.

Corinne wraps her arms round herself and is trying to control her breathing.

'Don't do anything,' Pollock whispers to the speaker. 'You have to trust the guards, you're only a patient.'

'Why hasn't anyone come in?' Johan Jönson says. 'The guards must have noticed what's going on, for God's sake?'

'If she acts, Jurek will kill her at once,' Corinne whispers, the stress making her French accent come to the fore.

'Don't do anything,' Pollock pleads. 'Don't do anything!'

## 134

Saga's heart is pounding in her chest. She can't make any sense of her thoughts as she gets off the running machine. It's not her job to protect other patients. She knows she mustn't step out of her role as a schizophrenic patient.

'I can break his kneecaps,' she tries. 'I can break his arms and fingers and—'

'It would be better if he just died,' Jurek concludes.

'Come on,' she says quickly to Bernie. 'The camera's hidden here—'

'Snow White, what the fuck?' Bernie snivels, moving closer to her.

She grabs hold of his wrist, pulls him closer and breaks his little finger. He screams and sinks to his knees, clutching his hand to his stomach.

'Next finger,' she says.

'You're both mad,' Bernie sobs. 'I'll call for help . . . my skeleton slaves will come . . .'

'Be quiet,' Jurek says.

He walks over to the running machine and removes the lead, yanking it out from the skirting board, sending a shower of concrete dust over the floor.

'Next finger,' Saga tries.

'Just stand back,' Jurek says, looking her in the eye.

Saga remains where she is, with one hand against the wall, as Bernie follows Jurek.

The situation feels absurd as she watches Jurek tie the lead round the handle on the side of the door facing the dayroom and throw it over the top of the door.

She feels like shouting out.

Bernie looks at her beseechingly as he climbs onto the plastic chair and puts the noose round his neck.

He tries to talk to Jurek, smiling and repeating something.

She stands there, immobile, thinking that the staff must surely see them now. But no guards come. Jurek has been in the unit for so long that he's learned their routines by heart. Maybe he knows that this is when they have a coffee break, or change shifts.

Saga moves slowly towards her own room. She doesn't know what she's going to do, can't understand why no one's come in.

Jurek says something to Bernie, waits a while, repeats the words, but Bernie is shaking his head as tears spring to his eyes.

Saga keeps walking backwards with her heart pounding. A sense of unreality is spreading through her body.

Jurek kicks the chair away, then walks through the dayroom straight into his own room.

Bernie is dangling in the air, with his feet only just off the floor, trying to pull himself up with the lead, but he isn't strong enough.

Saga goes into her room, walks over to the door and its reinforced glass window. She kicks at it as hard as she can, but all she can hear is a muffled thud from the metal. She pulls back, turns and kicks again, backs up and kicks, then kicks again. The solid door vibrates slightly, but the heavy sound of her kicks carries into the concrete walls. She goes on kicking, until finally she hears agitated voices in the corridor, followed by rapid footsteps and the whirr of the electric lock.

## 135

The lights in the ceiling go out. Saga is lying on her side in bed, with her eyes open.

God, what should I have done? She's burning up with anguish.

Her feet, ankles and knees ache from the kicks.

She doesn't know if she could have saved Bernie by intervening. Maybe she could have, maybe Jurek wouldn't have been able to stop her.

But there was no doubt that she would have exposed herself to danger and ruined any chance of saving Felicia.

So she went into her room and kicked at the door. Which had been desperate and pathetic, she thinks.

She kicked on the door as hard as she could, hoping that the guards would wonder where the noise was coming from and finally glance at their monitors.

But nothing happened. They didn't hear her. She should have kicked harder.

It felt like an eternity before any voices and footsteps approached.

She's lying on her bed and trying to tell herself that the

staff got there in time, that Bernie is now in intensive care, that his condition is stable.

The outcome depends on how tightly the noose squeezed the arteries in his neck.

She's thinking that Jurek might have tied a bad noose, even though she knows that wasn't the case.

Since Saga returned to her room all she's done is lie on her bed, feeling frozen. Dinner was dished out by the girl with the piercings, but she's only eaten the peas and two mouthfuls of potato from the fish gratin.

Saga lies in the darkness thinking about Bernie's face as he shook his head with a look of total helplessness in his eyes. Jurek moved like a shadow. He conducted the execution dispassionately, simply doing what he had to, kicking the chair away and then walking to his room without hurrying.

Saga switches on the lamp by her bed, then sits up and puts her feet on the floor. She turns her face towards the CCTV camera in the ceiling, towards its black eye, and waits.

As usual, Joona was right, she thinks as she stares at the camera's round lens. He thought there was a chance that Jurek would approach her.

He had actually started talking to her in such a personal way that even Joona ought to be surprised.

Saga thinks of how she broke the rule about not talking about her parents, her family. She just hopes that the officers listening don't think she lost control of the situation. She persuades herself it was an attempt to deepen the conversation,. She was perfectly aware of what she was doing when she told serial killer Jurek Walter about one of the most difficult periods of her life.

She's never forgotten what Jurek Walter has done, but she hasn't felt threatened by him. That's probably benefitted the infiltration, she thinks. She's been more scared of Bernie. Up until the moment when Jurek hanged him with the lead.

Saga massages her neck with her hand, and goes on staring at the eye of the camera. She must have been sitting like that for over an hour now.

## 136

Anders Rönn has logged in and is sitting in his room trying to summarise the day's events in the unit journal.

Why is everything happening now?

The same day every month the staff go through the medicine store and other perishable goods.

It takes no longer than forty minutes.

He, My and Leif were outside the medicine store when they suddenly heard the noise.

Deep rumbling, echoing within the walls. My dropped the inventory list on the floor and ran to the surveillance control room. Anders followed her. My reached the large monitor and cried out when she saw the image from patient room 2. Bernie was hanging lifeless against the door to the dayroom. Urine was dripping from his toes, forming a puddle beneath him.

Anders's skin is still crawling. As a result of the suicide in the ward he was summoned to a crisis meeting of the hospital committee. The hospital manager came straight from a children's party, annoyed to have been called away in the middle of a game. The manager had looked at him and said that perhaps it had been a mistake to allow an inexperienced doctor to assume the role of senior consultant. His round face with its deeply dimpled chin quivered.

Anders gulps and blushes when he recalls how he stood up and apologised, stammering and trying to explain that, according to his medical notes, Bernie Larsson had been extremely depressed, and that he had found the transfer difficult.

'Are you still here?'

He starts and looks up to see My standing in the doorway, smiling wearily at him.

'The hospital management want the report first thing tomorrow morning, so you're probably going to have to put up with me for a few more hours.'

'Tough shit,' she says with a yawn.

'You can go and lie down in the rest-room if you like,' he says.

'Don't worry.'

'I mean it. After all, I have to be here anyway.'

'Are you sure? That's really sweet of you.'

He smiles at her.

'Get a couple of hours' sleep. I'll wake you when I'm ready to leave.'

Anders hears her walk down the corridor, past the changing room and into the rest-room.

The glow from the computer screen fills Anders's little office. He clicks to open the calendar, then adds some newly arranged meetings with relatives and care workers.

His fingers pause above the keyboard as he thinks about the new patient again. He feels caught in that moment, the seconds when he was in her room, pulling down her trousers and underwear, and saw her white skin turn red after the two injections. He touched her as a doctor, but he looked between her thighs at her genitals, her blonde hair and closed vagina.

Anders makes a note about a rearranged meeting, then

clicks to open up past assessments, unable to concentrate properly.

He reads through the report for Social Services, then gets up and goes out to the surveillance control room.

As he sits down in front of the large screen to look at the nine squares, he immediately notices that Saga Bauer is awake. Her bedside light is switched on. She is sitting quite still and staring at him, directly into the camera.

Feeling a peculiar weight inside him, Anders looks at the other cameras. Patient rooms 1 and 2 are dark. The airlock and dayroom are quiet. The camera outside the room in which My is resting shows nothing but a closed door. The security company's staff are beyond the first security door.

Anders highlights patient room 3, and the image instantly fills the other screen. The lamp in the ceiling of the surveillance control room reflects off the dusty screen. He moves his chair closer. Saga is still sitting there, staring up at him.

He wonders what she wants.

Her pale face is lit up, and the skin on her neck is taut.

She massages the back of her neck with one hand, rises from the bed and takes a couple of steps forward, all the while looking up at the camera.

Anders clicks away from the image, gets up, looks at the guards and the closed door of the rest-room.

He goes over to the security door, runs his card through the reader and walks into the corridor. The nocturnal lighting has a flat grey tone. The three doors are glowing dully, like lead. He walks up to her door and looks in through the reinforced glass. Saga is still standing in the middle of the floor, but turns to look towards the door as he opens the hatch.

The light from the bedside lamp is shining behind her, between her legs.

'I can't sleep,' she says with big, dark eyes.

'Are you scared of the dark?' he smiles.

'I need ten milligrams of Stesolid, that's what I always used to get at Karsudden.'

He's thinking that she's even more beautiful and slender in reality. She moves with a strange awareness, confident in her body, as if she were an elite gymnast or a ballerina. He can see that her tight, thin vest is damp with sweat. The perfect curve of her shoulders, her nipples beneath the fabric.

He tries to recall if he's read anything about sleeping problems in her notes from Karsudden. Then he remembers that it really doesn't matter. He's in charge of decisions about medication.

'Wait there,' he says, then goes and gets a tablet.

When he comes back he can feel sweat between his shoulder blades. He shows her the plastic cup, she reaches her hand through the hatch to take it, but he can't resist teasing her:

'Can I have a smile?'

'Give me the tablet,' she says simply, still holding out her hand.

He holds the plastic cup in the air, out of reach of her outstretched hand.

'One little smile,' he says, tickling the palm of her hand.

## 137

Saga smiles at the doctor and maintains eye-contact with him until she has the plastic cup. He closes and locks the hatch, but remains outside the door. She retreats into the room, pretends to put the pill in her mouth, gets some water and swallows, tipping her heard back. She's not looking at him, isn't sure if he's still there, but she sits down on the bed for a while and then turns out the light. Under cover of darkness she quickly slips the pill under the inner sole of one of her shoes, then lies back on the bed.

Before she falls asleep she sees Bernie's face again, the tears filling his eyes as he put the noose round his neck.

His silent cramps, the little thuds as his heels hit the door, follow her into sleep.

Saga sinks steeply into deep sleep, into healing, falling sleep.

At some point the hourglass gets turned over.

Then, like warm air, she drifts up towards wakefulness and suddenly opens her eyes in the dark. She doesn't know what's woken her up. In her dream it was Bernie's helplessly kicking feet.

A distant rattling sound, perhaps, she thinks.

But all she can hear is her own pulse, deep inside her ears.

She blinks and listens.

The reinforced glass in the door gradually appears as a rectangle of frozen seawater.

She closes her eyes and tries to go back to sleep. Her eyes are stinging with tiredness, but she can't relax. Something is heightening her senses.

The metal walls are clicking, and she opens her eyes again and stares over at the grey window.

Suddenly a black shadow appears against the glass.

She's instantly wide awake, ice-cold.

A man is looking at her through the reinforced glass. It's the young doctor. Has he been standing there the whole time?

He can't see anything in the darkness.

But he's still standing there, in the middle of the night.

There's a faint hissing sound.

His head is nodding slightly.

Now she realises that the rattling sound that woke her was the key slipping into the lock.

Air rushes in, the sounds expands, grows lower and fades away.

The heavy door opens and she knows she must lie absolutely still. She ought to be sleeping soundly because of the pill. The nocturnal lighting from the corridor falls like shimmering powder on the young doctor's head and shoulders.

She's wondering if he saw that she only pretended to take the pill, that he's coming to get it from her shoe. But staff aren't allowed in patients' rooms alone, she thinks.

Then it dawns on her: the doctor has come in because he thinks she's taken the pill and is fast asleep.

## 138

This is madness, Anders is thinking as he shuts the door behind him. It's the middle of the night, and he's gone in to see a patient and is now standing in her darkened room. His heart is pounding so hard in his chest that it actually hurts.

He can just make out her figure in bed.

She'll be sound asleep for hours yet, practically unconscious.

The door to the rest-room where My is sleeping is closed. There are two guards by the most distant security door. Everyone else is asleep.

He doesn't actually know what he's doing in Saga's room, he can't think ahead, all he knows is that he has to come in and look at her again, has to come up with an excuse that will let him feel her warm skin beneath his fingers.

It's impossible to stop thinking of her perspiring breasts and the look of resignation she gave him when she tried to get away and her clothes pulled up.

He repeats to himself that he's only making sure everything's OK with a patient who's just taken a sedative.

If anyone spots him, he can say he detected signs of sleep apnoea, and decided to go in and check, seeing as she's so heavily medicated.

They'll say it was an error of judgment not to wake My, but the intrusion itself will be regarded as justified.

He just wants to make sure everything's OK.

Anders takes a couple of steps into the room, and suddenly finds himself thinking of fishing nets, lobster pots and fyke traps, large openings leading you on towards smaller ones, until eventually there's no way back.

He swallows hard and tells himself he hasn't done anything wrong. He's exceptionally conscientious about his patients' welfare, that's all.

He can't stop thinking about the time he gave her the injection. The memory of her back and buttocks are like a great weight inside him.

He walks slowly over and looks at her in the darkness. He can see she's lying on her side.

Carefully he sits down on the edge of the bed and folds the covers back from her legs and backside. He tries to listen to her breathing, but his own heartbeat is pounding too hard in his ears.

Her body is radiating warmth.

He strokes her thigh softly, a gesture that any doctor might make. His fingers reach her cotton underpants.

His hands are cold, they're shaking and he's far too nervous to be sexually excited.

It's too dark for the camera in the ceiling to be able to register what he's doing.

He lets his fingers slip cautiously over the underpants and in between her thighs, and feels the heat of her genitals.

Gently he presses a finger into the fabric, running it along the lips of her vagina.

He'd like to stroke her to orgasm, until her whole body is crying out for penetration, even though she's asleep.

His eyes have got used to the darkness and now he can make out Saga's smooth thighs and the perfect line of her hips.

He reminds himself that she is fast asleep, he knows that, and he pulls her underpants down without ceremony. She groans in her sleep, but is otherwise completely still.

Her body is shimmering in the darkness.

The blonde pubic hair, sensitive inner thighs, her flat stomach.

She'll carry on sleeping, no matter what he does.

It makes no difference to her.

She won't say no, she won't shoot him a look that's pleading with him to stop.

A wave of sexual excitement crashes over him, filling him, making him pant for breath. He can feel his penis swelling, straining against his clothes. He adjusts it with one hand.

He can hear his breathing – and the thud and roar of his heartbeat. He has to get inside her. His hands fumble with her knees, trying to part her thighs.

She rolls over, kicking gently in her sleep.

He slows down, leans over her, pushing his hands between her thighs and trying to spread them.

He can't do it – it feels like she's putting up resistance.

He rolls her over onto her stomach, but she slips to the floor, sits up and looks at him with wide eyes.

Anders hurries out of the room, telling himself that she wasn't properly awake, she won't remember anything, she'll think she was only dreaming.

## 139

Veils of snow are blowing across the motorway outside the roadside café. The vehicles thundering past make the windows rattle. The coffee in Joona's cup is trembling with the vibrations.

Joona looks at the men at the table. Their faces are calm and weary. After taking his phone, passport and wallet, they just seem to be waiting for instructions now. The café smells of buckwheat and fried pork.

Joona looks at his watch and sees that his plane out of Moscow departs in nine minutes.

Felicia's life is ticking away.

One of the men is trying to solve a sudoku, while the other is reading about horse racing in a broadsheet newspaper.

Joona looks at the woman behind the counter as he goes over his conversation with Nikita Karpin.

The old man had acted as if they had all the time in the world, until they were interrupted. He smiled calmly to himself, wiped the condensation from the jug with his thumb and said that Jurek Walter and his twin brother only stayed in Sweden for a couple of years.

'Why?' Joona asked.

'You don't become a serial killer for no reason.'

'Do you know what happened?'

'Yes.'

The old man had run his finger over the grey file and once again started talking about the highly trained engineer who had probably been prepared to sell what he knew.

'But the Swedish Aliens Department was only interested in whether or not Vadim Levanov could work. They didn't understand anything . . . they sent a world-class missile engineer to work in a gravel pit.'

'Maybe he realised you were watching him and had enough sense to keep quiet about what he knew,' Joona said.

'It would have been more sensible not to have left Leninsk . . . He might have got ten years in a labour camp, but . . .'

'But he had his children to think of.'

'Then he should have stayed,' Nikita said, meeting Joona's gaze. 'The boys were extradited from Sweden and Vadim Levanov was unable to trace them. He contacted everyone he could, but it was impossible. There wasn't a lot he could do. Of course he knew that we'd arrest him if he returned to Russia, and then there was absolutely no way he'd find his boys, so he waited for them instead, that was all he could do . . . He must have thought that if the boys tried to find him, they'd start by looking in the place where they'd last been together.'

'And where was that?' Joona asked, as he noticed a black car approaching the house.

'Visiting workers' accommodation, barrack number four,' Nikita Karpin replied. 'That was also where he took his own life, much later.'

Before Joona had time to ask the name of the gravel pit where the boys' father worked, Nikita Karpin had more visitors. A shiny black Chrysler turned in and pulled up in front of the house, and there was no doubt that the conversation was over. Without any apparent urgency, the old man switched all the material on the table concerning Jurek's father for information about Alexander Pichushkin, the so-called chessboard killer – a serial killer in whose capture Joona had played a small part.

The four men came in, walked calmly over to Joona and Nikita, shook their hands politely, talked for a while in Russian, then two of them led Joona out to the black car while the other two stayed with Nikita.

Joona was put in the back seat. One of the men, who had a thick neck and little black eyes, asked in a not unfriendly voice to see his passport, then asked for his mobile phone. They went through his wallet, called his hotel and the car-hire company. They assured him that they would drive him to the airport, but not just yet.

Now they're sitting at a table in the café, waiting.

Joona takes another small sip of his cold coffee.

If only he had his phone he could call Anja and ask her to do a search for Jurek Walter's father. There had to be something about the children, about the place where they lived. He suppresses an urge to overturn the table, run out to the car and drive to the airport. They've got his passport, as well as his wallet and mobile.

The man with the thick neck is tapping gently at the table and humming to himself. The other one, who has close-cropped ice-grey hair, has stopped reading and is sitting sending texts from his phone.

There's a clatter from inside the kitchen.

Suddenly the Russian's mobile rings, and the grey-haired man gets up and moves away a few steps before answering.

After a while he ends the call and explains that it's time to go.

## 140

Mikael is sitting in his room watching television with Berzelius. Reidar is heading downstairs, looking out through the row of windows at the snow lying on the fields outside like a grey glow. The sun never came up today, and it's been dark since morning.

Birchwood is burning in the open fireplace and the post has been laid out on the table in the library. Beethoven's late piano sonatas are streaming from the speakers.

Reidar sits down and glances quickly through the pile of post. His Japanese translator needs to know the exact titles and ages of various characters for the manga film adaptations of the books, and a producer from an American television company wants to discuss a new idea. At the bottom of the pile is a plain envelope with no sender's address. Reidar's address looks as if it had been written by a child.

He doesn't know why his heart starts beating faster before he's even opened the envelope and read the note:

*Felicia is asleep at the moment. I arrived here at Kvastmakarbacken 1B a year ago. Felicia has been here much longer than that. I'm tired of giving her food and water. You can have her back if you like.*

Reidar's hands are shaking as he gets to his feet and calls Joona. His phone is switched off. Reidar walks towards the hall. Obviously he's aware it could be another hoax, but he has to go, he has to go at once. He takes the car keys from the bowl in the hall table, checks that his nitroglycerine spray is in his coat pocket, then rushes out.

While he's driving to Stockholm he tries calling Joona again, then manages to get through to Joona's colleague, Magdalena Ronander.

'I know where Felicia is!' he yells. 'She's on Södermalm, in a flat on Kvastmakarbacken.'

'Is that Reidar?' she asks.

'Why's it so damn difficult to get hold of anyone?' Reidar roars.

'You're saying you know where Felicia is?' Magdalena asks.

'Kvastmakarbacken 1B,' Reidar says, trying to sound calm and collected. 'I received a letter this morning.'

'We'd like to see the letter—'

'I need to talk to Joona,' Reidar interrupts, dropping the phone.

It slips down beside his seat and he swears to himself and hits the wheel angrily as he overtakes a grey articulated lorry. The windscreen gets soaked in dirty snow, and the car shudders in the wind.

# 141

Reidar pulls up onto the pavement and leaves the car with its door open by the red railings leading to Kvastmakarbacken. His phone is ringing under his seat, but he doesn't bother trying to retrieve it. His legs are shaking as he climbs over the fence and runs through the deep snow towards the entrance that's been cleared of snow.

Number 1B is an old stone building that stands alone on a hill. Beyond it there's nothing but main roads and industrial estates. Reidar slips on the steep stone steps, hitting his knee hard enough to make him cry out.

He's trying to breathe calmly, and limps on up the steps, even though the pain is making him groan.

Leaning on the wrought-iron railing, he tugs at the locked door as he feels blood trickling from his knee inside his trousers.

An illuminated sign bearing the number 1B is glowing dull yellow from the entrance.

Reidar bangs on the door as hard as he can, and eventually the window alongside creaks as someone pushes it open.

'What are you up to?' a bald old man asks through the gap.

'Open the door,' Reidar gasps. 'My daughter's in here . . .'

'Oh,' the old man says, then closes the window.

Reidar starts banging on the door again and after a while the lock begins to turn. Reidar yanks the door open, marches in and shouts into the stairwell:

'Felicia! Felicia!'

The old man looks scared and backs away towards his door, and Reidar follows him.

'Who are you?' he asks. 'Was it you who wrote the letter?'

'I'm just—'

Reidar forces his way past the man and marches straight into his flat. On the left is a cramped kitchen with a table and one chair. The man remains standing in the doorway as Reidar walks into the next room. In front of a red sofa covered in blankets is a television on legs. Reidar's feet leave wet marks on the linoleum floor. He pulls the wardrobe open and hunts through the clothes hanging inside it.

'Felicia!' Reidar yells, looking in the bathroom.

The old man steps out into the stairwell when he sees Reidar coming.

'Unlock the basement!'

'No, I—'

Reidar follows him. His eyes are darting about the walls, doors, and the worn stone steps leading down.

'Open it!' Reidar shouts, grabbing the man's tanktop.

'Please,' the man begs, pulling the keys from his trouser pocket.

Reidar snatches the keys and runs down the steps, weeping as he opens the steel door and rushes in amongst the storage compartments.

'Felicia!' he cries.

He's coughing as he walks round the chicken-wire walls, calling for his daughter, but there's no one there and he runs back upstairs again. His chest is starting to hurt, but he carries on to the next floor and kicks on the door. He opens the letterbox and calls for Felicia, then goes up to the next floor and rings on the door. The building smells of damp and rotten wood.

Sweat is pouring down his back and he's starting to have trouble breathing.

A young woman with her hair dyed red opens the door and Reidar forces his way past her without saying anything.

'What the fuck do you think you're doing?' she yells.

'Felicia!'

A man in a leather waistcoat and long black hair stops Reidar and shoves him backwards. Reidar sticks out an arm and manages to pull a calendar onto the floor. He tries to get past the man again, but is struck so hard he stumbles back, tripping over shoes and junk mail and falls to the floor. He hits the back of his head on the doorstep, loses consciousness for a few moments, then rolls onto his side as he hears the woman shouting that they need to call the police.

Reidar stands up and comes close to falling again, pulling a coat down off its hanger and muttering an apology as he turns back towards the flat.

'I have to get in,' he says, wiping blood from his mouth.

The man with long black hair is holding a hockey stick in both hands and is glaring at him intently.

'Felicia,' Reidar whispers, feeling tears pricking his eyes.

'I've got her, but I don't think she's very well,' a woman says behind his back.

Reidar turns to see an old woman in a blonde wig with bright red lips. She's standing on the dimly lit staircase, a couple of steps down, cradling a striped cat in her arms.

'What did you say?' he gasps.

'You were calling for Felicia,' she smiles.

'My daughter . . .'

'She was stealing food from me.'

He walks towards the woman on the stairs. She's frowning and holding the cat out in front of her. Now he can see that the cat's neck is broken.

'Felicia,' the woman said. 'She was in the flat when I moved in, and I've been looking after her and—'

'The cat?'

'It says Felicia on the collar . . .'

## 142

Her unease after the doctor's nocturnal visit is like rain on a window – it's not too close, but is keeping her shut inside.

Her medication is making Saga feel oddly cut off from reality, but she still has a very strong sense that her cover is about to be blown.

That doctor would have raped me if I'd really been asleep, she thinks. I can't let him touch me again.

She just needs a bit more time to complete her mission. She's so close now. Jurek is talking about escape with her. And if her cover isn't blown he'll soon give her a location, a clue, something that could lead to Felicia.

He was on the point of confiding in her yesterday. Maybe today.

As long as the microphone is working.

Time and time again, thinking about Felicia helps Saga. She needs to concentrate on what she came here to do. Not feel sorry for herself.

She's going to save the captive girl.

The rules are simple. Under no circumstances must she let Jurek escape. But she can plan the escape with him, she can show interest and ask questions.

The most common problem with escapes is that people have nowhere to go once they're out. Jurek won't make that mistake. He knows where he's going.

The lock on the door to the dayroom whirrs. Saga gets up from her bed, rolls her shoulders as if preparing for a bout, then goes out.

Jurek Walter is standing by the wall opposite, waiting for her. She can't understand how he could have got out into the dayroom so quickly.

There's no reason to stay close to the running machine now that the lead is gone. She just hopes the range of the microphone is wide enough.

The television isn't turned on, but she goes and sits on the sofa.

Jurek is standing in front of her.

It feels as if she hasn't got any skin, as if he has a strange ability to see straight into her bare flesh.

He sits down beside her and she discreetly passes him the tablet.

'We only need four more,' he says, looking at her with his pale eyes.

'Yes, but I . . .'

'And then we can leave this terrible place.'

'Maybe I don't want to.'

When Jurek Walter reaches out his hand and touches her arm she almost jumps. He notices her fear and looks at her blankly.

'I've got a place I think you'd love,' he says. 'It's not that far away from here. It's only an old house behind an old brick factory, but at night you could go outside and swing.'

'A real swing?' she asks, trying to smile.

Jurek needs to keep talking to her, she thinks. His words are little pieces that will form a pattern in the puzzle Joona is putting together.

'It's just an ordinary swing,' he replies. 'But you can swing out over the water.'

'What, a lake, or—'

'You'll see, it's lovely.'

'I like apple trees as well,' she says quietly.

## 143

Saga's heart is beating so hard it seems to her that Jurek must be aware of it. If the microphone is working, then her colleagues will be identifying every derelict brickworks, they might even be on their way already.

'It's a good place to hide until the police give up the hunt,' he goes on, looking at her. 'And you can stay in the house if you like it there —'

'But you'll be moving on?' she says.

'I have to.'

'And I can't come with you?'

'Do you want to?'

'Depends where you're going.'

Saga's aware that she might be pushing him too far, but right now he seems keen to involve her in his escape attempt.

'You have to trust me,' he says curtly.

'It sounds like you're planning on dumping me in the first house we come to.'

'No.'

'Sounds like it,' she persists, sounding hurt. 'I think I'll stay here until I get discharged.'

'And when will that be?'

'I don't know.'

'Are you sure they're going to let you out?'

'Yes,' she replies honestly.

'Because you're a good little girl who helped your sick mum when she—'

'I wasn't good,' Saga interrupts, pulling her arm away. 'Do you think I wanted to be there? I was only a child, I was just doing what I had to.'

He leans back on the sofa and nods.

'Compulsion is interesting.'

'I wasn't forced into it,' she protests.

He smiles at her. 'You just said you were.'

'Not like that . . . I mean, I managed to do it,' she explains. 'She was only in pain in the evenings, and at night.'

Saga falls silent, thinking about one morning after a particularly difficult night, when her mother was making breakfast for her. She was frying eggs, making sandwiches, pouring milk. Then they went outside in their nightdresses. The grass in the garden was damp with dew, and they took the cushions with them down to the hammock.

'You gave her codeine,' Jurek says, in a strange tone of voice.

'It helped.'

'But they're not very strong – how many did she have to take that last evening?'

'A lot . . . she was in such terrible pain . . .'

Saga rubs her hand across her forehead and realises to her surprise that she's perspiring heavily. She doesn't want to talk about this, she hasn't thought about it for years.

'More than ten, I suppose?' Jurek asks lightly.

'She used to take two, but that evening she needed far more . . . I spilled them on the rug, but . . . I don't know, I must have given her twelve, maybe thirteen pills.'

Saga feels the muscles in her face tighten. She's scared

she's going to start crying if she stays, so she gets up quickly to go to her room.

'Your mum didn't die of cancer,' Jurek says.

She stops and turns towards him.

'That's enough,' she says sternly.

'She didn't have a brain tumour,' he says quietly.

'OK . . . I was with my mum when she died, you know nothing about her, you can't—'

'The headaches,' Jurek interrupts. 'The headaches don't subside the following morning if you have a tumour.'

'That's how it was for her,' she says firmly.

'The pain is caused by the pressure on brain tissue and blood vessels as the tumour grows. That doesn't pass, it just gets worse.'

She looks into Jurek's eyes and feels a shiver run down her back.

'I . . .'

Her voice is no more than a whisper. She feels like shouting and screaming, but she's suddenly powerless.

If she's honest, she's always known that there was something odd about her memories. She remembers yelling at her father when she was a teenager, saying he lied about everything, that he was the biggest liar she'd ever met.

He had told her that her mother hadn't had cancer.

She's always thought he was lying to her in an effort to excuse his betrayal of her mum.

Now she's standing here, no longer sure where the idea of her mother's brain tumour came from. She can't remember her mum ever saying she had cancer, and they never went to any hospital.

But why did Mum cry every evening if she wasn't sick? It doesn't make sense. Why did she make me call Dad all the time and tell him he had to come home? Why did Mum take codeine if she wasn't in pain? Why did she let her own daughter give her all those pills?

Jurek's face is a sombre, rigid mask. Saga turns away and starts walking towards the door. She wants to run away, she doesn't want to hear what he's about to say.

'You killed your own mother,' he says calmly.

Saga stops abruptly. Her breathing has become shallow but she forces herself not to show her feelings. She has to remind herself who's in charge of this situation. He may believe that he's deceiving her, but in actual fact she's the one deceiving him.

Saga adopts a neutral expression, then turns slowly to face him.

'Codeine,' Jurek says, smiling joylessly. 'Codeine phosphate only comes in the form of twenty-five-milligram tablets . . . I know precisely how many it takes to kill a human being.'

'Mum told me to give her the pills,' she explains hollowly.

'But I think you knew she'd die,' he says. 'I'm sure your mum thought you knew . . . She thought you wanted her to die.'

'Fuck you,' she whispers.

'Maybe you deserve to be locked up here for ever.'

'No.'

He looks at her with terrifying gravity in his eyes, with metallic precision.

'Maybe it will be enough if you get one more sleeping pill,' he says. 'Because yesterday Bernie said he had some

Stesolid wrapped in a piece of paper, in a crack under his sink . . . Unless he only said it to buy time.'

Her heart speeds up. Bernie hid sleeping pills in his room? What's she going to do now? She has to stop this. She can't let Jurek get hold of the sleeping pills. What if there are enough for him to carry out his escape plan?

'Are you going into his room?' she asks.

'The door's open.'

'It would be better if I did it,' she says quickly.

'Why?'

Jurek is giving her a look that seems almost amused, while she tries desperately to come up with a reasonable answer.

'If they catch me,' she says, 'they'll just think I'm addicted and—'

'Then we won't get any more pills,' he retorts.

'I think I can get more from the doctor anyway,' she says.

Jurek considers this, then nods.

'He looks at you as if he were the one who was captive.'

She opens the door to Bernie's room and goes inside.

In the light from the dayroom she can see that his room is an exact copy of hers. When the door closes behind her, everything goes dark. She walks over to the wall, feeling her way round, picking up the smell of stale urine from the toilet, then she reaches the sink, the edges of which are wet, as if it's recently been cleaned.

The doors to the dayroom will be closing in a few minutes.

She tells herself not to think about her mother, just concentrate on the job at hand. Her chin starts to tremble, but she manages to pull herself together, stifling the tears even though her throat feels as if it's going to burst. She kneels down and runs her fingers across the cool underside of the sink. She reaches the wall and feels along the silicone seal, but can't find anything. A drop of water falls on her neck. She blinks in the darkness, reaches further down, touches the floor.

Another drip falls between her shoulder blades. She suddenly notices that the basin is sloping slightly. That's why the water on top is dripping onto her instead of draining back into the bowl.

She pushes the basin up with her shoulder and feels along the underside where it joins the wall. Her fingers find a crack. There it is. A tiny package, tucked inside. Sweat is running from her armpits. She pushes the basin up further. It creaks as she tries to grab hold of the package. Carefully she manages to pull it out. Jurek was right. Pills. Tightly wrapped in toilet paper. She's breathing hard as she crawls out, tucks the package in her trousers and stands up.

As she feels her way to the door to the dayroom she thinks about having to tell Jurek she didn't find anything, that Bernie must have been lying about the pills. She reaches the wall, quickly moves along it until she finds the door and emerges into the dayroom.

Blinking hard against the bright light, Saga looks round. Jurek isn't there. He must have returned to his room. The clock behind the reinforced glass tells her the doors to the dayroom will be locked in a few seconds.

## 145

Anders Rönn taps lightly at the door of the surveillance control room. My is sitting there reading a copy of *Expo* in front of the large monitor.

'Have you come to say goodnight?' she asks.

Anders smiles back at her, sits down beside her and watches Saga leave the dayroom and go into her room. Jurek is already lying on his bed, and of course Bernie's room is dark. My yawns widely, then leans back in the revolving chair.

Leif is standing in the doorway, draining the last drops from a can of Coca-Cola.

'What does male foreplay look like?' he asks.

'Is there such a thing?' My asks.

'An hour of begging, pleading and persuasion.'

Anders smiles and My laughs so hard the piercing in her tongue glints.

'They're a bit short of staff up on Ward 30 tonight,' Anders says.

'Funny how we're so short of staff when there's such high unemployment,' Leif sighs.

'I said they could borrow you,' Anders says.

'There always have to be two of us here,' Leif says.

'Yes, but I'm going to have to stay and work until at least one o'clock anyway.'

'OK, I'll come back down at one o'clock.'

'Good,' Anders says.

Leif tosses the can in the bin and leaves the room.

Anders sits silently beside My for a while. He can't take his eyes off Saga. She's pacing anxiously in her cell, with her thin arms wrapped round her body.

The image is so sharp that he can see the sweat on her back.

He can feel himself aching with desire. All he can think about is how to get into her room again. He's going to give her twenty milligrams of Stesolid this time.

He makes the decisions, he's the responsible clinician, he can have her put in a straitjacket, tied to her bed, he can do whatever he wants. She's psychotic, paranoid, there's no one she can talk to.

My yawns again, stretches and says something Anders doesn't hear.

He looks at the time. Only two hours until the lights go out and he can let My go and get some sleep.

## 146

Saga is pacing around the floor of her cell, feeling the little package from Bernie's room moving in her pocket. Behind her back she hears the electronic lock whirr and click. She ought to wash her face, but can't be bothered. She goes over to the door to the corridor and looks through the toughened glass to see if she can see anything, then leans her forehead against the cool surface and closes her eyes.

If Felicia is in the house behind the brickworks, I'll be free tomorrow. Otherwise I've got a couple more days in me before this gets unbearable, before I have to put a stop to the escape attempt, she thinks.

Her facial muscles ache – she's been willing herself not to break down.

She hasn't let the pain in, all she can think about is completing her mission.

She's breathing faster again, and knocks her head gently against the cold glass.

I'm in charge of this situation, she tells herself. Jurek thinks he's controlling me, but I've got him to talk. He needs sleeping pills in order to escape, but I went into

Bernie's room, found the package and I'm going to hide it, say it wasn't there.

She smiles anxiously to herself. The palms of her hands are wet with sweat.

As long as Jurek believes he's manipulating me, he'll carry on giving himself away, piece by piece.

She's sure he's going to tell about his escape plan tomorrow.

I just have to stay a few more days, and I need to stay calm, not let him inside my head again.

She can't understand how it could have happened.

It was incredibly cruel of him to say she had killed her mother on purpose, that she would have wanted to kill her.

Now she feels the tears welling up. Her throat aches and she swallows and feels sweat running down her back.

Saga bangs her hands against the door.

Could her mum have thought . . .?

She turns, grabs the back of the plastic chair and hits the basin with it. She loses her grip and it spins round, but she grabs it again and bashes it against the wall, then the basin.

She sits down on the bed, panting.

'I'm going to be OK,' she whispers to herself.

She can feel she's on the brink of losing control of the situation, she can't stop thinking. Her memory is only showing her the long strands of the rug, the pills, her mum's wet eyes, the tears running down her cheeks, her teeth hitting the edge of the glass as she swallows the pills.

Saga remembers her mum shouting at her when she said Dad couldn't come, she remembers her mum forcing her to call him, even though she didn't want to.

Maybe I was angry with Mum, she thinks. Tired of her.

She gets up, trying to calm down, and repeats to herself that she's being deceived.

Slowly she walks over to the basin and washes her face, then carefully bathes her aching eyes.

She has to find a way back to herself, she has to become herself again. It's as if she's scrambling about outside her body, as if she can't be inside her body any more.

Maybe the neuroleptic injection is what's stopping her from just crying and crying.

Saga lies down on the bed and makes up her mind to hide Bernie's package, tell Jurek she didn't find anything. Then she won't have to ask the doctor for sleeping pills. She can just give Jurek the ones she got from Bernie's room.

One at a time, one per night.

Saga rolls over onto her side and turns her back on the CCTV camera in the ceiling. Covered by her own body, she takes out the package. She carefully unrolls the toilet paper, little by little, until she sees that it contains just three pieces of chewing gum.

Chewing gum.

She forces herself to breathe calmly, lets her eyes trace the streaks of dirt on the walls, and thinks with strange, vacant clarity that she's done exactly what Joona warned her against.

I've let Jurek inside my head, and everything has changed.

How can I possibly stand myself?

It's wrong to think like this, I know I'm being deceived, but that's how it feels.

Her stomach is aching with anguish as she thinks about her mum's cold body that morning. A sad, immoveable face with an odd froth at the corner of her mouth.

It feels as if she's about to fall.

I mustn't lose it, she thinks, and struggles to regain control of her breathing, and come up with a strategy that works.

I'm not sick, she reminds herself. I'm here for one reason alone, that's all I have to think about. My task is to find Felicia. This isn't about me, I don't care about myself. I am undercover, I'm following the plan, I'm accumulating sleeping pills, pretending to go along with the plan and talking about escape routes and hiding places for as long as I can. I'm doing my duty, for as long as it's possible. It doesn't matter if I die, she thinks with sudden relief.

# 147

It's been almost twenty-four hours since Joona Linna was picked up from Nikita Karpin's house by the men from the FSB, the new Russian security service. They haven't answered any questions at all, and he hasn't been given any explanation as to why his passport, wallet, watch and mobile have been confiscated.

After sitting in a café for hours, they took him to a bleak concrete block of flats, led him along one of the walkways and into a two-room apartment.

Joona was taken to the furthest room, which contained a dirty sofa, a table with two chairs, and a small closet concealing a toilet. The steel door was locked behind him and then nothing happened until a couple of hours later, when they gave him a warm paper bag containing soggy food from McDonald's.

Joona has to get in touch with his colleagues and ask Anja to look for Vadim Levanov and his twin sons, Igor and Roman. Maybe the names would lead to new addresses, maybe they'd be able to identify the gravel pit where the father worked.

But the metal door has remained locked, and the hours are passing. He's heard the men talk on the phone a couple of times, but apart from that it's been silent.

\*

Joona has been dozing off and on, curled up on the sofa, but snaps awake towards morning at the sound of footsteps and voices in the next room.

He turns the light on and waits for them to come in.

Someone coughs, and he hears voices talking irritably in Russian. Suddenly the door opens and the two men from the previous day come in. They've both got pistols in their shoulder-holsters and are carrying on a rapid-fire conversation in Russian.

The man with silver-grey hair pulls out one of the chairs and puts it in the middle of the floor.

'Sit down here,' he says in good English.

Joona gets up from the sofa and notices the man step back as he walks slowly over to the chair and sits down.

'You're not here on official business,' the thick-necked man with black eyes says. 'Tell us why you went to see Nikita Karpin.'

'We were talking about the serial killer, Alexander Pichushkin,' Joona replied in a toneless voice.

'And what conclusions did you reach?' the man with the silvery hair asks.

'The first victim was his presumed accomplice,' Joona says. 'We were talking about him . . . Mikhail Odichuk.'

The man tilts his head, nods a couple of times, then says amiably:

'Naturally, you're lying.'

The man with the thick neck has turned away and drawn his pistol. It isn't easy to see, but it might be a high-calibre Glock. He's hiding the gun with his body as he feeds a bullet into the chamber.

'What did Nikita Karpin tell you?' the man with grey hair goes on.

'Nikita believes that the accomplice's role was—'

'Don't lie!' the other man roars, and turns round, holding

the pistol behind his back. 'Nikita Karpin no longer has any authority, he isn't in the security service.'

'You knew that – didn't you?' the man with black eyes asks.

Joona is thinking that he might be able to overpower the two men, but without his passport and money it would be impossible to get out of the country.

The agents exchange a few words in Russian.

The man with cropped white hair takes a deep breath and then says sharply:

'You discussed material that has been declared confidential, and we need to know exactly what you were told before we can take you to the airport.'

For a long time none of them moves. The white-haired man looks at his phone, says something to the other one in Russian, and gets a shake of the head in response.

'You have to tell us,' he says, putting his phone in his pocket.

'I'll shoot you in your kneecaps,' the other man says.

'So, you drive out to Ljubimovka, meet Nikita Karpin and—'

The white-haired man breaks off as his phone rings. He answers, looking stressed, exchanges a few short words, then says something to his colleague. They have a short conversation that gets more and more heated.

## 148

The man with black eyes is stressed, and moves aside and takes aim at Joona with the pistol. The lino floor creaks under his feet. A shadow slips away and the light from the standard lamp reaches his hand. Joona can now see that the black pistol is a Strizh.

The white-haired man rubs one hand over his head, barks an order, looks at Joona for a few seconds, then leaves the room and locks the door behind him.

The other man walks round and stops somewhere behind Joona. He's breathing hard, and having trouble standing still.

'The boss is on his way,' he says in a low voice.

There's the sound of angry shouting behind the steel door. The smell of gun-grease and sweat is suddenly very noticeable in the small room.

'I have to know – do you understand?' the man says.

'We were talking about serial ki—'

'Don't lie!' he yells. 'I have to know what Karpin said!'

Joona can hear his impatient movements behind his back, can feel him coming closer, and sees a faint shadow flit across the floor.

'I have to go home now,' Joona says.

The man with black eyes moves quickly, presses the barrel of the pistol hard against the back of Joona's neck, from a position just to the right of him.

His rapid breathing is clearly audible.

In a single movement Joona pulls his head out of the way, twists his body, moves his right arm back and knocks the gun aside, then stands up. He throws the man off balance and grabs the barrel of the pistol, twisting it down before jerking it upwards and breaking the man's fingers.

The man howls and Joona concludes his violent movement by ramming a knee into his kidneys and ribs. One of the man's legs is lifted from the floor by the force of the blow, and he tumbles backwards, crushing the chair beneath him.

Joona has already moved out of the way and turned the pistol on him when he rolls onto his side, coughing, and opens his eyes. He tries to get up but coughs again, then lies there with his cheek to the ground, inspecting his wounded fingers.

Joona removes the magazine and puts it on the table, takes the bullet out of the chamber and then dismantles the entire pistol.

'Sit down,' Joona says.

The man with black eyes groans with pain as he gets up. His brow is beaded with sweat, and he sits down and frowns at the pieces of the gun.

Joona puts his hand in his pocket and pulls out a sweet. *'Ota poika karamelli, niin helpottaa,'* he says in Finnish.

The man looks at Joona in astonishment as he unwraps the yellow cellophane and pops the sweet in his mouth.

The door opens and two men come in. One is the man with silver-grey hair, the other an older man with a full beard, wearing a grey suit.

'Sorry for the misunderstanding,' the older man says.

'I need to get home urgently,' Joona says.

'Of course.'

The bearded man accompanies Joona out of the flat. They take the lift down to a waiting car and drive off to the airport together.

The driver carries Joona's bag and the bearded man goes with him through check-in, the security control, all the way to the gate and onto the plane. Only when boarding is complete does Joona get his mobile phone, passport and wallet back.

Before the bearded man leaves the plane, he hands Joona a paper bag containing seven small bars of soap and a fridge magnet of Vladimir Putin.

Joona barely has time to send a text to Anja before he is told to switch his phone off. He closes his eyes and thinks about the bars of soap, and wonders if the entire interrogation could have been arranged by Nikita Karpin as a test to see if Joona had the sense to protect his source.

## 149

It's already evening by the time Joona's plane lands in Stockholm after a connection in Copenhagen. He switches his phone on and reads a message from Carlos, telling him that a big police operation is underway.

Maybe Felicia's already been found?

Joona tries to get hold of Carlos as he hurries past the duty-free shops, down into the baggage collection area and through the arrival hall, then over the bridge to the garage. Tucked inside the compartment for the spare wheel is the shoulder-holster containing his black Colt Combat Target .45 ACP.

He drives south as he waits for Nathan Pollock to answer his phone.

Nikita Karpin said that Vadim Levanov had expected the boys to make their way to the place where they were last together if they ever tried to find him.

'And where was that?' Joona had asked.

'Visiting workers' accommodation, barrack number four. That was also where he took his own life, much later.'

Joona is heading down the motorway towards Stockholm at a hundred and forty kilometres an hour. The pieces of the puzzle have been coming thick and fast, and he's confident that he'll soon be able to see the overall picture.

Twin brothers forced to leave the country, and a father who commits suicide.

The father was a highly educated engineer, but was doing manual labour in one of Sweden's many gravel pits.

Joona puts his foot down as he tries to get hold of Carlos again, then Magdalena Ronander.

Before he has time to pull up Nathan Pollock's number, his phone rings and he answers at once.

'You should be grateful I'm here,' Anja says. 'Every police office in the whole of Stockholm is out at Norra Djurgården . . .'

'Have they found Felicia?'

'They're busy searching the forest beyond the Albano industrial estate, they've got dogs and—'

'Did you read my text?' Joona interrupts, his jaw clenched with stress.

'Yes, and I've been trying to work out what happened,' Anja says. 'It hasn't been easy, but I think I've managed to track down Vadim Levanov, even if the spelling of his name has been westernised. It looks like he arrived in Sweden in 1960, with no passport, from Finland.'

'And the children?'

'I'm afraid there's no mention of any children in the records.'

'Could he have smuggled them in?'

'During the fifties and sixties Sweden absorbed loads of visiting workers, the welfare state was being expanded . . . but the regulations were still very old-fashioned. Visiting workers were thought incapable of looking after their children and Social Services used to place them with foster families or in children's homes.'

'But these boys were extradited,' Joona says.

'That wasn't unusual, especially if there was a suspicion that they were Roma . . . I'm talking to the National Archives tomorrow . . . There was no migration authority in those days, so the police, Child Welfare Commission and Aliens Department used to take the decisions, often fairly arbitrarily.'

He turns off at Häggvik to refill the tank.

Anja is breathing hard down the phone. This can't be allowed to slip away, he thinks. There has to be something here that can lead them forward.

'Do you know where the father worked?' he asks.

'I've started investigating all the gravel pits in Sweden, but it may take a while because we're dealing with such old records,' she says wearily.

Joona thanks Anja several times, ends the call, and pulls up at a red light as he watches a young man push a pram along the footpath at the side of the road.

Snow is blowing along the carriageway, swirling up into the man's face and eyes. He squints as he turns the pram round to pull it up over a bank of snow.

Joona suddenly remembers what Mikael said about the Sandman being able to walk on the ceiling, and other muddled things. But he had said three times that the Sandman smells of sand. It may just have been something from the old fairytales, but what if there was a connection to a gravel quarry, a sand pit?

A car horn sounds behind Joona and he starts driving again, but pulls over to the side of the road shortly afterwards and calls Reidar Frost.

'What's going on?' Reidar asks.

'I'd like to talk to Mikael – how is he?'

'He feels bad about not being able to remember more – we've had the police here several hours each day.'

'Every little detail could be important.'

'I'm not complaining,' Reidar says hurriedly. 'We'd do

anything, you know that, that's what I keep saying, we're here, twenty-four hours a day.'

'Is he awake?'

'I can wake him – what did you want to ask?'

'He's said that the Sandman smells of sand . . . is it possible that the capsule is near a gravel pit? At some gravel pits they crush stone, and at others—'

'I grew up near a gravel pit, on the Stockholm Ridge, and—'

'You grew up near a gravel pit?'

'In Antuna,' Reidar replies, slightly bewildered.

'Which pit?'

'Rotebro . . . there's a large gravel works north of the Antuna road, past Smedby.'

Joona pulls out onto the opposite carriageway and drives back to the motorway, heading north again. He's already fairly close to Rotebro, so the gravel pit can't be far away.

Joona listens to Reidar's weary, rasping voice whilst hearing simultaneously – like a double-exposure – Mikael's peculiar fragments of memory: *the Sandman smells of sand . . . his fingertips are made of porcelain and when he takes the sand out of the bag they tinkle against each other . . . and a moment later you're asleep . . .*

## 150

The traffic thins out as he heads north. Joona is driving faster and faster, thinking that after all these years, three of the pieces of the puzzle are finally fitting together.

Jurek Walter's father worked in a gravel pit, and killed himself in his home there.

Mikael says the Sandman smells of sand.

And Reidar Frost grew up near an old gravel pit in Rotebro.

What if it's the same gravel pit? It can't be a coincidence, the pieces have to fit together. In which case this is where Felicia is, not where all his colleagues are searching, he thinks.

The ridges of snowy slush between the lanes make the car swerve. Dirty water is spraying up at the windscreen.

Joona pulls in ahead of one of the airport buses and carries on down the slip road and past a large car park. He sounds his horn and a man drops his bags of groceries as he leaps out of the way.

Two cars have stopped at a red light, but Joona veers into the other lane and turns sharp left. The tyres slide on the wet road surface. The car lurches across the snow-covered grass and straight through a bank of snow. Compacted snow and ice rattle over and underneath the car. He speeds up again, past Rotebro shopping centre and up the narrow Norrviken road that runs parallel to the high ridge.

The streetlights are swaying in the wind, lighting up the driving snow.

He reaches the top and sees the entrance to the gravel works a little too late, turns sharply and brakes hard in front of two heavy metal barriers. The wheels slide on the snow, Joona wrenches the steering wheel, the car spins and the rear end slams into one of the barriers.

The red glass from the brake-light shatters across the snow.

Joona throws the door open, gets out of the car and runs past the blue barrack containing the office.

Breathing heavily, he carries on down the steep slope towards the vast crater that has been excavated over the years. Floodlights on tall towers illuminate this strange lunar landscape with its static diggers and vast heaps of sifted sand.

Joona thinks that no one can be buried here, it would be impossible to bury any bodies here because everything is constantly being dug up. A gravel quarry is a hole that gets wider and deeper every day.

The heavy snow is falling through the artificial light.

He runs past huge stone-crushers with massive caterpillar tracks.

He's in the most recent section of the pit. The sand is bare and it's obvious that work is still going on here every day.

Beyond the machinery there are some blue containers and three caravans.

Joona's shadow flies past him on the ground as the light from another floodlight hits him from behind a pile of sand.

Half a kilometre away he can see a snow-covered area in front of a steep drop. That must be the older part of the pit.

He makes his way up a steep slope where people have

dumped rubbish, old fridges, broken furniture and trash. His feet slip on the snow but he keeps going, sending cascades of stones down behind him, until he shoves a rusty bicycle aside and makes it to the top.

He's now at the original level of the ridge, more than forty metres above the current ground level, and has a good view of the pitted landscape. Cold air tears at his lungs as he gazes out across the illuminated pit with its machines, makeshift roads and piles of sand.

He starts to run along the narrow strip of snow-covered meadow grass between the steep drop and the Älvsunda road.

There's a crumpled car-wreck by the side of the road in front of the wire-mesh fence with its warning signs and notices from the security company. Joona stops and peers into the falling snow. At the far corner of the very oldest section of the gravel pit is an area of tarmac, on top of which is a row of single-storey buildings, as long and narrow as military barracks.

## 151

Joona steps over some rusty barbed wire and heads towards the old buildings with their broken windows and graffiti tags sprayed on the brick walls.

It's dark up here and Joona gets his torch out. He aims the beam at the ground, carries on, then shines the light between the low buildings.

There's no door on the first building. Snow has blown in over the first few metres of blackened wooden floor. The beam of the torch sweeps quickly across old beer cans, dirty sheets, condoms and latex gloves.

He carries on through the deep snow, going from door to door and peering through broken or missing windows. The guest workers' old housing has been abandoned for many years. Nothing but dirt and dereliction. In some places the roofs have caved in, and whole sections of wall are missing.

He slows down when he sees that the windows in the last but one building are intact. An old supermarket trolley is lying on its side by the wall.

On one side of the building the ground drops away steeply towards the bottom of the quarry.

Joona switches the torch off as he makes his way to the

wall, where he stops and listens before turning the torch on again.

All he can hear is the wind sweeping across the rooftops.

In the darkness a short distance away he can make out the last building in the row. It seems to be little more than a snow-covered ruin.

He goes over to the window and shines the torch through the dirty glass. The beam moves slowly across a filthy hotplate connected to a car battery, a narrow bed with some rough blankets, a radio with a shiny aerial, some tanks of water and a dozen tins of food.

When he reaches the door he can make out an almost vanished number 4 at the top left corner.

This could be the number four of the visiting workers' accommodation that Nikita Karpin mentioned.

Joona carefully pushes the handle down and the door slides open. He slips inside, shutting the door behind him. It smells of damp old fabric. There's a bible on a rickety shelf. There's only one room, with one window and door.

Joona realises that he is now quite visible from the outside.

The wooden floor creaks under his weight.

He shines the torch along the walls, and sees piles of water-damaged books. In one corner the light flashes back at him.

He moves closer and sees that there are hundreds of tiny glass bottles lined up on the floor.

Dark glass bottles, with rubber membranes.

Sevoflurane, a highly effective sedative.

Joona pulls out his phone and calls the emergency control room, and asks for police backup and an ambulance to be sent to his location.

Then everything is silent again, and all he can hear is his own breathing and the floor creaking.

Suddenly from the corner of his eye he sees movement

outside the window, draws his Colt Combat and releases the safety catch in an instant.

There's nothing there, just some loose snow blowing off the roof.

He lowers the pistol again.

On the wall by the bed is a yellowed newspaper cutting about the first man in space, the 'Space Russian' as *Expressen's* headline-writer describes him.

This must be where the father killed himself.

Joona is just thinking that he ought to search the other buildings when he catches sight of an outline on the filthy rag-rug where something underneath is protruding. He pulls the rug aside and exposes a large hatch in the wooden floor.

Carefully he lies down and puts his ear to the hatch, but he can't hear anything.

He looks towards the window, then shoves the rug aside and opens the heavy wooden hatch.

A dusty smell of sand rises from the darkness.

He leans forward and shines the torch into the opening, and sees a steep flight of concrete steps.

## 152

The sand on the steps crunches under Joona's shoes as he heads down into the darkness. After nineteen stairs he finds himself in a large concrete room. The torch beam flickers across the walls and ceiling. There's a stool almost in the middle of the floor, and on one wall is a sheet of polystyrene with a few drawing pins and an empty plastic sleeve.

Joona realises that he must be in one of the many shelters built in Sweden during the Cold War.

There's an eerie silence down here.

The room tapers slightly, and tucked beneath the staircase is a heavy door.

This has to be the place.

Joona puts the safety catch back on his pistol and slips it into the holster again to leave his hands free. The steel door has large bolts that slide into place when a wheel at the centre of the door is turned.

He turns the wheel anticlockwise and there's a metallic rumble as the heavy bolts slide from their housings.

The door is hard to open, the metal fifteen centimetres thick.

He shines the torch into the shelter, and sees a dirty mattress on the floor, a sofa and a tap sticking out of the wall.

There's no one here.

The room stinks of old urine.

He points the torch at the sofa again and approaches cautiously. He stops and listens, then moves closer.

She might be hiding.

Suddenly he has the feeling that he's being followed. He could end up trapped in the same room as her. He turns and at that instant sees that the heavy door is closing. The immense hinges are creaking. He reacts instantly, throwing himself backwards and jamming the torch in the gap. There's a crunch as it gets squeezed and the glass shatters.

Joona shoves the door open with his shoulder, draws his pistol again and emerges into the dark room.

There's no one there.

The Sandman has moved remarkably quietly.

Strange light formations are flickering in front of his eyes as they try to make out shapes in the murky gloom.

The torch is only giving off a faint glow now, barely enough to illuminate anything.

All he can hear are his own footsteps and his own breathing.

He looks over towards the concrete steps leading up to the building above. The hatch is still open.

He shakes the torch, but it carries on getting dimmer.

Suddenly Joona hears a tinkling sound and holds his breath as he finds himself thinking about porcelain fingertips. At the same moment he feels a cold cloth pressed to his mouth and nose.

Joona spins round and lashes out hard, but hits nothing and loses his balance.

He turns, holding his pistol out, the barrel scrapes the concrete wall, but there's no one there.

Panting, he stands with his back to the wall, extending the torch towards the darkness.

The tinkling sound must have come from the little sedative bottles when the Sandman was pouring the volatile liquid onto the cloth.

Joona is feeling giddy, and swallows hard, forcing himself not to empty the magazine of the pistol into the darkness.

He desperately wants to get out into the fresh air, but forces himself to stay where he is.

It's completely silent, there's no one here.

Joona waits a few seconds, then returns to the capsule. His movements feel strangely delayed, and his gaze keeps slipping to the side. Before he goes inside, he turns the wheel of the lock so that the bolts slide out, preventing the door from closing.

In the weak glow of the torch he makes his way forward once more. The light bounces round the grey walls. He reaches the sofa and nudges it carefully away from the wall, and sees a skinny woman lying on the floor.

'Felicia? I'm a police officer,' he whispers. 'I'm going to get you out of here.'

When he touches her he can feel that she's boiling hot. She has an extremely high fever, and is no longer conscious. As he picks her up from the floor she starts to shake in fevered cramps.

Joona charges up the stairs with her in his arms. He drops the torch and hears it clatter down the steps. He realises that she's going to die soon unless he manages to get her fever down. Her body has gone completely limp again. He doesn't know if she's still breathing as he climbs up through the hatch.

Joona runs through the small building, kicks open the door, lays her down on the snow and sees that she's still breathing.

461

'Felicia, you've got a really bad fever . . . you poor thing . . .'

He covers her with snow, speaking to her in a soothing, reassuring voice, all the while keeping his pistol trained on the door of the building.

'The ambulance is on its way,' he says. 'Everything's going to be fine, I promise, Felicia. Your brother and your dad are going to be so happy, they've missed you so much, do you hear?'

## 153

The ambulance arrives, its blue lights flashing across the snow. Joona stands up as the trolley is wheeled past the old buildings. He explains the situation to the paramedics, the whole time keeping his pistol aimed at the entrance to barrack number four.

'Hurry up,' he cries. 'She's running a really high fever, you've got to get her temperature down . . . I think she's lost consciousness.'

The two paramedics lift Felicia out of the snow. Her hair is hanging in black, sweaty locks over her impossibly pale forehead.

'She's got Legionnaires' disease,' he says, then starts walking towards the open doorway with his weapon raised.

He's about to go back inside when he sees the flickering blue light of the ambulance playing over the remains of the last building. There are fresh footprints in the snow, leading away from the building and into the darkness.

Joona runs towards them, thinking that there must be another exit, that the two buildings share an underground shelter.

He follows the footsteps at a run, through clumps of grass and scrub.

As he rounds an old diesel tank he sees a thin figure walking quickly along the edge of the pit.

Joona is running as quietly as he can.

The figure is leaning on a crutch, limping, then realises he's being pursued and tries to move faster along the steep cliff.

There are sirens in the distance.

Joona races through the deep snow, his pistol in his hand.

I'm going to get him, he thinks. I'm going to arrest him and drag him back to the waiting cars.

They're approaching an illuminated section of the gravel pit containing a large concrete factory. A single floodlight is lighting up the bottom of the steep crater.

The figure stops, turns, and looks at Joona. He's standing right on the edge, supported by a crutch, breathing with his mouth open.

Joona slowly approaches, his pistol pointed at the ground.

The Sandman's face is almost identical to Jurek's, just much thinner.

Far in the distance Joona can hear the police cars arrive at the old barracks, but only thin arrows of blue light reach that far.

'It all went wrong with you, Joona,' the Sandman says. 'My brother managed to tell me to take Summa and Lumi, but they died before I got the chance . . . fate sometimes chooses its own path . . .'

The strong beams of the police officers' torches are circling round the old barracks.

'I wrote to my brother and told him about you, but I never found out if he wanted me to take anything else away from you,' he says quietly.

Joona stops, feeling the weight of the weapon in his tired arm, and looks into the Sandman's pale eyes.

'I was sure you'd hang yourself after the car accident, but

you're still alive,' the skinny man says, shaking his head slowly. 'I waited, but you just went on living . . .'

He falls silent, then smiles suddenly, looks up and says:

'You're still alive because your family isn't really dead.'

Joona simply raises his pistol, aims the barrel at the Sandman's heart and fires three shots. The bullets go straight through his skinny frame, and black blood sprays out from the exit wounds between his shoulder blades.

Three gunshots echo round the gravel pit.

Jurek's twin brother falls backwards.

His crutch remains where it is, stuck in the snow.

The Sandman is dead before he even hits the ground. His emaciated body rolls down the slope until it hits an old cooker. Light snowflakes drift down from the black sky.

## 154

Joona is sitting in the rear seat of his own car with his eyes closed, while his boss Carlos Eliasson drives him back to Stockholm, talking to him as if he was his dad.

'She's going to be OK . . . I spoke to a doctor at the Karolinska . . . Felicia's condition is serious, but not critical . . . They're not making any promises, but even so, it's great news . . . I think she's going to make it, I . . .'

'Have you told Reidar?' Joona asks, without opening his eyes.

'The hospital are dealing with that, you just need to go home and get some rest, and—'

'I tried to reach you.'

'Yes, I know, I saw I had a load of missed calls . . . You might have heard that Jurek mentioned an old brickworks to Saga. There were never that many, but there used to be one in Albano. When we went into the forest the dogs identified graves all over the place. We're busy searching the whole damn area.'

'But you haven't found anyone alive?'

'Not yet, but we'll carry on searching.'

'I think you're just going to find graves . . .'

Carlos is driving with exemplary caution, and it's now so warm inside the car that Joona has to unbutton his coat.

'The nightmare's over, Joona . . . First thing tomorrow the Prison Service Committee will pass the decision to transfer Saga again, and we can go and pick her up and clear all her details from the databases.'

They reach Stockholm, and the light around the street-lamps looks like fog because of the snow. A bus pulls up beside them, waiting for the lights to change. Weary faces look out through the steamed-up windows.

'I talked to Anja,' Carlos says. 'She couldn't wait till tomorrow . . . she's found the records for Jurek and his brother in the Child Welfare Commission's files in the council archive, and she's tracked down the decision of the Aliens Department in the National Archive in Marieberg.'

'Anja's smart,' Joona says to himself.

'Jurek's father was allowed to stay in the country on a temporary work permit,' Carlos says. 'But he didn't have permission to have the boys with him, and after they were found the Child Welfare Commission was brought in and the boys were taken into care. Presumably the authorities thought they were doing the right thing. The decision was hurried through, but because one of the boys was ill the cases were dealt with separately . . .'

'They were sent to different places.'

'The Aliens Department sent the healthy boy back to Kazakhstan, and then a different caseworker took the decision to send the other boy to Russia, to Children's Home Number 67, to be precise.'

'I see,' Joona whispers.

'Jurek Walter crossed the border into Sweden in January 1994. Maybe his brother was already at the quarry by that time, maybe not . . . but by then their father was dead.'

Carlos pulls up smoothly in an empty parking space on

Dalagatan, not far from Joona's flat at Wallingatan 31. They both get out of the car, walk down the snow-covered pavement and stop outside the door.

'As I mentioned, I knew Roseanna Kohler,' Carlos says with a sigh. 'And when their children disappeared I did all I could, but it wasn't enough . . .'

'No.'

'I told her about Jurek. She wanted me to tell her everything, wanted to see pictures of him, and . . .'

'But Reidar didn't know.'

'No, she said it was better that way. I don't know . . . Roseanna moved to Paris, she used to call all the time, she was drinking far too much . . . It wasn't that I was bothered about my career, but I thought it was embarrassing, for her as well as me . . .'

Carlos falls silent and rubs his neck with one hand.

'What?' Joona asks.

'One night Roseanna called me from Paris, screaming that she'd seen Jurek Walter outside her hotel, but I didn't listen . . . Later that night, she killed herself . . .'

Carlos hands Joona the car keys.

'Get some sleep,' he says. 'I'm going to head down to Norra Bantorget and get a taxi.'

## 155

Anders is thinking that My looked slightly bemused when he told her she could get some sleep in the rest-room again.

'I just can't see any reason for us both to be awake,' he said in a measured voice. 'I don't have any choice, I've got to do a couple more hours' work to get finished. After that you and Leif can divide things up however you like.'

Now he's alone. He walks down the corridor, stops outside the door to the rest-room and listens.

Silence.

He carries on to the security control room and sits down in the operator's seat. At last it's time to turn the lights out. The large screen is showing nine different scenes. Jurek went to bed early. Anders can see his thin frame outlined beneath the covers. Jurek Walter is lying unnervingly still. It's almost as if he isn't breathing. Saga is sitting with her feet on the ground. Her chair is on its side on the floor.

He leans closer to the screen and looks at her. His eyes follow the outline of her shaved head, her slender neck and shoulders, the muscles in her thin arms.

There's nothing to stop him.

He can't understand why he got so scared last night when

he was in her room. There was no one at the monitors, and even if there had been, the room was so dark that they wouldn't have seen anything.

He could have slept with her ten times, he could have done whatever he wanted.

Anders takes a deep breath, inserts his ID card into the computer, types the code and logs in. He opens the unit's administrative programme, highlights the patients' zone and clicks on nocturnal lighting.

All three patients' rooms go black.

Seconds later Saga turns on her bedside lamp and lifts her face up towards the camera.

It's as if she's looking at him because she knows he's looking at her.

Anders checks on the two guards; they're standing talking to each other by the entrance. The male one is saying something that makes the tall female guard laugh – he's smiling as he mimes playing a violin.

Anders stands up and looks at Saga again.

He gets a pill from the medicine store and puts it in a plastic cup, goes over to the security door and runs his card through the reader.

As he approaches her door his heart starts thumping hard. Through the thick glass he can see her sitting on her bed with her eyes fixed on the camera, as if she were a little mermaid.

Anders opens the hatch and sees her turn her head in his direction. She gets to her feet and walks slowly towards him.

'Did you sleep well last night?' he asks in a friendly voice.

When she reaches her hand through the hatch he holds her fingers for a few moments before giving her the plastic cup.

He closes the hatch and sees her walk back into the room. She puts the pill in her mouth, fills the cup with water and swallows it, then turns out the lamp by the bed and lies down.

Anders goes and gets the straps that fit the bed, removes the plastic covering and then stands outside the steel door watching her through the reinforced glass.

## 156

Under cover of darkness Saga hides the pill in her shoe, then lies down on the bed. She doesn't know if the young doctor is still standing outside the glass in the door, but she's sure he's planning to come into her room as soon as he thinks she's asleep. She could see quite clearly in his eyes that he wasn't finished with her.

Yesterday she was so taken aback by his abuse of power that she let it go way too far. Today she doesn't even know if she cares what happens.

She's here to save Felicia, and maybe she'll have to put up with this place for a few more days.

She tells herself that tomorrow or the day after Jurek will reveal everything to her, and then this will be over, then she can go home and forget what she's been through.

Saga rolls onto her other side, glances at the door and immediately catches sight of the silhouette behind the glass. Her heart begins to beat harder in her chest. The young doctor is waiting outside the door until she's knocked out by the medication.

Is she prepared to let herself be raped in order to conceal

her mission? It doesn't really matter. Her thoughts are far too chaotic for her to be able to prepare herself for what seems to be happening.

Just let it be over quickly.

There's a metallic scraping sound as the key is slipped into the lock.

The door opens and cooler air sweeps in.

She doesn't bother pretending to be asleep yet, and keeps her eyes open, watching the doctor close the door behind him and walk over to the bed.

She shuts her eyes and listens.

Nothing happens.

Maybe he just wants to look at her.

She tries to breathe out soundlessly, then waits for ten seconds before breathing in again, waits, imagining a mental square in her mind, where each side is a moment.

The doctor puts his hand on her stomach, following the movement of her breathing, then it slides to her hip and takes hold of her underwear. She lies quite still and lets him pull her pants off, easing them over her feet.

She can feel the warmth of his body clearly now.

Carefully he strokes her right hand and raises it gently above her head. At first she thinks he's going to measure her pulse, then she realises that she can't move. When she tries to pull her hand away, he puts a broad strap over her thighs and tightens it with terrible strength before she has a chance to wriggle off the bed.

'What the hell are you doing?'

She can't kick out, and realises that he must have tied her ankles while she was trying to free her right hand with her left. He switches on the bedside lamp and looks at her, wide-eyed. Her fingers are trembling, slipping on the thick strap round her wrist, and she has to try again.

The doctor stops her, quickly pulling her free hand away.

She jerks to get loose, tries to twist round, but it's impossible.

When she slumps back he starts to attach another strap across her shoulders. The angle is almost impossible, but when he leans over her she punches him in the mouth with her clenched fist. As the blow connects, he stumbles back and sinks down onto one knee. Shaking, she starts to untie the strap round her right wrist.

He's back at the bed now, shoving her hand away.

There's blood running down his chin as he roars at her to lie still. He tightens the strap round her right wrist again, then moves behind her.

'I'll kill you,' she shouts, trying to follow him with her eyes.

He's quick, and grabs her left arm with both hands, but she pulls free, gets hold of his hair and yanks him towards her. As hard as she can, she rams his forehead against the frame of the bed. She pulls him forward again and tries to bite his face, but he hits her so hard across the neck and one breast that she lets go.

Gasping, she struggles to grab hold of him again, fumbling with her hand behind her. Using all her strength she tries to twist her body, but she's completely stuck.

The doctor takes hold of her head and bends it hard to one side, almost dislocating her shoulder. The cartilage in the joint makes a creaking sound and she howls with pain. She's struggling to pull one foot free, but the strap is cutting into her skin and her ankle is clicking. She hits him on the cheek with her free hand, but without any real force. He pushes her hand down to the top of the bed, fixes the strap round her wrist and tightens it.

474

The young doctor wipes the blood from his mouth with the back of his hand, panting, then takes a couple of steps away and just looks at her.

## 157

The doctor walks slowly up to her, places the last strap across her chest and fixes it in place. Her left hand is stinging after her desperate blows. He stands there for a while, just staring at her again, then goes to the foot of the bed. Blood is trickling from his nose, over his lips. She can hear him taking shallow, excited breaths. Without any hurry, he tightens the straps round her ankles, pulling her thighs further apart. She looks him in the eyes and thinks that she can't let this happen.

He strokes her calves with shaking hands, and stares up between her thighs.

'Don't do this,' she tries to say in a composed voice.

'Just keep quiet,' he says, removing his doctor's coat without taking his eyes off her.

Saga turns her face aside, doesn't want to look at him, can't believe that this is happening.

She closes her eyes, desperately trying to think of a way out.

Suddenly she hears a strange rattling sound beneath the bed. She opens her eyes and sees a figure mirrored in the stainless-steel basin.

'You should get out of here,' she gasps.

The doctor picks her pants up from the bed and stuffs them roughly in her mouth. She tries to scream as she realises what the reflection in the shiny metal of the basin is.

It's Jurek Walter.

He must have hidden himself away in her room while she was looking for Bernie's sleeping pills.

With growing panic she struggles to free herself.

She can hear the buttons of Jurek's shirt clicking against the struts under the mattress as he moves.

One button comes loose and flies out across the floor. The doctor looks at it in surprise as it rolls round in a large circle and spins to a stop.

'Jurek,' the doctor mutters at the moment a hand grabs his legs and pulls him to the ground.

Anders Rönn falls flat on the floor, hitting the back of his head and gasping, but he rolls over onto his front, kicks out and crawls away.

Run, Saga thinks. Lock the door, call the police.

Jurek rolls out onto the floor and gets to his feet at the same time as the doctor. Anders Rönn makes for the door, but Jurek gets there first.

Saga is struggling to get the underpants out of her mouth, coughs, takes a deep breath and starts to feel sick.

Anders Rönn moves sideways, walks straight into the plastic chair and backs away, staring at the elderly patient.

'Don't hurt me,' he pleads.

'No?'

'Please, I'll do anything.'

Jurek comes closer, and his wrinkled face is completely expressionless.

'I'm going to kill you, my boy,' he says. 'But first you're going to experience a great deal of pain.'

Saga screams through the fabric gag, and tugs at the straps.

She can't understand what's happened, why Jurek hid in her room, why he changed their plan.

The plastic chair tumbles to the floor.

The doctor is shaking his head, retreating and trying to fend Jurek off with one hand.

His eyes are open wide.

Sweat is running down his cheeks.

Jurek is following him slowly, then suddenly he grabs his hand and forces the doctor down on the floor. With terrible force he stamps on the arm, close to the shoulder. There's a crunch and the young doctor screams out loud. With military precision, Jurek pulls in the opposite direction and twists the arm round. It's completely detached from its socket now, just hanging from muscle and skin.

Jurek yanks the doctor to his feet, holds him up against the wall, and slaps him several times to stop him losing consciousness.

His loose arm is slowly turning darker from internal bleeding.

Saga coughs, she's having trouble breathing.

The doctor is weeping like an overtired child.

Saga manages to shift position slightly and pulls her left arm so hard that her vision starts to go black before her arm suddenly comes loose.

She tugs the underpants from her mouth, gasps for breath and coughs again.

'We can't escape now – there weren't any sleeping pills in Bernie's room,' Saga says quickly to Jurek.

The hand she's just pulled free hurts like hell. She can't tell how badly wounded it is. Her fingers are burning like fire.

Jurek starts to go through the doctor's clothes, finds the keys to the cell door and slips them in his pocket.

'Do you want to watch while I cut his head off?' he asks, glancing quickly at Saga.

'Don't do it, please . . . there's no need, is there?'

'There's never any need to do anything,' Jurek says, grabbing the doctor by the neck.

'Wait.'

'OK, I'll wait . . . for two minutes, for your sake, little police officer.'

'What do you mean?'

'The one mistake you made was when you only broke one of Bernie's fingers,' Jurek says, taking the doctor's pass card.

'I was thinking of killing him slowly,' she tries, even though she knows there's no point.

Jurek slaps the doctor again.

'All I need is the two codes,' he says.

'Codes,' the doctor mumbles. 'I can't remember, I . . .'

Saga tries to loosen the other straps, but the fingers of her left hand are so badly injured that it's impossible.

'How could you tell?' Saga asks.

'I got a letter.'

'No,' the doctor whimpers.

'Saying that Mikael Kohler-Frost had escaped and been found alive . . . so I assumed the police were going to send someone.'

Jurek finds the doctor's phone, drops it on the floor and crushes it beneath his foot.

'But why—'

'I haven't got time,' he interrupts. 'I need to go and destroy Joona Linna.'

Saga watches as Jurek Walter leads the doctor out of the cell. She hears their footsteps in the corridor, then the sound of the pass card being pulled through the reader, the code being tapped in, followed by the whirr of the lock.

## 158

Joona rings his own doorbell and smiles to himself as he hears footsteps on the floor. The lock rattles and the door swings open. He walks into the dimly lit hall and takes his shoes off.

'You look completely wiped out,' Disa says.

'It's nothing.'

'Do you want something to eat? There's some left . . . I can warm it up . . .'

Joona shakes his head and gives her a hug. He's thinking that he's too tired to talk now, but later he'll ask her to cancel her trip to Brazil. There's no need for her to go now.

She helps him get his clothes off and a load of sand falls on the floor.

'Have you been playing in a sandpit?' she laughs.

'Only for a little while,' he replies.

He goes into the bathroom and gets in the shower. His body feels sore as the hot water courses over him. He leans against the tiles as his muscles slowly start to relax.

The hand that was holding the gun as he pulled the trigger and shot an unarmed man is burning.

If I can get used to the thought of what I'm guilty of having done, I can be happy again, he thinks.

Even though Joona knows the Sandman is dead, even though he saw the bullets go straight through his body, even though he saw him tumble into the quarry like a corpse into a mass grave, he still went down after it. He slid down the steep slope, trying to stop himself going too fast, and made his way to the body. Keeping his pistol aimed at the back of the man's head, he felt his neck with the other hand. The Sandman was dead. His eyes hadn't deceived him. The three bullets had all passed straight through his heart.

The thought that he no longer has to fear Jurek's accomplice is so warm and comforting that he can't help letting out a groan.

Joona dries himself and brushes his teeth, then suddenly stops and listens. It sounds like Disa's talking on the phone.

When he walks into the bedroom he sees that Disa's getting dressed.

'What are you doing?' he asks, lying down on the fresh sheets.

'My boss called,' she says with a weary smile. 'Apparently they're filling in a pit out at Loudden. The ground is being cleared, but it sounds as if they've found a backgammon set. I've got to get out there and stop them at once, because if it really is—'

'Don't go,' Joona begs, feeling his eyes prick with tiredness.

Disa hums to herself as she takes a folded sweater from the top drawer of the chest.

'Have you started using my drawers?' he mutters, closing his eyes.

Disa walks back and forth in the room. He hears her brushing her hair, then lifting her coat off the hanger.

He rolls onto his side and feels memory and dreams start to join up, like snowflakes.

The Sandman's body tumbles down the steep slope and stops when it hits an old cooker.

Samuel Mendel scratches his head and says: 'There's nothing at all to suggest that Jurek Walter has an accomplice. But you have to stick a finger in the air and say איפכא ודילמא.'

# 159

Saga makes a fresh attempt to loosen the strap round her right wrist, but fails and slumps back again, out of breath.

Jurek Walter is escaping, she thinks.

Panic is bubbling in her chest.

She has to warn Joona.

Saga twists her body to the right, but has to give up.

In the distance she can hear a noise.

She holds her breath and listens.

There's a squeaking sound, then several heavy thuds, before everything is silent once more.

It dawns on Saga that Jurek never needed the pills, all he wanted was for her to entice the doctor into her room. Jurek had seen through Anders Rönn's intentions, and realised he wouldn't be able to resist the temptation to go into her room if she asked for sleeping pills.

That had been the plan all along.

That was why he had taken her punishment, because the fact that she was dangerous had to be concealed.

She was a siren, just as he had said on the first day.

Jurek needed to lure the doctor into her room without a guard or a carer keeping an eye on proceedings.

Her fingers are so badly damaged that she whimpers with pain as she stretches to the side and picks at the catch of the strap across her shoulders.

Now she can move her shoulder and raise her head.

We all walked into his trap, she thinks. We thought we were deceiving him, but he had as good as put in an order for me. He knew someone would be sent, and today he found out for certain that I was his Trojan horse.

She lies still for a few seconds, catching her breath and feeling the endorphins in her body. She gathers her strength, then cranes her head to the side, trying to grab the strap round her right wrist with her mouth.

She slumps back, panting, thinking that she has to alert the staff and get them to call the police.

Saga takes a deep breath and tries again. Straining hard to hold her position, she manages to sink her teeth into the thick strap, loosen the catch and release another centimetre or so of the strap. She falls back, feeling nauseous, then twists and pulls her hand and succeeds in freeing it.

It doesn't take long for her to remove the remaining straps. She puts her legs together and slips onto the floor. Her inner thighs are aching and her muscles shake as she pulls on her trousers.

She runs out into the corridor barefoot. One of the doctor's shoes is wedged in the doorway, preventing the security door from closing.

Cautiously she opens the door, listens, then hurries on. The secure unit is ghostly quiet and abandoned. She can hear the sound of her feet sticking to the vinyl flooring as she creeps into the room to her right and over to the operator's desk. The screens are dark, and the lights on the alarm unit are all switched off. The electricity supply to the whole secure unit has been cut.

But somewhere there has to be a phone or a functioning alarm. Saga carries on, past a number of closed doors, until she reaches the staff kitchen. The cutlery drawers are open, and there's a toppled chair on the floor.

In the sink there's a vegetable knife and some browning apple peel. Saga quickly snatches up the little knife, checks that the blade is sharp, and moves on.

She can hear a strange buzzing sound.

She stops and listens, then continues forward.

Her right hand is squeezing the knife too hard.

There ought to be security staff and carers here, but she daren't call out. She's scared of Jurek hearing her.

The buzzing is coming from the corridor. It sounds like a fly caught on a piece of fly-paper. She creeps past the inspection room, feeling more and more apprehensive.

She blinks at the darkness and stops again.

The buzzing is closer now.

She takes a few cautious steps forward. The door to the staffroom is open. There's a light on. She reaches out her hand and opens the door wider.

For a moment there's total silence, then she hears the hissing, buzzing sound again.

She moves closer and sees the end of the bed. Someone's lying on it, their toes twitching. Two feet in white socks.

'Hello?' she says tentatively.

Saga convinces herself that the carer is lying there listening to music and has missed everything that's been going on before she steps further into the room.

The bed is completely drenched in blood.

The girl with pierced cheeks is lying on her back, her body is quivering, her eyes are staring up at the ceiling but she may well have lost consciousness.

Her face is twitching, and from her pursed lips a mixture of blood and air is bubbling out with a hissing sound.

'God . . .'

The girl has a dozen knife-wounds to her chest, deep cuts into her lungs and heart. There's nothing Saga can do, she needs to get help as soon as she possibly can.

Blood is dripping onto the floor, beside the remnants of the girl's crushed phone.

'I'll get help,' Saga says.

The girl's lips hiss as a bubble of blood inflates.

## 160

Saga leaves the room with a horribly empty feeling inside.

'Dear God in heaven, dear God in heaven . . .'

She runs along the corridor, oddly numb with shock as she approaches the security airlock. The guard is sitting on the other side of the far door. The toughened glass makes him look indistinct and grey.

Hiding the little vegetable knife in her hand so as not to frighten him, Saga slows down and tries to control her breathing as she walks up to the glass and knocks on it.

'We need help in here!'

She knocks louder, but he doesn't react, so she moves to the side, towards the door, and sees that it's open.

All the doors are open, she thinks as she walks through.

Saga is about to say something when she sees that the guard is dead. His throat has been cut so brutally that it's sliced right through to the vertebrae. His head looks almost as if it's hanging limply from a broom-handle. The blood has run down his body and gathered in a pool around his chair.

'OK,' she says to herself, and she runs across the wet floor with the knife in her hand, then up the steps and through the open gate.

She tugs at the door leading to secure forensic psychiatric Ward 30. It's locked, it's the middle of the night. She bangs on it a few times, then carries on along the corridor.

'Hello,' she calls out. 'Is there anyone here?'

The doctor's other shoe is lying on the floor in the harsh glare of the fluorescent ceiling light.

Saga runs on, and sees movement up ahead, through several panes of glass at different angles. It's a man, standing and smoking. He flicks the cigarette away, then disappears off to the left. Saga runs as fast as she can, towards the glassed-in exit and the passageway leading to the main hospital building. She turns the corner and suddenly notices that the floor beneath her feet is wet.

The light is blinding her, and at first it looks like the floor is black, then the smell of blood becomes so tangible that it's all she can do not to throw up.

There's a large puddle, and footsteps lead away from it towards the entrance.

In an almost dreamlike state she carries on, and sees the young doctor's head. It's lying discarded on the floor, beside the rubbish bin against the wall to her right.

Jurek aimed and missed, she thinks, as she starts breathing far too quickly.

She keeps moving forward, out over the dry floor, while her thoughts drift hollowly, unable to make sense of things.

It's impossible to understand that this is happening.

Why has he taken the time to do this?

Because he didn't just want to get out, she tells herself. He wanted revenge.

Suddenly she hears heavy steps from the passage leading to the main building. Two guards are running towards her, with bulletproof vests, guns and black clothing.

'We need doctors to the secure unit,' Saga calls.

'Lie down on the floor,' the younger one says, walking closer.

'It's only a little girl,' the other one says.

'I'm a police officer,' she says, throwing the knife away.

It bounces across the vinyl floor and stops in front of them. They look at it, open their holsters and draw their service pistols.

'Down on the floor!'

'I'm lying down,' she says quickly. 'But you've got to warn —'

'Fuck,' the younger one exclaims when he sees the head. 'Fuck, fuck . . .'

'I'll shoot,' the other one says in a shaky voice.

Saga slowly gets down on her knees and the guard hurries over, pulling the handcuffs from his belt. The other guard moves aside. Saga holds out her hands and stands up.

'Nice and fucking slow now,' the guard says in a jagged voice.

She shuts her eyes, hears boots on the floor, feels his movements and takes a little step backwards. The guard leans forward to cuff her hands, and Saga opens her eyes at the same moment as she throws a right hook. There's a crunch as she hits him hard above his ear. She swings round and meets the jolt of his head with her left elbow.

The only sound is a brief thump.

Saliva sprays from his open mouth.

The two blows were so hard that the guard's field of vision shrinks to a pinpoint of light in a tenth of a second.

His legs give way and he doesn't notice Saga snatching his pistol from him. She releases the safety catch and fires before he hits the floor.

Saga shoots the other guard twice, right in his bulletproof vest.

The shots echo in the narrow passageway and the guard

staggers back. Saga rushes over and knocks the pistol out of his hand with the butt of hers.

The gun clatters across the floor towards the bloody footprints.

Saga kicks both his legs out from under him, and he falls flat on his back with a groan. The other guard rolls over onto his side, clutching his face with one hand. Saga grabs one of their radios and takes a few steps away.

## 161

Joona is wrenched from his dreams by the sound of the phone ringing. He hadn't even realised he was dozing off, just plunged straight into deep sleep while Disa was changing into her work clothes. The bedroom is dark, but the glow from his phone is casting a pale elliptical shape on the wall.

'Joona Linna,' he answers with a sigh.

'Jurek's escaped, he's managed to get out of—'

'Saga?' Joona asks, leaping out of bed.

'He's killed loads of people,' she says, a note of hysteria in her voice.

'Are you hurt?'

Joona walks through the flat, adrenalin coursing through him as the realisation of what Saga's saying sinks in.

'I don't know where he is, he just said he was going to hurt you, he said—'

'Disa!' Joona cries.

He sees that her boots are gone, opens the front door and calls her name down the stairwell, his voice echoing in the darkness. He tries to remember what she said just before he fell asleep.

'Disa's gone to Loudden,' he says.

'Sorry to—'

Joona cuts the call off, pulls his clothes on, grabs his pistol and holster and leaves the flat, not bothering to lock it behind him.

He runs down the stairs and out onto the pavement, then off towards Dalagatan where Carlos parked his car. As he runs he calls Disa. No answer. It's snowing heavily, and when he sees the snow piled up along the edge of the pavement, he wonders if he's going to have to dig the car out.

His path is blocked by a bus passing so close that the ground shakes. The wind is blowing fresh snow from a low, wide wall.

Joona rushes over to the car, gets in and drives straight through the bank of snow, scraping the side against a parked car and putting his foot down.

As he accelerates past Tegnérlunden and down towards Sveavägen, the loose snow flies off the car in soft clouds.

Joona is suddenly aware that everything he's afraid of is going to flare up like a firestorm tonight.

The transition is instant, from one moment to the next.

Disa is alone in her car, on her way out to Frihamnen.

Joona can feel his heart pounding against his holster. Snow is falling heavily on the windscreen.

He's driving very fast now, thinking of how Disa's boss called and asked her to look at something that had been found. Samuel's wife Rebecka got a call from a carpenter, asking her to go out to their summer house earlier than arranged.

The Sandman must have mentioned Disa in the letter that Susanne Hjälm gave Jurek. His hands are shaking as he brings up Disa's name in his contacts and calls again. As the phone rings, he feels sweat trickling down his back.

She doesn't answer. Joona turns sharply into Karlavägen and drives as fast as he possibly can.

It's probably nothing, he tries to convince himself. He just has to get hold of Disa and tell her to turn round and drive home. He'll hide her away somewhere until Jurek has been recaptured.

The car slides on the brown slush on the tarmac and a lorry swerves violently out of his way. He calls again. Still no answer.

He heads past Humlegården as fast as he can. The road is lined with grubby banks of snow, and the streetlamps reflect off the wet tarmac.

He calls Disa again.

The traffic lights have turned red, but Joona turns right into Valhallavägen. A cement-mixer swerves out of his way, and a red car pulls up sharply with a shriek of brakes. The driver blows his horn as Disa suddenly answers.

## 162

Disa drives carefully over the rusty railway tracks and carries on into the huge harbour of Frihamnen with its ferry and container traffic. The night sky is low and full of swirling, falling snow.

The yellow glow of a hanging streetlight sways across a hangar-like building.

People are walking with their heads bowed to stop the snow getting in their eyes, to protect themselves from the cold. Far off through the snow she can just make out the large Tallinn ferry, lit up but as indistinct as a dream.

Disa turns right, away from the illuminated premises of one of the big banana import companies, and drives past a succession of low industrial units as she peers into the gloom.

Articulated lorries start to drive on board the ferry to St Petersburg.

A group of dock workers are standing smoking in an empty car park. Darkness and snow make the world around the little gathering seem muffled and isolated.

Disa drives past warehouse number five, and in through the gates of the container terminal. Each container is the size of a small cottage, and can weigh more than thirty tons.

They stand there stacked on top of each other, maybe fifteen metres high.

A plastic bag is being blown about by the wind. The ice on the puddles crunches beneath the car's tyres.

The stacks of containers form a network of passageways for the huge lorries and terminal tractors. Disa heads down one of the gangways that feels oddly narrow because its sides are so high. She can see from the tracks in the snow that another car has driven this way very recently. Some fifty metres ahead the passageway opens up onto the quayside. The vast bulk of Loudden's oil tank is just visible through the snow beyond the cranes that are loading containers onto a ship.

The men with the backgammon set are probably waiting for her up ahead.

Snow is blowing across the windscreen and she slows down, switches the wipers on and brushes the light snow away.

In the distance a large piece of machinery resembling a scorpion stops in the middle of a sideways movement: it's holding a red container quite still, just above the ground.

There's no one in the driver's cab, and the wheels are quickly being covered by snow.

She's starts when her mobile suddenly rings, and smiles to herself as she answers:

'You're supposed to be asleep,' she says brightly.

'Tell me where you are right now,' Joona says, his voice intense.

'I'm in the car, on my way to —'

'I want you to skip the meeting and go straight home.'

'What's happened?'

'Jurek Walter has escaped from the secure unit.'

'What did you say?'

'I want you to go home right away.'

The headlights are forming an aquarium full of glowing,

swirling snow in front of the car. She slows down even more, looks at the red container held in the claw of the machine, and reads:

'Hamburg Süd . . .'

'You have to listen to me,' Joona says. 'Turn the car round and drive home.'

'OK then.'

He waits and listens to her over the phone.

'Have you turned round?'

'I can't right now . . . I need to find a suitable place,' she says quietly as she suddenly catches sight of something odd.

'Disa, I can see that I might be sounding a bit—'

'Hang on,' she interrupts.

'What are you doing?'

She slows down still further and drives cautiously towards a large bundle that's lying on the ground in the middle of the passageway. It looks like a grey blanket tied with duct tape, and it's slowly being covered with snow.

'What's happening, Disa?' Joona asks, sounding agitated. 'Have you turned round yet?'

'There's something in the way,' she says as she stops. 'I can't get past.'

'You can reverse!'

'Just give me a moment,' she says, and puts the phone down on the seat.

'Disa!' he shouts. 'You mustn't get out of the car! Reverse away from there! Disa!'

She can't hear him, she's already out of the car and walking away. Snow is swirling gently through the air. It's almost totally quiet, and the light from the tall cranes doesn't reach into the deep gulley between the stacks of containers.

The wind forcing its way between the containers high above her is making strange noises.

In the distance she can see the warning lights of a huge

forklift truck. The flashes of yellow are caught by the falling snow.

Disa is filled with a sense of sombre ceremony as she walks on in silence. She's thinking that she'll drag the bundle to the side so she can drive past, but stops and tries to focus her gaze.

The forklift disappears round a corner a long way ahead, leaving just the ice-cold light of the car's headlights and the endlessly falling snow.

It looks as if there's something moving under the grey blanket.

Disa blinks and hesitates.

Everything in this moment is astonishingly silent and peaceful. Snowflakes are sailing slowly down from the dense sky.

Disa stands still, feeling her heart beating hard in her chest, then she walks the rest of the way.

## 163

Joona is driving too fast when he turns left at the roundabout, the front bumper thuds into the banked-up snow, the tyres rumble over the packed ice. He wrestles with the steering wheel as the car slides sideways, then puts his foot down and the car leaves the pavement and carries on along Lindarängsvägen without losing much speed.

The vast grassy expanse of Gärdet is covered with snow, stretching like a white sea up towards Norra Djurgården.

He overtakes a bus on the straight, hits one hundred and sixty kilometres an hour, and flies past yellow-brick blocks of flats. The car slides between the edges of the deep tracks through the snow as he brakes to turn left towards the harbour. Snow and ice are thrown up across the windscreen. Through the tall wire fence surrounding the harbour he can see a long, narrow ferry being loaded with containers in the blurred light from a crane.

A rust-brown goods train is on its way into Frihamnen.

Joona peers through the swirling snow, the murky shadows surrounding the deserted warehouses. He turns sharply into the harbour, bouncing across a traffic-island as slush flies around the car and the tyres spin.

The railway barriers are already starting to close but Joona accelerates across the tracks and the barriers scrape the roof of the car.

He drives on at speed through Frihamnen. There are people leaving the Tallinn ferry terminal, a scant line of black figures vanishing into the night.

She can't be far away. She stopped the car and got out. Someone rebooked her meeting. Forced her to come out here. Got her to leave the car.

He sounds his horn and people leap out of his way. One woman drops her luggage trolley and Joona drives straight over it.

An articulated lorry is moving slowly down the roll-on, roll-off ramp and onto the ferry to St Petersburg. It leaves great clods of compacted brown snow on the ground behind it.

Joona drives past an empty car park between warehouses five and six and in through the gates of the container terminal.

The area is like a city, with narrow alleys and tall, window-less buildings. He sees something from the corner of his eye and brakes sharply, then reverses with a shriek of tyres.

Disa's car is standing in the passageway ahead of him. A thin layer of snow has settled on top of it. The driver's door is open. Joona stops and runs over to it. The engine is still warm. He looks inside, there's no sign of violence or a struggle.

He breathes ice-cold air into his lungs.

Disa got out of the car and walked in front of it. Snow is filling her tracks, making them soft.

'No,' he whispers.

There's a patch of downtrodden snow ten metres ahead of her car, and a track has been left by something being dragged off to the side a metre or so between the tall containers before it stops.

A necklace of drops of blood is just visible under the powdery, freshly fallen snow.

Beyond that the snow is smooth and untouched.

Joona stops himself calling Disa's name.

Ice-crystals are falling on the containers, making a tinkling sound. He takes a few steps back and sees five ISO containers hanging in the air twenty metres up. The one at the bottom has white writing on a red background: Hamburg Süd.

He heard Disa say those words just before their conversation was cut off.

Joona starts to run through the passageway towards the crane holding the container. The snow is deep, he slips on a piece of metal, hits his shoulder against a yellow container, but keeps on going.

He emerges onto quay number five and looks round. His heart is beating fast in his chest. A dock worker in a helmet is speaking into a walkie-talkie. Snow is falling through the glare of the floodlight, swirling out over the black water.

A vast crane on rails is loading a container ship bound for Rotterdam.

Joona catches sight of the red container bearing the words Hamburg Süd and starts running.

Hundreds of containers, all different colours, bearing different shipping companies' names, have already been loaded beyond these latest ones.

Two dock workers are walking quickly along the quayside in their bulky outfits and bright yellow tunics. One of them is pointing up at the lofty bridge of the ship.

## 164

Joona peers through the heavy snowfall, jumps over a concrete plinth and reaches the edge of the quay. Sludgy ice is floating in the black water, rattling against the hull. The smell of the sea is mixed with the diesel fumes from four caterpillar trucks.

Joona clambers on board and hurries along the railing, shoving a box of shackles out of the way and finding a shovel.

'You there!' a man behind him calls.

Joona rushes straight through a damp cardboard box, running along the edge, and sees that there's a sledgehammer next to the railing, among the wrenches, lifting hooks and a rusty chain. He drops the shovel, grabs the sledgehammer instead and runs over to the red container. It's big enough for four cars. He hits it with his hand, and the metal echoes back dully.

'Disa,' he shouts, as he hurries round it.

A heavy container lock is fastened to the double-doors. He swings the sledgehammer across the deck, then twists it back and round with incredible force. There's a crash as the lock shatters. He drops the sledgehammer and opens the doors.

Disa isn't there.

All he can see in the gloom are two BMW sports cars.

Joona doesn't know what to do. He looks back towards the quayside, at the vast stacks of containers.

One of the terminal's tractors is moving loose goods with its lights flashing.

Far in the distance Loudden's oil tank is barely visible through the heavy snowfall.

Joona wipes his mouth and starts to walk back.

One mobile crane is lifting a number of containers onto a goods train, and at the end of the quay, more than three hundred metres away, an articulated lorry covered in filthy tarpaulin is driving on board a roll-on, roll-off ferry to St Petersburg.

On the ramp behind the lorry is another one, pulling a red ISO-container behind it.

On the side of the container are the words Hamburg Süd.

Joona tries to work out the quickest way to get there.

'You're not allowed up here,' a man shouts behind him.

Joona turns and sees a thickset dock worker in a helmet, bright-yellow tunic and heavy gloves.

'National Crime Police,' Joona explains quickly. 'I'm looking for—'

'I don't care who you are,' the man interrupts, 'you can't just climb on board a—'

'Call your boss and tell him that—'

'You're going to wait right here and explain everything to the security guards who are—'

'I haven't got time for this,' Joona says, turning away.

The dock worker grabs hold of him by the shoulder. Out of reflex Joona swings round, wraps his own arm over the man's and twists his elbow up.

It all happens very fast.

The dock worker is forced to lean back because of the pain in his shoulder, and Joona kicks his feet out from under him at the same moment, and he starts to fall.

Instead of breaking the dock worker's arm, Joona lets go and allows him to collapse onto the deck.

The large crane rumbles and everything suddenly goes dark when the glare of the floodlights is obscured by the cargo dangling from the crane, directly above him.

Joona picks up the sledgehammer and starts to walk away quickly, but a younger dock-worker in high-visibility clothing is standing in his way, holding a large wrench in his hand.

'Be very careful,' Joona says ominously.

'You need to wait until the security guards get here,' the dock worker tells him. There's a worried look in his eyes.

Joona shoves him in the chest with one hand to force his way past. The dock worker takes a step back, then strikes out with the wrench. Joona blocks the blow with his arm, but it still hits him on the shoulder. He groans with pain and lets go of the sledgehammer. It falls to the deck with a clang. Joona grabs the back of the man's helmet and pulls it down, then hits him hard over the ear, making him sink to his knees and howl with pain.

## 165

Joona runs through the snow along the edge of the quay, with the sledgehammer hanging by his side. He can hear shouting behind him. Large blocks of ice are rolling in the sludgy water. The water rises, hits the quayside and sprays up.

Joona tears up the ramp of the roll-on, roll-off ferry to St Petersburg. He carries on past the rows of warm, steaming private cars, trailers and lorries. Light is coming from lamps along the bulkheads. Behind a grey container towards the stern he can just make out a red one.

A man tries to get out of his car, but Joona shuts the door on him so he can get past. The sledgehammer hits a bolt in one of the ship's bulkheads. He can feel the vibration moving through his arm and shoulder.

The steel deck under the cars is wet with melted snow. Joona kicks some cones blocking his path out of the way and keeps moving.

He reaches the red container, bangs on the doors and shouts out. The lock is high up. He has to climb up onto the car behind – a black Mercedes – and stand on the bonnet to reach it. The bonnet buckles beneath his feet and the paint cracks. He swings the sledgehammer and smashes the lock with his first blow. The noise echoes off the bulkheads and roof. Joona leaves the sledgehammer on the car bonnet. He opens the container. One of the doors swings open and scrapes the car's bumper.

'Disa!' he calls into the container.

It's full of white boxes with the name Evonik on their sides. They're tightly packed, and strapped down on pallets. Joona picks up the sledgehammer again and carries on towards the stern, past the cars and lorries. He can feel that he's starting to get tired. His arms are trembling from the exertion. Loading of the ferry has finished now and the bow is being lowered into place. There's a rumble of machinery and the deck shakes as the ferry pulls away. Ice knocks against its hull. He's almost at the stern when he sees another red container with the words Hamburg Süd on the side.

'Disa,' he calls.

He runs round the cab, stops and looks at the blue lock on the container. He wipes water from his face, grabs hold of the sledgehammer, and fails to notice the person approaching from behind.

Joona raises the sledgehammer and is about to strike when he receives a hard blow in the back. It hurts, his lungs roar and he almost blacks out. He drops the sledgehammer and falls forward, hitting his forehead against the container and collapsing on the deck. He rolls to the side and gets to his feet. Blood is running into one eye, and he stumbles and reaches out to a nearby car for support.

In front of him is a fairly tall woman with a baseball bat over her shoulder. She's breathing quickly and her padded jacket is pulled tight across her chest. She takes a step to the side, blows a lock of blonde hair from her face and takes aim again.

'Leave my cargo the fuck alone!' she yells.

She strikes again, but Joona moves quickly, heading straight at her, grabbing her throat with one hand, stamping his foot down at the back of her knee so that her leg buckles, then throws her to the deck and points his pistol at her.

'National Criminal Police,' he says.

She lies on deck, whimpering and looking at him as he picks up the sledgehammer, grasps it with both hands, swings it and shatters the lock. A piece of metal casing lands with a clatter right in front of her face.

Joona opens the doors, but the container is full of large boxes of televisions. He pulls a few out to see further in; Disa isn't there. He wipes the blood from his face and runs off between the cars, past a black container, and hurries up some steps to the open deck.

He rushes over to the railing, gasping for breath in the cold air. In front of the ship he can see the channel that an icebreaker has cleared through the archipelago to the open sea.

A mosaic of crushed ice is bobbing around a buoy.

The ferry is now twenty metres from the quay, and Joona suddenly has a view of the whole harbour. The sky is black, but the harbour is lit up by floodlights.

Through the heavy snow he sees the large crane loading a waiting goods train. Joona feels a spasm of anguish as he realises that three of the wagons have similar red containers on them.

He carries on towards the stern, takes his phone out and calls the emergency control room. He asks for all traffic from Frihamnen in Stockholm to be stopped. The duty officer knows who Joona is, and puts his call through to the regional police commissioner.

'All rail traffic from Frihamnen has to be stopped,' he repeats breathlessly.

'That's impossible,' she replies calmly.

Heavy snow is falling over the vast container terminal.

He clambers up the mooring winch and out onto the railing. He can see a reach-stacker carrying a red container to a waiting lorry.

'We have to stop all traffic,' Joona says again.

'That can't be done,' the commissioner says. 'The best we can do is—'

'I'll do it myself,' Joona says abruptly, and jumps.

Hitting the practically freezing water feels like being struck by icy lightning, like getting an adrenalin injection straight to the heart. His ears are roaring. His body can't handle the abrupt chill. Joona sinks through the black water, loses consciousness for a few seconds and dreams of a bridal crown of woven birch-root. He can't feel his hands and feet, but thinks that he has to get up to the surface, kicks out with his legs and finally manages to stop himself sinking any deeper.

## 166

Joona breaks the surface of the water, emerging through the icy slush and trying to stay calm and get some air into his lungs.

It's incredibly cold.

The sub-zero temperature is making his head pound, but he's conscious.

His time as a paratrooper saved him – he managed to ignore the impulse to gasp and breathe in.

With numb arms and heavy clothes, he swims through the black water. It's not far to the quayside, but his body temperature is dropping alarmingly quickly. Lumps of ice are tumbling over all round him. He's already lost all feeling in his feet, but he carries on kicking with his legs.

The waves roll and lap over his head.

He coughs, feeling his strength draining away. His vision is starting to fade, but he forces himself on, takes more strokes, and finally reaches the edge of the quay. With trembling hands he tries to grab onto the blocks, onto the narrow gaps between them. Panting, he moves sideways until he reaches a metal ladder.

The water splashes beneath him as he starts to climb. His

hands freeze to the metal. He's on the point of fainting, but wills himself to keep going, step after heavy step.

He rolls onto the quay with a groan, gets to his feet and starts walking towards the lorry.

His hand is shaking as he checks that he hasn't lost his pistol.

His wet face stings as snow blows into it. His lips are numb and his legs are trembling badly.

He runs into the narrow passageway between the stacks of dark containers to reach the lorry before it leaves the harbour. His feet are so numb he can't help stumbling and he hits his shoulder but carries on regardless, leaning against one of the containers as he clambers over a bank of snow.

He emerges into the glare of the headlights of the lorry carrying the red Hamburg Süd container.

The driver is behind the vehicle, checking that the brake lights are working, when he sees Joona approaching.

'Have you been in the water?' he asks, taking a step back. 'Bloody hell, you'll freeze to death if you don't get indoors.'

'Open the red container,' Joona slurs. 'I'm a police officer, I need to—'

'That's down to Customs, I can't just open it—'

'National Criminal Investigation Department,' Joona interrupts in a weak voice.

He's having trouble keeping his eyes focused, and is aware how incoherent he sounds when he tries to explain what powers the National Crime unit has.

'I don't even have the keys,' the driver says, looking at him kindly. 'Just a pair of bolt-cutters, and—'

'Hurry up,' Joona says, then coughs tiredly.

The driver runs round the lorry, climbs up and leans into the cab, peering behind the passenger seat. An umbrella tumbles out onto the ground as he pulls out a set of long-handled bolt-cutters.

Joona bangs on the container, shouting Disa's name.

The driver runs back, and his cheeks turn red as he presses the handles together.

The lock breaks with a crunch.

The door of the container swings open on creaking hinges. It's packed full of boxes on wooden pallets, strapped into place, right up to the roof.

Without saying a word to the lorry driver, Joona takes the bolt-cutters and walks on. He's so frozen he's shaking, and his hands hurt terribly.

'You need to get to hospital,' the man calls after him.

## 167

Joona walks as quickly as he can towards the railway line. The heavy bolt-cutters keep hitting compacted banks of snow, jarring his shoulder. The goods train by the warehouse has just started to move, its wheels squealing as it rolls forward. Joona tries to run, but his heart is beating so slowly that his chest feels like it's burning. He scrambles up the snow-covered railway embankment, slips and hits his knee on the gravel, drops the bolt-cutters but gets to his feet and stumbles onto the railway track. He can no longer feel his hands or feet. The shaking is now uncontrollable and he is experiencing a frightening sense of confusion because he's so severely frozen.

His thoughts are strange, slow and disintegrating. All he knows is that he has to stop the train.

The heavy train has started to build up speed and is approaching with its wheels screeching. Joona stands in the middle of the track, raises his eyes towards the light and holds up his hand to stop it. The train blows its whistle, and he can just make out the driver's silhouette inside. The track is shaking with vibrations under his feet. Joona draws his pistol, raises it and shoots out the windscreen of the train.

Fragments of glass fly up over the roof and swirl away. The

echo of the shot resounds quickly and harshly between the stacked containers.

Paper is flying round the cab of the train, and the driver's face is completely expressionless. Joona raises the pistol again and takes aim straight at him. There's a thunderous sound as the train brakes. The rails scrape and the ground shakes. The train slides forward with its brakes squealing, and stops with a hiss just three metres away from him.

Joona almost falls as he steps off the track. He picks up the bolt-cutters and turns to the train driver.

'Open the red containers,' he says.

'I don't have the authority to—'

'Just do it,' Joona shouts, throwing the bolt-cutters on the ground.

The driver climbs down and picks up the bolt-cutters. Joona goes with him along the train, and points at the first red container. Without a word the driver clambers up onto the rust-brown coupling and sheers the lock. There's a rumble as the door opens and large boxes containing television sets tumble out.

'Next one,' he whispers.

Joona starts walking, drops his pistol, picks it up out of the snow, and carries on towards the rear of the train. They pass eight containers before they reach the next red one bearing the words Hamburg Süd.

The train driver breaks the lock, but can't open the heavy catch. He hits it with the bolt-cutters, and the sound of metal against metal echoes desolately around the harbour.

Joona staggers forward, shoves the catch up with a scraping sound and the big metal door swings open.

Disa is lying on the rusty floor of the container. Her face is pale and there's a look of bewilderment in her wide-open eyes. She's lost one of her boots, and her hair is stiff and frozen round her head.

Disa's mouth is frozen in a grimace of fear and sobbing.

There's a deep cut on the right side of her long, slender neck. The pool of blood beneath her throat and neck is already covered by a film of ice.

Gently Joona lifts her down from the container and takes a few steps away from the train.

'I know you're alive,' he says, falling to his knees with her in his arms.

Some blood is trickling over his hand, but her heart has stopped. It's over, there's no way back.

'Not this,' Joona whispers against her cheek. 'Not you . . .'

He rocks her slowly as the snow falls. He doesn't notice the car stopping, and is unaware of Saga Bauer running towards him. She's barefoot, wearing just trousers and a T-shirt.

'We've got people on their way,' she cries as she gets closer. 'God, what have you done? You need to get some help . . .'

Saga shouts into her radio, swears, and, as if in a dream, Joona hears her force the train driver to take his jacket off, then she wraps it round his shoulders. She sinks down behind him and holds him while the sirens of police cars and ambulances fill the harbour.

The snow is blown from a large circle of ground as the yellow air-ambulance helicopter lands, settling onto its runners. The sound is deafening and the train driver backs away from the man sitting there with the dead woman in his arms.

The rotors are still turning as the paramedics leap out and run over, their clothes flapping round their bodies.

The draught from the helicopter is blowing rubbish up against the high fence. It feels as if all the oxygen is being blown away from them.

Joona is on the point of losing consciousness when the paramedics force him to let go of Disa's dead body. His eyes are unfocused, and his hands white with cold. He's muttering incoherently and resists when they try to get him to lie down.

Saga is crying as she watches him being carried away on the stretcher and into the helicopter. She realises that it's urgent now.

The noise of the rotors changes as the helicopter rises off the ground, swaying in a side wind that's picked up.

The angle of the rotors shifts, the helicopter leans forward and disappears across the city.

As they cut his clothes off, Joona starts to sink into a death-like torpor. His eyes are still open, but his pupils have expanded and are so fixed that they no longer react to light. It's impossible to detect any pulse or sign of breathing.

Joona Linna's body temperature has sunk below 32 degrees as they descend to land on the helicopter pad on building P8 at the Karolinska Hospital.

## 168

The police are quickly on the scene at Frihamnen, and after just a few minutes they are able to put out an alert for a silver-grey Citroën Evasion. Jurek Walter's car was registered by several different surveillance cameras as it drove into the harbour fifteen minutes before Disa Helenius's car arrived. The same cameras recorded the car leaving the area seven minutes after Joona Linna got there.

Every police car in Stockholm is involved in the search, as well as two Eurocopter 135s. It's a massive deployment, and just fifteen minutes after the alarm is sounded, the vehicle is observed on the Central Bridge before it disappears into the Söderleden Tunnel.

Police cars are on their way, with sirens and flashing lights, and roadblocks are being set up at the exits when the shock wave from a huge explosion blasts out of the entrance to the tunnel.

The helicopter hovering above lurches and the pilot only just manages to parry the force of the wave. Dust and debris is scattered across the carriageways and railway tracks, all the way down to the snow-covered ice of Riddarfjärden.

*

It's half past four in the morning and Saga Bauer is sitting on a rustling sheet of protective paper on top of a couch as a doctor sews up the wounds on her body.

'I have to go,' she says, staring at the dusty flat-screen television on the wall.

The doctor has just started bandaging her left wrist when the item about the big traffic accident comes on.

A sombre-voiced reporter explains that a police chase in the centre of Stockholm has ended with a single car crashing with fatal consequences inside the Söderleden Tunnel.

'The accident happened at half past two this morning,' the reporter says, 'which probably explains why no other vehicles were involved. The police have given assurances that the road will be reopened in time for the morning rush-hour, but have otherwise declined to make any comment about the incident.'

The screen shows a cloud of black smoke billowing out of the entrance to the tunnel at a peculiarly high speed. The cloud covers the whole of the Hilton Hotel with rolling veils, then slowly disperses over Södermalm.

Saga refused to go to hospital until she received confirmation that Jurek Walter was dead. Two of Joona's colleagues from National Crime told her. To save time, their forensics experts had accompanied the fire crews into the tunnel. The violent explosion had torn Jurek Walter's arms and head from his body.

On the screen, a politician is sitting in the studio with a female presenter. Their faces heavy with sleep, they discuss the problem of dangerous police pursuits.

'I have to go,' Saga says, slipping down onto the floor.

'The wounds on your legs need . . .'

'Don't bother,' she says, and leaves the room.

## 169

Joona wakes up in hospital, feeling frozen. His arms are itching where infusions of warm liquid are slowly being fed into him. A male nurse is standing by his bed, and smiles at him when he opens his eyelids.

'How are you feeling?' the nurse asks, leaning forward. Joona tries to read the name-badge, but can't get the letters to stay still long enough.

'I'm freezing,' he says.

'In two hours your body temperature should be back to normal. I'll give you some warm juice . . .'

Joona tries to sit up to drink, but suddenly feels a pain in his bladder. He lifts the insulating blanket off and sees that two thick needles are sticking into his abdomen.

'What's this?' he asks weakly.

'A peritoneal lavage,' the nurse says. 'We're warming your body up from inside . . . You've got two litres of warm liquid in your abdomen right now.'

Joona shuts his eyes and tries to remember. Red containers, icy slush, and the shock as he jumped from the ship straight into the incredibly cold water.

'Disa,' Joona whispers, and feels goosebumps rising on his arms.

He leans back on the pillows and looks up at the heater above him, but can't feel anything but cold.

After a while the door opens and a tall woman with her hair pulled up and a tight silk sweater under her doctor's coat comes in. It's Daniella Richards, he's met her many times before.

'Joona Linna,' she says in a heavy voice. 'I'm so sorry—'

'Daniella,' Joona interrupts hoarsely. 'What have you done to me?'

'You were on the point of freezing to death, in case you hadn't noticed. We thought you were dead when you were brought in.'

She sits down on the edge of the bed.

'You have no idea how incredibly lucky you were,' she says slowly. 'No serious damage, from the look of it . . . We're warming up your internal organs.'

'Where's Disa? I have to . . .'

His voice cracks. There's something about his thoughts, his brain. He can't put the words together properly. All his memories are like crushed ice in black water.

The doctor lowers her gaze and shakes her head. She has a small diamond on a necklace round her neck.

'I'm so sorry,' Daniella repeats slowly.

As she tells him about Disa, her face starts to quiver with sad little spasms. Joona looks at the veins in her hand, sees her pulse beating, and her ribcage rise and fall under her green sweater. He tries to understand what she's saying, shuts his eyes, and suddenly everything that's happened crashes into his consciousness. Disa's white face, the cut on her neck, the scared set of her mouth and her bare foot in just her nylon tights.

'Leave me alone,' he says in a hollow, hoarse voice.

## 170

Joona Linna is lying still, feeling the glucose running through his veins and the warm air from the heater above his bed, but he's not feeling any warmer.

Waves of cold are rolling through his body, and every so often his vision switches off and everything goes black and turns to flaring darkness.

An impulse to grab his gun, put the barrel in his mouth and shoot himself flickers through his thoughts.

Jurek Walter has escaped.

And Joona knows he'll never be able to see his daughter or wife again. They've been taken from him for good, in the same way Disa was torn from his hands. Jurek's twin brother worked out that Summa and Lumi were still alive. Joona knows it's only a matter of time before Jurek realises as well.

Joona tries to sit up, but doesn't have the energy.

It's impossible.

He can't escape the feeling that he's sinking deeper and deeper through the mosaic of ice with every passing second.

He can't stop feeling frozen.

Suddenly the door opens and Saga Bauer walks in. She's wearing a black jacket and dark jeans.

'Jurek Walter's dead,' she says. 'It's over. We found him in the Söderleden Tunnel.'

She stands at the foot of the bed and looks at Joona Linna. He's closed his eyes again. It feels like her heart's about to stop. He looks terribly ill. His face is almost white, his lips pale grey.

'I'm heading out to see Reidar Frost now,' Saga goes on. 'He needs to know that Felicia's alive. The doctors say she's going to make it. You saved her life.'

He hears what she says, and turns his face aside, keeping his eyes closed to hold back the tears, and suddenly he understands the pattern.

Jurek is closing a circle of revenge and blood.

Joona repeats the thought to himself, moistens his mouth, takes some deep breathes, then says quietly:

'Jurek's on his way to Reidar.'

'Jurek Walter's dead,' Saga repeats. 'It's over now—'

'Jurek's going to take Mikael again . . . he doesn't know that Felicia is free . . . he mustn't find out that she—'

'I'm about to go out and see Reidar, to tell him you saved his daughter,' she says again.

'Jurek's only let Mikael out on loan, he's going to take him back.'

'What are you talking about?'

Joona looks at her and the expression in his grey eyes is so cold it makes her shiver.

'The victims aren't the ones who were locked up or ended up in graves,' he says. 'The victims are the ones who were left behind, the ones who were waiting . . . until they couldn't bear to wait any more.'

She puts a calming hand on his.

'I have to go . . .'

'Make sure you're armed,' he says.
'I'm only going to tell Reidar that—'
'Do as I say,' he interrupts.

It's still a long time before dawn when Saga reaches the manor. The old house is nestled in the cold and the depths of the dark morning. There's only one light visible, in a window on the ground floor.

Saga gets out of the car and walks across the drive, shivering. The snow is untouched and the darkness stretching off over the fields is ancient.

There aren't even any stars twinkling in the night sky.

The only sound comes from an open stretch of water nearby.

She approaches the house and sees a man sitting at the kitchen table with his back to the window. There's a book on the table next to him. He's drinking slowly from a white cup.

Saga carries on across the snow-covered gravel, up the stone steps to the big front door, and rings the bell. A short while later the door is opened by the man who had been sitting in the kitchen.

It's Reidar Frost.

He's wearing striped pyjama trousers and a white T-shirt. He's got white stubble, and the look on his face is exhausted and brittle.

'Hello, my name's Saga Bauer, I work for the Security Police.'

'Come in,' he says in a voice that's close to breaking.

She takes a couple of steps into the dimly lit hall with its broad staircase leading to the upper floor. Reidar moves backwards. His chin has started to tremble and he puts one hand to his mouth.

'No, not Felicia, not—'

'We've found her,' Saga says quickly. 'She's alive, she's going to be all right . . .'

'I . . . I have to . . .'

'She's seriously ill,' Saga explains. 'Your daughter has advanced Legionnaires' disease, but she's going to be OK.'

'She's going to be OK,' Reidar whispers. 'I have to go, I have to see her.'

'She's being moved from intensive care to the infectious diseases unit at seven o'clock.'

He looks at her with tears trickling down his cheeks.

'Then I've got time to get dressed and wake Mikael and . . .'

Saga follows him through the rooms to the kitchen she saw through the window a few minutes before. The ceiling-light is casting a pleasant glow over the table with the coffee cup on it.

The radio is on, playing gentle piano music.

'We've been trying to call,' she says. 'But your phone—'

'That's my fault,' Reidar says, wiping the tears from his cheeks. 'I've had to start switching the phone off at night, I don't know, so many crazy people keep calling with tip-offs, people who . . .'

'I understand.'

'Felicia's alive,' Reidar says tentatively.

'Yes,' Saga says.

His face cracks into a broad grin, and he looks at her with bloodshot eyes. It appears he's going to ask her again, but he just shakes his head and smiles. He picks up a large pot of coffee from the black stove and pours a cup for Saga.

'Some warm milk?'

'No thanks,' she says, taking the cup.

'I'm just going to wake Mikael . . .'

He starts to walk towards the hall, but stops and turns back to look at her.

'I have to know . . . Have you caught the Sandman?' he asks. 'The man Mikael calls the—'

'He and Jurek are both dead,' Saga says. 'They were twin brothers.'

'Twin brothers?'

'Yes, they were working togeth—'

Suddenly the light in the ceiling goes out and the music on the radio goes quiet. It's pitch-black and silent.

'Power cut,' Reidar mutters, trying the switch a couple of times. 'I've got candles in the cupboard.'

'Felicia was locked up in an old bomb shelter,' Saga explains.

After a while the glow of the snow outside starts to penetrate the darkness of the kitchen, and Saga can see Reidar feeling his way towards a large cupboard.

'Where was the shelter?' he asks.

Saga hears a rattling sound as Reidar searches a drawer.

'In the old quarry out in Rotebro,' she replies.

Saga sees him stop, take a step back and turn round.

'That's where I'm from,' he says slowly. 'And I remember the twins. I don't know why, but it must have been Jurek Walter and his brother . . . I played with them for a few weeks when I was little . . . but why, why have . . .'

He falls silent and just stands there, staring into the darkness.

'I'm not sure there are any answers,' she says.

Reidar finds some matches and lights a candle.

'I lived fairly close to the quarry as a child,' he says. 'The twins were a year or so older than me. They were just sitting in the grass behind me one day when I was fishing for roach . . . in the river that runs into Edssjön . . .'

Reidar takes an empty wine bottle from under the sink, pushes the lit candle into it and sets it on the table.

'They were a bit odd . . . But we started to play, and I went back home with them. I remember it was spring, and I was given an apple . . .'

The light from the candle spreads through the room, making the windows black and impenetrable.

'They took me to the quarry,' Reidar goes on, evidently remembering as he speaks. 'It was out of bounds, but they'd found a hole in the fence and we'd meet to play there every evening. It was exciting, we would clamber up the mounds and roll down in the sand . . .'

Reidar falls silent.

'What were you about to say?'

'I've never thought about it, but one evening I heard them whispering to each other, then they just vanished . . . I rolled down and was about to go looking for them when the foreman suddenly appeared. He grabbed me by the arm and began shouting . . . you know, saying he'd tell my parents and all that . . . And I was terrified, said I didn't know it was out of bounds, that the boys had said we could play there . . . and he asked about the boys and I pointed to the house . . .'

Reidar lights another candle from the first. The light bounces off the walls and ceiling. A smell of wax spreads through the kitchen.

'I never saw the twins again after that,' he says, then leaves the kitchen to go and wake Mikael.

## 172

Saga is standing at the kitchen table drinking the strong coffee and looking at the reflections of the two candles in the double layer of glass in the window.

Joona's so badly hurt, she thinks. He didn't even hear her when she said Jurek was dead. He just repeated that Jurek was on his way to get Mikael.

Saga turns her weary body and feels the weight of her Glock 17 against her side, then moves away from the window and listens to the sounds of the large house.

Something makes her suddenly alert.

She takes a few steps towards the door, stops and imagines she can hear a faint metallic scraping sound.

It could be anything, a loose window ledge moving in the wind, a branch against a window.

She waits for a moment, then goes back to the table and drinks some coffee. She looks at the time, takes her phone out and calls Nils Åhlén on his mobile.

'Nils Åhlén, Forensic Medicine Department,' he answers after a few rings.

'This is Saga Bauer,' she says.

'Good morning, good morning.'

A gust of cold air suddenly sweeps across the floor round Saga's legs. She goes and stands with her back to the wall.

'Have you looked at the body from the Söderleden Tunnel?' she asks, as she sees the candlelight flicker.

'Yes, I'm here now, they dragged me out of bed to deal with a body that . . .'

She sees the candle flicker again and hears Åhlén's nasal voice echo off the tiled walls of the post-mortem room at the Karolinska Hospital.

'The body suffered severe burns, it's all cracked, pretty much charcoal, the heat shrivelled it up badly. The head's missing, as well as both—'

'But have you been able to identify him?'

'I've only been here quarter of an hour, and it's going to be several days before I can come up with any sort of reliable identification.'

'Of course, but I was wondering—'

'All I can say right now,' Åhlén goes on, 'is that this man was approximately twenty-five years old, and he's—'

'So it isn't Jurek Walter?'

'Jurek Walter? No, this . . . Did you think it was Jurek?'

There's the sound of rapid footsteps upstairs. Saga looks up and sees the kitchen lamp quivering, and, caught in the candlelight, it casts a wavering shadow over the ceiling. She pulls her pistol from her holster and says in a low voice into the phone:

'I'm at Reidar Frost's house – you have to help me get an ambulance and police backup out here, as soon as possible.'

## 173

Reidar is walking through the silent rooms upstairs. His left hand is shielding the candle from draughts. The light flickers over walls and furniture, and its reflection is multiplied on the rows of black windows.

He imagines he can hear steps behind him, but when he stops and turns round all he can see is the shiny leather furniture and the big bookcase with its glass doors.

The door to the sitting room that he's just walked through is a gaping black rectangle. It's impossible to tell if anyone's in there. He takes a step forward, and something glints in the shadows then disappears.

Reidar turns again, sees the light shimmer in the windows, and carries on. Hot wax is running over his fingers.

The floor creaks beneath him and unease is spreading through his body as he stops outside Mikael's room.

He looks back down the long corridor with its rows of old portraits.

The floor is creaking slightly after his footsteps.

Reidar knocks cautiously on Mikael's door, waits a few moments, then opens it.

'Mikael?' he asks into the dark room.

He holds the candle up towards the bed. The walls sway in the yellow light. The covers are bunched up, and are hanging over the edge, down onto the rug.

He goes in and looks round, but Mikael has vanished. Reidar feels beads of sweat break out on his forehead as he bends over to look under the bed.

Suddenly he hears rustling behind him and spins round so fast that the candle almost goes out.

The flame shrinks and turns a tremulous blue before growing again.

His heart is beating faster and his chest is starting to ache.

There's no one there.

He walks slowly towards the doorway, trying to see something.

There's a scraping, creaking sound from inside the wardrobe. Reidar looks at the closed doors, then walks over, hesitates, reaches out a hand and opens one of the doors.

Mikael is sitting huddled up among the clothes.

'The Sandman's here,' he whispers, creeping further into the wardrobe.

'It's just a power cut,' Reidar says. 'We're going—'

'He's here,' Mikael whispers.

'The Sandman's dead,' Reidar says, holding out his hand. 'Do you understand what I'm saying? Felicia's safe. She's going to be fine, she's getting the same treatment as you, we're going to go and see her now—'

A scream rips through the walls, it's muffled but sounds bestial, like the cry of a man in terrible pain.

'Dad . . .'

Reidar pulls his son out of the wardrobe. Drops of wax fall to the floor. It's completely silent again. What's going on?

Mikael tries to curl up on the floor, but Reidar drags him to his feet.

Sweat is running down Reidar's back.

They leave the bedroom together and start to walk down the corridor. A cold draught is blowing across the floor.

'Wait,' Reidar whispers as he hears a creak from the floor of the sitting room in front of them.

A slender figure emerges from the doorway at the far end of the corridor. It's Jurek Walter. His eyes are shining in his butcher's face, and the knife hanging in his right hand glints heavily.

Reidar backs away and loses his slippers. He throws the candle at Jurek. It goes out in midair and hits the ground.

They turn and run down the corridor without looking back. It's dark and Mikael runs into a chair, he almost falls and stumbles against the wall, his hand flailing over the wallpaper.

A picture crashes to the floor and the glass shatters, spreading splinters around the room.

They push open a heavy door and stumble into the old reception room.

Reidar has to stop, he's coughing and fumbling for something to lean on. Rapid steps are approaching along the corridor.

'Dad!'

'Close the door, close the door!' he pants.

Mikael slams the heavy door shut and turns the key in the lock three times. A moment later the handle is pushed down and the frame creaks. Mikael backs away across the parquet floor, staring at the door.

'Have you got your phone?' Reidar says, then coughs.

'It's still in my bedroom,' Mikael whispers.

Pain is spreading through Reidar's chest and down his left arm.

'I have to rest,' he says weakly, feeling his legs getting unsteady.

The heavy wood of the door creaks as Jurek thuds against it with his shoulder, but it doesn't give way.

'He can't get in,' Reidar whispers. 'I just need a few seconds . . .'

'Where's your nitroglycerine spray? Dad?'

Reidar is sweating, and the pressure in his chest is so bad he can hardly speak.

'Downstairs in the hall, in my coat . . .'

## 174

Saga sweeps the corridor with her pistol as she creeps towards the staircase in the hall.

She has to reach Mikael and Reidar, and get them out to the car.

The sky may actually have brightened up slightly, because it's now possible to make out the pictures on the walls and the shapes of the furniture.

The adrenalin in her body makes her icily alert.

The sound of her footsteps vanishes as she walks over a rug and past the black grand piano. Something glints in the corner of her eye. She turns her head and sees a cello with its endpin extended.

The walls are clicking, as if the temperature outside has suddenly fallen several degrees.

Saga creeps along quickly, with her pistol aimed down at the floor. Slowly she moves her finger to the trigger, squeezing it carefully, past the first notch.

She stops mid-step and listens. The house is completely silent. The hall ahead of her is darker than the other rooms, its double doors almost closed.

Saga is moving forward when she hears a rushing sound

behind her. She spins round quickly and sees snow that has slipped off the roof of the bay window sliding past the glass.

Her heart is thudding in her chest.

When she turns back towards the hall she sees a hand at the door. Someone's skinny fingers are reaching round the edge of the door.

Saga aims her pistol at the door, ready to shoot through it, but suddenly there's a terrible scream and the hand slides down and disappears, followed by a thud as something hits the floor, and both doors swing open.

A man is lying on the floor. One leg is twitching spasmodically.

She goes over and sees that it's Wille Strandberg, the actor. He's gasping and clutching his stomach.

Blood is bubbling out between his fingers.

He stares at Saga in confusion, then blinks rapidly.

'I'm a police officer,' she says, as she hears the stairs creak under someone's weight. 'The ambulance is on its way.'

'He wants Mikael,' the actor groans.

## 175

Mikael is whispering to himself and staring at the locked door, when the key is suddenly pushed out and falls onto the parquet floor with a muffled clunk.

Reidar is standing with his hand pressed against the pain in his chest. His face is wet with sweat. He's in agony now. He's tried several times to tell Mikael to run, but he has no voice left.

'Can you walk?' Mikael whispers.

Reidar nods and takes a step. There's a scraping sound from the lock as Mikael puts his father's arm over his shoulder and tries to lead him towards the library.

Behind them the scraping sound from the lock continues.

They carry on slowly past a tall cupboard, along a wall lined with large tapestries stretched over wooden frames.

Reidar stops again, coughing and gasping for breath.

'Hold on,' he says.

He slips his fingers along the edge of the third tapestry and opens a concealed door leading to a servants' staircase down to the kitchen. They creep into the narrow passageway and gently close the door behind them.

Reidar fastens the little catch and then leans against the

wall. He coughs as quietly as he can, feeling the pain radiating down his arm.

'Keep going down the stairs,' he whispers in a muffled voice.

Mikael shakes his head and is about to say something when the door in the other room crashes open.

Jurek's broken in.

They stand there as if paralysed and watch him approach through the fabric covering the hidden door.

He's creeping forward, crouched down, with the long knife in his hand, peering around him like a predator.

His soft breathing is clearly audible through the door.

Reidar clenches his teeth and leans against the wall; his chest hurts badly, and the pain is spreading to his jaw.

Jurek is so close now that a cloying smell of sweat hits them through the tapestry.

They both hold their breath as Jurek walks past the tapestry door, heading towards the library.

Mikael tries to get Reidar down the narrow staircase before Jurek realises he's been deceived.

Reidar shakes his head and Mikael looks at him in anguish. He stifles a cough, tries to take a step, then stumbles, making a floorboard creak under his right foot.

Jurek turns and looks straight at the hidden door, and his pale eyes become strangely calm when he realises what he's looking at.

There's the sound of a loud bang in the corridor, and splinters from the edge of the tall cupboard fly through the air.

Jurek slips aside like a shadow and takes cover.

Mikael pulls Reidar with him down the narrow staircase towards the kitchen.

Behind them Berzelius comes into the passageway leading to the library. He's holding Reidar's old Colt in his hand.

The little man's cheeks are red as he pushes his glasses further up his nose and moves forward.

'Leave Micke alone!' he shouts, walking past the tall cupboard.

Death comes so quickly that Berzelius's main reaction is surprise. At first he feels the tight grip on the wrist holding the revolver, then there's a burning pain in his side as the rigid knife-blade penetrates his ribs and hits his heart.

There isn't much pain.

It's more like a protracted attack of cramp, but at the same time a profuse quantity of warm blood runs down his hip as the blade slips out again.

He realises that he's wetting himself as he falls to his knees and suddenly recalls the time when he was courting his wife Anna-Karin, long before the divorce and her illness. She had looked so surprised and happy when he came home early from Oslo and stood below her low balcony, singing 'Love Me Tender' with four bags of crisps in his arms.

Berzelius slumps over onto his side, thinking that he ought to try to crawl and hide somewhere, but an overwhelming tiredness sweeps over him like a storm.

He doesn't even notice when Jurek sticks the knife into his body a second time. The blade goes in at a different angle, straight through his ribs, and stays there.

Saga reaches the top of the broad staircase and hurries through the rooms on the upper floor. There's no one there, no voices. Tactically she tries to check off every dangerous angle and secure each zone as she passes through, but she keeps having to take risks so she can move more quickly.

She aims the pistol at a shiny leather sofa as she passes it, then points it towards the doorway, left, then in.

There's a wax candle lying on the floor of the long, portrait-lined corridor.

The door to one of the bedrooms is wide open, and the bedclothes are on the floor. Saga hurries past, catching a glimpse of herself as a fleeting shadow in the window to her left.

Then there's a loud bang from a firearm in one of the rooms up ahead. Keeping close to the right-hand wall, Saga starts to run towards the noise with her pistol raised.

'Leave Micke alone!' a man cries.

Running, Saga leaps over an upturned chair, covers the last stretch and stops in front of a closed door.

Carefully she pushes the handle down and lets the door swing open on its hinges.

The smell of a recently fired gun is heavy in the air.

The room is dark and still.

Saga moves more cautiously now.

She's starting to feel the weight of the pistol in her shoulder. Her finger is trembling on the trigger. She tries to breathe calmly as she leans to her right to get a better view.

There's a damp thud with a slightly metallic echo.

Something's moving – a shadow vanishing.

She sees a pool of blood gleaming on the floor next to a tall cupboard.

Stepping forward, she sees a man on the floor with a knife sticking out of him. He's lying on his side, completely still, with a fixed stare and a smile on his lips. Her first impulse is to rush over to the man, but something stops her.

The room is too hard to read.

She lowers her pistol and rests her arm for a few seconds before raising it again and moving further to the right.

One section of tapestry on the wall is open. Through it Saga can make out a short passageway leading to a narrow staircase. She can hear steps and dragging sounds from below, and raises her Glock towards the opening before moving closer.

The door at the other end of the room is open, leading to a dark library.

There's a faint click, as though someone were moistening their mouth.

She can't see anything.

The pistol is shaking in her hand.

The windows in front of her are black and she takes a step forward, holds her breath, then hears someone breathing behind her.

Saga reacts instantly and swings round. It's still too late. A strong hand grabs hold of her throat and she's dragged into the corner towards the cupboard with great force.

Jurek's grip on her neck is so tight that the blood-supply to her brain has been cut off. He looks at her perfectly calmly, holding her quite still. Her vision is starting to go black and the Glock simply drops from her hand.

Impotently, Saga tries to twist free, and just before she loses consciousness she hears Jurek whisper:

'Little siren . . .'

He slams her against the cupboard and her head hits the corner, then he smashes her temple against the stone wall. She falls to the floor, her eyes flickering. She sees Jurek bend over the dead man and pull the knife out of his body. A moment later everything goes black again.

## 177

They're no longer trying to keep quiet. Mikael supports Reidar down the staircase to the narrow servants' passageway. They turn left and walk slowly along it, past the old cupboard with the Christmas dinner service, and out into the kitchen.

Reidar has to stop, he can't go any further, he needs to lie down, the cramps in his chest are unbearable.

'You have to get out of here,' he gasps, then coughs weakly. 'Run, run out to the main road.'

On the kitchen table the candle is still burning, its flame flickering. The wax has run down one side of the bottle and onto the linen tablecloth.

'Not on my own,' Mikael says. 'I can't . . .'

Reidar takes a deep breath and starts walking again. His eyes are flaring as he leans against the wall, knocking the big Cullberg painting askew.

They walk through the music room and Reidar can hardly feel the floor under his naked feet.

There's blood on the parquet, but they just continue into the hall. The front door is open and snow has blown in, across the Persian rug and all the way to the broad staircase.

Mikael runs to the wardrobe, pulls out Reidar's coat and

finds the pink nitroglycerine spray. With shaking hands Reidar lifts it to his mouth, opens wide and sprays some under his tongue, he takes a few more steps, stops and sprays again.

He points at the dish containing the car keys on the other side of the room.

Now they can hear heavy footsteps in the rooms leading from the kitchen. There's no time. They rush out into the black winter morning.

The air is icy cold.

Snow has blown up over the stone steps. Mikael is wearing trainers, but the cold burns Reidar's naked feet.

The pain in his chest has vanished and they can move much faster now. Together they run over to Saga Bauer's car.

Reidar pulls at the door, looks in and sees that the keys are missing.

Jurek Walter emerges onto the steps and catches sight of them in the gloom. He shakes the blood from his knife, then heads straight for them.

They run through the snow up towards the stables, but Jurek is far too quick. Reidar glances across the fields. The dark ice of the river is visible as a curling band through the snow, leading off in the direction of the roaring rapids.

## 178

Saga wakes to find blood running into her eyes. She blinks and rolls over onto her side. Her temple is throbbing. She has a splitting headache, her throat feels swollen and she's having trouble breathing.

She tentatively touches the wound on her temple and groans with pain. With her cheek to the floor she can see that her Glock is lying in the dust under the large chest of drawers by the window.

She shuts her eyes again and tries to work out what's happened. Joona was right, she thinks. Jurek wants Mikael back.

She has no idea how long she's been unconscious. It's still almost dark in the room.

She rolls over onto her stomach and whimpers.

'Oh, God . . .'

With a great effort she gets up on all fours. Her arms shake as she crawls across the pool of blood from the dead man towards the chest of drawers.

She stretches for the gun, but can't reach it.

Saga lies down on the floor, reaches in as far as she can, but only manages to nudge the Glock with her fingertips. It's impossible. She's so dizzy that the room is tilting in violent lurches and she has to close her eyes again.

Suddenly she sees light through her closed eyelids. She looks up and notices a strange white glow. It's bouncing shakily across the ceiling. She turns her head and sees that it's coming from the park, sparkling in the ice-crystals on the outside of the window.

Saga forces herself to stand up, gasping as she leans against the chest of drawers for support. A string of bloody saliva is dripping from her mouth. She looks out of the window and sees David Sylwan running over, holding a burning flare in his hand. The bright light spreads out in a blazing circle around him.

Everything else out there is black.

David moves off through the deep snow. He's holding the flare in front of him, and its glow reaches all the way to the stables in the distance.

That's when Saga catches sight of Jurek's back and the knife in his hand.

She bangs on the window and tries to open the latches. She tugs at them, but they've rusted into place and are impossible to move.

## 179

With ice-cold fingers Reidar tries to open the combination lock on the stable door. The little numbered dials are stiff. His fingertips are sticking to the frozen metal. Mikael whispers to him to get a move on.

'Hurry up, Dad, hurry up . . .'

Jurek is pushing through the snow with the knife in his hand. Reidar blows on his fingers and manages to get the last digit. He undoes the lock, slides the catch back and tries to open the door.

There's too much snow on the ground.

As he tugs at it, he can hear the horses moving in their stalls. They're snorting quietly and stamping in the darkness.

'Come on, Dad,' Mikael shouts, pulling at him.

Reidar opens the door a bit further, turns round and sees Jurek Walter approaching with his vicious-looking knife.

With a practised gesture, he wipes the knife-blade against his trousers.

It's too late to run.

Reidar holds his hands up in self-defence, but Jurek grabs his neck and forces him back, against the wall of the stable.

'Sorry,' Reidar manages to say. 'I'm sorry that—'

With immense force Jurek thrusts the knife straight through Reidar's shoulder and pins him to the wall. Reidar screams with pain and his vision flares. The horses whinny anxiously, their heavy bodies rubbing against the dividing walls of their stalls.

Reidar is stuck. His shoulder is burning with pain. Every second is unbearable. He can feel hot blood running down his arm and hand.

Mikael is trying to squeeze into the stable, but Jurek catches up with him. He grabs hold of the young man's hair from behind, pulls him out and slaps him so hard across the face that he collapses in the snow.

'No, no,' Reidar pants as he sees a bright light approaching from the manor.

It's David, running towards them with an emergency flare in his hand. It's crackling with white light.

'The air ambulance is on its way,' he yells, but stops when he sees Jurek turn.

## 180

Saga tugs at the chest of drawers and manages to pull it a few centimetres away from the wall. Her head is aching and she still feels horribly dizzy. She spits out some blood, then bends over and takes hold of the bottom of the chest with both hands and overturns it with a roar. It topples forward, crashes to the floor and rolls over.

She quickly snatches up her pistol and smashes the window pane with the butt. Glass rains down onto the floor and tinkles off the window ledge outside.

She blinks and sees the bright light shimmering across the snow. It looks like a white jellyfish deep in the ocean. Jurek is heading towards the man with the flare. The man backs away and tries to hit him with the burning flare, but Jurek is too quick, grabs the man's arm and breaks it.

Saga knocks the last pieces of glass from the bottom of the window.

Jurek is standing over his prey like a lion, moving quickly and efficiently, hitting the man in the neck and kidneys.

Saga holds out her pistol and blinks the blood away from her eyes so she can see.

The man is lying on his back in the snow, his body jerking. The flare beside him is still casting a bright glow.

Jurek slips out of the way just as Saga fires her pistol. He moves away from the light and into the shadows.

The glow from the flare is illuminating a circle of white snow. The man stops moving and is now lying completely still. The red stable is only visible in brief bursts. Otherwise there is nothing but darkness.

## 181

Reidar is gasping for breath. He's pinned to the wall. The pain from the knife is excruciating. It feels as if that one burning point is all that exists. The warm blood is steaming as it runs down his body.

He sees Jurek vanish right after the shot. David is lying completely still in the snow. There's no way of telling how badly wounded he is.

To the east the sky has brightened slightly and Reidar can see Saga Bauer in a window on the first floor.

It had been her who had fired and missed.

Reidar is breathing far too quickly, his heart is racing and he realises that he's going into shock as a result of the loss of blood.

Mikael coughs, puts a hand to his ear and gets unsteadily to his feet.

'Dad . . .'

He has no time to say more before Jurek is back. He knocks him down again, then grabs him by one leg and starts to drag him off into the darkness.

'Mikael,' Reidar screams.

Jurek drags his son off through the snow. Mikael is flailing with his arms, trying to find something to grab hold of. They disappear towards the rapids, Reidar can only see them as pale shadows now.

Jurek came here to get Mikael, he thinks in confusion.

It's still far too dark for Saga to be able to tell the figures apart from her vantage point in the window.

Reidar howls as he grabs the handle of the knife and pulls. It's stuck fast. He pulls again, shifting the angle down slightly to get a better grip, and it cuts into his flesh.

Warm blood runs over the handle and his fingers.

He screams and pulls again, and finally the point comes free from the wall behind him. The knife slips out and Reidar falls forward onto the snow. The pain is so bad that he's sobbing as he crawls forward and tries to get to his feet.

'Mikael!'

He stumbles over to the burning flare in the snow, picks it up and feels the sparks prick his hand. He almost falls but manages to keep his balance. He looks towards the open water of the rapids, and can just make out Jurek's figure against the snow. Reidar starts to follow them, but has no energy left. He knows that Jurek is planning to drag Mikael into the forest and vanish with him for good.

## 182

Saga is pointing her pistol out through the window and sees Reidar Frost in the glow of the flare. He's picked it up, and blood is pouring down his body, he stumbles and looks like he's going to fall, then he throws the flare.

Saga wipes the blood from her eyebrows and sees the flare spin through the darkness in a wide arc, and follows it with her eyes, seeing it land in the snow. In its white glow she can clearly make out Jurek Walter. He's dragging Mikael behind him. They're more than a hundred metres away.

They're a long way off, but Saga rests her arm against the window frame and takes aim.

Jurek is moving away. The pistol's sights keep shaking. The black figure keeps moving out of the line of fire.

Saga tries to hold the gun steady. Taking slow breaths, she squeezes the trigger, past the first notch, and sees Jurek's head slide away.

She keeps losing focus and blinks quickly.

A moment later the angle of fire is better and she squeezes the trigger three times as the sights slip gradually lower.

The harsh, sharp blasts echo between the manor and stable block.

Saga manages to see that at least one of the bullets hits Jurek in the neck. Blood is squirting out, hanging like a red haze in front of him in the bright white light.

She fires off several more shots and sees him let go of Mikael, fall into the shadows and disappear.

Saga backs away from the window, turns and runs through the hidden doorway.

She rushes down the stairs. The pistol in her hand clatters against the banisters. She emerges into the kitchen, runs through the rooms, into the large hall and out into the snow. Gasping, she approaches the glowing light with her pistol raised. Further away she sees the black water of the rapids glint like a metallic fracture in the white landscape.

She carries on through the deep snow and tries to make out anything through the darkness, off towards the forest.

The light of the flare is weaker now, it will soon go out. Mikael is lying on his side in the snow, gasping for breath. There's blood spattered at the very edge of the trembling circle of light, but the body isn't there.

'Jurek,' she whispers, pushing into the light and spotting his tracks through the snow.

Saga's head is aching badly as she picks up the flare and holds it aloft, then carries on moving forward. The glow flickers ahead of her. Shadows and light play across the snow, and suddenly she sees movement from the corner of her eye.

Jurek stands up and moves away through the snow.

Saga fires before she has time to aim properly. The bullet goes through the top of his arm and he lurches to one side, almost falling, then takes a few steps down the steep slope leading to the rapids.

Saga follows, with the flare held high. She catches sight of him again, takes aim and hits him in the chest with three shots.

Jurek falls backwards, over the icy fringe and straight into the black water of the rapids. Saga fires as he's falling, and hits him in the cheek and ear.

He gets sucked down into the water and she runs over and manages to shoot him in the foot before he disappears. Saga replaces the cartridge, slides down the steep slope, falls and hits her back on the ground, sliding under the snow, but gets unsteadily to her feet and fires into the black water. She holds the flare up above the swirling rapids. The light penetrates the surface, past the spinning bubbles and all the way to the dark-brown bottom. Something large is tumbling round down there, and suddenly she catches a glimpse of a wrinkled face among the stones and swirling weeds.

Saga fires again and a cloud of blood billows out in the dark water. She takes aim and goes on firing, releases the cartridge and slides in a fresh one, then shoots again. The flashes from the barrel flicker on the racing water. She walks along the shore, following the current, and goes on shooting until she has no more ammunition and Jurek Walter's body vanishes beneath the ice where the rapids spread out.

Panting, Saga stands at the edge of the water as the flare dies away to a shimmering red glow.

She just stares down at the water as tears run down her face, like a tired child.

The first rays of sunlight are starting to reach over the treetops, and the warm light of dawn spreads out across the sparkling snowy landscape. There's a sound of helicopters approaching in the air, and Saga realises that it's over at last.

Saga was taken by ambulance to Danderyd Hospital, where she was examined and given a bed. She lay for a while in her room, but left the hospital by taxi before she received any treatment.

Now she's limping along a corridor in the Karolinska Hospital, where Reidar and Mikael were taken by air ambulance. Her clothes are dirty and wet, her face is streaked with blood, and all she can hear in her right ear is a loud buzzing sound.

Reidar and his son are still in emergency room 12. She opens the door and sees the author lying on an operating table.

Mikael is standing beside him, holding his hand.

Reidar is telling the male nurse over and over again that he has to see his daughter.

The moment he sees Saga he falls silent.

Mikael takes some clean compresses from the trolley and gives them to Saga. He points at her forehead, where blood has once again started to trickle from the blackened wound on her eyebrow.

The nurse comes over, looks at Saga, then asks her to accompany him to an examination room.

'I'm a police officer,' Saga says, looking for her ID.

'You need help,' the nurse tries to say, but Saga interrupts him and asks for them to be taken to Felicia Kohler-Frost's room in the infectious diseases clinic.

'I have to see her,' she says gravely.

The nurse makes a call, gets the go-ahead and wheels Reidar's bed towards the lift.

The bed's wheels squeak faintly on the pale vinyl floor.

Saga follows, suddenly feeling the urge to cry.

Reidar is lying with his eyes closed, and Mikael is walking alongside, holding his father by the hand.

A young nurse meets them and shows them into an intensive care room with subdued lighting.

The only sound is the slow wheezing and ticking of the machines monitoring heart rate, breathing, blood oxygenation and ECG.

In the bed lies an extremely slight woman. Her long black hair is spread out over her shoulders and pillow. Her eyes are closed and her small hands are lying by her sides.

She's breathing rapidly, and her face is covered with beads of sweat.

'Felicia,' Reidar whispers, trying to reach her with his hand.

Mikael leans his cheek towards his sister and whispers something to her with a smile.

Saga stands behind them, staring at Felicia, the captive girl who has now been rescued from the darkness.

# epilogue

Two days later Saga is walking through the park towards the headquarters of the Security Police. There are birds singing in the bushes and snow-covered trees.

Her hair has started to grow out again. She has twelve neat stitches on her temple, and five across her left eyebrow.

Yesterday her boss, Verner Zandén, called and told her to report to his office at eight o'clock this morning to receive the Security Police Medal of Honour.

The ceremony strikes her as being rather odd. Three men died out at Råcksta Manor, and Jurek Walter's body was washed away, deep under the ice covering the lake.

Before she was discharged she managed to visit Joona in hospital. He had a distant look in his eyes as he patiently answered her questions about why Jurek and his brother had done what they did.

Joona's body was shaking as if he were still frozen as he slowly told her what was behind it all.

Vadim Levanov fled from Leninsk with his two sons Igor and Roman after the disastrous accident in 1960, when an intercontinental missile exploded on the launch pad. He eventually reached Sweden, was granted a work permit and given a job at the big quarry in Rotebro, with accommodation in the guest labourers' barracks. His children lived with him in secret; he would school them during the evenings and keep them hidden during the day, all the while hoping that he would be granted Swedish citizenship and the chance of a new life for him and his sons.

Joona had asked for a glass of water and when Saga leaned forward to help him drink she could feel him shaking as if he were freezing, even though his body was radiating heat.

Saga recalls Reidar's account of how he met the twins by Edssjön, and started playing with them. The twins took Reidar back to the quarry where they played in the great mounds of sifted sand. One evening Reidar got caught by one of the foremen. He was so scared of reprisals that he blamed everything on the older boys, and pointed out where they lived.

The twins were taken into the custody of the Child Welfare Commission, and because they weren't listed on any Swedish registers the case was passed to the Aliens Department.

Joona asked a nurse for a warm blanket and explained to Saga that Jurek's brother had pneumonia and was being treated in hospital when Jurek was extradited to Kazakhstan. But because Jurek didn't have any family there he ended up in a children's home in Pavlodar.

From the age of thirteen he worked on the barges trafficking the Irtysh River, and during the troubles that followed Stalin's death he was forcibly recruited by a Chechen militia group. They took the fifteen-year-old Jurek to a suburb of Grozny and turned him into a soldier.

'The brothers were sent to different countries,' Joona said in a low voice.

'But that's crazy,' Saga whispered.

Sweden had little experience of migrants in those days, and had no effective way of dealing with them. Mistakes were made, and Jurek's twin brother was sent to Russia as soon as he was well enough. He ended up at Children's Home 67 in the Kusminki district of south-east Moscow, and was written off as retarded because of the after-effects of his illness. When Jurek, after many years as a soldier, left Chechnya and managed to track down his brother, he had been transferred to a mental hospital, the Serbski Institute, and was a complete wreck.

Saga is so absorbed in her thoughts about the twin brothers that she doesn't notice Corinne Meilleroux walking towards the security doors at the same time as her. They come close to colliding. Corinne's hair is tied up and she's wearing a black trench-coat and high-heeled boots. For once Saga is conscious of the way she's dressed. Maybe she should have chosen something different from her usual jeans and thick parka.

'Very impressive,' Corinne smiles, and gives her a hug.

Saga and Corinne get out of the lift and walk side by side down the corridor leading to their boss's large office. Nathan Pollock, Carlos Eliasson and Verner Zandén are already waiting for them. On the table is a bottle of Taittinger and five champagne glasses.

The door closes and Saga shakes hands with the three men.

'Let's start with a minute's silence in memory of our colleague Samuel Mendel and his family, and all the other victims,' Carlos says.

Saga lowers her head and has trouble maintaining a steady gaze. In front of her she can see the first pictures of the police operation in the industrial estate where the old brickworks used to be. Towards morning it had become clear to everyone that no victims were going to be found alive. In the muddy snow the forensics officers had started placing numbered signs by the fourteen different graves. Samuel Mendel's two sons had been found tied together in a shaft covered by a sheet of corrugated metal. Rebecka's remains were found buried ten metres away in a drum fitted with a plastic air-tube.

The voices drown in Saga's tinnitus and she shuts her eyes and tries to understand.

The traumatised twins made their way to Poland, where Roman killed a man, took his passport and became Jurek Walter. Together they caught a ferry from Swinoujscie to Ystad, and then travelled up through Sweden.

Now middle-aged, the brothers returned to the place where they had been separated from their father, to barrack number four in the guest workers' accommodation at a quarry in Rotebro.

Their father had spent decades trying to trace the boys, but couldn't travel to Russia himself because he'd be sent to the gulag. He had written hundreds of letters in an effort to find his children, and waited for them to come back, but just one year before the brothers arrived in Sweden the old man gave up and hanged himself in his cellar.

Before Saga left the hospital, Joona had closed his eyes and tried to sit himself up as he explained that finding out about his father's suicide had wrecked what little was left of Jurek's soul.

'He started to draw up his circle of blood and revenge,' Joona said, almost soundlessly.

Everyone who had contributed to the break-up of his family would experience the same fate. Jurek would take their children from them, their grandchildren and wives, sisters and brothers. The guilty parties would be left as alone as their father in the quarry, they would have to wait year after year, and only when they had killed themselves would those of their relatives that survived be allowed to return.

That was why the twins didn't kill their victims – it wasn't the people who were buried who were being punished, but those left behind. During the wait for the suicides, the victims were placed in coffins or drums with air-tubes. Most of them died after just a few days, but some lived for years.

The bodies that were found in Lill-Jan's Forest and in the vicinity of the Albano industrial estate cast a cruel light on Jurek Walter's terrible revenge. He was following an entirely logical plan, which was why his actions and the choice of victims didn't seem to fit the pattern followed by other serial killers.

It was going to take a while for the police to fill in all the details, but it was already apparent who the victims were. Apart from Reidar Frost, who revealed the boys to the foreman in the quarry, they included those responsible at the Child Welfare Commission, and the case-officers at the Aliens Department.

Saga thinks about Jeremy Magnusson, who was a young man when he dealt with the twins' case at the Aliens Department. Jurek took his wife, son and grandson, then finally his daughter Agneta. When Jeremy eventually hanged himself in his hunting cabin, Jurek went to the grave where Agneta was still being kept alive to let her out.

Saga repeats to herself that Jurek actually had disinterred her, just as he'd told Joona. He had opened the coffin, sat by the graveside and watched her blind fumbling. In this terrible circle, she was a version of him, a child doomed to return to nothing.

Joona explained that Jurek's brother was so psychologically damaged that he lived among their father's old possessions in the abandoned barracks. He did everything that Jurek told him to do, learned to handle sedatives and helped him to seize people and watch over the graves. The shelter that their father had built in anticipation of a nuclear war acted as a sort of holding cell before the victims could be placed in graves.

Saga is torn from her thoughts by her boss tapping a glass and asking for silence. With great solemnity he fetches a blue box from the safe, snaps it open and takes out the gold medal.

A wreathed star on a blue-and-yellow ribbon.

Saga's feels her heart clench unexpectedly when she hears Verner say that she has demonstrated remarkable courage, bravery and intelligence.

The atmosphere in the room is one of gentle solemnity.

Carlos's eyes are moist, and Nathan smiles at her with a sombre look in his eyes.

Saga takes a step forward and Verner attaches the medal to her chest.

Corinne claps her hands and gives her a big smile. Carlos opens the champagne, firing the cork at the ceiling.

Saga drinks a toast with them, and receives their congratulations. Every so often her hearing is interrupted by a howl of tinnitus.

'What are you going to do now?' Pollock asks.

'I'm on sick leave, but . . . I don't know.'

She knows there's no way she can sit around in her dusty flat with its withered pot-plants, guilt and memories.

'Saga Bauer, you have done a great deed for your country,' Verner says, then goes on to explain that unfortunately he's going to have to keep her medal locked in the safe, seeing as the whole case is confidential and already erased from all public records.

He carefully removes the medal from Saga again, puts it back in its box and closes the safe door securely.


The sun is shining in a hazy sky when Saga emerges from the underground into the swirling snow.

After they arrested Jurek, Samuel Mendel and Joona Linna ended up on his revenge list. His twin brother seized Samuel's family, and was closing in on Summa and Lumi when they were killed in a car crash.

The only conceivable explanation as to why Mikael and Felicia were kept in the capsule was that Jurek never had time to give his brother any orders about where they were to be buried. Whereas Samuel Mendel's family was buried, Mikael and Felicia were held captive for all the years that Jurek was in solitary confinement in the secure psychiatric unit. His brother gave them scraps of food and made sure they couldn't escape while he waited for orders from Jurek, as usual.

Presumably Jurek hadn't foreseen how restrictive the verdict of the Court of Appeal would be.

An unlimited sentence and no contact with the outside world, locked away in the secure unit of the Löwenströmska Hospital.

Jurek Walter bided his time and formulated a plan as the years passed. The brothers had probably each been trying to work out a solution when Susanne Hjälm chose to give Jurek a letter from a lawyer. It's impossible to know what the encrypted letter said, but the evidence suggests that Jurek's brother simply gave him a status report about Joona Linna.

Jurek needed to get out, and realised that there was a chance to make a dent in his isolation if he could only smuggle a letter out to the PO box that the brothers sometimes used to communicate to each other.

The twins had learned advanced cryptography from their father, and Jurek managed to make his letter look like a plea for legal help. In actual fact it was an order to release Mikael. Jurek knew the news would reach Joona Linna, and that the police would contact him to try to find out where Felicia was. He didn't know what form this contact would take, but he was convinced it would give him the opportunity he had been waiting for.

Because no one had attempted to negotiate with him about finding the girl, he realised that one of the unit's new patients must be a police officer, and when Saga tried to save Bernie Larsson, he knew for certain that it was her.

Jurek had been watching the young doctor, Anders Rönn, as he overstepped his authority and enjoyed the power he wielded in the secure unit.

When Jurek noticed his undisguised fascination for Saga, he knew how his escape could be accomplished. All he had to do was lure the young doctor – with his keys and pass card – into Saga's cell. There was no way the doctor would be able to resist this sleeping beauty. Jurek spent several nights wetting toilet paper, drying it against his face, and creating a head that would make it look as if he was asleep in his bed.

Saga stops outside the bakery in the cold wind sweeping along Sankt Paulsgatan, unsure whether she feels up to going in right now.

She recalls what Joona had said about Jurek lying to everyone. Jurek listened and pieced together everything he found out, using it to his own advantage, and mixing lies with truth to make his lies stronger.

Saga turns and makes her way across Mariatorget towards Hornsgatan. She walks through the swirling snow as if she is isolated in a tunnel of grief with only the winter light and her memories of herself as a little girl.

She didn't want to kill her mum, she knows that, it wasn't intentional.

Saga carries on walking slowly, thinking about her dad. Lars-Erik Bauer. A cardiologist at Sankt Göran Hospital. She hasn't spoken to him properly since she was thirteen years old. Yet Jurek made her remember how he used to push her on the swing at her grandparents' when she was little, before Mum got ill . . .

Suddenly she stops, and feels a shiver run down her neck and through her arms.

A man walks past, pulling a little girl on a sledge as it scrapes along the ground.

Saga thinks that Jurek lied to everyone.

Why does she think he was telling her the truth?


Saga sits down on a snow-covered park bench, takes her phone out of her pocket and calls Nils Åhlén.

'Nils Åhlén, Forensic Medicine Department.'

'Hello, Saga Bauer here,' she says. 'I'd like—'

'The body's been identified now,' Åhlén interrupts. 'His name's Anders Rönn.'

'That wasn't what I wanted to ask.'

'What is it, then?'

A short silence follows as Saga watches the snow blowing off the statue of Thor raising his hammer against the Midgard Serpent, then suddenly she hears herself ask:

'How many codeine phosphate pills would it take to kill someone?'

'Child or adult?' Åhlén asks, without seeming remotely surprised.

'Adult,' Saga replies, swallowing hard.

She hears Åhlén breathe through his nose as he taps at his keyboard.

'It would depend on size and tolerance . . . but between thirty-five and forty-five pills would probably be a fatal dose.'

'Forty-five?' Saga asks, clutching her ear as the tinnitus flares up. 'But if she was only given thirteen, could that kill her? Could she die from thirteen pills?'

'No, she couldn't, she'd fall asleep and wake up with—'

'So she took the rest herself,' Saga whispers, standing up unsteadily.

She can feel tears of relief in her eyes. Jurek was a liar; that was all he did, he destroyed people with his lies.

All her life she has hated her father for leaving them. For never coming, for letting her mum die.

She has to find out the truth. There's no other option.

She gets her phone out again, calls directory inquiries and asks to be put through to Lars-Erik Bauer in Enskede.

Saga walks slowly across the square and the phone rings.

'This is Pellerina,' a child's voice says.

Saga is rendered speechless, and ends the call without saying anything. She stands quite still and looks up at the white sky above St Paul's Church.

'Bloody hell,' she mutters, and dials the number again.

Saga waits in the snow until the child's voice answers a second time.

'Hello, Pellerina,' she says in a steady voice. 'I'd like to talk to Lars-Erik, please.'

'Who shall I say is calling?' the girl asks, sounding much older than she is.

'My name's Saga,' she whispers.

'I've got a big sister called Saga,' Pellerina says. 'But I've never met her.'

Saga can't speak. There's a lump in her throat. She hears Pellerina pass the phone to someone and say that Saga wants to speak to him.

'This is Lars-Erik,' a familiar voice says.

Saga takes a deep breath, and thinks that it's too late for anything but the truth.

'Dad, I have to ask . . . when Mum died . . . were the two of you married?'

'No,' he replies. 'We'd got divorced two years earlier, when you were five. She never let me see you. I'd got hold of a lawyer who was going to help me to . . .'

He falls silent and Saga closes her eyes and tries to stop shaking.

'Mum said you'd abandoned us,' she says. 'She said you couldn't deal with her illness and that you didn't want me.'

'Maj was ill, she was mentally ill, bipolar and . . . I'm so sorry you had such a bad time.'

'I called you that night,' she says, in a voice that sounds very lonely.

'Yes,' her dad sighs. 'Your mum used to force you to call . . . She would call as well, all night long, thirty times, maybe more.'

'I didn't know that.'

'Where are you? Just tell me where you are. I can come and get you . . .'

'Thanks, Dad, but . . . I have to go and see a friend.'

'How about after that?' he asks.

'I'll call.'

'Please, Saga, make sure you do,' he says.

She nods, then walks through the snow to Hornsgatan and hails a taxi.

Saga is waiting at reception in the Karolinska Hospital. Joona Linna is no longer in intensive care, but has been moved to a smaller room. As she walks towards the lifts, she thinks of the look on Joona's face after Disa's death.

The only thing he asked of her when she last visited him was to find Jurek Walter's dead body and let him see it.

She knows she killed Jurek, but she still has to tell Joona that Carlos has sent police divers under the ice for several days without finding the body.

The door to his room on the eighth floor is half-open.

Saga stops in the corridor when she hears a woman say she's going to fetch a thermal blanket. A moment later a smiling nurse comes out, then turns back towards the room again.

'You have very unusual eyes, Joona,' she says, then walks off.

Saga stands still and closes her burning eyelids for a little while before walking over.

She knocks on the open door, walks into the room, and stops in the light of the sun shining through the dirty window.

Saga stares at the empty bed, then draws closer. The drip is dangling from its support with blood on the needle. The tube is still swaying in the air. There's a broken wristwatch on the floor, but the room is empty.


Five days later the police put out an alert, but Joona Linna had vanished. After six months the search was called off. The only person who carried on looking was Saga Bauer, because she knew he wasn't dead.

# THE
# HYPNOTIST

## COME FACE TO FACE WITH FEAR ITSELF

Detective Inspector Joona Linna is faced with a boy who witnessed the gruesome murder of his family. He's suffered more than one hundred knife wounds and is comatose with shock. The killer's on the run and there are no clues.

Desperate for information, Linna enlists the help of disgraced hypnotist, Dr Erik Maria Bark. And as the hypnosis begins, a terrifying chain of events unfurls with reverberations that go far beyond the case.

# THE
# NIGHTMARE

## THEIR FEARS ARE HIS MASTERPIECE

A young woman's body is discovered aboard an abandoned boat. The likely cause of death is drowning. Shortly afterwards, a man is found hung in his apartment in an apparent suicide.

The deaths seem unrelated, but Detective Inspector Joona Linna suspects something more sinister. The woman is linked to a peace organisation campaigning against an arms committee led by the hanging man. As the death toll rises it becomes clear Linna is chasing a serial killer.

# THE
# FIRE WITNESS

## WAKE UP TO TRUE EVIL

Detective Inspector Joona Linna has been called to a home for troubled girls, north of Stockholm. A young girl has been found brutally murdered in her bed.

Vicky Bennet is the only girl unaccounted for. When a bloody hammer is found under her pillow, she quickly becomes the prime suspect. Refusing to accept the easy answers, Joona embarks on a search that leads him into a dark, violent territory and a shocking confrontation with his past.

# KILLER READS

## DISCOVER THE BEST IN CRIME AND THRILLER.

### SIGN UP TO OUR NEWSLETTER FOR YOUR CHANCE TO WIN A FREE BOOK EVERY MONTH.

### FIND OUT MORE AT
### WWW.KILLERREADS.COM/NEWSLETTER

Want more? Get to know the team behind the books, hear from our authors, find out about new crime and thriller books and lots more by following us on social media:

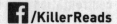 /KillerReads
 /KillerReads